Brian Strause was born in ▓▓▓▓▓▓▓▓▓▓▓▓▓▓▓▓▓▓▓▓▓▓▓ the American Film Institute with an MFA in producing and worked as an associate producer for *The 90s* for PBS. He has also written TV and film scripts. He lives in Los Angeles.

Praise for *Maybe a Miracle*:

'I'm reading a book called Maybe a Miracle by Brian Strause. It's narrated by an 18-year-old-boy who saves his sister after she's found floating face down in a pool. After she recovers she begins performing miracles and healing people who come into contact with her. Whenever I see a first-person narrator done extremely well - and by that I mean a narrator who never really breaks out of character no matter what goes on in the plot of the book - I'm always driven to want to go to my computer and do something just as good as that. I really hope we hear from this writer again in the future.' Jodi Picoult

'...unique and intriguing... An original take on a boy's coming-of-age and a sly, thoughtful look at the complexities of faith.' *Kirkus Reviews*

'*Maybe a Miracle*, by Brian Strause is a first novel with an irresistible premise. Teenager Monroe Anderson goes to grab a smoke before his senior prom only to discover that his sister, Annika, is floating facedown in a pool. He dives to the rescue, but she's sunk into a coma. Annika's hands bleed as if she has stigmata. Rose petals flutter from the sky. The media go wild, and religious pilgrims begin to flock to the hospital to worship, to wish, to beg for healing. So is this a miracle or not? The delight in this book is that Strause doesn't give any definitive answers. Monroe reacts with sarcasm. If his sister can heal others, how come she can't heal herself or cook all the throngs of pilgrims pancakes? But while Monroe occasionally provokes the pilgrims, he's surprised by his own sense of awe about what's going on, and his questions about faith and miracles become more pointed, until even ordinary life becomes majestic.' *Boston Globe*

MAYBE A MIRACLE

Brian Strause

PIATKUS

Copyright © 2005 by Brian Strause

First published in Great Britain in 2006 by
Judy Piatkus (Publishers) Ltd of
5 Windmill Street, London W1T 2JA
email: info@piatkus.co.uk

First published in the United States in 2005 by Ballantine Books,
an imprint of The Random House Publishing Group,
a division of Random House, Inc., New York

This edition published 2006

The moral right of the author has been asserted

A catalogue record for this book is available from the British Library

ISBN 0 7499 3684 3

Data capture by Phoenix Photosetting, Chatham, Kent
www.phoenixphotosetting.co.uk

Printed and bound in Great Britain by
Mackays of Chatham Ltd, Chatham, Kent

For my parents

There are two ways to live your life –
Believing everything is a miracle or that nothing is.

– Albert Einstein

Maybe a Miracle

Chapter 1

THERE'S A BOW TIED around my neck and I'm dying for a smoke.

Tonight's the senior prom and there's no way I'm going to get through this ordeal sober. I wouldn't be going at all, but I promised my girlfriend, Emily. She said the prom happens only once in your life and I'd regret it if I blew the whole thing off. "Humor me," she said. On the off chance she's right, I agreed to take her—a decision I now regret.

I figure if I catch a buzz before I pick her up, maybe the night won't be a total disaster. Emily always says she can't stand being around stoners, but then again she can never tell when I'm stoned.

Besides, there's no use complaining now. I have the whole thing lined up—the black tux, the white limo, the red corsage. I even rented a room at the Hyatt. It's something you're supposed to do, I guess. It's not like I think some cheesy hotel room will make Emily want to sleep with me. I know she won't. It's not even worth trying. I probably won't even tell her I got it. If she ever wants to go all the way, she'll let me know. Her parents left her home alone for an entire weekend last month and she still wouldn't put out. A hotel room isn't going to make any difference.

The most we ever do is kiss, sometimes until our lips are chapped. Every time I try to push it a little further, she pulls away and I stop. Supposedly, most guys don't. Like the guys she used to go out with. From what I can figure, they didn't take no for an answer and I don't want to be like them, so I always apologize and say, "Whenever you're ready." You might think that makes me a good guy, but most people around here would say it just makes me a pussy.

I've heard people say that Emily was a slut at her old school, Fairview High. It's only a couple miles away from Chelsea. News gets around and sometimes I listen. Not that it really matters. People say a lot worse about their so-called best friends.

From the very beginning she told me she wanted to take things slow and that was fine with me. After three years of high school I'd never even been on a date, so going slow sounded a lot better than going nowhere at all.

I'm pretty sure Emily doesn't care about the prom anyway. She wants to shed her old skin. Going to the prom is really about making a new memory to replace the old ones she wants to forget. Deep down I'll bet she knows it's a big joke, but you'd have to ask her. That's the only way you ever know what's going on in someone else's head and even then you can't be too sure.

Emily doesn't talk about her past much, just in bits and pieces. She once told me how her dad found her drunk at Larry's down on High Street, sitting in some guy's lap. Another time she got so wasted at a Beastie Boys concert she had to have her stomach pumped. She's been arrested for shoplifting, but she won't tell me what she stole. Like she says, it doesn't matter. But if you put all the pieces together it looks like a blur, a girl out of control. She's not like that anymore; so maybe going to the prom is a small price for me to pay.

My sister, Annika, on the other hand, cares *a lot* about the prom. Even though she's only in the fifth grade and I'm about to go to college, in a lot of ways I think of her as my best friend. I can tell her anything and know she'd never rat me out. That's a lot rarer than it ought to be. In a few years she'll drift away. When she gets into sixth grade, it'll all change. That's when girls start thinking about boys. That's when they turn mean.

Last week Annika was begging me to help pick out my tux. Not that she had to, I would have taken her anyway. Without her or someone else from the family in the car, I'm not allowed to drive. Dad says *driving is not a right but a privilege.* He says he's doing it *for my own good*. If I had a gallon of gas for every time I heard that, I could have escaped to California by now. Dad figures with Annika in the car I won't try anything stupid and if I do, he's under the false impression she'll report back to him. The truth is, I'm really not such a bad driver; I've just had some bad luck.

First of all, I should point out in my defense—and despite objections from the insurance company—that it was completely not my fault when I totaled the driver's ed car. That distinction belonged to Mr. Bailey, the so-called *instructor*. The one who was there *to teach* me how to drive. He was hard to take seriously. After all, no one grows up wanting to be a driver's ed instructor. In order to get that job, some serious vocational errors must be made along the way. Throw in the facts that he smelled like broccoli, never cleaned his glasses, and spoke often of Freemasonry and it's not so hard to see how it came to *this*.

Mr. Bailey didn't have too many driving tips to share, but he frequently ranted about how all the kids around here have been bred to be cogs in the machine and they don't even know it.

Maybe I was going a little too fast, but I only wanted to get out of the car. Bailey was babbling on and on about how fluoride is the main ingredient in rat poison. "It lowers your IQ, crumbles your bones, and causes cancer. People think it's the TV that makes everyone slaves to the system, but it's the *fluoride*."

After a while, he wasn't so hard to tune out.

Later, Mr. Bailey would tell the cops, "I told him to slow down." More than once, he said that. That's the thing about conspiracy theorists—they never take personal responsibility for anything. Whatever happens is the result of some sinister plot.

Even though he wasn't at the wheel, Mr. Bailey was in control. He had his own set of brakes. He could do what he wanted. Any objective observer could see, it was Mr. Bailey who panicked, not me. Had he not freaked out and slammed on the brakes, we never would have fishtailed into the plaza in front of City Hall, headed straight for a statue of our city's namesake.

When Christopher Columbus hit the ground, his head fell off

and rolled down Front Street. You might have seen a picture of it in the paper. No one got hurt, but everyone acted like it was a sign of the coming apocalypse.

At the time, though, I couldn't stop laughing, which is probably why the cops thought I was drunk. But what was even funnier was Mr. Bailey. He was having a fit, wheezing about how he wasn't going to be framed.

I don't know why he was so upset. He'd only told me a dozen times how Columbus was a slave trader and a rapist and how if the natives didn't bring him all the gold he wanted, he'd chop off their arms. Mr. Bailey often said, "Everything they teach you in that stuck-up school is a lie, *a goddamn lie.*"

The destruction of such an esteemed civic icon really would have been a wonderful opportunity for Mr. Bailey to initiate a city-wide dialogue over why our landlocked town is named after the seafaring Christopher Columbus in the first place. But all he could talk about was how I was trying to ruin his life. Like he hadn't already done that all on his own.

I WAS WEARING jeans and a T-shirt. It wasn't really a big deal to me, going to a department store to get fitted for a tux, but Annika has always loved getting dressed up. Any occasion will do. She's old-fashioned that way.

"Monroe, we're going to the Lazarus *downtown*, right?"

"That's right."

"Not the one at the *mall.*"

"Yes, we're going downtown."

"And you're going to wear *that*?"

The Lazarus store downtown used to be a pretty elegant place, unlike the one at the Chelsea mall, which is a fortress made of glazed turquoise brick. Mom calls it architectural vomit. But the downtown Lazarus is different. It's like 1948, not that I know what 1948 was like; but when you walk through the cast-iron doors you could be walking into a black-and-white movie.

Lazarus keeps the tuxedoes on the fourth floor in the back. I wanted to get one in baby blue, just to make it clear I wasn't taking the prom seriously, but Annika would have none of that. "Monroe," she said, "you'll look back at pictures of yourself and wonder what you were thinking. Is that what you want?"

I look at myself in the mirror and cringe as it is. I can't imagine how looking back on photos will be any different.

She insisted on a classic cut. "You'll look like William Powell and Emily will be Myrna Loy . . . or better yet Ginger Rogers and Fred Astaire." Annika wants to be a dancer. She watches those old movies all the time.

When I came out of the dressing room, she came right up to me all serious, brushed off my lapels, and asked, "May I have this dance?" I'm telling you, she's going to break some hearts someday, she really will. You'll see.

"Of course, my lady." I know it sounds kind of gay, dancing with your sister like that, especially in public. But we've always danced together. It's the one thing my mother insisted on, dance lessons. "There are a lot of things you can fake in this life and dancing is not one of them," she said. It's right up there with, "People always say dance like no one's watching, but the thing to remember is this: they *are* watching and you can bet they wish they were dancing too."

Annika and I used to dance all the time. It didn't matter that I have about a foot and a half on her; she could always keep up. It wasn't cheesy, you know, like at weddings when you see old people dancing with little girls. She really knew what she was doing.

People at school used to call me a faggot because I took dance class, like it was something to be ashamed of. And it worked. I was ashamed. Being called a faggot will do that to you. I wanted to quit and Mom would have let me too. But first she asked me one question: "So what do the boys who call you names do at the school dances?" I told her they all hang around on the edges. They don't dance at all. "That's interesting. You're dancing with girls and they're not, yet you're the faggot." Sometimes the most obvious things go right over your head when you're a kid.

We finished with a big dip and the clerks all clapped. It figures, they sell clothes.

Annika never worried if people laughed at her. She always assumed everyone else was in on the joke and I've always assumed the joke was on me. When I was eleven I was mortified if I wasn't wearing the right shoes to school. But Annika just never cared what other people thought. Maybe if you don't care, other people don't care much either. Maybe it's like how dogs only bite people who are afraid of them.

After they made some alterations, we got milk shakes at the old-fashioned fountain on the fourth floor. There was no one else there. It was just us and Sam, the old black man who works the counter. He's been working at Lazarus forever. Sam's a nice man, but kind of slow. Mom says he's thick—just like his shakes.

"It doesn't look like anyone comes here much anymore," I said.

"They don't, son, they sure don't," Sam said as he continued polishing the counter, not missing a beat. He concentrated his efforts on one spot, gliding his hands over and over it again.

I inhaled my shake, but Annika took her time. She said, "Mr. Sam, you make the best milk shakes in the world."

He just smiled and kept rubbing that one spot, considering the praise. Then he looked up at us and said, "I wish I could make more."

When I was a kid, before they built a new mall next door, Lazurus was packed on Saturdays. But sitting there looking at Sam, it felt like we were at a museum visiting a relic from the past, like the way they have blacksmiths banging out horseshoes and women spinning lamb's wool at the Ohio Historical Society. If they ever close the store, maybe that's where Sam will end up. In a museum. The mall next door—which was so new and popular just a few years ago—quickly filled with ghosts. New, better malls with more things to do popped up on the outskirts, effectively killing the downtown renaissance before they even had a chance to build an IMAX.

If you've already done the math, then you'd know I was seven years old when Annika was born. It was kind of an unexpected bonus—no longer being the youngest. I could hardly wait for her to arrive. I learned so much about the infliction of pain from my older brother, I was eager to impart my wisdom to the younger generation.

I SPENT MY first seven years as an unwitting scientific experiment. *Scientific*, however, suggests it was all documented for a greater good. But nothing was written down. There were no lab notes. No charts. No graphs. Only a constant stream of misery. Dad always said our family was part Austrian, but all you had to do was see my brother, Ben, in action to realize our German roots ran deep. I could have written a book like Anne Frank, detailing the occupation, but Ben would have found it and rubbed every word in my face like broken glass.

I'm ashamed to admit that I, the persecuted, became the persecutor. When Annika was five years old she won a goldfish at the Ohio State Fair by tossing a Ping-Pong ball in his bowl. She named him Ping. For three weeks she took that goldfish with her wherever she went. She put his bowl in her wagon and walked him around the neighborhood like he was a dog. Like it was the most natural thing in the world.

Maybe I was jealous to see her make a connection with a fish. Maybe I couldn't handle seeing her so happy. Maybe it annoyed me to hear the neighbors say how cute she looked, like they used to say about me. Maybe I was just being a boy. All I know is that it didn't go down the way I planned.

The thing is, I just wanted to put a scare in her. I thought it'd be funny. So I dumped the fish in the blender and made like I was going to whip Ping up into a frothy Orange Julius, just like at the mall. Annika was hysterical, begging me not to.

I'd never seen her so desperate, I'd never seen *anyone* want something so much as she did in that moment. And all she wanted was for me to stop what I was doing. But the more she pleaded, the more I was determined to deny her. Something clicked in my head when she started to cry. You'd think I'd have shown some compassion, but instead, I lost it.

"You want something to cry about? Watch this."

I remember being disappointed in myself, but it didn't matter. I did it anyway. I flicked the switch of the blender, and in an instant, Ping was no more.

Annika crawled under the coffee table and cried for the rest of the day. When Mom asked her what was wrong, she didn't even tell on me. I probably felt worse than she did. I promised myself I'd never do anything to hurt her ever again. I don't know if she even remembers that day. We've never talked about it and I hope we never do. I'm hoping it's one of those memories that's so bad, your mind forces you to forget, because if she ever remembers what I did, she'll probably hate my guts.

MOM INSPECTS ME in my tuxedo. She's impressed with my bow tie–tying abilities until she realizes it's a clip-on. She says, "Oh, Monroe, you'll never score with one of these." That makes me blush, which is always happening to me. It's a curse, blushing. I'll never be able to play poker. I'll never be one of the guys.

Despite her prim and proper exterior, Mom's always been pretty open about sex. I must have been eight years old when I called her a dildo and she asked me if I knew what a dildo was. "Sure," I said. "A dildo is a bird. They're *extinct*." I probably said it like she was stupid to even ask, but I was the stupid one. "That's a *dodo* bird," she said. "A *dildo* is something a woman uses for sexual gratification. It's a substitute for a penis—it could be a cucumber or a carrot."

I never thought of salad the same way again. Whenever I get the chance in the kitchen, I like to ask her if she washed that cucumber, but I don't think she gets the reference. It's kind of an in-joke with myself.

Mom's talking about how handsome Dad was last time he wore this tie at some fund-raiser. She shows me how to tie the bow without making me feel like an idiot. That's what Dad would do. Not that he'd mean to make me feel like an idiot, he just would. He doesn't have a lot of patience and that makes me nervous and when I'm nervous I screw things up and, well, you can imagine the vicious cycle. Truth is, it's really not hard, tying a bow tie. Even though Mom is good at it, it kind of makes me sad it's not Dad teaching me, but he's not here. He practically never is.

Mom says seeing Dad in his tuxedo at that fund-raiser made her think of her wedding all over again. It was like taking a step back in time.

I tell Mom I probably should get going. "I think I left my wallet in the pool house." But what I really want to do is get high.

Chapter 2

I'M ON MY WAY to the pool house—that's where I hide my pot—when I see Annika floating face-first in the pool. We had watched *Harold and Maude* about a week ago and the first thing I think is she's just trying to get a rise out of me. You know how Harold tries to shock his mom by pretending he drowned in the pool? But she's been through it all so many times, she just jumps in and swims on by? Like he's not even there? Annika couldn't stop laughing about that, so I figure she's trying to pull the same stunt on me.

She's just floating, not a ripple in the water . . . it's a very convincing performance. So, just to make sure, I pick up a tennis ball and chuck it at her, not too hard, but hard enough. It hits her head and bounces into the bushes. She doesn't flinch. She just keeps floating, facedown, her back to the world, the ripples of her spine in stark contrast to the stillness of the pool.

Annika's threshold of pain is much too low to fake her way through a beaning, no matter how soft. Clearly this isn't some stunt to get attention, not that she would do that anyway. She gets all the attention she could ever want. So I dive in. Some people say this makes me some sort of a hero, but it's what anyone would have done. You probably would have done it too, unless you're in a wheelchair or something. It's really no big deal.

She's in the deep end, near the diving board. When I get to her she's limp. I hang her over my shoulder—no struggling, no nothing—

and swim toward the steps. It feels like surrender, her rag doll body, like I got there too late. Her mouth is right next to my ear, but nothing is coming out of it, not a gurgle, not a breath. I swim her to the shallow end, walk her up the steps and out of the pool, screaming for help.

When we get out of the water, I give her the Heimlich maneuver. On the second thrust, about a gallon of water comes gushing out, but still there is no gasping for breath, no wheezing. Just silence. It's not like TV where they start gulping for air, so I lay her on the stone patio and feel for a pulse. Nothing. Maybe I'm not doing it right. Maybe I'm just making it *worse*. I scream for help again, for someone to dial 911.

But it's so quiet, all I can hear is the water lapping against the sides of the pool and in the distance the Gormans' sprinkler is going around and around. Water everywhere. I guess I should be scared, but in moments like this you don't really think, there's no time for that. You just do what you have to do, so I try CPR. They gave us a class in gym once, but I'd never done it on a real person, only on some plastic dummy.

I hold her nose while I place my mouth to hers, pumping my breath into her lungs, when finally Mom comes to the second-story window. She must have seen me hunched over Annika, my lips locked with hers. She screams down at me, "Monroe, what the hell are you doing to your sister?" It's such a weird thing to say, like what does she think I'm doing? Making out with her?

I blow another breath into her lungs and I yell, "Call 911!" Again, I check Annika's pulse, but there isn't one there. I look up at the window, but Mom's gone.

This is the part where you jump-start their heart. I'd hoped it wouldn't come to this. You can really screw someone up. You'd think a sternum would be pretty sturdy, but they're not. Maybe nothing really is. Maybe everything is just hanging by a thread.

Even if the ambulance is on its way, there isn't much time left, so I start pushing down on her chest, afraid I might be hurting her, afraid I'm making it worse. But I don't know what else to do. After about a dozen times, she starts to breathe, her chest rising and falling all on its own.

The doctors say I got there just in time. A minute later and she probably wouldn't have made it.

There are times I wonder if she would have been better off if I hadn't been going to the pool house to get high that day. I know that's a terrible thing to say, not that I would ever say it out loud. I just know if it were me, I probably would have just let go.

As I watch them load my sister into the ambulance, water drips from my tuxedo, forming a puddle at my waterlogged shoes. Mom is losing her mind, but they let her ride in the back anyway. After all, who can blame her? That's what she's *supposed* to do. But what I'm supposed to do now, I'm not quite sure. I'm given a hint, though, before the technician closes the doors. "We're headed to Riverbend," he says. That's the hospital where I was born. As they pull out of the driveway, their siren screaming, a bunch of kids pull up on their bikes to see what all the fuss is about.

Josh Gorman from next door asks me what happened. He's always coming over to play with Annika. They're friends. He wants to know if she's going to be okay. I don't know what to say, so I don't say anything. I should say, "I hope so," but I just stand there, staring at the ambulance as it pulls away. He may have asked me again, I'm not sure. He rejoins his friends and the boys pedal fast, trying to keep up with the ambulance, their bikes' safety flags flapping in the wind.

Even though it's humid and sticky outside, a chill comes over me. The street is suddenly empty. It happens so fast I wonder for a second if it happened at all. But that's just wishful thinking; the wail of the siren fading away tells a different story.

I don't know how long I stand there, just staring down the street. When Stevie Robbins drives by on his bike and throws the weekly Chelsea newspaper at my feet, I snap out of it. I look at the paper, but I don't pick it up. I leave it there and go around back. The pool is so still it could be empty. I take off my wet tuxedo and go inside, leaving the monkey suit in a pile by the door. It's the only evidence left that something out of the ordinary happened here.

I put on some dry clothes before I get into Mom's new car, a blistering red BMW convertible that Dad gave her for their anniversary last year. "A cherry on top of twenty-five years," he said. It's the first time I've ever driven by myself. Dad will understand. He'll make an exception.

Annika loves this car, especially when the top is down, which I hate. I always feel like such a dick in a BMW, a red one no less. But Annika will hear nothing of it. She says I'm a *snob*. Somehow, not wanting to drive a snobby car makes *me* a snob. Why? I don't really understand. But I don't say anything. There's really no use getting into it with my little sister. Very little joy comes from winning an argument with an eleven-year-old.

I think maybe we'll be able to stop at the Dairy Queen on the way home. She'll want a Blizzard with chopped-up Butterfinger, maybe some onion rings. I tell myself everything is going to be okay, but I don't believe it. I can't get that last image of her out of my mind. Even though she was breathing, her lips were blue when the medics arrived, so blue it looked like she'd just eaten a blueberry sno-cone.

I might as well be drunk. The drive is a blur until I pull into the hospital parking lot, press the button, and get a ticket. Until then I don't even realize I'm listening to Neil Diamond singing "Forever in Blue Jeans." Mom loves Neil Diamond, but she doesn't play him in the house anymore. She probably got tired of listening to everyone complain, especially me. I've always hated "Forever in Blue Jeans" and now, here it has me crying. I can't bring myself to credit Neil's emotionally penetrating baritone. It's just I always thought forever seemed so far away, but now it feels like forever might just end today.

A guy pulls up next to me and looks me over like I'm some sort of freak, crying to the stupidest song in the world. I don't care. I just turn it up louder and let the tears fall.

When I get inside the hospital, the first thing I do is call Emily. I tell her about the accident and how it doesn't look like I'm going to be able to make it to the prom tonight. I tell her, "I'm really sorry. There's nothing I can do."

"Monroe, you're not funny. I'm ready to go. My dad's already taking pictures, it's torture. Just get the fuck over here."

"I'm serious." There might have been a few times when I made up stuff, so I guess I can't blame her for not believing me. "Do you hear me laughing?"

"God damnit, Monroe. Look, I know you don't want to go, but it's too late for that now."

"Emily, I'm at Riverbend Hospital." She still doesn't believe me, so I tell her to hold on for a second. I pull over a nurse and I ask her if she'll tell my friend where we are. She takes over the phone and confirms my location.

"See, I told you."

"If this is your way of breaking up with me and going out with someone else, it's pretty shitty, Monroe."

"Jesus, Emily, she's like fifty years old. She's a *nurse*." The nurse looks at me and scowls, but there's nothing I can do about that. "If you don't believe me, why don't you come over and see for yourself. . . . We don't even know if she's going to make it. She probably could use your help."

I feel bad saying that—*we don't know if* . . . I haven't even gone into the emergency room yet, I don't know *anything*. I only want Emily to believe me. But now they're out there, these words—and it feels like I've mentioned a no-hitter is in progress, jinxing the whole thing.

"Oh my God" is all Emily can say. She's on her way.

MOM'S IN THE WAITING ROOM all by herself. Dad should be there too, but he's in Detroit taking depositions. He's always somewhere else. It doesn't really matter where. It's not like he ever brings back any presents, even stupid crap from the airport gift shop. Not that I need a snow globe or some retarded T-shirt. It would just be nice to know he's thinking of me. The truth is, I barely even know the guy.

Dad's a big-shot lawyer. He's never lost a case. Not once. What's scary about him is that he's so persuasive it takes him only a few minutes to get you to agree with whatever it is he has to say. He'll have you believing kittens could be a healthy alternative to chicken if you give him half a chance. At least that's what people say, people who probably know him a lot better than I do.

Dad almost never talks about his cases with anyone in the family. Not even my mom. If you ask, he'll just change the subject to sports, or the weather, or if he's feeling particularly conversational he'll just answer with a short burst of condescension and *you'll* change the subject all on your own to sports or the weather. . . . Truth is, it makes me not want to talk to him at all, which is probably exactly what he's shooting for. It wouldn't bother me so much; it's just that he's never that way with my brother, Ben. He'll talk to Ben about anything.

Emily says my dad is evil—an allegation based largely on the fact that he represented a waste management company that leaked some plutonium into a nearby river. Her parents are always protesting anything nuclear, so that's where she got the idea that Dad's evil. I never held it against Emily's parents for turning her against my dad. After all, plutonium is pretty vicious stuff. I wouldn't want it anywhere near me either. They say if you dab some on the tip of a needle, there's enough to kill 250,000 people. Dad's client, Waste Disposal Inc., somehow managed to dump *seven pounds* on the banks of a river within a hundred yards of a subdivision. When the people who lived there found out what happened, they were understandably concerned. The plutonium quickly became the cause of everything that ever went wrong in their lives . . . and they were pissed.

Mom and Dad had a party once and I overheard Dad say, "I don't know why they were so upset. Finally, they had something to blame for all their problems. How often in life do people get a chance to do that? It's kind of attractive, really, to think whatever's gone wrong in your life is not your fault." Like most Republicans, Dad talks a lot about personal responsibility; yet he spends his life making sure corporations never have to take responsibility for anything they ever do.

It was no surprise when Dad proved those people weren't in any danger—after all, the plutonium was stuck in mud. In the paper, he said it was as dangerous as a gun encased in concrete. And a jury believed him. They always do. At that same party, one of the guests, well out of Dad's earshot, said, "Jesus Christ is probably afraid to come back, because if he did, Larry would drop a civil action suit on his ass for breach of contract." Then another one of his friends added, "Yeah, Larry would keep JC bogged down in court for so long he'd beg to be put back up on the cross."

They all thought that was pretty funny.

Mom is a mess of tears in the waiting room, surrounded by strangers. Historically, emotional displays aren't our family's specialty, but for once in her life it seems Mom doesn't care what anyone thinks. I sit down next to her and put my arm around her, which I've never done before. She's still wearing her tennis clothes and I can't take my eyes off the white sock with the little green ball on the back of her ankle. I just keep staring at it, wondering why it's even there, what possible function it serves—that little green ball just hanging there like some sort of fungus. You don't see those little fuzzy balls very much anymore. Some genius probably figured out that they impede peak aerodynamic performance. Or maybe they just realized how stupid they look.

She's crying uncontrollably now. My arm around her shoulder isn't working. I don't know what else to do, so I try to hold her hand. But that only makes it worse. It's not something we'd ordinarily do, holding hands, and now she's crying harder. She must think if it's come to this—*holding hands*—it must be really bad, worse than she ever could have imagined. I tell her everything will be all right. *Annika will be okay.* I don't know what else to say.

Thankfully, Aunt Sally shows up and I'm off the hook. Aunt Sally's not really an aunt; she was Mom's roommate in college. They've been best friends ever since, so she's more of a pseudo-aunt. We call her Aunt Sally for no other reason than that it would be weird to call her *Mrs. Hamilton.* She's also my godmother; if Mom and Dad die, she has to take care of us, although I'm eighteen now, so I'd probably just be on my own.

Aunt Sally takes over for me and holds Mom. She's telling her everything will be all right too, but she's a lot more convincing than I was. It probably helps that she didn't see Annika's blue lips.

I go over to the other side of the room and look out the window at the fountain, its flumes reaching high into the air and exploding into a ball of white spray like an exclamation point screaming just how serious this all is. People in wheelchairs circle the water and orderlies hold their patients' hands. It's too much reality, so I ask if anyone minds if I turn on the TV. No one says anything. They probably don't even hear me. They have their own dramas to worry about.

There's a Reds game on. Annika and I were planning to go see them play next month after I graduate, just the two of us. It was going to be our secret. The plan was to tell Mom we were spending the day at the country club playing tennis and swimming, but instead we'd drive down to Cincinnati. We'd never done anything like that before. Mom probably would have let us go, but for some reason it was more fun to lie. It was practically all Annika talked about for the last week, always in hushed tones, always looking over her shoulder. When she was done with the bathroom, I'd find GO REDS GO written on the steamed mirror.

UNBELIEVABLY, MY BROTHER, BEN, shows his face. It's a Friday night about eight o'clock. By now he's usually wasted. All day Ben plays golf, but once the sun goes down he starts drinking. Ever since Ben was fourteen, people around here started calling him the next Jack Nicklaus. That's pretty high praise, not only because Nicklaus may just be the best golfer ever, but because he learned to play golf about two par-fives from our front door. He's a local legend and I guess now Ben is too. After one more year of college, he'll go pro. He's that good. Whenever people start their Jack Nicklaus talk, I always tell them Ben's really more like the next John Daly. It's pretty generous of me, I know. I don't come out and say *Ben's a stupid, self-destructive drunk*. They can figure that out on their own.

I guess it sounds like sour grapes and maybe it is. I never really understood the big deal about golf. People are always talking about it like they're mapping DNA or sending a man to Mars. But really they're just hitting a stationary ball into a stationary hole. It's not baseball, that's for sure.

When I see Ben come through the door, I start leafing through a *Sports Illustrated* from a couple of months ago. It's an instinctive self-defense mechanism I've honed over the years. Avoid Ben and no one gets hurt. Especially me.

As I scan predictions for the Reds' future, I keep an eye on Ben. It would be hard not to. He's still wearing the clown clothes he plays golf in. He's like flashing neon; you can't help but look at the striking combination of patch madras pants and a lime green shirt. It should surprise no one that Jimmy Buffett is his favorite musician.

Ben looks at Mom crying like she's an animal at the zoo, an animal he's never seen before. It startles him enough that he deigns to come over and sit next to me.

"What the fuck is going on here?" He always talks like that. *Fuck this. Fuck that. Everyone is a fucker. Fuck you.*

So I tell him what happened, concluding with, "That's all we know. The doctors are still working on her."

"Wait a second, *you* did CPfuckingR on her? You sure you knew what the fuck you were doing?"

"Yeah, I knew what I was doing."

"Because if you don't, you can make it a fuck of a lot worse."

You can see why I really don't like Ben very much. Fortunately, that's when Emily comes running into the waiting room. She's still wearing her prom dress. I've never seen her look so beautiful. I've never even seen her in a dress. Her blonde hair is accented with a blue iris, her lips painted red. She hugs me hard, like someone who wants you to catch them from a fall.

"Is she going to be all right?"

"We haven't heard anything yet."

"I'm so sorry, Monroe. I'm so sorry I didn't believe you."

Emily's an only child, so maybe it's not surprising she's always treated Annika like a sister. Every time she came over, she'd give Annika stuff she had left over from when she was a kid. Like plastic horses. Emily had a ton. Once she gave all her horses away, she'd move on to something else, like dolls, or barrettes to put in her hair. Stuff girls like.

"I don't know what to say."

I tell her, "You don't have to say anything."

She sits down next to me and holds my hand. It never feels weird holding hands with Emily. It's practically all we ever do.

We sit there waiting, like everyone else. No one is saying anything, mainly I suppose because there's nothing you can really say in a waiting room. Everyone just wants their people to be okay, so there's no sense talking about it. All you can do is hope for the best.

I keep my eye on the baseball game, careful to pretend I don't really care. In the bottom of the fifth inning, Barry Larkin puts one out of the park, giving the Reds the lead. I'm inclined to rub it in Ben's face—he *hates* the Reds—but instead I pick up a *Time* magazine and act like I don't notice.

It's forever until a doctor finally comes into the waiting room. He addresses my mother. "Mrs. Anderson? Hello, I am Dr. Singh. I have been attending to your daughter."

"Is she okay?"

"For now, yes. She is a very lucky young lady. After two minutes underwater, one loses consciousness. After three to five minutes, we have to worry about brain damage. Do you have any idea how long she was under?"

Mom looks at me and I shrug, *I don't know.*

"The next twenty-four hours will be of paramount importance."

"The next twenty-four hours?" she asks.

"Mrs. Anderson, your daughter is in a coma."

A coma? My mother's eyes unleash a waterfall of tears. He could have at least come up with some clever euphemism, like saying she's currently unresponsive, but *coma*? It just sounds so stupid, like a bad soap opera. Since when do people in real life fall into comas?

He tries to reassure us. "A coma can be a very positive development. It is often the body's way of preserving itself. In fact, sometimes we induce them ourselves. She's on a respirator right now. Her breathing was irregular. This too is quite normal. We will know much more tomorrow. There's not a lot more we can do right now."

Later, I learned they could have done a lot more right then, right there. Waiting until tomorrow was only going to make it worse. I'm sure if Dr. Singh had known more about traumatic head injuries, he would have done it all differently.

I was never very good at science. I didn't know then how the brain floats on a cushion of spinal fluid, but Dr. Singh should have. When the brain gets injured, sometimes it swells and the swelling restricts the flow of blood, and well, nothing good can come from that. It's a slow strangulation. A lot of doctors think the first thing you should do with someone in a coma is to monitor the pressure on the brain. If it's so high the blood flow is cut off, you release some of the spinal fluid to bring the pressure back down and keep the blood flowing. It sounds simple, but Dr. Singh didn't do that. I guess he didn't know any better, but like Dad always says, "Sometimes doing your best just isn't good enough."

Mom asks, "Can we see her?"

The doctor says, "Of course," like it's the first thing he's been sure of all day.

Chapter 3

ANNIKA'S ROOM SMELLS LIKE ROSES. Before this day, I always thought roses smelled disgusting, like the cheap rose perfume worn by my dead grandmother who always left behind a sickly sweet, polyester trail—a smell so bad it only made sense when I found out she was trying to hide the stench of an embarrassing case of gangrene.

This rose smell, though, is the real thing, soft and clean. But there are no roses to be seen. The room is so full of machines it would be hard to find a place to put them. For a second, it looks like Annika might just be sleeping, but to believe that, you'd have to ignore the tubes going up her nose, down her throat, and in her arm. And they're pretty hard to ignore.

Mom starts to cry again and falls down on her bare knees. It's amazing she has any tears left. She's still wearing her tennis whites—I know it sounds stupid to be even thinking about that, but I am. I'm thinking how just a few hours ago she was running around the court hitting balls with her friends just having a good life, never imagining something so horrible could be right around the corner. Who would? But now, here she is saying, "Hail Mary, full of grace, the Lord is with thee; blessed art thou among women, and blessed is the fruit of thy womb." And she keeps saying it over and over again. I've never heard her say a Hail Mary before. Not once. I wish I could say I never heard it again.

Mom's never been particularly religious, but she does go to church. It used to be you could lure me to Saint Victor's with the doughnuts they sold after Sunday school, but I got over that in the fifth grade when I asked Father Ferger why all the people in Africa were starving while we were jamming doughnuts in our faces and he said it was all part of God's bigger plan, that God doesn't give anyone anything more than they can handle, to which I replied, "How much starvation do you think *you* could handle?" He laughed and told me he could probably stand to go on a diet, like it was some big joke.

After that, I told Mom I didn't want to go anymore. I told her I thought the whole thing was a scam. She said *fine,* I didn't have to go anymore if I didn't want to. She said it like she thought for sure I'd feel too guilty to take her up on it, but apparently I didn't inherent the Catholic guilt gene. Now, I'm willing to go to Midnight Mass on Christmas, but that's about it. It seems Dad and Ben feel pretty much the same way. Mom and Annika, though, frequently go on their own.

Don't get me wrong. It's not like the church doesn't have some decent ideas—like some of the Ten Commandments. *Don't steal. Don't kill. Don't commit adultery. Don't bear false witness. Don't covet your neighbor's stuff. Honor your mother and your father*—those are pretty respectable guidelines, I guess, but then again, they're pretty obvious. Even a retard can tell you not to kill, steal, or lie. Curiously, the rest of the commandments are about not painting pictures of God, or taking His name in vain, or being sure to take a day out of the week to pray to Him. And whatever you do, don't pray to any other gods—in fact, that's the first one. The least He could have done is save that one for last: *By the way, don't go praying to anyone else.* It's bad enough, making everyone capitalize pronouns. It's a big pain in the Ass. If Christians are right about God, He sure has a big ego. I hate to say that, but four out of the Ten Commandments are about how you're supposed to get down on your knees and pray to Him, like He's some sort of genius for coming up with six rules any three morons could have figured out.

~~~

BEN AND I are standing by the bed. We're the only other ones there, besides the doctor and Mom. They said only the family could come into the ICU, so Emily and Aunt Sally have to stay outside. Looking at Mom, I think I should be crying too, but the tears aren't coming. I think I should be praying, but I don't know who to pray to. I think I should say something, but I don't know what to say.

Then Ben says, "She looks so peaceful," which sounds like something you'd say at an open casket funeral. I hate him so much for saying that. I hate him for saying anything at all. Ben doesn't know Annika. Not like *I* do. He should just shut the fuck up. But, I don't say that. Instead, I nod my head, as if he's right, as if I actually agree with him.

"Glory be to the Father, and to the Son, and to the Holy Spirit." That's Mom. There's something so unseemly about praying to God only when you really need help. It's like the flip side of people who root for a sports team only when they're winning, and just as bad.

I can't take it anymore and go back to the waiting room.

Emily's still there, her face wet from her tears. "How'd she look?" Emily asks. I lie and say Annika looks good. I say I think she's going to be okay. Emily's face softens; it's what she wants to hear. She hugs me and I start to feel better too. If you think of lies as wishes you want to come true, they're really not so bad, but the Ten Commandments don't say anything about that.

A woman comes up to us. Her shoulders are hunched over like she's been caught in the rain all of her life. She says, "Hi, I'm Lynne Erickson from *The Dispatch*. I understand you're quite a hero."

"Not really."

"Do you think I could talk to you for a few minutes about what happened?"

"I saw my sister floating in the pool and I pulled her out. It's pretty much that simple."

"And then you gave her CPR. She'd be dead if it weren't for you."

"I happened to be the one who was there."

"Ahhh," she says. "The reluctant hero. Our readers will love that."

I'm thinking, "What the hell kind of thing is that to say?" Even though the words don't come out of my mouth, the question must have been etched on my face. Shell-shocked, I don't say a word. I just shake my head, like I don't understand her.

Emily chimes in. "An eleven-year-old girl hanging by a thread—I can see how that would sell a lot of papers. Seriously, I can. People are just that lame. The only thing lamer is giving the people what they think they want. Why don't you just leave him alone? Can't you see this isn't really the best time?"

"Unfortunately, I specialize in *not the best of times*." The reporter says it like she's said it a thousand times before.

Emily takes me by the hand, "Let's go get something to eat in the cafeteria." For a second I think I don't need her help, I can defend myself, but that's not true. The only time I ever defend myself is in my imagination and by then it's usually way too late.

When we get to the elevator and as Emily pushes the button, the door opens and, like some magic trick, out comes my dad.

"Hi, Mr. Anderson."

Dad doesn't acknowledge Emily, but not in a rude way. He's just doing what anyone would do.

"Where is she?" He's so focused on the task at hand you can almost see the bulldog marine tattoo popping through his shirt sleeve. Dad was in the marines during Vietnam; it's no big deal. At least, that's what he says if you ask him.

I point down the corridor. "Room 712."

And off he runs, his wing tips sliding down the hall. I want to go after him, to be there for him, but I wouldn't know where to begin.

BY THE TIME Emily and I get to the basement cafeteria it must be around nine o'clock. If all had gone as planned, we'd be finishing up dinner at the Riverfront Gardens, this new restaurant downtown. It was supposed to be really romantic. I had already paid the band to play the Beatles' "Something" right after they served dessert. That's

Emily's favorite band, the Beatles. Deep down she's quite a traditional girl.

People litter the cafeteria, just waiting for the day to end. It's a tough battle—the flickering fluorescent lights fighting back time. It's a bunker mentality down here; everyone's bracing for the worst.

I feel like an insect trapped in amber, something we'd study in Mr. Yatkov's science class back in eighth grade. In a way I guess they're lucky—those bugs trapped in amber. They've acquired a degree of immortality no man has ever achieved. Most old people hope their kids remember to call once a week, but to be remembered a million years after you were feeding off dinosaur dung? That's a pretty big accomplishment. It should be enough to give hope to us all.

Here in the cafeteria, we're specimens under the light—not much different than the not-so-rare roast beef drying out under the heat lamp. To take the edge off, to help everyone relax, they pipe in Muzak. But the thing about Muzak is this: once you notice it's there, it's not so relaxing at all.

Despite the enticing kaleidoscope of Jell-O and whipped cream dessert concoctions, we settle for a pair of Cokes and pay the cashier.

"It's a little early for the prom casualties, isn't it?" says the puffy cashier.

Before I can say, "Well, actually . . ." Emily says, "I guess not. My best friend is in critical condition. They say they may never be able to get all the glass out of her face."

"I'm so sorry," says the cashier in full retreat.

"Save it."

If there was a moment I could point to and say I was in love, that would be it.

We head to a corner and sit down, people staring at us—well, actually just at Emily—all the way to our table. Emily looks so good, who could blame them? She's in white, her back bare. Her hair, straight and full, shines across her shoulders. I always thought she was pretty, but not like this. Not like some picture out of a magazine.

"Thanks a lot for coming. I know how you really wanted to go to the prom."

"Without you? What would be the point?"

"Well, for starters, you would have been the most beautiful girl there."

"Tell it to Kelly Kirkwood." Like most girls, Emily can't take a compliment. Around here, if you don't show outward signs of hating yourself by fifth grade, everyone calls you *conceited*.

"I'd be happy to tell Kelly she's not half as hot as she thinks she is."

"Yeah, right. You're just looking for an excuse to talk to her."

The Muzak fills in the empty space. That's what it's for: killing uncomfortable silences in elevators and waiting rooms. Without Muzak, people might actually talk to each other.

"Raindrops Keep Falling on My Head" trickles through the invisible speakers, prompting Emily to ask, "Isn't that the song from *Butch Cassidy*?"

"Annika loves that movie." My dad had taken us all to see it last fall when the revival house did a Newman–Redford retrospective. Dad always liked taking us to movies, probably because then he didn't have to talk to us. For two hours he could just relax and no one could bother him.

"You know what I was looking forward to more than anything?" Emily asks.

"Riding in a limo?"

"You got a limo? Monroe, I told you you didn't have to do that."

"What did you think I was going to do? Pick you up on my bike?"

"*Dancing.* That's what I was looking forward to the most. We've never danced before."

"I didn't know you liked to dance."

"What girl doesn't?"

"Okay, let's dance." I take her arm and lead her to an open space by the salad bar.

Raindrops keep falling on my head . . .

We dance slow.

"Wow, Monroe, you're really good."

"Thanks," I say. I never told her I used to take lessons and I'm not going to tell her now. It would just spoil the illusion. I think Annika would approve, at least I hope so.

We dance like we've been doing it every Friday night of our lives, but usually on Friday nights we end up at a coffeehouse or a movie and if I'm lucky we have enough time to make out in her car before she has to get home. I shouldn't be surprised Emily's a really good dancer. She takes my lead, not that we're doing anything fancy, but I can feel her trust. It's easy, like a conversation you don't have to think about—when you're really listening to what the other person is saying, not worrying about what you're going to say next.

As the tune slips effortlessly into the first sugared-down notes of "Everyone Plays the Fool," a few people applaud. Us. Until then, for those few minutes gliding across the floor, I'd forgotten where we were. Emily looks at me, her lips flush with red. When she was twelve she split her lip open trying to fly her banana bike over a creek. The scar is still there. I think it embarrasses her, but that only makes it sexier than it already is.

"I don't know what I'd do without you," I say way too seriously.

"You'd probably collapse into a fetal ball, roll away, and never be heard from again."

THEY FINALLY KICK us all out of the hospital at eleven. Except Mom and Dad. They get to stay. Ben, remarkably, hasn't left. He's probably been casing the place, trying to figure out a way to get to the drugs. That'd make him quite the hero at the frat house, I'm sure. We head down the elevator with him. He hasn't said a word to Emily all night.

"Nice dress."

"I would let you borrow it, but you'd just stretch it out."

He's not used to people giving him shit, so he just scowls. It's not that he's gay; he just prefers stupid girls. If I'd said that to him, he'd kick my ass; but in an unprecedented move, he plays nice. He says there's a party down on campus. Emily and I can come if we want.

I say, "I really don't feel much like partying."

"And I do?" he replies. "I just want to forget this day ever happened." It's the most compassionate thing I've ever heard him say.

The plan is for Emily to drive me home; I gave Mom her keys back. We're both pretty cashed, but as we're pulling out of the parking lot, I say, "We could probably catch the tail end of the dance. You know, if you want."

"That's sweet of you, Monroe, but I don't really feel like being around anyone—except you."

I don't want to go either. "I just thought I'd throw it out there."

As the Grateful Dead start into the first few bars of "Fire on the Mountain," Emily pulls into the circular driveway in front of our house. I really can't stand the Dead, but in this moment they actually don't sound so bad.

"How come everything always sounds better on the radio?" I ask.

"I don't know," Emily says, even though she does. "I guess sometimes if you're listening to a CD and you're all alone, the music just makes you feel *more* alone. Maybe you want to dance, but there's no one there to dance with or maybe you want to cry and there's no one there to lean on, but with the radio, even if you're listening all by yourself, there're still all these other people listening with you, and all of a sudden it's like you're not alone anymore. You're part of something bigger than just you, you know?"

"I'm glad I'm not alone now," I say.

When she kisses me, the day falls away. It's just the two of us. This was the way this evening was supposed to end.

The band breaks into a jam I'd ordinarily say you'd need to be on acid to appreciate. But my head is clear, clear as it can be, and warm waves of cascading guitar and rolling drums are wrapping and bending around my neck like Emily's fingers do sometimes when she kisses me.

Chapter 4

The sprinklers kick in, waking me up, but I don't move. The car's foggy windows filter the sun in shades of honey. Emily is still sleeping, her face nuzzled on my chest, gently rising and falling with my every breath. There are moments like this, moments you want to hold on to forever, but they're always gone when you realize how great they are. Not this one, though. I know right now I want this one to last as long as it can; so I just stay here, barely breathing, looking at the light on Emily's face, the way each tiny hair on her cheek glows like wheat in the sun. I want to kiss her so badly, but that would just ruin everything.

I see him coming. The windows are encased in fog but I know it's him—the torso in a gray suit. But I'm not going to move. I still have a few more seconds to let this last. Even though it's pretty much ruined for me, it's not yet for her.

He taps on the window hard with a *crack*, his wedding ring taking the brunt of the impact. Emily stirs, her head pushing into my neck, her fingers gripping my shoulder. Two more cracks and she's up: looking around, all mole-eyed and confused, getting her bearings. She looks at me, smiles, and rests her head back on my chest; but the tapping isn't going away. Her mom always says she's hard to get up. I guess I shouldn't have worried about my breathing. Dad keeps rapping over and over again on the driver's-side door. He's nothing if not persistent; that's what people always say. I can't take it anymore and say, "You better get that, Emily." And finally, like she's turning off an alarm clock, Emily rolls down the window.

"Hi, Mr. Anderson."

"Good morning. What are you two doing?" I swear, even though she's eaten dinner with us about a hundred times, Dad still doesn't know her name.

"Hi, Dad, I guess we must have fallen asleep. How's Annika? Anything change?"

"She's still unresponsive. This will be a big day for her. Monroe, we need to talk about what happened." Despite the bags under his eyes, the disheveled suit, the pasty skin, Dad is the consummate professional. He may not even realize it yet, but he's thinking about who he's going to sue.

"Okay."

Then he walks away.

There are so many things I want to say to Emily, but none of them are coming to me. I guess they could be encompassed in one big "I love you," but saying that will probably just screw everything up. Instead, I look at her like a doofus. *That,* she's used to.

With a kiss she's gone. Just that fast. And as I watch her round the corner it's hard to believe that only minutes ago I never felt so connected to anyone in my life.

DAD'S IN THE KITCHEN trying to make coffee. He looks perplexed, as if brewing a cup of coffee is the most difficult thing he's ever done.

"Monroe, it doesn't look good."

"First you put the filter in, *then* the coffee," I say, trying to lighten the mood. But it doesn't.

"Monroe, I'm talking about your sister."

"What do the doctors say?"

"She could snap out of it any time, but they don't really know anything, any more than we do."

"How's Mom doing?" I ask.

"Father Ferger stayed with us most of the night. He seems to help your mother."

Then, just like a lawyer, he says, "Monroe, I need to know *exactly* what happened yesterday. Start from the beginning." It's like all of a sudden I'm on the stand. My palms are sweating. My heart is racing. This is the way Dad likes it.

"I was going out to the pool house to uh . . . look for my wallet, you know before the prom . . . and Annika was just floating. I thought she was joking, so I threw a tennis ball at her. She didn't move, so I dove in. . . . It all happened really fast."

"Damnit. I knew we shouldn't have gotten that pool."

I don't know what to say. I've always been a big fan of the pool.

"The doctor said you saved her life."

"I just happened to be there. Even Ben probably would have done the same thing." I probably shouldn't have said that. Ben is Dad's favorite, but he lets it go.

"You know your mother and I love you very much."

"Yeah, I know." Actually, I had never given the matter much thought: the depth of their emotions for me. He'd never actually uttered those words before—*I love you*. Neither had Mom. Not once out loud. It's not like they have to. It's not like I walk around feeling *unloved*. Every year I get a birthday card from them that says just that: *Love, Mom and Dad*. Each of them signs it. Just because someone at Hallmark wrote whatever else came before it, it doesn't necessarily mean the sentiment's not true. It's enough for me. Still, hearing the words for the first time—that's when I know this is *serious*.

Dad follows up his proclamation of love with a hug, continuing an avalanche of firsts. He's holding on tight, so I pat his back. I don't know why. It just seems like the thing to do. Like you see on TV. It's supposed to be reassuring, I guess. Whatever it does, it's working. You'd think Dad would be stiff after so many years with a stick up his ass, but right now, he's melting.

He pulls away from me, like he's forgotten where he is. "God damnit, I don't think I've ever made a pot of coffee in my life." I think he's about to cry. He turns his back on me and starts picking at a pack of filters, but he's having trouble peeling one off.

I'VE SEEN MY FATHER get emotional only once before, but he didn't know I was there.

It was like this: Ben started drinking along the stretch of campus bars that runs up and down High Street the day he turned sixteen. You'd have hated him at first sight—preppy, tanned, square-jawed.

It happened at a red light. Ben was driving the Audi convertible Dad got for him when he won the Junior Nationals. No one likes a kid in a car like that. Sure, in Chelsea it's expected, but beyond these borders it's a different story. So when some rednecks in a pickup started calling Ben and his buddy faggots, it was only natural. As rednecks, that's kind of their job, to keep a lookout for preppy rich kids and give them shit. And despite his proclivity for torturing me, Ben wasn't one to get in a fight with someone his own size.

He probably thought he was safe on such a busy street, even if the top was down. Besides, he wasn't alone; one of his meathead friends was with him. I don't know what Ben said. He probably called them trailer trash. He probably said they could be bought and sold with his spare change. That would be just like him. Ben's considered quite witty among his frat boy friends.

Whatever he said, it was enough to prompt one of the rednecks to jump out of the truck at a stoplight and pull Ben from the driver's seat—not all the way—just far enough so he could open and slam the door on Ben's head. Over and over again. By the time the light turned green, Ben was all red, a bloody husk, slumped on the pavement.

If the call from the hospital hadn't woken me up, I might have missed the whole thing. After Dad sped out of the driveway, I went downstairs to see what was going on, but Mom told me not to worry and go back to bed. *Everything was okay.* But I couldn't sleep. So when Dad's car pulled in the driveway, I was watching through the bars of the banister.

I saw it all. Ben wore a white button-down shirt when he went out that night. When he came through the door at three in the morning, the shirt was red with blood, and his face a puffy mass of black and blue. His left eye swollen shut. It was days before they were able to find the contact lens lodged somewhere in the bruised mess of flesh. He looked awful, his head striped in bandages, but he was so drunk when he came through the door, he couldn't stop laughing.

When Mom saw him she couldn't stop crying. Annika slept through the whole thing. I guess she always has been a heavy sleeper.

I'd never seen Dad cry before that night. Not at a funeral, a wedding, or a movie. Never. I certainly didn't see it coming. After Ben passed out, I watched through a crack in the door while he sat in the master bedroom with my mom, listing all the ways he figured he had failed as a parent. It was like he was putting himself on trial. Exhibit A: "I'm never around." Exhibit B: "I can't even remember my children's birthdays." Exhibit C: "I never should have let him take sips of my Heineken." Exhibit D: "I should have gone to more golf tournaments." Exhibit E: "I should have eaten at home more, you know, like a family." Exhibit F: "I spend so much time planning for the future, I never enjoy the present."

I was surprised to see him take responsibility for anything; he had spent his entire life assigning blame to everyone else. That's his job. That's what lawyers do. Now here he was blaming himself because his son is a drunken asshole. He could list exhibits until he got to triple z, but it wouldn't matter. They're just excuses. Ben's a drunk because he likes to drink. It's that simple; it makes him feel good. Even though he's this gifted golfer, he's like most everyone else—he doesn't really like who he is very much. In his case, it's for a good reason and when he's lit, he manages to forget that troubling fact for a little while. That's probably why most people drink—to forget what assholes they are. I've done it myself. And the drunker I got, the bigger asshole I became.

Maybe it's just in us. We have no choice in the matter. We're programmed that way. It's genetic. After all, my dad's father was a boozer. Like anything else that's interesting around here, no one told me about it. I had to find it out myself. I knew both my grandparents died in a car crash, but that was about it. That was long before they ever got a chance to be grandparents. They only gained that distinction in death. No one ever mentioned it happened because my grandfather was wasted. I would have thought it was an accident, like everyone else, but in sixth grade I had to do a report on them for school. Since I didn't know them and Dad was nowhere to be found, I looked them up at the library. Even though that was a long time ago, when even less probably happened around here than it does now, I figured I'd find an obituary. Just a few *facts*. I didn't expect it to be front-page news. I didn't expect to see a picture of my grandfather's arm hanging out of the car, a broken bottle of whiskey on the ground.

So Dad was blaming himself for Ben. It was refreshing to see him be so human for once in my life. While it didn't stop me from being afraid of him, it helped.

For a lawyer, Dad never had much of a sense for justice. He'd probably say justice just gets in the way of practicing law. *It's an occupational hazard.* It would have been nice, though, if he could have treated all us kids the same. My driving privileges get revoked after one little accident, while Ben drives drunk and not only gets to keep his car, but gets to continue driving it wherever and whenever he wants. His punishment? A weekend in rehab. It was supposed to last a week but they kicked him out because he wouldn't admit that he had a problem. You have to say you're powerless to alcohol and he wouldn't do it. No one seemed to have a problem with that. After all, if Ben wanted to deny he was a drunk, everyone else could too. So Ben kept his car while I've spent my high school career riding around on my bike. I wasn't even allowed to get a moped. It wasn't worth bringing up this inconsistency with Dad; he would have just said I was whining. After all, Ben, the gifted golfer, had places to go. I didn't.

Back in the kitchen, Dad wonders, "How can a grown man not know how to make a cup of coffee?"

"I don't know, Dad. I guess you've led a charmed life."

"Again with the sarcasm."

"Sorry, Dad."

Dad says sarcasm is a mark of the passive-aggressive and weak. And maybe it is. But when you're eighteen there aren't many other weapons in your arsenal. The real trouble with my sarcasm is that half the time people think I'm being sarcastic, I'm actually being quite sincere.

I go up to my room and lie down just for a minute, resting my eyes, gathering the strength to take off my clothes.

WHEN MOM WAKES me up, it's two in the afternoon. She says I should go over to the hospital. "Annika would like it if you did."

"She's awake?" I ask.

"No, not yet. But she knows we're there. I can feel it."

Even though it sounds like wishful thinking to me, I don't say anything. I put the pillow over my head and hope she'll go away. I hope maybe I'll fall back asleep and when I awake yesterday will be erased and everything will be like it was before.

Mom always wanted to be a ballet dancer. It's not the most original dream for a girl, I know, but it was hers. However, there's a difference between Mom and the millions of other girls dreaming that dream. Mom actually made a pretty good run at making it come true. At fifteen years old she was accepted to the summer program at the School of American Ballet in New York, a small-town girl from a farm outside Toledo.

It was a rainy Sunday when my mom got off the bus in front of the Metropolitan Museum of Art. She had only been in New York for about two days and she was alone. She wanted to see Degas' dancers. I guess it's something you have to do if you're a ballerina, make a pilgrimage to the Met and pay homage to the dancers. But she never made it into the museum. As she got off the back of the bus, the belt buckle from her jacket got stuck in the door. She was tangled up but managed to run along with the bus, that is, until she tripped on a sewer grate. That must have been when the bus ran over her ankle. To make matters worse, she was dragged about a hundred feet down the street before the driver finally realized what was going on. By then it was too late.

Mom didn't dance again until the night she married my dad.

Mom always says she's lucky. After all, she could have died like Isadora Duncan. Isadora was a dancer too, but not ballet, more like modern dance, which always seems to me like playing baseball without any rules. I don't really know much about art, but it's hard to respect something when you can't tell if someone's making a mistake. That's what I told Mom, but she said that beauty is beauty, whether you're coloring inside the lines or not.

Isadora was driving a convertible along the French Riviera in 1927, her scarf flowing in the wind behind her. She must have been beautiful, a postcard in motion. But somehow that scarf got caught in her back wheel. I guess it was a pretty long scarf. It couldn't have taken many rotations of the tire to snap her neck. One second she's driving along enjoying the view, the next second she's dead. She probably never knew what happened. I guess that's the most you can hope for when anyone dies.

Mom says Isadora's life wasn't easy, that it's a wonder she could bring herself to dance at all. Isadora grew up in poverty and suffered more than her share of tragedies. In fact, she had two children who drowned when their car rolled into the Seine River as their nanny watched, helpless. Now, it looks like Mom has something else in common with Isadora . . . well, almost.

While Isadora was pretty much a bohemian and Mom, well, *isn't*, you never know, they might have gotten along. If they met at a cocktail party, they could talk about how much they don't like cats. Isadora could tell the story about how she used to live next to a cat sanctuary. The cats didn't pay much attention to her fence and started hanging out in her garden. Isadora didn't like that much, so in retaliation she ordered her servants to kill any and all trespassing cats. And as a warning to their cat friends, their cat corpses were to be hung around the perimeter.

It worked; the surviving cats got the message. This solution may seem cruel, perhaps even barbaric. But it sounds like a fair warning to me. It sounds like the work of someone who doesn't really want to kill any more cats, but will only if they have to. Cats have a way of pushing the envelope. This way, at least, they knew the score.

Mom has a story of her own. She could tell Isadora about how when I was a kid I used to spend a lot of time in the sandbox. That is, until the neighborhood cats started using it as a litter box. Soon after that startling discovery, I got sick. Mom did the math, although science would have probably been more appropriate, and concluded the cats got me sick. She was thoroughly appalled and banned me from playing there anymore (as if I needed to be told).

I thought that was that, but soon thereafter, posters for lost cats began popping up on lampposts throughout the four-block radius around our house. Rumors abounded: satanic teenagers were sacrificing them, mysterious black panthers were eating them, the local Chinese restaurant was serving them. . . . Articles were written in the paper. Emergency teas were held. *Something needed to be done.* I had no idea there were so many cat lovers among us. There hadn't been this level of community activism around here since they banned gasoline-powered leaf blowers.

There's an abandoned quarry across the river. There's a hole in the fence—you can get through if you want. It's not like anyone's going to stop you, although everyone knows you're in big trouble if you get caught there, let alone swim in the water. Hidden in the bushes, I used to watch my brother and his friends drink beers on the edge of the cliff, until they got enough courage to dive in. They never even knew I was there.

Until, one day they spotted me. I didn't hang around to find out what would happen next. I knew. As I beat it through the brush, rocks rained down all around me.

The weird part was when I saw Mom's Volvo parked by the side of the river. I slipped behind a tree and watched her. I thought maybe she was there like me—to spy—that she was there to bust Ben. But that wasn't it at all. When she got out of the car, she looked around, as if to check to see if the coast was clear. Convinced she was alone, she opened the back door of the wagon. In there, she had two cages, one cat in each one. When she opened the latches, they bolted into the brush. Satisfied, Mom got back in her car and drove away. Mission complete.

That day, I knew my mother loved me. I knew that she really cared. "I love you" weren't just words on a birthday card; she was actually willing to back them up.

I never let on that I saw her. It would be our secret. She just doesn't know we share it. She could tell that story to Isadora; but I guess if it ever came to that, secrets wouldn't matter much anyway.

Chapter 5

I GO BY MYSELF to see Annika. Mom has finally passed out; Dad's drained. Someone has to keep watch, so I take the baton, which comes to me in the form of Dad's car keys. I've been waiting for the moment when Dad gives me the keys to his car for two years and here it is. As you might imagine, it's not nearly as fulfilling as I'd hoped it would be.

Dr. Singh is looking in on her when I arrive. He tells me again how I saved my sister's life, how I got there just in time.

I tell him I wish I'd gotten there sooner. Then maybe she wouldn't be here at all. He pats me on the back, not knowing what to say. Dr. Singh really needs to work on his bedside manner. He could at least tell me I shouldn't blame myself. Even though I know that, it would be nice to hear it. I know I shouldn't be feeling guilty, so I tell myself if I weren't slinking around getting stoned, I wouldn't have been there at all. Annika would be dead now. It's pretty much that simple.

As the doctor jots down a few notes, I stare out the window at a big brown stain on the wall across the way.

The doctor leaves and I return to watching Annika breathe. There's something so peaceful about it, so rhythmic and reassuring in its repetition. And she's doing it all on her own now; the respirator is gone. That's a good sign. Still, I feel like I'm in the reptile hut at the zoo, looking at the lizards. They're barely moving. It's easy to wonder if they're alive at all. It says not to tap on the glass and that only makes me want to tap more. But there's no glass between me and Annika. I put my hand on her wrist. I can feel her pulse, gulps of blood passing through her, going in circles, and suddenly she doesn't seem so far away anymore.

There's a tube going through her nose, down her throat. She looks like a grouper. In slow motion her lips move, barely opening, never quite closing. Maybe she's trying to say something? Maybe there's nothing to say at all.

We used to come back late at night whenever we visited our grandparents. Annika would be wide awake, that is, until we were about fifteen minutes away from home. Then she'd curl up and shut her eyes. It was as if the Columbus city limits induced narcolepsy, an altogether not surprising development. As we drove by downtown, not even the sweet smell of turpentine-drenched dough emanating from the Wonder Bread factory would stir her. Once we pulled in the driveway, everyone would be opening and closing doors, dragging junk out of the trunk; but still Annika wouldn't move. Once the car was empty, Dad would pick her up, carry her up the stairs into her room, and tuck her in.

Everyone knew she was faking, but no one ever said anything. Not even Ben. It was just something we always did, letting Annika play sleeping beauty. She got such a kick out of it, it would have been cruel not to.

You could always count on Annika to keep up a conversation, but now it's all on me. "You know I love you, right? I know I've never said it before, but you know that, don't you?"

A bubble of saliva forms on the side of her mouth.

"Come on, Annika, just wake up, okay? We'll take a ride in Mom's car. We'll put the top down and drive out to Jasper's Farm and get some apple fritters."

The mere mention of apple fritters is usually enough to bring Annika out of any corner in the house, but she doesn't stir. She just breathes, the same as before: in and out, in and out. . . .

I start telling her about the Reds and how we're going to go see them next week. How she'd better not flake out on me. I tell her that if she doesn't wake up soon, there's no way the Reds will win this year. Their season will be *over* and it'll all be her fault. I know that's pretty harsh, but I don't know what else to say.

There's not a TV in here, that's how serious this room is. I sit and listen to the machines that monitor every beat of her heart, every blip of her brain. It's a symphony of blips and beeps. Even Annika joins in—breathing in, breathing out. All I can think is, "Annika, just *breathe* . . . please just keep *breathing.*"

I never saw that movie *Coma*, but I saw the box at the video store. In the picture there's a room of coma patients and they're all suspended in the air by strings. It's like they're marionettes hooked up to the clouds, but God can't be bothered to make them move. He just leaves them hanging. Annika is the opposite of that. She's so deeply rooted to the ground, tethered to machines, the mattress might as well be swallowing her.

I wonder for a second if all she wants is to be tucked in her own bed, that maybe she's faking. That all she wants is a ride up the stairs. We always let her get away with it. Maybe that's what she's waiting for, a piggyback ride home.

"Come on, Annika, this is really getting old, really *fucking* old. Let's just go home." I guess I'm getting kind of upset. I've never said "fuck" in front of her in my life, not that it matters. Ben says it all the time.

Beep, blip, blip, blip, beep . . . Nothing.

"I know all about your tricks." I'm practically yelling right in her ear. "It's not funny anymore!"

Then I get that feeling you get when someone is watching you. I look over and there's a priest, his face halfway in the door. "Hi, Monroe, sorry to intrude," he says. I must have been looking at him blankly, because he adds, "Father Ferger?" His skin is like an old, wrinkling peach. His bulging body suggests that his vow of poverty clearly does not extend to food. His blond hair is as thin as the forced smile on his face.

"Of course, Father. Come on in," I say.

It's not that I want him to come in—I would rather sit here with Annika by myself—but I don't really have a choice. After all, even though we never really go to church, he *is* the family priest. Dad's always giving the church a ton of dough, so he has no choice but to comfort us.

To further perpetuate the charade, I stand up to shake his hand. And with that small gesture, he takes me into his arms and hugs me. That's the thing about priests; they're always trying to get their hands on you. And I don't necessarily mean in a sexual way. It's more like they all went to some sales seminar where they were told if you touch the customer you have a 33 percent higher chance of getting them to walk home with something they definitely don't need, but think they can't live without.

When he finally lets me go, he says, "You sure have grown, Monroe." I hate when old people say that. It's like every party my parents have ever had. All anyone ever talks about is how much I've grown, even though I haven't grown an inch in the last three years. I must be some sort of walking optical illusion. I should have said that it looks like he's lost a lot of hair—at least that's true, but I don't. Instead, I just smile like an idiot.

"How's our patient today?" he says, squeezing Annika's foot. Annika's feet are usually really ticklish, so ticklish it's not even fair to *pretend* to touch them. I want to tell him to get his mitts off her, but she doesn't move, so I guess it doesn't really matter anyway.

"The same, I guess."

"We hope to change that," he replies. "It should be really cool."

I swear to God, that's exactly what the balding priest with the growing paunch said: *It should be really cool.*

TURNS OUT, FATHER FERGER isn't here just to comfort the family, he's here to help *heal* Annika—that is, if you think prayer can do that kind of thing. I always figured you'd have almost as much of a chance dialing up God with a prayer as you do getting roadside assistance off one of those plastic cell phones full of bubble gum. But maybe I was thinking about it all in the wrong way. God is pretty busy, I imagine, so perhaps it's more fruitful to go through the proper channels. It's like how if you want to get a senator to do something you better send a lobbyist. It's the same with the Catholic God; instead of lobbyists, you use saints to get your message across. If your prayer is considered worthy, your chosen saint *might* be willing to petition God on your behalf. That's what Catholics believe—that saints have the ear of God, they're right by His side. You can't have a personal relationship with God; you have to go through a middle man. It's quite the spiritual bureaucracy.

"Take a look out the window, Monroe."

I pull open the drape. We're on the seventh floor. There must be thirty or forty people down there, milling around in the front of the building.

They see us looking down on them and they hold up their signs: "ANNIKA, WE LOVE YOU" "GOD IS ON YOUR SIDE." "YOU'RE NOT ALONE."

"Pretty good turnout, don't you think?"

"Who are those people?" I ask.

He says they're from the church, that they want to do whatever they can to help. While it sounds like a stupid idea to me, I don't say that. After all, he's only trying to help and it probably can't hurt. Even though Father Ferger is wearing a collar, truth is, it's hard not to like him. He has a way about him, like everything is going to be all right. Like you could say anything to him and he wouldn't really judge you, even though that's his job. This likeability, however, does not make me trust him more; in fact, it makes me suspicious. Being nice may be his diabolical way of lulling unsuspecting boys into his clutches. Granted, it's not like he ever tried anything with me or as far as I know with anyone I know; but then again, I got out early. Maybe he likes his boys a little older. Or maybe he already had his way with me and I'm repressing memories of abuse. I saw a movie about that once. It happens.

"Father, do my parents know about this?"

"Actually, it was my idea." Mom says that, arriving with Dad in tow. Immediately, she's at Annika's side. "How is my little baby?" she coos as she caresses her face.

Dad goes to the window and says something about it looking like a lot more people from up here. Father Ferger puts his arm around his shoulder. "Larry, we're going to get through this. It's going to work out. I can *feel* it." Even I almost believe him, but Dad's expression never changes. He might as well be on a plane looking out the window, lost in the clouds.

"Look," Ferger says, way too excited, "They're doing the circle of prayer. I better get down there."

When Father Ferger leaves, no one really knows what to say, although I bet Annika would if she could. She actually *likes* going to church.

Annika used to sneak a couple of extra Communion wafers and slip them in her pockets. Then when she got home she'd come into my room while I was still in bed and she'd offer one to me, saying, "Would you like a wafer-thin wafer?" And even though I was kind of annoyed to be woken up, I'd say, "Yes, I'd love one." Then she'd give it to me and once it was in my mouth, she'd say, "Ha. That wasn't a wafer at all. It was the *body* of Jesus Christ! You just ate Jesus Christ's *flesh*." And then I'd say, "Now I vant to drink his blood," you know like Dracula, and she'd run out of the room and I wouldn't see her again until the pancakes were ready and it was time to come down for breakfast. There, at the table, everyone else would have orange juice, but at my place, Annika always had a glass of grape juice waiting for me.

I'm staring at a painting of sunflowers behind Annika's bed, wondering if there'll ever be any more Sunday mornings like that. The painting is nothing special. It's not even a van Gogh reproduction, just an afterthought—the kind of art they sell in hotel banquet rooms on Saturday afternoons. It's a little crooked. I keep staring at it until the flowers become a yellow and green blur. It looks better that way, as swirling colors, but then I blink and it comes back into focus—sunflowers in a field. I want the blur to come back, so I start staring again, thinking about how Mom's got all these art books at home, the kind that people put on the coffee table but never really look at. If it wasn't for Annika, ours would have been like that too—crisp with unbroken spines; but she couldn't keep her hands off them, especially the one on Jackson Pollock. I always thought it was a joke that people made such a big deal about him. All I could ever see were splatters of paint, but Annika said that if you looked hard enough, you could see dancing. I really tried, but I couldn't see anything like that, even when I was stoned. The sunflowers here in the hospital room are different, though. Once I stare right through them, they do kind of dance. At the very least, they sway in the wind. Who knows? Maybe religion is kind of like art. You can look at it all day and in the end, you see whatever you want to.

Dad was raised Catholic, but he's a busy man and thinking about God probably only gets in the way. It's not like it's something we ever talk about, religion. I overheard someone at a cocktail party describe my dad like this: "You know how it is when you find a stray dog who's been living off the streets? Scavenging from meal to meal? So, you bring the dog into your home, give him everything it wants; but every time you lay down some food for it, the dog devours it like it may never eat again? Well that's the way Larry Anderson practices law." He said it like it was a compliment. Everyone laughed, even my dad.

See, Dad grew up poor, so poor that he never wanted to talk about it. Not even to brag, not even to say, "See how easy you have it compared to me?" He's not like that. He only wanted to put it all behind him and to his credit he's done just that. He was only thirty-one when he bought the house on Stoneridge Road. He'd just made a ton of cash suing an air-conditioning company. Their air conditioners were leaking some noxious carcinogens into the cooled air. The company knew what the problem was, but they figured it was easier to do nothing than to have a recall; besides, they probably figured no one would ever notice. There's so much junk floating around in the air as it is, who's to say where it all comes from? No one thought he had a chance. He was David. They were Goliath.

At the time, it was the biggest settlement ever against an industrial manufacturer; but that was long before I was ever born. It's just a story I read about in the library. He may have been David then, but ever since I've known him, he's always been Goliath.

Finally, Dad turns away from the window and says, "I wonder if it's going to rain?" But there isn't even a cloud in the sky. Mom doesn't answer; she keeps stroking Annika's creamy yellow hair, saying, "Oh, sweetheart, everything's going to be okay."

"So, I guess you guys got this shift?" I ask.

"You're welcome to stick around," Mom encourages.

"I don't think I've eaten yet today."

"Well, don't go out, the house is full of food. . . . Everyone has been so nice."

That means macaroni and cheese from Mrs. Geiger, a casserole from Mrs. Haverford, a chocolate cake from Mrs. Otis, a meat loaf from Mrs. Rawlins. . . . They did the same thing when Mom had her hysterectomy three years ago.

"Okay, Mom."

As I head out the door, Dad follows me, reaching for his wallet. He pulls out a twenty.

"Here you go, get yourself a pizza."

"Thanks, Dad."

"Be sure to save your old dad a slice. Okay?"

"Sure, Dad," I say.

I HAVE TO GO by the prayer group to get to the car—there's no way to avoid them. Father Ferger spots me.

"Monroe, would you like to join us?"

"No thanks, Father, I'd love to, but I'm kind of in a hurry."

"I'll be around if you ever feel like talking."

"I've got this . . . ummmm thing," I stutter as I flee.

His flock, his parishioners, his *drones*—whatever you want to call them—wave to me. I give them the thumbs-up sign and immediately I want to kill myself. *Thumbs-up?* I skulk away in shame, thinking, *What will I do next? Flash the peace sign? High-five complete strangers?* I'm not saying I don't appreciate what they're trying to do. I do. I really do. It's not like it can make anything worse than it already is.

I sit in the car; I don't know where to go. Home sounds so depressing: a kitchen full of aluminum foil, an empty room where Annika should be, and a pool filled with one big bad memory.

What I want to do is forget, like Ben said. Maybe I should go down to campus and track him down. Ben has always liked to get me drunk. He thinks it's funny. He thinks it's funny to get dogs drunk too. That's the way he is. The first time he introduced me to alcohol was at my twelfth birthday party. Peach schnapps over ice. He said it was a special birthday treat, that schnapps was a rare nectar and there wasn't enough to go around. *Don't tell anyone.* Made sense at the time.

We were at the go-cart track with all my so-called friends. I remember going fast and having no fear. I remember feeling strangely focused, yet completely out of control. I remember slicing through the cool autumn night and the faces blurring by. I remember pumping the gas, wanting to go faster, faster; but I could never go fast enough. I don't really remember running into the wall and spinning across the track, but I do remember laughing my head off like it was the funniest thing in the world.

Ben was laughing too. Only later would I figure out why. While I'm sure Ben thinks it's funny to see me drunk, I know what he *really* likes is for me to get into trouble. I don't know why he cares so much; he'll always be the favorite son. Just insurance, I guess. The thing is, when he gets caught, nothing happens, but when I get caught, the world comes tumbling down. That's probably what he finds so entertaining.

I should go over to Emily's instead. I don't need to be drunk; I only want to feel like everything is going to be all right. Maybe that's as much of an illusion as being drunk, but at least I won't have a hangover in the morning.

Emily lives on the edge of the Chelsea school district. Her parents work at Ohio State. Her dad's a psychology professor and her mom's a molecular biologist. They like to be called Bob and Lily.

They're the nicest adults I ever met, definitely not like my parents' friends, who never fail to ask me a string of stupid questions. Seriously, they must think I'm a retard, always asking how tall I am, always wondering how school is going. Talking real slow. Don't they remember what it was like to be young? Or is that what it means to be an adult—you forget? And, sadly, the more they forget, the more they try to recapture what they had. It doesn't really give you much to look forward to.

Through the screen door, I can see Lily singing along with Janis Joplin as she chops up some carrots. She's got a beautiful voice, she really does. I hate to interrupt her, but I guess I must have been standing in her light. She turns around, sees me, and drops her knife on the ground.

I barely manage, "I'm sorry, I didn't mean to . . ." before she takes me into her arms and hugs me, not saying a word. She smells like cinnamon. Her hair is soft against the side of my face, like Emily's. In fact, people sometimes think they're sisters, a comparison that goes beyond the way they share long, dirty blonde hair and the kind of deep blue eyes that make oceans seem shallow. When people say they look alike, it's a mirror that relies on the way Lily's smile easily washes ten years off her face.

When she rubs my back, that's when I start to cry. When it all really hits me. No heaves and sighs, just tears flowing down my cheeks. Most people would have given you a hug and let go; but Lily holds on, like she's trying to make sense out of it all too. Like she needs the hug as much as I do.

Emily hollers from upstairs, "Mom!" cutting the moment in two. "Have you seen my polka-dot shirt?!" In a second, she's in the kitchen, where she can see for herself—her shirt is covered with my stupid tears.

"Monroe, you're here. I was about to call you." But when she sees my face she must have thought the worst. "OhmyGod, what happened?"

"Nothing's changed," I say, wiping my face. "She's still the same."

"Do you want me to go over to the hospital with you?"

"I was just there. There's a bunch of people from the church praying outside."

Lily says, "At least that won't hurt." Considering that she's an atheist, it's a very diplomatic thing to say. Lily says that she has some things to do down in the basement and she disappears, leaving the kitchen to Emily, me, and the warm smell of slowly bubbling vegetable soup. Emily smiles her crooked split-lip smile and right here, right now, I feel like maybe everything really will be okay.

"I wish I knew what I could do," she says, holding me in her arms.

"You're already doing it."

THE WORST THING that ever happened in Chelsea was when Heidi Morgan went missing. I was in sixth grade. She was in third. There were only two weeks left of school. It might as well have already been summer. When she didn't come home by three-thirty, her mother lost it. Heidi *always* came home on time.

It didn't take long to find her, only a few hours. Heidi was in a drainage culvert about a hundred yards from her house. She'd been raped, and her head was smashed with a rock. A few hours before she was just a nine-year-old walking home with her books. Then she was dead and it wasn't even dark out yet.

At school the next day, they brought us all into the gymnasium to tell us what happened; but thanks to the papers and the television, everyone already knew. Her sister, Allison, was in my class, but she wasn't in school that day, not that anyone expected her to be. She didn't come back to school again that year.

No one really knew what to do, but we wanted to do something, so Mrs. Ansel, our teacher, got us all to make a card and send it to the family. We did the same thing for the Oklahoma City bombing. We sent Oklahoma a card too. No one could figure out why that happened either. *Sending a card*—it made us think we'd done something good and maybe we did; but now it feels like we should have done something *more*—not that there's anything you can really do besides letting Oklahoma know how much you care. That they're not *completely* alone.

When school let out for the summer, no one ever saw Allison at the pool or at the mall or at the park. Then that fall, when the new school year started, we were in junior high, and like a lot of people, she fell between the cracks. It's easy to do around here when you're not one of the beautiful people or an athlete. But Allison was more invisible than most; she went through the day like a ghost.

In high school, Allison became sort of a hippie, which basically means she was probably high most of the time. A lot of kids were like that, so it didn't really make her stick out. It's not like being a hippie exactly takes a lot of work. If you can put up with the music, pretty much anyone can pull it off.

Sometimes I'd talk to her behind the gym, but she never said much. She wanted to be left alone, her sadness as blatant as the cloud of smoke hanging around her head. All that changed, though, when she danced. It didn't even matter to what kind of music. Even when the marching band played at a mandatory pep rally or something stupid like that, she'd start twirling around in Tasmanian Devil swirls. I always wondered what was going on in her head when she danced. But it was probably nothing. Maybe that's why she looked so happy.

After Heidi was killed, orange "safety spots" popped up all over—houses you could run to if you were in trouble, but after about a year, the cardboard cutouts in the windows disappeared. Maybe acknowledging that danger lurked even here in our sanitized little enclave was too much for people to handle. People said the safety spots were bad for property values. That seemed to be what people cared about the most—*property values*. And those orange dots were like measles; they said that our neighborhood wasn't well. But when they came down, it's not like we were cured. After all, they never caught the killer. While people didn't talk about Heidi much, no one ever forgot. We lived less than a mile from Annika's school, but not once in her life did she ever get to walk there by herself or even ride her bike. That's just the way it was. It's not like she ever knew what she was missing.

Every time I see the Chelsea police pull someone over, which is all the time, I always think of Heidi. If they ever stop me, the first thing I'll say is, "So you find out who killed Heidi yet?" and they'll say they haven't and I'll say, "And you have nothing better to do than give me a ticket?"

It won't exactly keep them from writing me up, but since I'm not a girl, it's not like there's anything I can do to stop them anyway.

Emily says, "Maybe we should get out of here for a while."

I HAVE THE TWENTY DOLLARS Dad gave me in my pocket, so we decide to go to Antoine's Pizza. Emily thinks it might be a good idea to ride her parents' bikes. She says I look kind of pale, that a little exercise will do me some good. I'm in no position to disagree. Besides, I like the idea of bikes. I won't have to talk, but I also won't have to be alone. People always expect you to talk to them, but Emily never seems to mind the silences between us. Sometimes that silence seems to glue us together. Like words only get in the way of what we're really thinking.

We get to Antoine's too fast. I wish we could have kept pedaling. Antoine's is practically the only pizza I've ever had in my life. It's hard to imagine anywhere else being better. Josie has been working there ever since I can remember and probably a lot longer than that. She likes to remind everyone that she used to be good-looking and with very little prodding she'll point to a picture on the wall as proof. If it is her, it's true. She really was hot.

Josie always greets me by saying something like, "Monroe, nice face, looks like you'll be providing the pepperoni"—but today she doesn't do that. Instead, she flashes a sympathetic smile and says, "How's Annika doing?"

"She's the same," I say.

"She's in all of our prayers, you know." I had never really pegged Josie as a religious person. But, then again, it's probably just one of those things people say.

She seats us at the best table in the house, a booth hidden in the corner. Usually, you have to hit a home run or score the winning touchdown to get to sit there, like it's a big deal or something. It doesn't feel that way today. There's a picture of Ben hanging over my head; he's holding up the state trophy he won as a freshman golfer at Chelsea High.

A television mumbles the local news. I don't know how they fill up a whole half hour around here. Not a lot happens, which is why a lot of people live here in the first place and why a lot more people say they want to move the first chance they get. The newscaster Cheryl Hanover has that look on her face too, like she's passing through. Her highlighted blonde hair, her collagen-lipped smile, her bursting bustline: they're all too big for this town. I can't hear what she's saying and it probably doesn't really matter.

Emily wants to know what it was like over at the hospital. But I don't have to tell her. All she has to do is look at the television. There must be less than nothing going on in the Buckeye capital; they're actually covering the crowd of well-wishers who've gathered below Annika's window. There's a reporter on the scene. The crowd must have tripled since I was there, or maybe like they say, everything looks bigger on TV.

They put Annika's picture up on the screen. It's the one they took at school last year. She's wearing a smile that looks like it could last forever. Thankfully, it's a short story and I don't think anyone is paying attention, but back here in the corner it's hard to tell.

When they cut to the commercials, Josie comes over with a pitcher of Coke. "It's on the house," she says.

"Thanks, Josie." It's weird having her be so nice. If she really wanted to make me feel better, she should have made fun of me. *Monroe, did Stevie Wonder cut your hair? Who dressed you today, Helen Keller? Is that a thimble in your pocket, or are you just happy to see me?*

"A pity pitcher," says Emily.

We aren't the only ones watching; the people in the next booth are watching too. One guy says, "Being in a coma must suck." Then another guy says, "It wouldn't suck because you wouldn't even know you were in a coma. You wouldn't know *anything.*"

"Yeah, dude, kind of like you are right now."

"All I know, man, is that if she doesn't wake up soon, *like in the next day,* she'll probably be a vegetable for the rest of her life. That's what my dad said. And he's a doctor, you know." Fuck, it's Alex Stephenson. I'd know his voice anywhere. He used to be my best friend, but that was about five years ago.

"Imagine being a fucking vegetable. No one would ever wanna fucking eat you." That's the wit of Todd Amberson, which prompts Alex to reply, "Look at you, Amberson; you're a piece of meat and no one wants to eat you either." Even though Todd always has been sub-mental, he used to be my friend too. His claim to fame is that last year he was in New York with his parents and on *David Letterman* he was picked from the audience to perform the stupid human trick of taking off his shoelace and running it up his nose and out his mouth, a stunt he's been perfecting since third grade.

Alex and Todd turned against me in junior high for the crime of allegedly calling them faggots, which is completely untrue. Of course, this information came from Andrew McGee, a notorious liar. I denied it, but they didn't believe me, only because deep down they probably knew it was true.

After school one day, they chased me down on my bike. In attempting to make a covert turn into our driveway, I crashed into a pine tree and racked myself on the gear shift. Rolling around on the ground with my pants covered in blood and tears in my eyes, it was definitely not one for the highlight reel. That wouldn't have stopped them from beating me up too, but my mom was unloading groceries at the time. Embarrassingly enough, she came to my aid. A couple kicks in the head surely would have been better than hearing them cackle as they pedaled away. It's the same laugh they're cackling now, the hyenas.

Over the years we developed an unspoken deal—ignore one another and everything will be fine. Mainly for me. After all, they can beat me up anytime they want.

Emily is more annoyed than me. They're assholes; that's who they are. I expect them to be jerks in the same way I expect fish to swim. Emily, though, is chewing her cheek, dying to rip into them. I tell her that it's okay, not to worry about it. "Just ignore them," I say.

Emily's jaw quivers in response.

When Josie comes back I ask her if we can get that pie to go. "Sure, whatever you want, Monroe."

She brings back the pizza and a six-pack of Coke—on the house. "Tell your mom and dad we all send our best," she says.

We get up to go and pass Alex and Todd's table. I want so badly to say, "Hey faggots, how's it going?" But I don't.

As we walk by, Alex says, "Hey, Anderson, sorry to hear about your sister."

Todd gets with the program and adds, "Yeah, we really hope she pulls through."

"That's really nice of you," I say.

I wish Emily hadn't said this, but she does. "If only everyone could be as sensitive as the two of you. It's sweet how we can live in a town where two jocks so obviously in love with each other can go to the local pizzeria on a Saturday night date without any fear of being harassed. It really is a beautiful world."

Alex is all like, "What did you say?"

"I'll give Annika your best wishes, we gotta get going," I say, taking Emily's hand, but she's not budging. She and Alex are staring each other down.

MAYBE A MIRACLE ~ 57

"You heard me."

Alex says, "What a cu—" but as Josie appears, he reverses himself—"kind young lady."

Josie wants to know, "Everything all right here?" I tell her we were just leaving. *Thanks for everything.*

Once we're outside, Emily says, "Monroe, I'm so sorry. I didn't mean to do that. They're just such fucking assholes."

I guess I should be mad. Having a girl stick up for you isn't exactly very cool, but the truth is I don't really care what those guys think of me. I only wish I'd had the guts to say it myself. I tell her not to worry about it; the look on Alex's face was almost worth the price of my emasculation.

OHIO STATE'S AGRICULTURE farm is right behind Antoine's. Fields and fields of corn and cows buffer Chelsea from the campus. It seems like a fine place for a picnic. The cows look so peaceful, their eyes glazed over with the delight that comes from a jaw full of moistly ground cud. Emily wonders, "What kind of experiments do you think they do on them?"

Emily doesn't eat cows. I do. That means, for me, I'm sitting in a field of potential food, while she's among friends. As a lifetime beef eater, I am complicit in bovine persecution. *Guilty.* I know where this is leading, so, in order to cut the inevitable off at the pass, I tell her I've been thinking about becoming a vegetarian, which I guess is true in the sense that I've been thinking about it for about ten seconds.

"Seriously?" she asks, probably skeptical because I'm always making fun of the MEAT IS MURDER bumper sticker on her car.

"I mean, just look at them. They're like big dogs."

She rewards me with a kiss. The truth is, I'm behind the times. Annika swore off meat a month or so ago. Her conversion came after she had to do a report on Earth Day for school, a report she also presented to the family right before we were about to dig into a steak dinner. "Do you guys have any idea how much oil it took to bring these steaks to our table?" she asked, to which Mom replied, "Honey, the grocery store is only a mile away."

"Mom, that's what I used to think too, but it goes a lot deeper than that. First of all, as everyone knows, they feed cows corn. But did you know that there's actually oil in the fertilizer they use to make the corn grow? How gross is that? Then there's the oil in the farm machinery and in the trucks they use to get the corn to the cows. It's a lot of oil, I don't know how much. But instead of A-1 maybe we ought to put oil on these steaks; then at least it would be truth in advertising. Ms. Foster says cows are like walking SUVs and until we release the cows, we'll never be free of the tyranny of global oil cartels. I'm not sure what that means, but I don't think I want to eat cow anymore."

Dad almost lost it. He said liberal fundamentalists had infiltrated her elementary school. "Steak," he said, "is an inalienable right."

"As American as the nuclear bomb," I added. "As patriotic as a Hummer."

Dad told Mom to save the uneaten steak. First thing tomorrow he was going to visit Annika's teacher and slam the wasted meat on her desk, demanding an explanation.

But I don't think he ever did.

It hits me. "You're the one who gave Annika all of that anti-cow propaganda, aren't you?"

"Actually, I'd prefer to think of it as *pro*-cow propaganda."

Crickets start flexing their wings. Annika used to say they were like an orchestra tuning up before a concert. I lean back, looking up at the sky. The sun will be setting soon. I ask, "Do you think prayers help?"

"I think mainly they help the people who pray. It makes them think they're doing something when they don't know what else to do. But who knows? Maybe if enough people get together it becomes something bigger. You know, like one of those things where the whole becomes greater than the sum of its parts."

"But you don't even believe in God."

"Maybe it's not what you believe in, just that you believe in the first place. It's like the Reds. Do you think it helps when you root for them?"

"Well . . . yeah."

"Well, maybe praying is like rooting for your favorite team, just quieter."

Chapter 6

Cars are lined up for blocks. I've never seen a traffic jam like this in Chelsea, but no one's even honking. No one seems to be in much of a hurry at all. We glide by on our bikes and when we get to the hospital we find Father Ferger's army firmly entrenched around the fountain in front of the entrance. There must be five hundred people, maybe more. They're holding hands, their heads bowed, murmuring in unison. Emily says they sound like bees.

It's insane, all these people here to pray for Annika. It's not like they know her. It's not like the church is that huge. It's not like Annika is the only little girl in Columbus hanging by a thread.

Security only lets us inside once I show them my driver's license. It's nice to have it come in handy for once. By the time we get to the elevator, it's oddly comforting to be standing under the fluorescent lights. I ask Emily, "If this was a *Twilight Zone* episode, how do you think it would end?" *The Twilight Zone* is pretty much the only show Emily knows, which somehow makes sense considering her family not only doesn't have cable, they don't have a color TV.

"In *The Twilight Zone* their prayers would bring Annika back . . . but they'd have to learn that you have to be careful about what you pray for. Once Annika woke up, she would denounce them all as charlatans, find salvation in rock 'n' roll, become the next Madonna, and systematically destroy religion as we know it."

~~~

BACK IN THE HOSPITAL ROOM, Mom combs Annika's hair while Dad stares out at the crowd. That's how I left them four hours ago.

"Do you think the prayers are helping?" I ask.

Without looking away from the window, Dad says, "She hasn't gotten any *worse*."

Mom assures us, "Yes, of course it's working. She squeezed my hand about twenty minutes ago." Then she asks Emily, "Would you like to help me braid Annika's hair? Your hair always looks so pretty."

It's the nicest thing Mom has ever said to Emily. She seems so calm and centered. Ordinarily, I'd think Mom would be worrying about how she was ever going to thank all those people for their prayers. What would Miss Manners say? Are thank-you notes appropriate? Or should you pray for them in return? *Pray back for payback* has its appeal—but if that's all you do, how will they ever know?

While Emily and Mom braid Annika's hair, I look out the window with Dad. He says it sure was lucky how I was there to jump in the pool. *Again*. I stifle a laugh; Dad always says that you make your own luck. Well, actually, he never said that at all. In lieu of giving out such fatherly nuggets of wisdom, sometimes he passes on this pamphlet to me called *Bits and Pieces,* which I think is published by the people who put out *Reader's Digest.* It's a motivational guide for upper management full of clichés and little anecdotes that tell you how to most effectively exploit the people around you. From what I can tell, that's one of the guiding principles for people who've made it big—*you make your own luck.* If you believed otherwise, you wouldn't be so special anymore. You wouldn't be so smart. You'd just be a lucky bastard sitting in a leather chair and every day you'd have to thank your lucky stars. I don't mention that if indeed I made my own luck in this instance, it was only because there was no way I could have dealt with going to my prom without getting stoned.

"Does Grandpa know?" I ask Mom.

"I don't want to get him all worried. She could snap out of it any minute."

~

NO ONE EVER tells anyone anything in our family. Dad could have cancer and Mom could be a diabetic. I swear, if they were dying, they wouldn't say a thing. Dad would silently go about his chemo, acting like the hair he lost was just because he was getting old. Mom would shoot up her insulin behind closed doors, pulling another layer of her life around her like a raincoat. And they'd rest assured they were doing you a favor.

Case in point: My favorite uncle, Ross, used to make the best pumpkin pie in the world. Actually, he was my great-uncle, old like grandparents. Not only were his pies the highlight of every Thanksgiving, but as an added bonus, he had the filthiest mouth of any adult I ever met. It wasn't even particularly offensive when he'd say, "Look at that monkey run" when describing Barry Sanders sprinting to the end zone during the annual NFL Turkey Day game. It was actually kind of funny. It must have been, because we all laughed. When you're an old racist, it's funny for some reason. I don't know why.

When Ross died of cancer, I was twelve years old, but no one told me. In fact, I never knew he had cancer in the first place. As Thanksgiving approached, I mentioned to Mom how I was looking forward to seeing Ross. Not only did he make the best pie, but he also used to give me old baseball cards, back from when he was a kid.

"Uncle Ross passed away . . . but, Monroe, you know that."

Now I liked Uncle Ross. I liked him a lot. But my affection did not run so deep that I would have needed to block his death from my memory.

"No one ever told me Uncle Ross died."

"He had cancer."

"He had cancer?" I think I would have remembered that. It's not like you die from cancer over night.

"He had it for a couple of years."

"He had cancer for a *couple of years* and no one thought to mention anything?"

"Monroe, I'm pretty sure we did."

"So when did he die?"

Even she was embarrassed when she said, "Four months ago."

"I missed the funeral?"

"You were at camp."

I don't know what they thought they were protecting me from. I had already dealt with lots of death. Every pet I ever had died. Turtles, lizards, and snakes; we're dealing with a very high mortality rate here. Yes, some escaped, but I'm sure most of them died premature deaths too. Sometimes I'd find them dried up behind the furnace. Oh yes, I knew about death. I didn't need to be protected.

That Thanksgiving went on pretty much like always, although it was a bit quieter, especially when the Lions took the field. Without Ross there to make comments like, "Look at him go—they must be giving out free watermelons in the end zone," it wasn't the same. His son, Ross Jr., a manager at the Toledo sanitation department, tried to take up the slack, but it wasn't as funny coming from him. Racism doesn't wear so well on a thirty-year-old. After all, he should know better. Ross, on the other hand, was a relic. If the Ohio Historical Society really wanted to be accurate, they'd fill their fake old Main Street with people like him. Then everyone would really know what they were missing from the good old days.

That night for dessert, Aunt Harriet, Ross's wife, brought out a batch of Ross's pumpkin pies. They'd been in the freezer. Making them was one of the last things he ever did. With each bite I felt like I was swallowing him good-bye. I think we probably all did. Not that anyone said anything.

Mom finishes braiding Annika's hair and says, "Annika, you look so beautiful. Now all we need is a prince to come by and give you a kiss."

Dad's not listening. He looks so lost. "You kids don't really need to stay here if you don't want," he says.

Fine, I can take a hint. As we head out the door, I give it a shot; I kiss Annika on the forehead. It's the first time I've ever kissed her.

Nothing.

In the hallway, Emily says that it was worth a try and then she holds my hand all the way until we get outside.

THE SUN IS about to set. The crowd is still here, even bigger than before. Police with loudspeakers are trying to get them to go home, but they aren't listening. The humidity has given way to an unexpected crispness, as if someone has turned on an air conditioner. People are looking around, their noses in the air, like dogs on the verge of catching a fresh scent.

It felt this way a few years ago, right before the blizzard, but in reverse. It was a cold Sunday in January. Dad and I were outside getting ready for a storm—it's all we heard about for two days. We'd just cleared the gutters and were taking the ladders back to the garage when a blast of hot air swept through the yard. It felt like it was seventy-five degrees, though it was probably more like fifty. We thought for sure that the weatherman must have gotten it all wrong—no way was it going to snow now. We stood in the driveway looking at the sky, the clouds chasing each other like chocolate syrup in a blender of vanilla ice cream. Dad said it must be snowing in Florida. Even though it wasn't really very funny, we laughed like it was. Then, after a slightly uncomfortable pause, Dad picked up the thread and said it looked like spring training is coming early this year; maybe we should get out our gloves and play catch. I'd never turned down a request to play catch with my dad in my life. Not once.

I bolted to the garage for our mitts, but before I got back, flurries were already filling up the sky. In no time at all they turned into shovels and shovels of snow. I'll never forget that day. Dad never asked me to play catch with him again. I'm not sure why. I was thirteen years old.

At the hospital, the wind starts blowing and a sweet smell fills the air.

"Roses," Emily says.

Just like Annika's room in the hospital. The cops put down their bullhorns—no one is listening to them anyway—and they too crane their necks upward. The sky is red, that red you get for only a few minutes after the sun goes down.

It's as if pieces of the sky are falling down on us. There are rose petals *everywhere*. It's snowing petals, a soft and lazy dusting of huge silky flakes. Hand in hand, Emily and I head deeper into the crowd. All eyes are to the sky, faces smiling. These people, these people who are here to pray for my sister, are looking to the sky like what they're seeing is the most natural thing in the world, a rose petal blizzard. Like they've been expecting it all along. Like this is what they came for.

Emily and I look at each other, but we don't say anything. We don't know *what* to say. Our mouths are open but nothing is coming out. She squeezes my hand and I take a deep breath, inhaling the sweet smell. Emily has rose petals hanging in her hair and her face is shining, filled with wonder. Whenever I think of her that day, that way, I practically fall in love with her all over again.

I look up to Annika's window. Mom's hands are pressed against the glass, like she's trying to reach out and touch the falling petals. My dad's hands rest on her shoulders. I'm so glad he's watching, because if I told him it snowed roses, there's no way he would believe me. First, he'd ask for a report from the American Meteorological Society or maybe he'd ask me what I was smoking—not because he really thinks I'm high, but because he had heard it somewhere and thinks it's a funny thing to say.

THE SKY CLEARS. As quickly as it came to life, it goes back to sleep.

"All right, folks, the show's over. It's time to go home," says a man with a bullhorn. He's a cop, and even though we're in Columbus, apparently he's already seen it all. But no one listens to him. Some people are looking at the sky, not sure if what they saw really happened. Waiting to see if maybe it will happen again. Others are on their knees. Not praying, but picking up the petals that have fallen on the ground, as if maybe they're proof that what happened here wasn't all just some dream. I pick one out of Emily's hair and put it in my pocket.

Emily says, "I don't know what to say."

"You don't have to say anything."

"But did you *see* that? Did you *feel* it?"

"I feel full, like I've just eaten Thanksgiving dinner, but I'm still hungry," I manage to say.

"Me too," Emily says.

"What do you think we should do?"

"Maybe we should go back inside and see Annika."

WHEN WE GET to Annika's room, Mom's smiling face is swimming in tears. She wants to know. *Did we see what happened? It was unbelievable. Were we there?* I manage to nod *yes.* A rose petal stuck in my hair dislodges and glides to the floor. Mom picks it up and holds it in her hand with the sort of reverence I'd reserve for a foul ball off the bat of a Cincinnati Red. Her tears should scare me, but they're as warm and inviting as a Jacuzzi.

The room is full of doctors and nurses and now *us.* Machines are being monitored. Annika's blood pressure is being taken. Fluids are being administered. Everything is happening so fast, it's like a time-lapse movie, but in real time.

Mom says that during the rose storm Annika tossed and turned. Dad says she looked like a cat trying to get out of a bag. Everyone thought she was waking up, that she was coming out of it, but once the petals stopped falling, she settled back down and it was like nothing ever happened.

She looks the same to me as she did a few hours ago.

It's already getting dark, but Dad keeps looking out the window, like maybe it's going to snow rose petals again.

Dr. Singh scans a printout and tells us that Annika's brain waves showed a substantial amount of activity. "Very encouraging indeed," he says. What he really means is that at least now we know she's not a vegetable.

Annika went as a banana last Halloween. While not a vegetable, it's close. She got the idea from a Woody Allen film—not *Bananas*, but *Everyone Says I Love You*. At every stop she sang a few verses of "The Banana Boat Song" and did a little dance—all to the instrumental accompaniment we'd rigged into her costume. You could barely see her eyes through the slit in the papier-mâché, but she still shined through—a luminous yellow banana. She was quite a hit and she had an overflowing bag of candy to prove it.

Father Ferger sticks his head in the room and asks, "Did you see what happened?" He says it like he can't believe it himself.

Mom excitedly welcomes him in with a hug. "It was a *miracle*, the most amazing thing I ever saw—all of those rose petals coming down." She says it as if Ferger personally dialed them up from above. "When the roses came down she started to shake and move her head back and forth. Father, she's dancing in there. We just need to get her to come out and dance with us."

Mom is giddy. The exaggerated calm that masked her face just hours ago has been replaced with the optimism of someone convinced they're on the verge of winning the lottery.

Father Ferger assures us that twice as many people will show up tomorrow.

"The hospital is not particularly equipped for that kind of . . . public display," warns Dr. Singh.

"Don't worry," Father Ferger assures Dr. Singh. "We'll be much more organized tomorrow. We won't get in anyone's way."

Ferger seems so happy, I can't help but wonder if he's been waiting his entire life for this opportunity—a chance to will someone back to consciousness, a mini-resurrection. If she comes back, it'll be thanks to God and it will have nothing to do with the doctors or modern medicine. If she doesn't, well . . . in that case, it's all part of God's larger plan and we all must have faith that this was the way it was meant to be. Either way, Ferger can't lose.

Father Ferger holds Annika's hand as he says a prayer. For the first time since she fell in the pool, there's some color in her cheeks. As he leads a prayer asking for her recovery, everyone bows their heads, including Dr. Singh. Emily holds my hand, bowing her head not in prayer, but out of respect. I pray along, not because I know who I'm praying to, or even because I think it will help. I pray for no other reason than that it can't hurt.

Chapter 7

UNDER THE FRONT-PAGE HEADLINE "Is Someone Listening?" *The Columbus Dispatch* features a picture of the rose petal shower in the Sunday morning edition. A shot of Father Ferger leading the crowd in prayer lies beneath the fold.

I bring the paper inside. It's about four a.m. and there isn't a light on in the house. Ordinarily, I'd be crucified for coming in this late. At least I think I would—I've never actually tried it before—but I figure Mom and Dad are probably still at the hospital. I should be okay. It's not like I've been out boozing. I fell asleep at Emily's, right in the middle of the living room. I guess no one had the heart to wake me up. I woke up alone on the floor, covered with a blanket. Everyone else had gone to bed.

I come in through the kitchen, figuring I'll get a drink of water before I head upstairs. When I open the refrigerator, the light reveals Dad sitting at the breakfast table.

"Hello, Monroe, nice evening?" he says without a hint of emotion.

"I hope you weren't waiting up for me," I say for the first time in my life. However, it quickly becomes clear that my curfew is the last thing on his mind.

"You'll be on your own in a few months anyway. . . . There's a certain point where you have to let go. There's nothing you can do." And with this bone of wisdom, he drains a glass of vodka. Then he pours another.

Dad is not the kind of guy to just let it go, the kind of guy who says there's nothing you can do. He's a man of action, the kind of guy who thinks there's *always* something you can do. *Someone's always to blame and there's always something you can do.*

A bottle of vodka sits in the middle of the table. He nods to me — *want some?*

I don't really like vodka, but this is the kind of offer a son doesn't refuse.

Dad busted me drinking back when I was a sophomore. Ben gave me a bottle of tequila and told me to go out and have some fun with my friends. It seemed like a good idea at the time, but I couldn't find anyone to drink with me. My best friend, Charlie, had just moved to Florida with his family. So I drank the bottle by myself on the golf course. Or most of it. I think.

I probably would have gotten away with it too, had the door not been so completely impossible to open when I got home. Dad just stood there at the window looking at me flail, until finally I realized the door wasn't locked after all.

I may have thrown up on his shoes when I got inside. I'll have to take his word for it. I don't really remember.

I didn't see Dad again until the next morning. The sun was just coming up when he came into my room with a pitcher of Bloody Marys. "Hair of the dog," he said, as he poured me a glass.

At the time I'm thinking, *Wow this is pretty cool.* He sat down on the side of my bed and told me about the first time he ever got drunk. He was already in the marines; he enlisted the day he graduated from high school to go to Vietnam. He must have been kind of a square, volunteering for such a lame war, but he'd say it was because it was the only way he could afford to pay for college. Anyway, he and his buddies tried to sneak some girls on the base. They got busted and spent the next two days cleaning out latrines. It was one of the best conversations we ever had. Dad doesn't often admit doing anything wrong.

By the time I finished the pitcher, I was wasted. All I wanted in the world was to go back to sleep.

"I don't think so," said Dad. "We've got a lot of work to do." By work, he meant I would be pulling weeds. "It's hard to screw that up," he said as he handed me some gloves. "And don't touch any of your mother's flowers."

The first hour or so of pulling weeds wasn't so bad; it was actually kind of fun. But it took a sharp turn somewhere along the way. One second I'm getting off on the joy of pulling weeds out, root and all; the next I'm dizzy, seeing stars . . . thinking maybe drinking tequila all by myself on the golf course, chucking pin markers into the pond, and breaking ball cleaners wasn't such a great idea after all.

I puked in the bushes that morning. The flowers survived, but I had a head full of gravel and a mouth full of cotton. The weeds dying in the sun looked like they had it pretty good.

"Sure, Dad," I say to his offer of a drink.

He pulls himself out of the chair to get me a glass. His body is stiff, like he's been sitting there all night. And maybe he has. Or maybe he's just getting old. He fills the glass too much and hands it to me. "To your sister."

"To Annika."

"She's a real good kid." He says it like he's just realized it for the first time. Maybe it is, because the next thing he says is: "I wish I knew her better."

"You're a busy man," I say as a way of apology, but he doesn't reply. It probably sounds sarcastic, but I don't mean it to. We both know it's not an excuse—*everyone is busy*—it's the problem.

"Monroe, I want you to answer this question. Answer it with *the truth*."

"Okay, Dad."

"I'm *serious*, Monroe. Do you swear to tell me the whole truth, nothing but the truth, so help you *God*?"

He sure is wasted. He's never made me take the oath before. Besides, Dad only asks questions he knows the answer to. It's what lawyers do, at least the ones on TV.

"Do you think I know you, son? Really *know you*?"

"I don't know, Dad."

"I'm serious. *Think*."

I don't need to think. I know the answer. He doesn't know me at all. But that doesn't make him much different than most other parents. When parents tell you they really, *really* want the truth, what they really want is for you to be an especially convincing liar. If I ever learned anything from Ben, it's that.

Dad knows most of the tricks, so I ask him, "Who's my favorite baseball player?"

"Johnny Bench," he says and he's right. Johnny Bench retired the year I was born. I never got to see him play. Maybe that's why I like him so much. He'll never have the chance to disappoint me. I only know him as the greatest catcher of all time. All I've ever seen are the highlight films.

"What if I were to tell you that Johnny Bench is a big asshole?" he says, changing the subject. I guess he's satisfied he knows me, *really knows me*.

Johnny Bench. An asshole? At least he's not saying it with the kind of glee that, say, Ben took when he told Annika that Santa Claus was just a fat drunk in a red suit who was pulled out of the gutter by the people who run the mall.

"I met Bench, you know." No, I didn't know. "It was at some corporate luncheon and he was the speaker. Ordinarily, I don't go to things like that, but I wanted to get his autograph." Dad has always made fun of autograph collectors. He says they're pathetic. "It wasn't for me. The autograph. Remember how I coached your brother's Little League team about ten years ago?"

How could I forget? Ben hated having Dad as a coach so much, after one game he ripped up his uniform and left it in the driveway. I would have done the same when Dad coached my team, but since he barely ever let me play I might as well not have had a uniform at all.

"The catcher on our team, Larry Stiggers, was having a rough time. He was a real good kid. Polite, even when he didn't think anyone was watching. Not like most kids. His mother died of leukemia right before the play-offs and I wanted to do something for him, something special. It seems kind of stupid now. . . ." He trails off and composes himself with a drink.

"So I waited around for like twenty minutes, you know, while people were taking pictures with Bench and having him sign stuff for their kids. It's my turn and I tell him the story about how Larry was the best catcher in our league and how he always said he was his favorite player, even though he was too young to have seen him play. Kind of like you. I told him about his mother and what a rough time he was having, how the kid could use a break. So, I ask him to autograph the ball and if he could make it out to Larry that would be great."

"Then Bench looks at me and says, 'So, *Larry*, what do I look like—a fucking idiot?' "

"He actually said *fucking*?"

He looks at me like it's completely beside the point, although it seems like rather pertinent information to me.

"Okay, if it makes him look better in your eyes, we'll say *goddamn*. But just so I don't get confused here, let me understand, taking the Lord's name in vain—a violation of one of the Ten Commandments, I might add—is a more attractive use of speech to you than utilizing a mere euphemism for the act of making love?"

"Yeah, I guess," I say, but I feel like saying, "What are you? A lawyer?"

"Anyway, where was I?"

"He called you Larry."

"Right. The bastard called me *Larry*. I look down and I've got this stupid MY NAME IS sticker on and I tried to explain that yeah I'm a Larry too, but it's not for me, it's for the kid. And he just laughed and said, 'You don't have to make up a story, it's nothing to be ashamed of. You like men. I get a lot of that.' As he's laughing, he signs the ball, putting Larry in quotation marks. . . . What a dick."

I crack a smile, but I don't laugh.

"So you think that's funny? Johnny Bench calling your dad a fruit?"

Of course, I think it's funny, but I don't say that. That story only makes me like Bench more than I ever did before, but I don't say that either. Obviously, Dad doesn't know me at all. Sure, he's found some cracks. I'm not perfect; that he knows all too well. But, to him, I *am* the cracks. When he looks at me, that's all he ever sees—the imperfections. I know because when I look in his eyes, that's all I see too. What a loser I am.

"I think I'll switch my choice to Barry Larkin."

"You're a good kid, you know that?"

You can't believe anything a drunk tells you . . . or maybe you should believe *everything*. I don't know. As far as I can tell, this is what my dad thinks of me. He thinks I'm smart, but I don't apply myself, which may be true. Somehow he thinks I want to be a lawyer like him, which is definitely not true, although it was when I was in sixth grade, which is probably when he got the idea. He thinks I habitually masturbate in the shower, which was once true, but is no longer. Since I got caught, it kind of took the fun out of it. He thinks I like the *Rocky* movies, but the truth is: I only watch them to humor him. He also thinks I'm serious when I say Barry Larkin is my new favorite player. But most of all, he thinks he can solve most of my problems with a twenty-dollar bill and with that notion he couldn't be more right.

So, it's not like he's *completely* clueless.

"I know I'm not around a lot," he says.

"Someone has to pay for all of this." He can't call me sarcastic for that. I'm only quoting him; he says it himself all the time.

He takes a drink. "God damnit, it's so easy to forget what's important. You know what I mean?"

Not really. But I nod *yes.*

He asks, "When's the last time we went to a baseball game together?"

That would be last season, August 12, Columbus Clippers versus the Rochester Red Wings. Dad likes to arrive an hour before the first pitch and leave by the end of the fourth inning. I can see how he might have forgotten. "We should go more often," he says, as if he doesn't have season tickets already. He almost always goes by himself. It's not like he's a huge baseball fan; mainly he just likes to go to the ballpark because no one ever bothers him there.

"I remember when I was your age. I remember how time used to go so slow. How it seemed like it'd be *forever* until I could drive a car, then it seemed like it would be *forever* until I could enlist in the marines, then it'd be *forever* until I would graduate from college."

He finishes off the glass and fills another.

"Now it's all just a blur. Sometimes I feel like when I'm about to put my finger on it all, it gets chopped off in a fan."

I've heard old people talking like this before, but it's weird to hear it coming from Dad. Even if he is wasted. When I was a junior, I had to volunteer at a convalescent home as part of a social studies class and all the old people were always saying *Slow down, enjoy yourself. These are the best years of your life.* It made me want to kill myself. If you're eighty-five years old and you're thinking the best years of your life were spent in high school, I'm sorry, but you should have cut bait a long time ago.

Besides, if these really are *the best years of our lives,* how come all we ever hear about is how we're supposed to prepare for the future?

Maybe that's why I like our next-door neighbor Paul Henderson. He doesn't seem to care so much about the future. Even though he's twenty-two, he still lives with his dad. And no, he's not retarded. In fact, he's one of the smarter people I've ever known. I guess you could call him my boss. For the past three summers, I've been on his payroll, cutting grass. In the winter, he shovels snow, but he does that all by himself. Once he got a plow for his Scout, it became a one-man job.

Like I said, Paul's pretty smart. He even went to Princeton for a semester. He didn't like it all that much and ever since he's lived in the room above the garage. Sometimes after we're finished working we go up there, have a smoke, and listen to music. He has the most amazing collection of records I've ever seen: mainly old blues, R & B, and funk. He's probably the best friend I have besides Annika. But I'm sure he doesn't think that way about me; I'm just the kid from next door who works for him. Still, that doesn't keep me from wishing *he* was my big brother and not Ben.

Dad always talks about Paul like he's a huge loser, but Paul's always smiling, so it's hard to see exactly what he's lost. Dad says Paul should grow up, that he should get a life. Paul was, after all, the valedictorian of his class. He had a *future*. Paul, however, will tell you that being a valedictorian is nothing special. "Take Weird Al Yankovic. He gave the speech and look at the contaminated legacy of toxic cultural debris he's left behind . . . or worse, what about Cindy Crawford? She was the quote smartest person unquote in her class and she's gone on to become a poster girl for impossible beauty standards, promoting self-hatred to millions of young girls across the globe. Believe me, we'd all be better off if both of them stayed in their parents' garages." Paul says stuff like that when people like my dad ask him how he could be satisfied doing manual labor when he had so much promise.

Johnny Bench was the valedictorian of his class too, but it's probably best not to mention that. At least, not now.

Dad's leaning back on his chair, teetering. "Just when you're about to put your finger on it all, it gets lopped off," he says smiling, repeating this observation as if it's been eluding him all of his life and now he finally gets it. As an exclamation point, he points his finger into an imaginary fan. It doesn't get lopped off. Instead, he falls over backward, spilling vodka all over himself—one big mess on the floor.

I help him get up and say, "Maybe it's a good time to go to bed."

"Hey, that's my line," he says, but he lets me walk him upstairs anyway. Since Mom's still at the hospital, it's left to me to get him into his bed and take off his wing tips.

By the time I unlace the second shoe, he's already snoring.

Chapter 8

Mom wakes me up at seven-fifteen. She's going to early Mass and she wants me to come; she's on a mission. My moans of protest elicit no sympathy from her, but down the hall, Dad is telling her to let me sleep. She says, "He can sleep anytime. This is important."

"Maybe I'll catch a later service," I lie, trying to get her to go away.

If I stare at the ceiling long enough, they'll leave without me. But when they finally do, it's a hollow victory. There's no way I'll be able to get back to sleep.

In the bathroom, I find myself looking into the mirror. Ordinarily, such an examination is cause for disappointment, but not today. Remarkably, my complexion is clear, not a single zit. I can't remember that being the case since I turned thirteen. I have brown hair and green eyes, which makes me pretty typical in this neck of the finely manicured woods. I'm skinny, all arms and legs. It makes it easy for people to call me a geek. My saving grace is the dimple in my cheek when I smile. Emily says it's cute, that it's why she first noticed me. Mom, who theoretically would be inclined to say I'm handsome, is more prone to noting that my earlobes have an aristocratic air to them. I'm not sure what that exactly means, but if Prince Charles is any indication, it means I look positively goofy. Clearly, when you're reduced to pointing out the positive aspects of someone's ears, you're making a stretch to be kind. Basically, I'm nothing special. If you were going to pick me out in a crowd, just look toward the back, maybe in the corner; that's where I'll be.

*　　*　　*

I'm waiting for the coffeemaker to spit out my morning cup. The paper's next to me and I start reading about the rose storm. Whetstone Park is just about a mile away from the hospital; they've got about five thousand rose bushes there. Bob Granada, the certified meteorologist from Channel 10, says it could have been a minitornado, a freakish gust of spiraling wind that sucked the petals off their blooms only to then deposit them minutes later at the hospital. He says it happens all the time. In fact, the paper has compiled a list of all the bizarre things that have fallen out of the sky over the years. In 1877, thousands of live snakes rained down on Memphis, Tennessee. Stroud, England, and its neighboring communities were treated to several downpours of albino frogs throughout the fall of 1987. "A silver sheet of rain" showered down on two acres of Australia in February 1989. The culprit? Thousands of *sardines*. Blood-colored clouds once filled the sky of Italy's Marche Province. Within an hour the air was filled with millions of small seeds. They were from the Judas tree, found only in central Africa. And let's not forget, when the Jews wandered the desert, they were showered with seed that tasted of fresh oil. They ground it up and baked it into cakes. No one knows exactly what it was, but they call it *manna from heaven*.

Apparently, a lot stranger stuff than rose petals falls from the sky all the time. Where those petals came from, though, is still a mystery. The leading candidate: Whetstone Park? The groundskeeper says the roses there weren't ruffled in the slightest.

WITH EVERYONE AT CHURCH, it should be pretty quiet at the hospital. I figure maybe I can spend some time with Annika without having to deal with the circus.

I figure wrong. As I come up to the entrance, six guys wearing scrubs are standing in a cloud of their own smoke, staring up at the wall. They look tough, like a motorcycle gang on their day jobs. They tilt their heads, to the left, then to the right, then back to the left again. They're looking at the rust stain on the wall. It's a lot bigger than it was yesterday.

The skinniest one says, "Man, I don't know what pills you've been swiping, but I don't see it."

Then the ringleader replies, "If you don't see it, you're not *looking*. It's as clear as the tattoo on your sister's ass." The others nod along as if they'd all had a piece of Skinny's sister too. Me? I don't see what the big deal is. It's just a stain. I'm sure the sides of their trailers are much worse.

"Hey man, you see it, don't you?"

He's talking to me. "I don't know, see *what?*"

The man addresses his cohorts. "All right, we have an impartial observer here. This will settle it." He puts his arm around me and says, "Just look at the wall and tell us what you see." He could crush me like balsa wood. Believe me, I'd really like to see what he sees.

"I bet you five bucks he don't see it," says Skinny, pulling out his wallet.

"Make it twenty," says the black one. "And I'll take your money too. I don't see shit up there."

"Fine, ye of little faith," my new friend says. "Anyone else?"

There are no other takers.

So, I look. I really do. "That big brown splotch? That's what I'm looking at, right?"

"Yeah, that's the one."

"The water stain?"

"Use your fucking imagination."

"I don't know? Mickey Mouse?"

"Five dollah, don't make me hollah," says Skinny, holding out his hand. Smiling like it's the first bet he's ever won in his life.

My new friend isn't so happy with me. He slaps a five into Skinny's palm and doles out a twenty to the black one. "No, man, what are you? *Blind?* It's *Jesus Fucking Christ.* Don't you see it?"

I look a little closer. "Jesus on a cross or just the head?"

"Shit, man, what did you just do? Get off the little yellow bus? It's Jesus's *face*. There ain't no cross up there."

"Oh sure, Jesus's face . . ." I lie.

I look again. If anything, it slightly resembles Karl Marx, but I don't say that. If they know who he is, they'll pummel me for sure.

"It's a friggin' miracle, is what it is. Don't you believe in miracles?"

"Sorry about the twenty-five bucks," I say as I keep walking.

As I head for the front door, I hear him say, "I'm telling you guys, that kid's retarded."

Skinny reconsiders his stance. "I guess if you look at it from this angle, it sort of does look like JC."

People are always seeing Jesus in the clouds, in the tiles of a roof, on the side of a barn, in the trunk of a tree, in a plate of macaroni. People are always seeing Jesus everywhere they look. Miracles? Probably not. The miracle is that anyone believes that's the way God would choose to reveal himself in the first place. As the all-knowing Creator, can't He come up with something better than a rust stain?

WHEN I STEP into Annika's room I'm hit with the smell of roses, just like yesterday. And just like yesterday, the only flowers to be seen are in the painting on the wall. Annika's lying there, her eyes closed. I can see why Mom's always calling her an angel. I give her a kiss hello.

She looks so peaceful as I sit down next to her. It's almost as if she's not there at all, leaving me wondering, *Where is what makes Annika Annika? Hiding beneath the sheets? Flowing through the wires of these machines? Stuck in her throat, trying to get out? Somewhere at the bottom of the swimming pool?*

I don't have any answers, only questions, so I look out the window. There are more people down below, staring up at the wall, staring up at *us*. I close the curtains and say, "The Reds won again last night. Barry Larkin hit another home run."

Annika always says Barry Larkin is her boyfriend; he just doesn't know it yet. I love it when she says that, especially around Dad. You can see it driving him quietly mad—the idea of a black man and his daughter. He would never say that, but whenever the subject comes up, you can see him gnawing on the inside of his cheek. I guarantee you, seven years of Annika as a teenager will leave him with another hole in his face. It'd be a small price to pay for her to come through this. I swear, she's going to break some hearts some day. She really is.

"They won the day before too."

A nurse comes in and says, "Hi, I'm Nurse Finnerty. Just checking to see if everything is okay."

"I was telling Annika about the Reds game last night."

I'm surprised I'm able to say *anything*. Nurse Finnerty might as well have walked out of a porno. Not that she's naked; she's not. It's more like the part before the nurse lets her hair down and takes off her glasses, you know, when all the pills have failed and the only way to heal the patient is with a healthy dose of love.

"She's so beautiful," the nurse says as she changes the sheets. "You know, people around here say your sister is an angel."

"My mom's been saying that ever since she was born."

"I mean for real. Didn't you see the rose storm yesterday?"

"Yeah, I was there."

"You seem pretty skeptical."

"Do I? Because I could be persuaded."

"If that didn't do it for you, I don't know what will," she says.

"Maybe if it rained frogs . . ."

She ignores that and asks, "You're still in high school, right?"

"Just for a few more weeks."

"I read about what you did in the paper. Pretty heroic."

I feel a flash of red invade my face. "Thanks," I say. "It was really no big deal."

That's when Ben shows up. Tanked. Already. It's not even nine o'clock. Everything about him is in three-quarter time.

"Any news?"

"I'll be back in a minute," says the nurse as Ben's eyes follow her ass out the door.

"She still hasn't come out of it."

"Fuck. Man, that fucking sucks."

He probably never went to sleep. "Don't you have a tee time to get to or something?"

Ben doesn't answer. He just stares at Annika like she's a science project, like he isn't even related to her. "Did you say something?"

"No."

"Man, you see that Jesus stain on the wall? Pretty fucking wild. There's a ton of people down there. They fucking carded me just to get up here."

"You might want to ease up on the fucks."

"Why the fuck would you say that? She can't hear a fucking thing."

"We really don't know what she can hear."

Ben tries to process this information. "This is all pretty fucked up. I saw what they said about you in the paper. Man, I bet that gets you some pussy."

I can't believe we share the same DNA, I really can't. "I sure hope so, otherwise I'd wonder if it was even worth it," I say.

"Although that slice you were with last night looked pretty tasty." Sarcasm never works on him. He's too fucking stupid.

"Ben, Emily and I have been going out for almost six months now."

"Which is exactly why you need a fresh piece of the pie. Let me give you a little glimpse into the future: When she goes away to college, she'll cheat on your ass within the first week. Believe me, they all do."

"You're such a dick."

"You think so, huh?"

"Well, Ben, let me give you a little glimpse into *your* future. After you drink away whatever little talent you have as a golfer, you'll consider yourself lucky to be the teaching pro at some second-rate resort in Florida where the sole fringe benefit of your miserable existence will be that you can fuck all the old ladies in their patch madras dresses to your heart's content."

Ben has that look in his eye. The look that says *I'm going to make you wish you'd never been born,* which, after all, is his main issue with me. I don't think he has the guts to do anything about it here in the hospital, though, so I add, *"Big fat* ladies from Cleveland. They'll be so fucking fat you'll have to roll them around in the sand trap to find the wet spot. That's all you'll get and the thing is, you'll be so drunk, you'll like it. You'll like it *a lot."*

I've been wanting to say that to him for years. It's not like I just thought it up.

"Interesting, Monroe," he says, as if he can see it all playing out right in front of him. He smiles. "Very fucking interesting." For a brief moment, I think maybe he's seen the light. "Fat chicks need love too," he philosophizes. Yes, maybe even Ben can redeem himself and if Ben can do it, well, maybe there really is a reason to have faith.

"Wait, hold on a second," he says. "I'm getting another vision from your immediate future."

I've seen this look on Ben's face before too. He used to get it when he'd stand in the driveway, menacingly bouncing a golf ball on the asphalt. He'd say, "I'll give you ten seconds to run." I'd look at him like *you can't be serious,* searching for a hint of humanity in his eyes, which was kind of like looking in the refrigerator for the fifteenth time when you know there's nothing there. He'd say "Ten . . ." and I'd start to run, but I never got too far. "Nineeightsevensixfivefourthree-twoone." Splat. The back of my leg tattooed with the Titelist insignia. He especially enjoyed performing this trick for an audience of my peers, because really what's the point of humiliating your little brother unless his friends are there to see him cry?

I know he's going to hit me. The only question is where.

"Here it comes," he says, landing a right hook across my jaw.

I fall back in the chair, holding my cheek, glaring. He's never hit me in the face before. I can't believe he'd actually do it, here in a hospital with our sister clinging to her life just a few feet away. Had I realized nothing is sacred, I would have kept my stupid mouth shut.

"I was positive there'd be tears," he says. "Guess I don't know much about the future after all."

"You're such an asshole."

"Watch your mouth. I'd hate for Mom and Dad to have two kids in the hospital at the same time."

The hot nurse comes back in and Ben flashes that same stupid smile he's been using to get whatever he wants all his life. She asks, "Are you boys okay?"

The sting of his punch hits me late and I'm doing my best not to cry. I mutter something about how it's all really hard, you know, seeing our sister like this. I'm not sure who I'm protecting here, him or me.

Okay, in case I didn't already mention it, I'm what is regularly referred to as a pussy. While I have been abused quite frequently by Ben, I've never been in a fight in my life. My initial reaction to conflict has always been to flee. That worked pretty well until sixth grade when Mason Jones, the only black kid in our class, was upset that I was "going out" with the object of his obsession—Heather Appadouklous. I don't know if you could even call it "going out"; all we ever did was talk on the phone. I never even got to kiss her. Nonetheless, Mason was under the impression that by pulverizing me, he'd be next in line for Heather's affections. He and a crowd of our bloodthirsty classmates waited for me at the bike racks after school, but instead of taking the beating, I hid out in a restroom stall. In retrospect, it's pathetic; but at the time it felt like a reasonable solution. Fear, apparently, has a way of making you blind to your own stupidity. My failure to show up for my beating led my classmates to conclude (if there ever was any doubt) that, indeed, Monroe Anderson is a pussy. To salt the wounds I never received, Heather dumped me through her intermediary, Stacey Oliver, and soon thereafter began *going out* with Mason. I would have been so much better off getting my ass kicked. A black eye and a broken arm would have been a small price to pay for my dignity. Once you lose it, it's hard, if not impossible, to get it back.

I look at my brother through tear-glazed eyes. I know it doesn't make a lot a difference whether the tears drop. Either way he's already won. I don't think I've ever hated anyone quite so much as I do right now. I wish it were him in the hospital bed and I wish he'd never wake up.

I've only gotten the better of him once in my life. I was in third grade. He was in seventh. It was Christmas Eve. I don't remember why he was chasing me around the house—pure sport, I imagine— but he ended up cornering me in the kitchen. I begged him to leave me alone, but begging never worked with him. It only made him want to hurt me more—after all, he's a sadist. At the time his favorite maneuver was to pin me down and jam his fingers under my collar- bone until I wet my pants. Being that we were on our way to Mass, I was wearing my suit and I really didn't want to sit through the service soaking in my own piss. The stakes were high, so I grabbed the first thing I could find off the kitchen counter—a meat thermometer. I didn't think to hesitate or threaten him. I simply jammed the spike into his arm until it hit the bone. I wish I could say the pointer went into the red zone, but all I remember is the look of disbelief on his face. And it was beautiful.

"Hey man, I'm sorry about that," he says about the right to my jaw. "I don't know what I was thinking."

"Don't worry about it."

"Just try not to be such a smart-ass."

Some apology. I get up out of the chair and say, "I'm gonna go down to the cafeteria and get a coffee."

"Get me one too. And don't forget the fucking sugar."

"Okay," I say.

THERE'S NO FUCKING way I'm getting him *anything*.

By the front desk, a man is taking a break from painting the wall. He's chatting up a nurse. With barely a thought in my head, I pick up the bucket of paint and head into the elevator. One swift move. I'm on a mission. It doesn't even feel like *me;* it's more the idea I have of me when I'm driving home, thinking *Coulda, shoulda, woulda.* I take the elevator as high as it will go and when I get there, I find the stairs and keep going *up, up, up* . . . until I get to the roof. A sign says AU-

THORIZED PERSONNEL ONLY but that doesn't scare me off. Not now. I open the door to find a bank of air conditioners wheezing under the heat. It's so hot, the black tar under my feet feels like a gigantic fly-trap. My shoes stick and unpeel, stick and unpeel as I walk around, trying to get my bearings. Tentatively, I inch to the edge and look over. I never would have thought so, but seven stories is pretty far down.

There must be a hundred people down there. Maybe if I were higher up they'd look like ants, but from here they're more the size of monkeys. The air conditioner next to me kicks in with a rattle. It heaves and sighs, gurgling like an old man with a wet cough. Rusty fluid hemorrhages out its side, follows a seam in the roof, and seeps down the wall. Jesus works in mysterious ways.

It quickly becomes apparent why I'm here. In the name of keeping up the community's high aesthetic standards, I pour the paint into the stream of air conditioner gunk and let gravity take over. I wish I had the guts to look down at the crowd and gauge its reaction, but my freshly discovered fear of heights will allow for only so much bravery in one day. Besides, I don't need to look. The crowd lets out a collective roar. What a rush to have my work so immediately appreciated. Most artists, I realize, never experience such instant gratification.

But I prefer to toil away in anonymity, so I toss the pail aside and make tracks down the stairs. As I'm spiraling down through the cold concrete, I hear the cry of a posse coming from down below. I slip onto the fourth floor, thinking it's as good a place as any to bide my time. I hate to disappoint my fans, but surely they'll understand my desire to remain nameless.

At first I think I've landed myself in the morgue, but a closer look reveals that these old people are merely moving in slow motion. I'm sure to be mistaken for someone's grandson any second, so I go into the first room I see. It belongs to Eloise Parker—that's what the chart says. Remarkably, Eloise is somehow able to sleep through the noise screaming from her TV, also known as Reverend Jim Pritchard—savior of souls and healer of the lame throughout the Ohio Valley. Like a rancher with a cattle prod, he jolts the believers with his touch. Unlike cattle, Pritchard's touch leaves the believers collapsing in ecstasy. It makes engaging TV, but the real show is watching the people—people you normally get to see only at the state fair—as they approach the altar, thinking their lives are about to completely transform. They have so much hope they're practically glowing.

"Do you want God to make you hear? Take those hearing aids out! You don't need 'em. God will take care of you!"

The TV is loud, *too* loud. I can barely think, so I reach up and turn it down. Eloise groans and shakes her head like she's about to wake up. I turn it back up and she relaxes. "Let God unclog your veins. . . . Let his words flow through your blood." Serene for her, not for me. I turn it back down and she flops like a fish, back up and she's calm. "You don't need chemotherapy if you have God!"

Eloise looks like she's been lying there forever. Or maybe it just smells like she has. I don't know what that stench is, but it sure isn't roses. They can keep people alive, even if they look like they're practically dead, for a long time. I bet Eloise never thought this is the way it would end.

Her face looks like a crumpled piece of paper someone threw away. Maybe that paper used to hold a shopping list or maybe it was the greatest poem ever written. Now it doesn't really matter. It's crinkled and yellowing as if it could turn to dust in your hands. On the bureau, there are pictures of Eloise from better days. She was no beauty, but she was cute, if that's her at all, pulling up her skirt, showing some leg over sixty years ago at the 1939 World's Fair in New York City. There are other pictures too, and if you cared you could probably stitch together a life between them all.

All these people, these smiling people; I wonder if any of them ever come to see Eloise. Or is she alone in the world, with only a few celluloid memories to keep her company? Then I think, maybe I'm looking at Annika fast-forwarded seventy years, lying on a bed comatose. Abandoned.

That's when Eloise opens her eyes.

"Who the hell are you? You been scewing with the TV?"

"Uuhhhh, no."

"I may be old, but I ain't stupid."

"Maybe a little bit."

"You think I'm a little stupid?"

"No, I may have screwed with the TV a little bit."

"Is that the way you treat your own grandmother?"

"Uhh, my grandmother is dead . . . both of them."

"Well I ain't gonna be your grandma. I got too many grandkids don't visit as it is."

"Okay . . . but I'm visiting you right now. Doesn't that count for something?"

"And you didn't even bring me a present. You visit someone in the hospital, you bring them a present. Don't you know anything?"

"I know that they're making great strides in euthanasia."

"Whoopie for you, you read. Now go downstairs and get me a strawberry milk shake."

"All right, just promise me you won't eat anything until I get back. I don't want you ruining your appetite."

"Ha. That's rich. I haven't had an appetite in three years."

I believe her; you can see the bones coming through her skin.

I tell her I'll be back in a little while, even though I probably won't be. It's kind of a shitty thing to do, I know.

THE SUN SHINES bright as a crowd looks up at the wall. The white paint is slowly descending, swallowing the brown ooze.

"It's looks like a big bird took a dump on Jesus's head," says one young, astute art connoisseur.

I didn't realize it at the time, but that's exactly what I was going for—a dump on Jesus's head. I'm feeling pretty happy with myself. As the white paint inches down Jesus's face, I think I've done something good.

Self-congratulations get me nowhere. Like oil separating from water, the white paint recedes from the brown streaks. The paint and the spent air-conditioner gunk don't mix. Now the stain is popping off the wall. There are *oohs*. There are *aaahs*. If you didn't think it looked like Jesus before, you would now. Even I can see it. Good ol' peace-loving, Birkenstock-wearing Jesus—his stringy hippie hair jumping off the wall, his hangdog expression asking, *Couldn't you just try to be nice?*

A news van pulls up and I head toward the car.

THE RELATIVES FROM Toledo find out about Annika from their local news and immediately come to Columbus. It's only a two-and-a-half-hour drive, which is nothing to them. They all drive down to Branson, Missouri, at least twice a year. On the way they blow their wad on riverboat keno and whatever's left once they hit Branson goes to Mickey Gilley, George Jones, and souvenirs from area gift shops. They're all serious collectors of farm implements that feature artistic renderings of Civil War battles.

My grandpa, Mom's dad and my lone surviving grandparent, is at the wheel of his two-tone silver-mauve Cadillac. He gets a new one every other year. As I turn into the driveway, he pulls up right next to me. Aunt Harriet is sitting next to him, while Aunt Betty and Uncle George are in back.

"We made it here in record time," Grandpa proudly exclaims as he hoists himself out of the car. "I can't believe we had to hear about Annika on the news. What is it with this family?"

"I don't know, Grandpa," I say, offering him my hand.

"God damnit, give your grandpa a hug."

I do and he says, "How's my little princess doing?"

"She's doing pretty much the same."

Grandpa hasn't looked this good in ten years. Grandma died from Alzheimer's two summers ago. It was a slow dive and Grandpa took care of her every second of the way down. People said he should put her in a home; even my mom wanted him to. It would have made sense. After all, Grandma didn't know where she was half the time, but Grandpa would hear nothing of it. He'd made his vow and he was going to stick to it. "I said 'in sickness and in health.' I said ' 'til death do us part' and God damnit, that's what I'm going to do." Personally, I never would have thought he had it in him. No one did.

In fact, we all thought it would happen the other way around. We thought Grandma would be taking care of Grandpa; the year Annika was born, Grandpa had a stroke. Now, you'd never know it, unless you knew why he was sporting a mustache. He won't admit it (he says the ladies like it), but really, he grew it to cover up a scar on his lip. He got it when a chain saw jumped off a piece of wet wood and bit him in the mug. Grandma found him passed out in the snow. His blood must have looked like a spilled slush puppy. She thought he was dead.

No one would have thought my grandfather would make a good caregiver, but he really stepped up to the plate. Even after Grandma pulled a shotgun on him, he still refused to lock her up. "She just got a little confused, is all," is what he said. Grandma was under the impression that Grandpa was cheating on her with Thelma Murphy, a spry seventy-four-year-old from their church. With her binoculars Grandma would watch them greet each other in the church parking lot down the hill from their farm. Apparently, that was all the evidence she needed. With the shotgun pointed at his head, he said, "Why don't you just shoot me now? Go ahead pull the goddamn trigger." Instead, she put the gun down and started to cry.

Uncle George and Aunt Betty are looking at me like they don't know who I am. Or maybe they're just disappointed that I'm not Ben. I get that a lot.

"Hi, Aunt Betty, Uncle George."

"Monroe, you get taller every time we see you."

Grandpa says they've been worried sick. He wonders again why no one in this family ever tells anyone what's going on.

Certainly it would have had nothing to do with the way he raised my mom. Like most rural kids, Mom was a 4-H'er. Up until the age of ten, the highlight of her life was winning the blue ribbon at the county fair for raising a milk cow named Pat. She loved that cow the way boys love their first dog. That's the way she always puts it. Mom had big plans for Pat. The next year she hoped to take home the prize for best cheese from the now prizewinning line of Pat's milk. But there would be no next year. Grandpa told her it was time for Pat to move to a bigger farm. He said Pat had become so big she needed more space. It would be for her own good. Mom had no choice but to suck it up. That's life on a farm.

Grandpa had Pat slaughtered. Dairy cows usually don't have to worry about the chopping block, but it had been a lean year on the farm and drastic measures were required. That's not such a shock, but the cruelty came in bite-sized morsels of red meat, as Mom unwittingly ate her best friend through the long, cold Ohio winter. She was none the wiser until their farmhand accidentally spilled the news. Mom laughs about it now, but Grandma told me she didn't stop crying for two weeks.

Aunt Harriet, my dead grandma's sister, wants to go inside and use the bathroom. "I have a bladder the size of a pea," she says. They all laugh like she's saying it for the first time, but her minuscule bladder is, in fact, her most notable characteristic. They probably stopped about a dozen times along the way. She ought to do everyone a favor and just wear a diaper.

I'VE GOT THE WHOLE DAY wide open and nowhere to go. There's a month left in school, but my fate is sealed. I'm going to Ohio State. Dad said it was the only place he would pay for if I didn't get an A average. It didn't matter to him that I was accepted to Oberlin, which is not only a pretty good school, but also where Emily is going. Dad said that if I go there, I'll turn into a terrorist-loving liberal. He says that's okay with him as long as I pay for it myself—as if there were any way I'll ever come up with thirty-five grand a year on my own.

Emily is probably getting tired of dealing with me, so I figure I'll leave her alone . . . but I need to do *something*. I can't just wait around like the rest of them. I can't just pray and hope someone, somewhere will not only hear me, but also do something about it.

That's asking a lot.

I feel like crying, but I can't. It felt good to cry in Lily's arms, but I don't think I'll be able to bring myself to do it again, especially alone. Maybe I should save my tears for if it gets worse—or if it gets better. Right now, though, I've got nothing. Annika's in a coma and I might as well be too. I guess I'm in shock. It's not that shock is bad. It stops you from feeling the pain. It's a defense mechanism. Like a coma. I'm generally all for avoiding pain, but right now it seems like there might be some comfort in feeling bad. In feeling at all.

I don't know where to go, so I go to the mall. Which is not to say I spend a lot of time in the mall. I don't. I *hate* the mall. It's just that it's hard to avoid. There aren't exactly a lot of other options around here. In Columbus malls are king. It's been that way since 1949 when Town & Country became the country's first regional shopping center. By all accounts, it was a groundbreaking and courageous development. Hard to believe, but no one thought a shopping center would succeed, so the opening-day festivities included the spectacle of an elderly woman named Grandma Carver diving from a hundred-foot perch into a five-foot pool of flaming water. Hundreds, if not thousands, of people jammed the parking lot to see her. In fact, she was such a tremendous draw that the promoters had her repeat this stunt on several occasions. She soon became a Columbus institution, that is, until a dim-witted teenage assistant replaced the usual flaming kerosene with gasoline. When she hit the water, the explosion nearly killed her.

I end up in the food court. Eating a lame taco. Drinking a Coke that's short on carbonation and high on ice.

That's when I spot Mason Jones. He buses tables. Don't feel too sorry for him. He got a scholarship to play football at the University of Michigan. He has a *future*. Even if he shatters his leg in the first practice, he'll be fine. At school, he's like some god, but right now you'd never know it. In his apron and paper hat and hairnet, he could be anyone. His shoulders are slumped, his eyes fixed on his shoes. If you didn't know who he was, you wouldn't notice him at all.

The most alive I've felt in the last two days was when Ben hit me. It didn't feel *good,* but at least it *felt*. That's what I'm thinking as Mason makes his way toward me, filling up a big plastic tray with trash. I should have let him beat me up six years ago when I had the chance. Maybe I wouldn't be such a pussy today. Maybe when I walked through the halls at school, I wouldn't be invisible.

I have no reason to hate him, but I do.

When he's about to pass by me, I knock over the Coke, spilling it everywhere.

"Oh man, sorry about that," I say. If you didn't know me, you might even think I'm being sincere.

"Don't worry about it," he says, not even looking up.

"Thought you'd get a promotion by now," I say. "You've been working here long enough."

He raises his eyes to mine. "Oh, it's you. *Anderson.*" I can't believe he remembers who I am.

He seems resigned to be doing what he's doing, but not embarrassed. Everyone says Mason is the best football player to come out of Ohio in the last ten years and here he is on his knees cleaning up my mess.

"Hey man, sorry about your sister," he says. "Man, I'd be dropping shit everywhere too, if I were you. Is she doing any better?"

"She's the same, but thanks for asking."

This is not going as planned. If you could call what I had a plan.

"I'll go get a mop," he says. "I'll be back in a minute."

I grab a fistful of napkins and fall to the ground. I want to clean up the soda before he gets back. I've never felt like such an asshole in my life. I succeed only in moving the soda around. Making a bigger mess.

Mason's back. He's looking down on me, a pail in his hand.

"Hey man, you don't have to do that."

"I'm really sorry," I say.

"Don't worry about it, it was just an accident," he says. "Where you going to school?"

"OSU."

"I'm going to be a Wolverine. You realize we're going to stomp your ass, right?"

"Yeah, I hope so," I say.

He just looks at me like *whatever,* like I'm a *moron,* and wrings out his mop.

I thought I wanted to get beaten up and even though a punch was never thrown, I guess I did. Mason didn't have to lay a hand on me to kick my ass. Sitting here with a half-eaten taco and a pile of wet napkins in front of me on a plastic tray, I've never felt so small in my life.

Chapter 9

A CARLOAD OF TEENAGERS died coming home from their prom in Pickerington. A man blew up a gas station with a cigarette. Someone capped a liquor store clerk on the south side. But the local news leads with Jesus's face on a hospital wall. *That* was such a big deal, Cheryl Hanover from the local CBS affiliate vacated her anchor's desk just long enough to get to the bottom of the story herself. She nods along as Father Ferger says, "Since the image was able to transcend the attempted vandalism, it seems all the more likely to be the work of God."

We're watching on TV at home. And by we, I mean Mom, Dad, Grandpa, and me. The other relatives went back to Toledo, but Grandpa is still here. He thinks maybe he can help around the house.

Mom wonders why anyone would ever want to vandalize the spontaneous image of Jesus Christ. Grandpa assures her there are a lot of sick people out there. He knows because his mailbox has been smashed three times in the last four months. "I just got a new one," he says. "And I'll tell you that next punk is going to be surprised. It looks *exactly* like a regular wood mailbox, but it's made out of *cement*. When the next little bastard hits it with a baseball bat, I bet it'll take the little prick's arm right off."

"You might want to be careful about that," Dad cautions. "It could open you up to some liability issues."

"You're talking like a goddamn lawyer, Larry."

Dad glares.

"Oh right, you *are* a goddamn lawyer." I've heard him tell that joke about a million times and every time I laugh, mainly because I can see how much it pisses Dad off. Dad and Grandpa don't really get along very well. In fact, I'm surprised Dad's sitting here with us at all. Usually he would have retreated upstairs to his room by now. But now that Grandpa has made fun of him, he *can't* leave. It would be admitting defeat. So, he's left to sink in his chair and grind his teeth.

I can't help myself. "Maybe the act of vandalism was an act of God. After all, it really brought out the sheen in Jesus's hair. Maybe the vandalism was all part of a bigger plan."

Mom nods along, while Grandpa adds, "All I know is this: If the Big Cheese were going to come down to earth and show Himself, He could come up with a helluva better stunt than spitting out a picture of His Son in rusty water."

Mom says, "Beauty can come from the most unlikely places. Maybe that's the lesson we're supposed to learn."

Mom isn't acting like herself at all. Beauty comes from uncracked glossy coffee table books and household tips courtesy of Martha Stewart, not from air-conditioner splooge, regardless of how well it's presented. In fact, a few years ago Mom spearheaded a campaign to "liberate" our neighborhood from a downed tree in the Harringtons' yard. While the dead tree was certainly an eyesore, the situation was exacerbated by Mr. Harrington, who painted the tree Day-Glo orange for the express purpose of pissing off people like my mom. And it worked. The more the neighbors demanded the trunk's removal, the more he was determined to make sure it stayed. At Christmas, he decorated it with lights to mock them. At Easter, he rigged cardboard bunny rabbits going back and forth, like a shooting gallery, daring them to take a shot. At Halloween, he lined the carcass with laughing pumpkins, but no one was amused. The neighbors, bound in solidarity against the evils of bad taste, bided their time, waiting to strike. Once all legitimate means of protest were exhausted, they did what they had to do.

When the Harringtons went away on their annual vacation, the tree miraculously disappeared in the middle of the night.

At the next commercial break, Dad admits defeat. He says he has a lot of work to do; he's going upstairs. Everyone is okay with that. But the thing is, Dad's a workaholic. So, for him to say he's going to do some work: it's no different than a drunk saying, *Man, I need a drink* or a junkie saying, *Excuse me for a minute while I go stick a needle in my arm*. Whichever way you dice it, it's an escape from reality. Alcohol, bad. Heroin, bad. But work? That's okay. Go knock yourself out.

Someone has to pay for all of this.

Grandpa tells Mom that everything is going to be okay. He says that Annika is a real tiger. We're all going to pull through this together. Then he goes into the kitchen and starts rifling through all the food the neighbors have brought over.

Chapter 10

FOUR WEEKS HAVE PASSED and nothing has changed. Annika's still in the hospital. Grandpa's still here, Mom's still praying, and Dad still has a lot of work to do. I repeat, *A lot of work. To do. Now.*

As of yesterday, I'm a high school graduate, which isn't really a big deal. The big deal would be if I weren't one. Lately, though, school has been the last thing on my mind. I spend most of my time at the hospital, in intensive care. It's not like I think Annika knows I'm there, but Mom says she does know, even though it looks like she doesn't. Emily comes with me sometimes, but not so much lately. She's been pretty busy with homework, trying to make sure she graduated summa cum laude—which she did, not that it really matters; she's going to Oberlin either way. It was kind of great, though, at graduation, seeing all the people who've called her a slut have to suck it up and clap when she got the award for highest grade-point average in our class. I've never seen such a big smile on her face.

At the hospital, I must have read a dozen books. Slipping into another world makes it easier to tune Mom out as she reads Annika her get-well cards and tells her stories. I sit in the corner with a book, because by just sitting there I'm able to create the illusion that I'm actually doing something, whereas if I was home doing what I'm doing now, I would be of no help at all.

JESUS DISAPPEARED A couple days after He showed up. The hospital had the good sense not to fix the air conditioner and Jesus eventually drowned in his own juices. It was really all quite beautiful. The local news caught it on time lapse film: Jesus slowly turning into rust-colored mud. It was all for the best. Too many people were showing up. Jesus had become a distraction. Nobody could get anything done.

Mom talks in Annika's ear and tells her how she's there for her, how she's never going to leave. They're in it together, like it's all a secret only the two of them share. After Mom says what she has to say, she kisses her on the cheek. If she's done it once, she's done it a thousand times.

But this time is different. "She kissed me back, she kissed me back," Mom says with the kind of joy generally reserved for contestants on *The Price Is Right*. I look up from my book, skeptical. "If you don't believe me, put your face next to her ear and tell her you love her."

It would have been futile to resist. So, I say, "Annika, I love you," my cheek next to her lips. Nothing.

"Say it like you mean it."

"I mean it."

"Then say it that way."

"Annika, *je t'aime*."

"Monroe, that's not very funny."

"What says *I love you* more than French?"

"*Monroe.*"

So, I lean in, but the way Mom is staring at me makes me squirm. "You're not helping," I tell her.

"Fine. I won't look."

Somehow, I manage to compose myself and tell Annika I love her without cracking up. Without sounding sarcastic. It's a lot harder to do than you might think. After I say those words, which are so hard to say, I let my cheek linger on her lips and yes, she puckers back, leaving a slight residue of drool.

"Yeah, Mom, she's a kissing machine." I'm thinking we could put up a sign and start taking donations: KOMA KISSES $5. But I don't say that.

Mom presses the NURSE button and says Dr. Singh has got to see this.

After about fifteen minutes, once every nurse on the floor has gotten a kiss, Dr. Singh finally shows up. He doesn't want to, but he puts his cheek up to her lips and she kisses him too, but the doctor is not impressed. He doesn't even look at Annika when he tells Mom, "That is a *primitive* response, like a baby suckling his mother's breast. You really shouldn't read too much into it. In fact, I'd be surprised if her lips *didn't* move."

"You don't understand," Mom says. "She *kissed* me."

"I understand that, Mrs. Anderson, she kissed me *too*." Mom's crestfallen, but the doctor isn't through yet. He says, "Mrs. Anderson, we need to talk. It's been four weeks and nothing has changed. The odds, they are not promising. Annika may come out of it tomorrow and she may come out of it in three days or three years—we just don't know. She may *never* come out of it. You need to prepare yourself for that, Mrs. Anderson. But, as far as this facility goes, there's nothing more that we can do here." This is the official medical diagnosis four weeks and two days after Annika fell in the pool. Then, like it's some sort of consolation prize, he says, "I wish there were."

The prayer group headed by Father Ferger still shows up, usually a couple dozen faithful congregate around the fountain at dinnertime. Our street is lined with yellow ribbons. So many flowers have been sent, we've farmed them out to every patient on the fifth floor. Nobody has forgotten us.

Still, it looks like it's going to take a lot more than prayers to make Annika well again. They can monitor her, they can keep her comfortable . . . but *there's nothing they can do*. It's funny that Dr. Singh should admit that now. Mom has been tending to Annika more than anyone in the entire hospital. She's been here every day, all day, holding her hand, talking in her ear, telling her stories.

In the last month Annika is all Mom has thought of. Every moment has been dedicated to her. It's written all over her face. In the lines I've never seen before. Lines I guess she used to fill with makeup so well it never would have occurred to me that's why she looks so young. That's what everyone always tells her—*Jeannie, you look so young.* Now, for the first time, gray hairs stray from her head. She's barely eaten, although sometimes the nurses bring her Jell-O. She tells them the best part of all this is how much weight she's lost. She laughs and calls it the coma diet. The thing is, now that Mom has surrendered her battle against old age, she looks younger than she has in years.

Mom wonders, "What does that mean, Dr. Singh—there's nothing more you can do?"

It means, Dr. Singh suggests, "Perhaps Annika should be placed in Oakside."

"Oakside? You want to put my baby in an *institution*? And just let her rot away? Are you *crazy*?"

"Oakside is a very fine facility," replies Dr. Singh, not blinking. Dr. Singh *never* blinks.

Everyone knows Oakside is a dead-end street. No one ever comes back from Oakside. In addition to the vegetable stand, they also have a psych wing. They're both one-way tickets. If you want to scare your kid into doing what you want, tell them you'll take them to Oakside and have them committed.

"Dr. Singh, are you familiar with immersion therapy?"

"Yes, Mrs. Anderson, if you're referring to the work pioneered by Dr. Ahmed Ghaloab of Saint Louis, Missouri. Yes I am. I see you have been surfing the Internet. I should caution you. Doctor—and I use the term loosely—Ghaloab has never published a paper. His results have never been substantiated. His methods are not accepted by any major American insurance carrier."

"And what do you suggest, Dr. Singh?"

"Mrs. Anderson, there are many different therapies and none have withstood medical scrutiny. Do you want your daughter to be an experiment? Because that is what will happen."

"What I want is for my daughter to get the kind of care she deserves. And from the minute we got here, I don't think you've given her that."

"I do not appreciate your implication, Mrs. Anderson."

"And I don't appreciate that you failed to alleviate the pressure on Annika's brain when we brought her in. Dr. Ghaloab says the brain floats on a cushion of spinal fluid and when there's swelling . . ."

Dr. Singh explains, "I don't need to listen to this. People read a few pages on the Internet and they think they can tell me how to practice."

But Mom's not intimidated. "That seems to be the problem, Doctor. You're just practicing, but we can't afford it when you make mistakes. All I want is for Annika to wake up. If she were *your* daughter, tell me, Doctor, would you just let her lie there?"

"If she were my daughter, my grief would be overwhelming."

"Dr. Singh, I'm taking Annika home."

"I would not recommend that, Mrs. Anderson. For Annika's sake, I hope you reconsider. Do you have any idea what kind of facilities Annika requires? The equipment? The medical expertise? Annika needs to be monitored all day, every day. The financial cost will be staggering."

"I appreciate your concern. We'll manage."

Mom isn't bluffing. Everyone tries to talk her out of it, even Father Ferger, but she will hear none of it. One doctor says Annika won't survive a month without around the clock professional care. Another tells Mom that Annika's life might be ruined, but there's no point in ruining her own.

Everyone says she has no idea what she's getting herself into.

Chapter 11

THE DELIVERYMEN COME to the door with a hospital bed and Mom tells them to put it right in the middle of the living room; that will be fine. "Perfect," she says. They say, "What a beautiful room." And she says, "It will be nice to actually put it to use." Dad watches from around the corner, not saying a word, but you can see that it's killing him.

I can guarantee you that they never discussed bringing Annika home. Mom probably figured there was nothing to discuss. She probably assumed Dad would feel the same way. After all, who'd want to leave their daughter out to rot in Oakside? *You'd have to be a monster.* That's what she calls Dr. Singh, *a monster.*

Dad exhales, like he's forgotten to breathe for about five minutes. He does that a lot lately, forgets to breathe. Then he grabs his keys off the kitchen table, slips out the door, and goes to work. He'll be back in twelve to fourteen hours.

The only person who ever used the living room—with the exception of parties thrown by my parents—was Annika; so it kind of makes sense for her to move in. Annika always liked to read in the living room, probably because it's the only room in the house that doesn't constantly have a television on.

It's like a museum: two or three paintings Mom and Dad got in Italy on their honeymoon, Oriental rugs, furniture so uncomfortable it's sure to alienate the guests it's supposed to attract. Everything about the room is so stiff, I feel like I just put on a starched shirt whenever I walk in.

Annika comes home just like she left, in an ambulance. The same boys on their bikes circle around the street, craning to get a look. The same sprinklers circle the lawns. Only the black circles under all of our eyes are new.

The hospital bed is adjustable like the ones they try to sell to old people on TV except that this one is wrapped with a metal railing. Mom put on Annika's Charlie Brown sheets—a nice touch. There's a stomach tube to feed her and monitors to keep tabs on her vitals. The whole room is full of flowers. People keep sending them—people we don't know. If they're not sending flowers they're sending pictures of the Virgin Mary or Jesus or Padre Pio.

Above the bed, Mom takes down a painting of the Italian coastline. Its defining characteristic lies in how beautifully it complements the sofa's soft robin's-egg blue hue. In its place she hangs a painting of the Virgin Mary, its dots lovingly connected by one of Annika's admirers.

Mom must have made the deal, the deal everyone makes when the going gets tough. She's given herself to God, as if somehow, by making this trade, she'll bring Annika back. She's always been a believer, but not like this. I don't hold it against her. People barter with God all the time, making promises they'll never keep. They might as well be asking for salvation on layaway. Back in the old days, when people sacrificed not only their pets but their kids too, that's when a deal meant something. They gave up the goods up front with only the *hope* of a return on their investment. Now it's the other way around and people rarely—if ever—pay up when the bill comes due.

I don't know exactly what promises my mom has been making, but she's constantly holding, rubbing, and caressing her rosary beads. Holding, rubbing, and caressing. Silently ticking off the prayers one by one. *All the time.*

It makes me think she's weak. I'm sure a believer would say that I'm the weak one—but you watch her rub these beads, all day all the time. It's utterly compulsive. How many times do you have to repeat yourself before God hears you?

Father Ferger is Annika's first visitor. He's here to perform the Eucharist. I don't stick around to watch. Theoretically, this ritual requires two. You can't just give someone the body and blood of Christ; they have to ask for it. That's why they make you kneel in front of the priest when he puts the wafer on your tongue. But Annika can't give her consent; she's going to eat the body of Christ whether she wants to or not.

On her first night home when everyone is asleep, I peek in on her. The moonlight illuminates her face, but the rest of the room is dark. Her freshly washed blonde hair is perfect, just as it will be tomorrow. There will be no tossing and turning for Annika.

"She looks just like a doll, doesn't she?" asks Grandpa. He's sitting on the couch no one ever sits on, looking at his granddaughter. It's two-thirty in the morning.

Grandpa always used to give Annika dolls. Every time he saw her he'd have a new one. I can see him now in the doll shop, picking them out. "Did I give her the one with this dress already?" "Are Princess Jennifer and Princess Alexandra the same, just with different hair?" Grandpa always saw himself as a bit of a Casanova. He is, after all, a charter member of Cleveland's Playboy Club. The girl behind the toy store counter must be really hot. Mom says he never got her a doll. Not once. He's probably trying to make up for it with Annika. Maybe that's why parents are so into becoming grandparents. It gives them a chance to redeem themselves for all the mistakes they made the first time around.

The dolls always came in a glass holder. Forever young, never touched by grubby hands. *Virgins*. Once Annika tore off the wrapping paper, the first thing she would do was break the seal and free them from the glass. Grandpa said they were collectibles and that they lost their value when you took them out of their case, but Annika never understood that. If you couldn't play with a doll, then what good was it? She'd make fun of Grandpa and put on a show with the prince and the princess in their glass shells. They'd bump into each other, like bubble boys and girls—trapped in their cages. She'd say the world is so polluted now, no one can breathe unless they're in a balloon. It's the only way you can survive. "Everyone's in a bubble, but no one can hold hands," she'd say. "It's sad, but it's better than being dead." Then she'd have the dolls trying to kiss each other through glass. She called it safe sex, which made everyone laugh mainly because they thought she had no idea what it really meant.

Annika looks like one of those dolls now. No glass, but she somehow seems unapproachable. Untouchable. Not that you can't feel her skin, but that her skin can't feel you. I know this is not the way it will always be. I know someday she'll wake up and we'll ride out into the country for apple fritters and the wind will blow through her hair and it will be like none of this ever happened.

Maybe this all means I have faith—not in God, but in the future. Faith that everything is going to be all right.

"I guess the old man should go to bed now," Grandpa says. "Be sure to keep the lights on."

He always says stuff like that, like whenever he sees me, he says, "You look so much shorter than the last time I saw you. You're getting so *short*." He's always pretending he's the opposite of an adult.

When we were kids, Ben and I put on a carnival in the backyard. All the money went to charity, not that there was much, but that's where it went. To UNICEF. That was our excuse, *charity. We're saving starving kids in Africa.* You can do almost anything if you say it's for charity, *especially* saving starving kids in Africa.

We had these carnivals for a couple of years before Ben decided it was stupid; then we didn't do it anymore. We had a petting zoo featuring all my turtles and we'd recruit the neighborhood dogs and dress them up as elephants and giraffes. We had a midway where you could knock down cans and fish for trinkets. You could bob for apples and eat sno-cones and play putt-putt golf. It was a lot of fun. It really was. Grandpa would always come so he could be the guy who'd guess your weight or age, whichever one you wanted. He'd tell fat people they weighed what they wished they weighed. He'd tell the ten-year-old girls they were fourteen and they'd squeal. It made them so happy. He'd tell all the mothers they couldn't be a day older than twenty-eight. Even if he gave everyone *two* prizes, we still would have made money.

Our biggest attraction was the freak show, featuring our neighbor Andy Albertson, who's two or three years younger than me. No need to call the ACLU or Amnesty International. It's not like he was deformed. It's not like people were making fun of him. If anything, Andy made the rest of us look like retards. Andy had a photographic memory and could recite almost anything—from all the *A*'s in the phone book to all the *Z*'s in the encyclopedia . . . and backward, if you asked. He just had to see it first on a printed page.

We made more money off of Andy than we did on everything else combined. You could give him a book, he'd read a page, and he'd recite it right back to you. For extra cash, he'd take requests. Speeches were his specialty. Then one day he wiped out on his bike, cracking his head open on the sidewalk. I didn't see it happen, but I saw the bloodstain. Everyone did. We were all crowding around looking at it the next day, until his dad came out of the house with a hose and a bottle of bleach and told us we were all sick.

Andy was okay. He was just never the same again. He could still remember stuff, but it was all out of order. Like he'd be reciting the Declaration of Independence and then he'd break into some letter he'd read in *Penthouse Forum*. Or he'd be reciting "I Have a Dream" and right when he got to the climax, he'd slip into that part in *Are You There God? It's Me, Margaret* where she has her period in the middle of class. Andy was like a radio whose dial kept spinning. Just when you thought he was tuned in, that maybe he was okay, he'd switch to another frequency and start reciting passages from *Mein Kampf.*

We couldn't really use Andy after the accident, even though technically he was more of a freak than he was before. His dad wouldn't let him do it anymore. Something about it being exploitative and sick. Andy's dad takes everything pretty seriously. So we had to come up with a new headliner. Ben, running with the idea that exploitative was a fine jumping-off point, christened Annika the missing link. She was only four at the time, but she was ready for the spotlight. All it took was a little glue and the contents of the vacuum cleaner bag to turn her into a living, breathing dust bunny, a twisted hybrid somewhere on the evolutionary scale between a marmot and a very lonely shepherd. It went over pretty well. She'd roll around, bare her teeth—it was quite primitive. While her wild ways were appreciated, the paying public demanded a glimpse of humanity . . . and the highly choreographed show indulged their basest desires. After a demonstration of her uncanny abilities to win at three-card monte, Annika finished her show with a lip-synched rendition of "Material Girl." Not surprisingly, whatever loose change the audience had left was soon on its way to Africa.

It may not have been politically correct, but at least the money went to a good cause. That was the intention. That was the plan. But who knows? Maybe our spare change and crumpled dollar bills landed in the mitts of some Somalian warlord bent on dragging dead American soldiers through the streets of Mogadishu. At the time, it was a risk we were willing to take, mainly because we didn't realize it was a risk that existed at all.

I used to think it was my job as Annika's older brother to protect her from the world; Ben sure wasn't going to do it. But now I know that you can't protect anyone from anything.

Chapter 12

I WAKE UP TO "Sweet Caroline," which isn't quite as bad as the time I woke up to Ben peeing on me, but it's close. I should stay in bed and surrender, let this day go, but Neil Diamond's voice cuts glass. He leaves me no choice but to go downstairs and see what this is all about. I'm in my robe, only now realizing what it must feel like to be so old that all you want in the world is *some peace and quiet,* all you want is for the kids to just *keep it down.*

When I get to the living room, I find Mom tying helium balloons to Annika's toes.

She says something. Her lips are moving, but all I can hear is Neil. He's having his way with the room. In a rare reversal of roles, I turn down the stereo. "We have to fight back gravity," she says. "She's sinking into the mattress, we can't let that happen." There must be fifty balloons in the room, get-well balloons, happy-face balloons, square balloons, balloons inside balloons.

"We really have to get our own helium dispenser," she says.

Mom's willing to try anything. She's always talking to Dr. Ghaloab on the phone from his clinic in Saint Louis and she's determined to put his special brand of immersion therapy to the test. Basically, the drill is this: bombard the patient with constant stimulation until they wake up. He told her, "The trick is to knock on the door as loud as you can, as often as you can, for as long as you can."

"And that's what we're going to do, keep knocking until the door opens."

I say, "You know, there is such a thing as headphones." I'm sounding more and more like her every minute.

" 'Sweet Caroline' is good for everyone," she says, "It gets the blood flowing." I'll remember that next time she complains about me cranking Lee Dorsey.

She asks me if I'd like to rub ice on Annika's feet. I figure I might as well get with the program, so I do. Annika's feet used to be so ticklish that just saying you were going to tickle them was enough to get her to practically pee her pants. But right here, right now, *nothing*. Not even a shudder. Not a flinch. She doesn't even have any goose bumps, but I do, it's so cold.

I've never seen Mom as happy as she has been since Annika came home and I've never seen less of my dad. Mom is determined to make sure that Annika doesn't lie there, wasting away. Dad is determined not to show his face.

"Dr. Ghaloab says that bedridden means we should rid Annika of her bed," explains Mom as she loads Annika into a wheelchair. "Get dressed and we'll go on a walk."

"A rolling stone gathers no moss," that's what Mom tells Mr. Albertson when he says how delighted he is to see Annika out and about. He says she looks really *great,* but he can barely even look in her direction. He'd love to stay and chat, but he really has to get to work. We continue our stroll down the yellow-bowed tree-lined streets and we come across Mrs. Latham. She's in the middle of a power walk, plastic weights Velcroed around her ankles. She stops long enough to say how adorable Annika is, how her prayers have been with us. She'd love to stay and chat, *but* . . . Everyone is full of smiles, but they never seem to stick around for long.

When I was a little kid I used to work these streets, selling bark out of my Radio Flyer. I'd go door-to-door with a stash of birch bark that had *fallen on the ground.* I emphasize that because sometimes people would accuse me of stripping it right off the trees. Even when I was seven, I knew better than that. It was five cents for a small piece, ten cents for a bigger one. I told the people that birch was great for writing notes, but now I realize they probably bought my wares out of pity. Maybe they thought it was cute. Maybe they thought they were on a hidden camera show.

Maybe they were just humoring me. That's what they're doing with my mom. I'm sure they must think she's lost her mind. Pushing her unconscious daughter down the street like it's any other day, the neighbors are always on the lookout for that kind of thing. For something out of the usual, something to talk about. Mom used to be like them, always looking for cracks in everyone's facade. Now, she doesn't seem to really care. She pushes that wheelchair around, like the pope himself is riding first class, and waves at everyone she sees.

It won't be long before they stop waving back.

Taking care of a patient in a vegetative state is a lot harder than you might think. By the way, that's what they're officially calling Annika's condition now—*a persistent vegetative state*. Apparently, it's a step up from being in a coma. When you're vegetating, your eyes open and close in accordance with the cycles of sleep, while when you're in a coma, your eyes never open, which I guess means you're pretty much *always* asleep. Unofficially, though, Annika's still in a coma. It's a lot easier to say than *persistent vegetative state*. And while a coma may be worse, it doesn't sound quite as bad as being vegetative. It doesn't sound so hopeless. After all, people sometimes wake up from a coma, while being persistently vegetative sounds like the best fertilizer money can buy.

Mom doesn't believe either one. She says Annika is *locked-in,* which basically means she's in there, but she can't get out. Of course, this diagnosis generally refers to patients who are paralyzed, and Annika is definitely *not* paralyzed. If you want to get clinical about it, the best-case scenario is that Annika is in a *minimally conscious state,* which unfortunately makes it sound like she's been exiled to Arkansas.

Whatever you call it, it may look like Annika's not so much trouble just lying around all day, but it's a lot of work, and it would be, even if she didn't get any therapy, which is pretty much what most unconscious patients get—*nothing.* Like at Oakside. Dad said it's too much work for Mom to do all on her own, so he hired a live-in nurse to help out. Her name is Maggie O'Shaunessy and she came to us highly recommended by Father Ferger. All it takes is one look at her to know that something bad happened. It's not like you can see any scars. In fact, when you look at her, you practically don't see anything at all. She might as well be disappearing right before your eyes.

I don't think Maggie likes men very much, which hardly accounts for why she should be afraid of me. As my father likes to remind me, it's not like I'm a man. I'm just a boy. Of course, he was already a man at my age, but that's what killing villagers in Vietnam will do—make a man out of you. If that's what it takes, somehow, I think I can wait.

Maggie can barely look at me, let alone speak a complete sentence. But that's okay. Even though she's kind of shy, she's still good to have around. After all, she changes the sheets, massages Annika, and keeps the food tube flowing. That's all pretty good stuff. She also reads her the Bible. Which is not. I don't think that's in her job description, but she does it anyway. I don't know if she thinks Bible stories are going to wake Annika up, but I seriously doubt it. It's a pretty boring book. I will say this for Maggie, though: She has a voice so constant, so devoid of emotion, it's practically hypnotic.

The only time Maggie ever leaves the house is to go to Mass. She's Irish, probably in her forties. Mom says her husband died in a construction accident while they were retrofitting Ohio State's football field. Under the by-laws of the Buckeye faithful, dying for such a worthy cause should make him a martyr. He's probably in a never-ending tailgating paradise with seventy-two virginal cheerleaders (if there is such a thing), slamming down all the Budweiser he can drink and all the Buffalo wings he can eat. As far as Maggie goes, you'd think she would have gotten some money out of her loss; but if she did, it's hard to imagine why she'd be working here.

Mom got Annika some headphones. *Finally.* Nice ones too, like DJs use. Annika better wake up soon or she just might go deaf. Everyone has an idea about what she should be listening to. Mom is all about Neil Diamond and show tunes; Maggie has her own personal collection of the Bible on CD. This is what I have to compete with. Me? I'm partial to the early groundbreaking work of Parliament and Funkadelic. If there is a track that can raise the dead, certainly it has to be "One Nation Under a Groove." Sometimes, I put it on REPEAT before I go to bed and Annika listens to it all night long.

Someday I hope she'll thank me.

CUBAN HORNS MIXED with fresh basil and garlic drifts through Emily's screen door as I coast up the driveway. Even though it's June, the Christmas lights in the bushes are on.

Emily and her parents have me over for dinner all the time. They're expecting me, so it's not like I'm eavesdropping. I just happen to hear what they're saying. It would have been hard not to.

As I park my bike, I hear Bob say, "Emily, we're so proud of you. We always have been."

Lily says, "Oh honey, it's going to be such an *adventure*. You're going to have so much fun. I wanna be like you when I grow up."

Emily says, "It's like a dream come true."

I hesitate before I knock. That's when they spot me. Right as they're about to clink glasses.

"Monroe, you're early."

That's when I know this isn't going to turn out well for me. They're *celebrating* and I'm *early*.

Lily doesn't know it's a secret. "Monroe, did you hear the good news?"

If she were looking at the horror scribbled on her daughter's face, she'd know the answer.

"Uhhh, no," I say.

Emily knows it's going to kill me.

She tries to explain. "It's totally a fluke. I practically forgot I even applied."

Lily adds, "No need to be so modest, honey." Lily's a feminist. She's all into girl power.

"I got into a summer program at the women's studies department at Harvard to go to Guatemala and work with a collective of basket weavers and textile designers."

"That's great," I lie.

"It's all about helping them use their indigenous skills to more effectively become a part of the global economy," she says, apparently reciting the brochure.

"They've been exploited for way too long," muses Lily.

"It's a once-in-a-lifetime opportunity," Emily explains.

"I'm really happy for you," I lie again, giving her a hug. What else am I supposed to say?

"When do you leave?"

"In two weeks."

GRANDPA GOES BACK to Toledo to pick up some more clothes. He's decided to stick around until Annika comes out of it. Ever since Grandma died, he's been looking for a new mission. I guess living with us is it.

He comes back with a gadget he says his mother used on his dad after he'd worked in the field all day. "Even though they call it quackery, it still works," he assures us.

It looks like luggage, what my grandma used to call a grip, but when you open it up it's not spilling over with jars and bottles full of whatever potions Grandma used to keep her face from falling apart. Instead, inside this box we find four or five glass tubes, all of different shapes and sizes. One looks like a stethoscope. One looks like a claw. Another looks like a pencil—apparently for those hard-to-reach places. You attach the glass pieces to a cord and plug it in.

Mom says, "You're not going to plug that thing *in an outlet* are you?" I can see why she might be concerned about the ancient electrical cord. It looks like merely bringing this thing inside could burn the house down.

"Don't worry about it," says Grandpa, turning on the box. Even though the tube glows blue with electricity, it's called a violet ray machine.

"You've got to be kidding," Mom says, coming closer, curious.

"I thought you might say that," Grandpa says as he takes off his shirt. "Watch this," he says, rubbing it on his surprisingly fit belly. "It's like a ray gun, but it feels *good*."

The hair on his chest stands up, like he has static cling. "It's invigorating," he says. "She's going to love it."

Mom tries it on her arm, "It's like everything is alive." I try it too. It feels like laser-guided Bengay. "You think it'll be okay?" Mom asks.

I say, "It couldn't be any worse than Neil Diamond."

She glares at me, but the point has been made. When the glass touches Annika's skin, she shudders, a fraction of the jolt you might get from the electric paddles they use for cardiac arrest—we all agree it's a good sign. Then as Mom runs it down her daughter's arm, Annika moans. It's anguished and low like the *baaing* of a lost lamb. It's the first noise she's made since she splashed in the pool.

Mom pulls the blue glow away. "Oh baby, are you okay?" she reflexively asks. A dribble of drool goes down Annika's face.

"I think it was a good moan," I say, optimistically.

"I think at this point, *any* moan is a good moan," Grandpa says.

Ever since then, the healing electrolight has become a part of the daily regimen. I think of it as an introverted laser light extravaganza. My experimentations have shown that more moans are yielded per kilowatt when accompanied by the soothing mind-bending tones of Marvin Gaye's "What's Going On."

When I'm not cutting grass for Paul, the rest of my day wraps itself around Annika. For about a half hour after breakfast, I sit with her and read her the sports page, giving her the official recap of the Reds' exploits from the night before—which, incidentally, we've invariably listened to already. I, however, don't consider it a completely redundant exercise since it's not entirely clear which parts she was paying attention to in the first place.

We listen to the Reds together most nights, unless I have something else to do, which unfortunately, I usually don't. I like the West

Coast games best. They don't start until ten o'clock. By then, everyone has gone to their bedrooms to watch their own TVs. It seems so long ago when we used to build forts with blankets and pillows and listen to the ball games with bowls of popcorn and sodas to keep us awake. Now it's only me, the radio, and a book. Annika's there too, but it's not like before when I had to keep *shhhing* her. Now, she hardly even stirs, although about every other inning or so, I wipe off the drool that accumulates on her chin. Sometimes I wonder if Annika is like me at a party. I always think I'm taking part in the conversation, then I realize I haven't said a word.

Someone's always with Annika, whether it's me, Mom, Maggie, Father Ferger, assorted friends, or people from the church. She always enjoyed her time alone and now she has none. Then again, maybe being in a coma is as alone as anyone could ever be.

Like everyone else, I wonder what's going on in her head. It can't be *nothing*. It's not like she's flatlining it in there. I've seen the EEG, the waves of lines cascading across the monitor. They call it brain activity, but what that really means, I don't quite know. And neither do they. We're just assured that it's good that they're there, these wavy lines. Otherwise, she'd be brain-dead—a condition that some people seem to be able to live with quite well. But these peaks and valleys, sometimes smooth, sometimes jagged—maybe they're just hieroglyphics that no one will ever be able to decipher, a map of a place where no one will ever be able to go.

EMILY'S BEEN BUSY getting ready to go to Guatemala and I practically haven't seen her since graduation. Apparently, living like they do in a Third World country requires a lot of shopping, which I'm informed is a pretty snotty thing to say. I told Emily I only said that because I wish she was spending more time with me, which scored me a kiss, but it still didn't stop her from going to Pennsylvania for a week to see her grandparents, effectively cutting whatever time we have left to spend together in half.

I thought this summer was going to be different. I'd never had a girlfriend before, especially not in the summer. I thought it would be about making out by the pool, maybe driving into the country, having picnics, you know, stuff like that. But that's not the way it's been.

Two nights before Emily leaves I think I might get lucky. Her parents are at a Rickie Lee Jones concert and we have the house to ourselves. We're up in her bedroom and I'm pretty sure the making out is about to begin, but then she says, "Monroe, there's something I need to tell you, but I'm not sure how you'll react. I hope it doesn't make you hate me."

I tell her she can tell me anything, I could never hate her.

"Okay, here it goes. You know how people say I was a slut at Fairview?"

"People don't say that," I say.

"That's sweet of you," she says, "but I know they do."

"It doesn't matter what anyone says anyway," I assure her. "I wasn't exactly planning on going back for any reunions."

"There was only one guy," she says. "It wasn't something I planned. It wasn't like I really wanted to sleep with him at all, but I did."

"He forced you?" I ask.

"No, not really. I'm not going to make any excuses; I only have myself to blame. But still, he's an asshole. He went and told everyone, and, well, you know how that story goes."

"Want me to kick his ass?" I ask. I'm joking, but still it hurts when she laughs.

Once she gets over the idea of me in a fight, she manages to say, "The thing is I got knocked up."

"He hit you?" I say, densely.

"No, Monroe, I got pregnant."

She lets the news hang in the air like a balloon. And it's a *big* balloon, the size of the Good Year blimp and I'm doing my best to pretend I don't see it suspended there, hogging up the horizon, blocking out the bamboo in the windows and the poster of Che on the wall.

She says, "You're the first person I ever told; you know, except for my mom. And I probably wouldn't have told her, but I had to, you know, to get the abortion."

An abortion? Surely my face must register surprise, even though I should see it coming. I'm in favor of abortions, at least I thought I was, but it sure doesn't evoke that "go team" spirit when you find out someone you care about had to get one. It's not like congratulations are in order.

"I just thought you deserved to know. So, I guess that's why I've been kind of gun-shy, you know, when it comes to sex. I've always really liked that about you, the way you're so understanding. The way you treat me more like a friend than a girl, you know? Most guys, all they think about is getting in my pants."

See how I have her fooled? I think about getting in her pants pretty much all the time.

"I thought coming to Chelsea would be a fresh start, but no one ever wants you to have one of those. You never held any of the rumors against me, though," she says, kissing me on the cheek.

"And you never held being a social outcast against me."

We end up watching a movie. Nothing quite kills the moment like bringing up an abortion.

The next time I see Emily is right before she leaves for Guatemala. She gives me a kiss. It's on the lips and long, but Bob and Lily are sitting in the car, waiting to take her to the airport. Her lips feel good on mine, but the rest of me just feels sad.

Chapter 13

IT'S JULY 16 and Annika and I are listening to the radio as the Reds take it to the Houston Astros. In a matter of moments, Marty Brennaman will declare, "And this one belongs to the Reds." Those words guarantee a pretty good day, but Reds pitcher Scott Williamson has other ideas. After getting two easy outs, he walks three guys in a row, putting the winning run at the plate.

For Williamson's trouble, he's taken out of the game, leaving it up to Danny Graves to finish this one off. When Marty announces Danny's name, Annika's hands start to shake. I can hardly blame her; Danny makes me nervous too, even though he's supposed to be the best guy we have in the bullpen.

Houston slugger Craig Biggio is at the plate. It seems like he kills us every time, but there's nowhere to put him. Danny's first pitch is in the dirt, prompting Annika's face to twist, just like it did when Mom used to try to make her eat lima beans. I reach over to hold her hand, thinking it might help settle her down.

It smells like roses in here. The smell of victory. The smell of parades. The smell of floats full of winners waving at you, smiling.

It hasn't smelled like this since back at the hospital.

I can feel Annika sweat. I've held her hands a lot lately and they've never felt like this, so warm and sticky. Marty says, "The bases are drunk." His partner Joe Nuxhall says, "But we're just an out away from happy hour."

I'm thinking if I keep holding on to Annika's hand, maybe Danny will do the same. *Hold on.* I know it's stupid, but I still think it might help.

It doesn't. When the ball leaves the park, Marty says, "It looks like it's going to be a long flight back to Cincinnati." You can practically hear Joe shaking his head as he says, "Defeat snapped from the jaws of victory." I pull my hand away from Annika's and run it through my hair. At least, I try to, but my fingers get stuck. My hand is covered with blood.

And I'm not the only one. Annika's not sweating; she's *bleeding.*

She sure is taking this loss hard. Her eyes are open and she's not looking through me or to the side. She's looking right at me and if her eyes could speak they'd say she's scared to death.

There's a hole in her palm and the blood is still flowing, flowing down the side of Snoopy's doghouse. I couldn't have been holding on *that* tight. I don't even have any nails. Then I see that her other hand is holding a pool of blood at Peppermint Patty's feet. I'm almost relieved. At least, now I know *I* didn't do it.

For a second I think we're just playing, acting out a scene from *Buffy the Vampire Slayer* on a rainy summer day in the basement. I think I'm just looking at two handfuls of corn syrup and red dye. I'm wondering if maybe it tastes like Kool-Aid. That's when she snaps her head to the side, her jaw clenched, all the muscles in her neck straining through her skin.

I call for Mom, but she's already here. She says, "It smells like roses."

Maggie is right behind her. When Mom sees Annika's hands, she's calm, like she's seen it a hundred times before. "Monroe, have you been playing with the corn syrup?"

I wish I had. Maggie, though, has no doubts. She drops to her knees and starts praying.

BLOOD IS DRAWN. Pictures are taken. Tests are conducted.

It's *not* bed sores. It's *not* lupus. It's *not* Kaposi's sarcoma. It's *not* an allergy. It's definitely *not* self-inflicted.

At least, we've got that straight.

With those possibilities out of the way, now, naturally, the leading diagnostic candidate is *stigmata*. Nothing special, just a manifestation of the wounds Jesus Christ endured when He was crucified. Basically, the logic goes like this: Annika's palms bleed, therefore God has chosen Annika to take on the suffering of Jesus Christ.

Seriously, that's what people say.

The Lord imprints these sacred wounds on souls he has chosen to partake in the ongoing saga of the Passion and Crucifixion of Christ. In doing so, these anointed few are here to aid in the redemption and salvation of the world, to serve as a living reminder of the suffering Jesus endured for us all.

Even Father Ferger says, "I know, it sounds like something out of *The Hobbit.*"

Well, that's the Bible for you, full of fairy tales. But I don't say that. In two thousand years, people will probably be poring over some long-lost videotape of *Star Wars* in the same way, piecing together the code of the Jedi into a cloak of religious dogma. Actually, there are people who already do that. I saw it on CNN. But I don't say that, either.

When the Romans tacked Jesus up on the cross, they put nails through His hands and His feet. Actually, Ferger says the nails went through His *wrists,* otherwise the weight of His body would have ripped those nails right through His hands. "But that didn't stop artists from painting the crucifixion that way for centuries." He says when people get stigmata, they practically never get the wounds on their wrists. He's always found that quite curious. "Either way," he says, "it must hurt like you wish there was no tomorrow."

Father Ferger says a lot of religions believe in Jesus, but only Catholics bleed like him. "Even Pentecostals don't bleed and for God's sake, *they speak in tongues.*"

Considering how crazy it's been around here, it's actually been kind of reassuring having Ferger around. It's not like he's always trying to jam God down your throat. He says stigmata is pretty rare. "More often than not, they're just crazy people looking for attention," he says. And as if not to be *too* judgmental, he adds, "God bless them."

I'VE HAD TO tell the story about the baseball game and how Annika started to bleed so many times, I'm happy when it happens again; because when it does, I'm not there. Mom was watching *Oprah* with Annika at her side. Oprah was doing a story on women who get beat up by their husbands, but haven't left them yet. Apparently, all these victims of domestic abuse need is a little encouragement from an audience of strangers to change their lives. When a woman showed Oprah the cigarette burns her husband had tattooed up and down her arms, Annika's hands promptly bled.

At least now they can't pin the whole thing on me. Not that anyone actually came out and said it was *my* fault, but if they were inclined to make such accusations, now they can't.

Cheryl Hanover sniffs out the stigmata story and promptly comes to our door bearing a pecan coffee cake, Mom's favorite. Just looking at Cheryl Hanover, you'd never think she possessed such well-honed investigative skills, but she's tricky that way—all decked out in dumb blonde's clothing. It's a very convincing disguise. I've always thought she was a complete idiot.

Mom is finishing up the tour when I get home from cutting grass. I'm used to seeing Cheryl Hanover in our kitchen, just not in the flesh. It's bizarre. But here she is, just feet away, smelling of freshly sprayed aerosol mint.

She says she was *hoping* I would be here, which is all it takes for me to transform from a skeptical cynic to her biggest fan. I'm just that easy. When Cheryl Hanover looks at you, you feel like you're the only person in the world. At least I do. So when she asks me to tell her what happened, I say "sure" before it even occurs to me that I could say no. It's like Cheryl—that's what she tells me to call her—knows me, *really knows me*. It's not sexual. It's *warm*. Like she *understands*. Like she actually *cares*.

When I tell her what happened, I don't say anything about stigmata or God or Jesus. I only tell her about the blood. She sits there, nodding like it's the most natural thing in the world. *So what did the blood feel like in your hands? What did you think was happening? Do you think your sister was in pain?*

She's not a conniving phony like I always thought she would be. She doesn't treat us like freaks—more like people stuck in the middle of something they don't quite understand. Like we could be anyone. It makes me want to tell her *everything*. At least everything I know, which admittedly isn't much.

I'm so glad Ben's not here—he's out on the road playing golf tournaments all summer. I guarantee, if he were around, he'd just screw everything up.

Mom invites Cheryl and her camera crew to stay for dinner. Cheryl says they'd love to, but she really has to get back to the studio. It seems like she really means it too. Like it's not just an *excuse*. After all, she's not merely an anchor reading off a teleprompter; she *reports* the news too.

When the segment on Annika airs the next day, I feel like the biggest moron in the world. It's a feeling I'm familiar with, but never like this. My voice sounds so stupid, I never want to say another word to anyone ever again. Every zit on my face looks like it could be easily picked up on a NASA satellite. Every pause is a testament to just how *uuuhhh* . . . dumb I am.

The story, though, it's not so bad. Ferger says the bleeding could have been from a lot of things. It's a bit too early to tell. Mom comes off as calm and caring. She doesn't even sound insane when she demonstrates how she ties helium balloons to Annika's toes and blasts Neil Diamond in her ears. It seems like the most normal thing in the world when she pushes Annika around the neighborhood in her wheelchair. It's what anyone would do. Isn't it?

Annika looks beautiful in her close-up; she's not even drooling.

Dad is in Denver, but he makes it home in time for the eleven o'clock reairing. Mom is bursting to tell him all about it and when she does, he says, "That's great, Jeannie." Then he heads straight for his room, adding, "I've got a lot of work to do."

Dad's not a big fan of the local news. About five years ago he represented a timber company that was trying to get its mitts on an old-growth stand in southern Ohio. Supposedly, a good clear-cut is what the forest needed to keep its healthy shine. Or so he had argued. While exiting the courthouse, Smokey the Bear tried to plant a pie in the CEO's face, but he missed and nailed Dad instead. The local news thought that was pretty funny and so did I. For two weeks Channel 10 aired that clip in its opening montage. But then Dad threatened to sue them, so they stopped.

IF CHERYL HANOVER is a snowflake, CNN is a snowball. They pick up the story and when they're through chewing it up and spitting it out, Annika doesn't seem so normal anymore. And neither do we.

From there, the tale grows, popping up in papers and bouncing around the Internet. But what really brings in the crowds are the local news anchors across the country who end their telecasts with a glimpse of the little miracle girl in Columbus, Ohio:

See how she makes rose petals fall from the sky?

Marvel as Jesus appears on her hospital wall!

Feel the presence of Jesus as blood flows from her hands!

For most people, it's a joke waiting for a punch line. For others, it's an invitation. The phone never stops ringing. There's always someone at the door. Mom can't even walk Annika around the block anymore without people falling down on their knees to pray.

When people come to our home to see Annika, Mom welcomes each and every one of them like she's been waiting for them all day.

The first ones show up minutes after Cheryl Hanover's story airs. *Jeopardy!* hasn't even started yet. It's a mother and her son. The boy couldn't be more than eight years old. His name is Allen. Mom asks them to come inside. "Allen, would you like some cookies? I just made a batch." She smiles and adds, "They're *chocolate chip*." The magic words. Allen smiles and says, "Yes, please."

Allen's mother says they both have AIDS. Allen, though, doesn't say much at all. He looks cowed, like he's been standing in a line for his entire life, and whenever he gets to the front they tell him, *Sorry, there's nothing we can do,* and he has to go to the back all over again.

Mom tells Allen's mom she wishes there was something *she* could do to help and the woman says she's already doing it, just letting them come inside. She says most people treat them like lepers, like they're *contagious.* They just want to see Annika. Allen's mom says she thinks it might bring them closer to God. "And we could really use some God right about now."

They sit with Annika for about ten minutes. I don't know if it helps or not, but Allen leaves with a smile on his face, which is at least an improvement from when he showed up.

And they keep coming. Dad says Mom's not helping matters by being so accommodating, but she ignores him. Mom calls the people who come here pilgrims. Dad calls them losers, but he says he doesn't really care as long as they're not here when he gets home.

I would be inclined to turn them away too, but once they tell you their sad stories, it's impossible. They're convinced that if only they could see Annika, their problems would go away. Maybe then they could find some peace. It's not like they're really asking for all that much.

Sure, they're *deluded.* No matter how you dice it, they think Annika is a *messenger from God.* They think that she might just *save the world.* They say it's a *blessing.* A *gift.* Not only is Annika essentially dead to the world, but she bleeds from her palms and they say it's a *gift from God.* I'll never understand that.

No one seems to care how she *feels.* No one seems to wonder about what *she's thinking.* But then again, as far as we know, there's not a thought in her head. Maybe that's what they like about her. Annika is a blank slate and they can write whatever they want on it.

It's hard to hold it against them. If they've come this far they've probably been through more than I'll ever know. That's what Mom tells me when I make fun of them. She loves it when the people come. It would be easy to say that Mom is so accommodating because when Annika bleeds, it makes her special. It makes her more than just a girl vegetating in a bed. It would be easy to say that, but it doesn't necessarily explain anything at all.

At first they come because they want to get closer to God, but then they start to believe Annika can heal them, which, if you stop to think about it for even just a second, is pretty funny. If Annika had the power to heal, wouldn't she heal herself first? Wouldn't she just get out of bed and go into the kitchen and make everyone pancakes?

Chapter 14

THEY SHOW UP AT NIGHT. Like the dew on the grass, you know they're there.

Tonight, I'm waiting for them. It's generally like this: They'll slowly approach, their dome lights on. They'll circle the block, but they'll come back and stop. They'll sit in their cars and stare at the house. Sometimes they'll drive away. Sometimes they'll get out and walk up to the door. Sometimes they'll knock. But, usually, this late, they'll come to their senses, get back in their car, and go away.

It's raining in San Francisco. Annika and I are listening to the radio as the Reds battle the Giants. It's midnight here and they're only in the second inning because of a rain delay. The room is dark, but the moon is full. I'm barely paying attention to the game. I'm just looking out the window at our perfect lawn. At our perfect street, thinking nothing is really perfect at all.

I see one coming. The telltale dome light flicks on and off like a firefly and lands across the street. And it really is a bug—a Volkswagen with Canadian plates. I can feel eyes studying our windows, wondering which one is Annika's.

Usually they stay in the car longer, but not this one. It's a woman. They almost always are. She gets out of the car and starts rummaging around the backseat until she finds what she's looking for. An offering? They almost always come with an offering. If so, it's a big one.

But instead of heading up the walk and leaving the gift on the steps—like they sometimes do—she goes straight for the oak tree in the front yard and lays down a sleeping bag. I guess she plans to spend the night. She won't be the first.

I'm by the front door, fingering a switch that'll turn the sprinklers on. And I'm not afraid to use it. I've done it before. It's the last thing they expect. They have no choice but to think that getting soaked is an act of God. That it was meant to be.

But it just doesn't feel right. Not tonight. Just to make sure, I confer with my companion. "Annika, you think I should give her the hose?"

Not a blink. Not a drop of drool. She appears to be entranced by the lilting drawl of Joe Nuxhall—longtime Reds announcer, but perhaps best noted at age fifteen as the youngest pitcher ever to play in a major league game. Clearly, Annika's neutrality is an endorsement to investigate our visitor.

Dutifully, I go out to meet her. "Separated from your troop?" I ask.

Her voice is slow and sweet, her face shrouded by shadows. She says her name is Katie. She's driven all the way from Montreal and she doesn't want to bother anyone. "I would have been here at a more reasonable hour, but I fell asleep at a rest area in Pennsylvania. They have really nice rest stops in Pennsylvania. Did you know that?" She *really, really* hopes she didn't wake me up, but she didn't know where else to go. "I forgot how expensive gas can be."

She says she's surprised she's actually here. "You ever wake up and forget where you are? Like after a nap or something?" She leans into the moonlight, revealing curly strawberry blonde hair, full lips, and high cheekbones. I'm struck dumb. Is that what they mean when they say a girl is a knockout? Her beauty punches you in the head and you don't know what to say?

She says, "I have leukemia." I don't know what to say to that either, so I ask her to come inside.

She wants to touch Annika's hand and say a prayer. That's all. "It won't take long," she says. "It'll be like I wasn't even here."

I've never brought a pilgrim inside before. I'm surprised to hear myself saying, "Okay."

We go into Annika's room and I turn on the light next to her bed. "Don't worry," I say, "it's not like we're going to wake her up."

Katie ignores me and says what everyone says: "She's so beautiful, she must be an angel."

It would have been impossible not to reply, "People must say that about you too."

She blushes and changes the topic. "I can't believe I'm here. I saw the story in the paper and I just started driving. I've been praying for a miracle for so long, but it never came. So I started to think that maybe miracles don't just come to you. You have to make them happen. You know?"

I don't really know, but I nod along like I do.

"What's she like?"

"You ever know someone who you could sit in a room with and not say a word, but it feels like you're talking to them? That's how it is with Annika and me. At least, it used to be. Maybe sometimes it still is. I guess since I don't know anyone else like that, it kind of makes her my best friend."

She's looking at Annika, lost. Like she didn't hear a word I just said. "I guess that sounds pretty lame," I say.

"No, no. Not at all," she says, disentangling herself from Annika's infinite gaze. "I was just thinking how me and my sister can hardly stand to be in the same room. . . . I wish that wasn't the way it is. But it is."

"Does she know you're sick?"

"I wouldn't give her the pleasure," she says. It's not a memory she wants to entertain, so she changes the subject. "What's it like living in the middle of a miracle?"

I tell her I never really thought of it that way.

She wonders what way I do think about it. "The rose storm, the Jesus picture, the stigmata. It must mean *something.*"

There are probably a hundred explanations for it, any of which would be just as convincing as the gargantuan leap over the Grand Canyon of logic that concludes Annika has taken on the suffering of Jesus Christ. But I don't say that. I just say, "I don't know." Sometimes it's better to let people believe what they need to believe. Besides, she came such a long way.

Such a long way, it makes me want to give her the full tour. That, and the fact that she's the most beautiful girl who's ever spoken to me. "You wanna see where the accident happened?" Shameless, perhaps, but Katie makes you want to do things for her and she doesn't even have to ask.

It's almost one a.m. and the neighborhood is quiet. The pool is so dark, it could be a pond. You can see the stars through the trees and hear the crickets chirping. We could be in the middle of nowhere. On nights like this, Annika used to say, "All it takes is a little imagination and it doesn't matter where you are."

I tell her no one really knows what happened; it's not like there were any witnesses. The doctors, however, say the crack in the back of her skull suggests she hit her head on the diving board. That sounds about right; Annika had said she wanted to get a double back-flip down by Memorial Day.

The diving board is gone now, but the holes where it was bolted down are still there. You have to be careful, you could stub your toe.

"They say drowning is the best way to go." I'm an idiot to be telling that to a girl, especially a pretty one. But still, I continue. "When your lungs fill up with water, you're at one with the world. It's supposed to be the most amazing high . . . but then you die." Of course, Annika wouldn't have been able to enjoy that last burst of euphoria. She was knocked out before she ever hit the water. That's what the doctors say.

"I always thought jumping off a building wouldn't be so bad. It'd almost be like flying," she says. Yeah, if by *almost*, you mean *the opposite of.* But I don't say that.

Katie says she's never really been high. She tried pot a few times, but it didn't work.

"These things sometimes take practice. We could smoke some now, you know, if you want."

"No, I better not." She says it automatic, like she's been saying those four words her entire life. Then she says, "Oh, what the hay?

Why not? Ever since they told me I have six months to live, I decided I wasn't going to say no to anything." She looks at me coyly, "Well, *almost* anything."

I ask how long ago that was. She says it's been five months.

One month to go.

But she doesn't say that. And neither do I.

If I thought I had only a month to live, what would I do? The obvious inclination is to cram as much life into those last thirty days as possible. To do everything I'd always wanted to do but never got around to. But I don't even know what those things are.

Sure, I always wanted to play guitar, but with only a month to go, I wouldn't get much past the opening to "Smells Like Teen Spirit."

Sure, it'd be great to bike to California, but I'd be dead by the time I got to Iowa. Even if it is where they filmed *Field of Dreams,* I don't think I want to die there.

Sure, it'd be great to get Emily back, but she'd probably figure out another way to break my heart before they bury me.

Did I not mention that Emily dumped me? I try not to think about it. She did it the old-fashioned way—in a letter that began warmly *Dear Monroe,* but it got chilly fast. Basically, she met someone in Guatemala. Oh, I can rest assured that she felt *terrible* about falling in love. She felt *terrible* about writing it in a letter. But mainly, she felt I deserved to know, apparently so I could feel *terrible* too. She was just being honest, that's what she said, like she deserved a medal or something for telling me the truth. I never wrote back. What was I supposed to say to that? *I'm happy for you? Good luck? Screw you?* So, I didn't say anything at all.

Katie and I head into the pool house and sit on the futon. I pull out my pipe from behind a panel in the wall and load up the bowl. It's the first time I've smoked since all this happened.

It's a hot summer night and I'm sitting in the pool house with a dying girl I've just met. She takes a hit and kisses me, blowing the smoke down my throat. I know this is all about to sound like a letter to *Penthouse Forum,* but every word is true.

She asks me, "You wanna take a swim?" I say, "Sure, why not?"

Then, she steps out of her clothes like she's walking out of one of those paintings of girls washing themselves by a river in France.

Not a hint of embarrassment.

Not a blush of self-awareness.

Not a man in sight . . . well, just me, and in case you haven't noticed, I'm in no real hurry to be a *man*. Whatever that means.

We float naked in the pool.

She says, "I can't believe this is me," and laughs. I could say the same thing, but I don't.

She wonders, "So, Monroe, you do this with all the girls who come to visit Annika?"

It would have been impossible not to say, "You're the first pretty one to show up."

She says I'm sweet, as if I've just told a lie. Then she kisses me.

I did mention that I've never slept with a girl before? Not Emily. Not a hooker. Not even Suzy James—and *everyone* around here sleeps with her. Which is all to say, I'm not exactly experienced with this kind of thing. Yet here I am with a naked girl in my arms and I know practically nothing about her, other than that she says she's dying and she believes touching my sister will somehow change that. Oh yeah, and she's Canadian.

I think I like Canadians.

I've always thought this pool would be a magnet for chicks, but Emily would never swim in it. She says pools are *bourgeois*. She says they're "too sterile." She'd rather swim in the Scioto River, which, incidentally, doubles as a sewer when it rains. I suppose on some level, Emily would consider that quite organic.

I know. I shouldn't be thinking about Emily. Or the Scioto River. Or sewage.

I kiss Katie and our tongues slowly dance as the water laps against the sides of the pool.

"How old are you, anyway?" she asks.

I say I'm eighteen and she says I don't kiss like an eighteen-year-old. "Most teenage boys kiss like they're starving."

Emily was always a really good kisser too. I guess I should thank her for all the practice. She's the only girl I've ever kissed. Until now. I know, I should quit thinking about her. I can be sure she's not thinking about me while she's making out with some guy under a Guatemalan moon.

Katie leads me over to the steps as she holds my hips. I'm feeling her breasts and she's biting my shoulder and before I know it, I'm inside her.

"Don't worry about a thing," she says, "I can't get pregnant."

Considering she's not due to make it past the first trimester, it's not exactly forefront on my mind. The only thing I'm worried about right now is waking up my parents.

She tells me to fuck her. Seriously, that's what she says: "Fuck me, Monroe. Fuck me." She says it over and again and each time she says it, Emily seems farther and farther away. It's like an exorcism. "Fuck me" is the last thing Emily would *ever* say. Even as a joke. She wouldn't even say it if you dropped a cement block on her fucking foot. "Fuck me" is permission to be in the moment, to forget about the rest of the world. But all I can think about is Emily and how I wish I were with her, making love. So, as far as an exorcism goes, I guess it's not really working.

We end up on the futon in the pool house tracing the shadows on each other's bodies. I tell her she's the most beautiful woman I've ever seen. I tell her she looks so healthy, it's hard to believe she's sick. I don't know what else to say. Having sex with her is simultaneously both the greatest and most depressing thing I've ever done.

And she says she's not through with me yet, her mouth sliding down my neck to my chest to my belly button to . . .

When she's done or I'm done or however you want to put it, she looks up and smiles. Her face is covered with blood.

"You're bleeding," I tell her. She touches her nose and looks at the blood on her hand.

"Damnit," she says. "It happens *all the time*. Guess I don't look so healthy now, huh?"

I tell her it's okay. She should lie down. I get a washcloth from the bathroom and clean up the blood. She says bloody noses are what got her to go to the doctor in the first place.

We're just lying there, not really saying anything. It feels like we've been talking all night, but the truth is—we've hardly spoken. Maybe that's what sex is all about. I barely know a thing about Katie, but in a way I feel like I know everything.

She wants to smoke some more. "It *definitely* worked." She hasn't felt this great all year.

I tell her, "You never know, maybe it has nothing to do with the sex or drugs and everything to do with meeting Annika."

"Oh yeah," she says, sort of laughing at herself, "if you believe in that kind of thing."

I ask her, "How are you supposed to deal with hearing you have only six months to live?"

"Well, the only way I know to deal is by not dealing at all. Besides, what do doctors know? A doctor can only tell you how you are. It's only a guess how you're going to be. It's like you can spend your whole life living up or down to other people's expectations, but in the end, the only thing that matters is living up to your own."

The night sky sighs ribbons of dark blue. Light sifts through the trees into the windows, falling on us, revealing secrets.

Katie's inner thighs are covered with bruises. She sees me staring and says she bruises kind of easily. I shouldn't worry about it. "Fucking white cells," she explains. I nod like that makes sense. Like that very diagnosis was on the tip of my tongue. *White cells.*

She changes the subject. "I read about you, you know. I thought what you did was really heroic."

I lean on the old "It's what anyone would do."

"Yeah," she says. "Anyone might have done the same thing, but you're not just anyone." In case I don't believe her, she kisses me again.

It's just like something Emily would do, kissing me like that.

Katie says she probably should get on the road, she's supposed to work tonight. She takes emergency calls for the police. "At this point,

I could just live off the dole and wait, but working makes the days go faster."

I tell her I'd want the days to go slow if I knew I didn't have too many left. She says she tried that at first. She tried doing all the things she always wanted to do, but never did.

She went canoeing.

She went to the top of the Empire State Building.

She went to Paris.

"But none of those things made me feel like I was really living. They just made me feel like a tourist. When I'm working, though, it's like the days mean *something*. I'm not just waiting around to die. I'm useful, you know?"

I don't really know what it feels like to be useful, but I nod along like I do.

Once she's dressed, I walk her out to her car.

"Will I ever see you again?" I say, more to myself than to her.

"I hope so," she says, more to herself than to me.

She pulls away into the fading darkness, her back lights leaving a sweeping red trail. It disappears as she turns the corner that leads to the highway. And like that, Katie is gone. Like a joke you don't want to forget, so you keep repeating it in your head over and over.

Chapter 15

FOR EVERY PERSON who shows up at our door, fifty send letters. Most of them are from people who are sick or from the people who love them, people who are running out of options. They all think my sister can heal them.

Mom reads each and every one of them to Annika. It takes about two hours a day. Sometimes they write back and say that they're better. Whatever Annika did worked. They're so thankful. Sometimes they write back and ask if maybe she could please try again. Occasionally, I leaf through them and read them too, but not out loud. Mom already does that and I can't imagine they're any more entertaining to Annika in reruns.

If you think people have it bad on the local news, it's just the tip of the iceberg. The bad things that happen to people on the news, those are just the ones that are "interesting." But most of the screwed-up things that happen to people *aren't* interesting. They're just *sad*. They're too typical to wade through a bunch of car commercials to watch. Most people's suffering isn't suitable for TV.

They're the ones who write to Annika. Mothers with paralyzed sons from motorcycle accidents. Mothers with daughters disfigured from drunk drivers. There are the wives with husbands taking the slow dive of Alzheimer's; all they want is just a flicker of memory so that maybe they can say "I love you" one more time and have it actually mean something more profound than "Do you want another cookie?" There are the mothers with children who have burns all over their bodies and the sisters with retarded brothers and the wives with husbands who beat them and they think maybe, *If I could shake loose the devil alcohol's grip, maybe he won't beat me anymore.* Then there are the people with cancer who have tried everything and have nowhere else to go—they have no hair on their heads and no skin on their bones; and they would come to visit, but they can barely even lift the pencils in their hands. And there are the people who can't walk and can't hear and can't speak and can't see. They all have a piece missing and they all just want their lives back. They don't want anything special, just what they had before.

And all these broken people have one other thing in common: they all think a little girl in a coma can make them whole again.

If the stories aren't bad enough on their own, they almost always come with a picture—in a hospital, in a wheelchair, with a respirator, with tubes going in and out, with walkers and canes and with smiles that look like they took every bit of effort they could possibly muster. Smiles that look more like grimaces of pain. Sometimes they come with "before" pictures too. Those are the ones that just kill me. Those are the ones that make you realize it can happen to anyone at any time. One second you're living life, probably not appreciating how good you have it. The next, you've fallen down and you can't get up. It doesn't matter how much you're loved. Or how much money you have. Or what you believe.

It's just who you are. *Broken.*

Maybe Annika hears the stories, but I'm glad at least that she can't see the pictures. There's something about them that's just *too* real. It's almost like pornography; not the airbrushed kind you see in *Playboy,* but like the pictures on the Internet where you can see the rashes on their thighs and the sadness in their eyes—that look that says they can't believe they're really doing this. It's not the way they had it planned at all. It just happened.

Mom puts them all up on the wall where an antique Japanese silk used to hang. They're always there looking at you, desperately hoping they won't be forgotten. If that's so, they've come to the right place.

Mom was reading Annika a letter from a girl in Midland, Texas, whose stepfather was molesting her. The girl didn't know what to do. She just prayed that he'd stop. "I'd kill myself, but I know it's a sin," she wrote. "I wish I could be like you, in a coma. When he touches me, that's what I wish for. Sometimes I get there in my head, so far away that it doesn't even hurt anymore. But it never lasts for very long and then he's back on top of me."

Annika's hands bled when Mom read that. I'm surprised it wasn't her *ears*. Mom called the police and told them what was going on and the girl's stepfather was arrested. Prayers really can come true. Maybe you just can't keep them between you and God. Maybe someone else needs to know.

PEOPLE KEEP COMING to the house. There are so many of them, at all hours, all the time, that the neighbors started to complain. Ordinarily, it's a quiet street, so it's hard to blame them for wanting to keep it that way. Nonetheless, it's easy to hate their spokesman—Mr. Oester, a notorious baseball thief. He impounded about a dozen of my baseballs before Dad finally went over there and scared the shit out of him.

On the news, in Mr. Oester's big moment in the sun, he says, "I guess people have so much faith that they can't help themselves. But it's not like Annika Anderson is going to cure cancer or heal a broken foot. Now that I'd like to see—healing a broken foot." Mr. Oester is such a jerk, even Annika says so. In her words: "What kind of person gives out *apples* at Halloween? They know you have to throw them away."

Flush with the high of media exposure, Mr. Oester next took the show to a city council meeting. Now, thanks to him, no one's allowed to park on the street anymore, unless you have a special placard in your window saying it's okay, you know someone who lives here. Gates and a guard can't be too far way.

Nonetheless, mere zoning restrictions will not be enough to thwart God's work. That's what Father Ferger told Mom when the vote was announced. Dad says that maybe we should give Father Ferger 15 percent for managing Annika's budding career as a religious icon. Mom says 15 percent of nothing is still nothing. Dad just shakes his head, refusing to argue. He's becoming less and less like himself every day.

To get around the draconian parking restrictions, Father Ferger has organized a shuttle from the church. Now three days a week from one to three p.m. people can come to visit Annika. In case you just show up, there's a sign by the front door, giving a number to call to make an appointment.

MY BOSS, PAUL, has to play golf with his dad this afternoon, so I'm taking the day off, lounging by the pool. Dad had the pool built three summers ago. Now Mom's talking about filling it up with cement. I figure I better enjoy it while I can.

While the pool is not officially part of the tour, the pilgrims occasionally wander from the flock and stick their heads over the fence. After all, this is where our story begins.

And sometimes if I'm in the mood, I might just tell the tale. I tell them the thing people don't really know about Annika is that she was training for the Olympics as a diver. I tell them she practiced for *six hours a day*. It wasn't the first time I had to drag her out of the pool, but usually it was just because she was exhausted, not drowning. I tell them I saw the face of Jesus reflected in the pool before I dove in. I tell them the ambulance driver was a dead ringer for Saint Francis, the original stigmatist. I tell them the puddle Annika left on the ground took three days to dry and looked like Mary in Prayer. Sometimes I say I could feel angels on my body as I scooped her out of the water.

They *love* it when I say stuff like that. It makes them feel good. Like the trip was worth their while. I know I'm only making it worse, but in the moment I can't resist. Their eyes are filled with so much *hope*. I can't help but give them a little bit of what they need. Is there really any harm in that?

I'm reading *The Sporting News,* drinking lemonade, enjoying the day when an old lady sticks her head over the fence and says, "You must be Monroe." She's startles me, so I confess. "Yeah, I'm Monroe." She says, "Bless you" and asks if I know the Virgin Mary had stigmata too.

I tell her I had no idea.

She takes my professed ignorance as an invitation to open the gate and come inside.

She's not surprised I don't know about Mary. She has a secret, a real insider scoop. After all, it's difficult to bear the wounds of Christ before Christ ever did. She says that Mary's heart was *figuratively* pierced by the Lord. She's a *victim soul.* I'd always thought Mary's *vagina* had been figuratively pierced by God, not her heart. But I don't say that. I just tell her I've heard Mary's statues and pictures sometimes bleed oil. She knows *all about it.* She's *seen* it happen, but with *real blood.* "It was in Brazil," she says. "You should go if you get a chance. *Everyone* should."

I say maybe I will.

She rewards me for my good humor with her trust. She has a snow-globe featuring the Virgin Mother rising up from the town of Bethlehem and she wants to make sure it gets to Annika. Mary's looking to the heavens, her hands clasped in prayer. The old lady asks if I'll put it by Annika's bed.

"Of course," I promise, shaking it up, mesmerized as the snowstorm swirls around Mary's head. It's like Mary's got the worse case of dandruff ever. But I don't say that. Instead, I tell her Annika would *absolutely love it* and I'm not even lying. I guarantee you, it's the first gift someone has brought she would truly appreciate.

The old lady is so happy to hear that, she can't stop thanking me. She says tonight I'll be in her prayers and then she leaves.

Alone, I dive into the pool and hold my breath on the bottom, trying to erase every thought in my head, trying to be anywhere but here. It feels like we've had house guests all summer and they're never going to leave. I just want to be alone, to take a break and forget this is really happening. But I can't stop thinking about all of these Mary statues bleeding. It sounds like bullshit, but maybe there is something to it all. I wouldn't have believed someone's hands could spontaneously bleed either, but I've seen the blood flow with my own eyes and I've felt it hot in my own hands.

Underwater, watching the waves of light reflect off the sides of the pool, I wonder: *How is anyone supposed to know what's real and what's not?*

Chapter 16

I SHOULD HAVE LET IT GO. I shouldn't have said anything. I should have let her think what she wants.

After all, it's not like Annika lies there like a mannequin. Her eyes are sometimes open. They're sometimes closed. They blink. She drools and she moves her head from side to side. She sucks her thumb. She kicks her feet. She curls up. She spreads out. She looks straight at you. She looks right through you. She closes her eyes. She opens them—it doesn't matter what you do. You can flick your finger a centimeter from her eye and she won't flinch, which I only know because I saw Ben do it.

Annika is listening. Mom's been saying that all along. Now she says she talks back. Maggie has the night off and Dad's out of town and Grandpa is asleep, so she tells *me.*

"Come look, *Annika talks back.* You just have to look for the signs," she says. By *the signs,* she means specifically, a systematic series of blinks. As in, *blink once for yes, blink twice for no*—I'm sure you get the picture. It's everyone's favorite way to communicate with the comatose and hopelessly paralyzed. I'm surprised she didn't break the code sooner.

We're in Annika's room when Mom says, "Honey, are you in any pain? Blink once for yes, twice for no."

Annika blinks once, her eyes blank as slate.

"Oh, honey, I know. *I know.* It's not going to always be like this. There's a reason for your suffering. There's *a plan.* I know you're strong enough to endure. Do you want me to massage your feet? Once for yes, twice for no."

It seems like *forever.* Annika holds Mom's gaze so long, you might think she's a fish. That she has no eyelids. That she couldn't blink even if she wanted to.

"She's such a little angel. She's afraid to ask for anything. All she wants to do is *give.* It's okay, honey. It's okay to ask for help."

Annika's eyelids drop. The curtain goes down. Looks like the show might be over; but right when I'm about to head back to my room, they open back up. *One long blink.*

"Oh, honey, you know I want nothing more than to make you feel better." As instructed, Mom starts massaging her feet, and almost immediately Annika's eyes start to flutter.

"See, she's *clapping.* That means she likes it." As Mom works her little feet through her hands, Annika's eyelids bounce up and down, flickering like an old movie reel, colored in tones of blue. Mom stops for a second, leaving Annika's eyes wide open. Then she starts the massage again and the eyes resume their applause.

"It's kind of like when you rub a dog's belly and their leg starts spazzing out."

"Don't say that, Monroe. Your sister is *nothing* like a dog."

Spell dog backward and it's a lot closer to God than Annika. But I don't say that. I also don't say that a dog can stay at home alone, knows how to ask to go out, and can catch a ball—all things that are well beyond my sister's current abilities, but I don't say that either. I never get credit for the things I don't say. I just say, "I'm sorry. You're right."

"Don't tell me. Tell *her.*"

"I'm sorry, Annika, I didn't mean to compare you to a dog."

She blinks three times. Mom interprets that to mean, "She says it's okay. Just don't do it again."

Then Mom asks, "Annika, are you looking forward to Father Ferger coming over to share Communion with you? One blink for yes, two for no."

This question takes a while to compute as Annika stares a hole in the picture of Mary on the wall. Father Ferger comes over practically every day to administer Communion. A piece of Jesus's flesh dissolves in her mouth each morning, the only food she ever eats—all the rest is fed to her through the tube that goes straight to her stomach.

Mom assures me that sometimes it takes Annika awhile to formulate an answer. Then, finally, two unqualified blinks.

"Oh, honey, you love it when Father Ferger comes to see you, don't you?"

That gets a blink. "*See?* She *knows* what we're saying."

If we still had a dog, this is where I'd say. "Okay, Blue, who's the greatest home run hitter of all time?" and he'd say, "Roof" and I'd say, "Good boy, Ruth is right. Here's a biscuit." But I don't say that either. Clearly dogs are off-limits in this discussion.

Still, I can't help myself. I should have just let Mom be happy, to let her see what she wants to see, but I can't let it go. "Mind if I ask her a couple questions, Mom?"

"Ask her anything you want."

"Annika, do you think the Reds will win their division this year? One blink for yes, two for no."

That gets one blink from Annika and a raised eyebrow from Mom. I say maybe we should go to Vegas and lay down some cash. The Reds are currently twelve games out of first place. "We'd get great odds." But Mom's all snake eyes.

I should have just stopped there, but I say, "Annika, what would you rather do, lie in bed all day or go to church? Two for church, one for bed."

That gets one blink. Just as I hoped.

"Monroe, if you're not going to take this seriously."

"Just one more, Mom, okay? I'll be totally serious."

"*Fine.*"

"Annika, who do you like more—me or Mom? One for Mom, two for me."

Mom is annoyed, but clearly she wants to know the answer. After a long stare, Annika blinks once and, despite herself, a glimpse of a smile sneaks across Mom's face; but just when you think Annika's eyelids are being held up with crazy glue, she blinks again. Mom's smile disappears as fast as you can shake up an Etch A Sketch.

"It's okay, Mom, that doesn't mean she doesn't love you *too*. She just loves me *more*."

"You're not funny, Monroe," Mom says as she turns around to leave, but before she can get away, I stop her, all sincere.

"Don't go. I'm sorry. I was just having fun. How about this. Let's see how she is at current events. Okay?"

Mom nods, willing to indulge me once more.

"Annika, how many priests were accused this year of pedophilia?"

"Monroe, Annika does not need to hear that kind of talk. And neither do I." And with that admonition, she leaves the room, disgusted. It's too bad because if she'd stayed, she could have seen just how keyed in Annika is to the news of the day. Her eyes are blinking like a butterfly—too many blinks to count, which is exactly the correct answer.

"Some people just can't take a—stop blinking, Annika, it's a new question—some people can't take a joke, can they, Annika? One for yes. Two for no."

She blinks once and I leave the room as fast as I can before she manages another one.

IN CASE YOU need any more evidence, here's why I'm a jerk: I don't just talk *to* Annika, I talk *with* her all the time too. She doesn't talk to me in blinks or in teaspoons of drool. It's not like that. I can hear her voice, you know, in my head. I can hear what she would say if only she really were here.

I tell her how Emily met some guy in Guatemala and dumped me. I tell her about how I think I loved Emily, but now I think maybe I hate her. I tell her how now it's like I can't even trust anyone and I don't want even to try to trust someone because in the end they're just going to leave you and you'll feel like an idiot. I tell her at night sometimes I dream that my teeth are falling out. I tell her sometimes I wish I could marinate in nothingness like her.

She tells me I'm idiot. Get over it. And by the way, she says, don't ever say I want to be like her, in a coma. *It's not funny.* Even though she likes Emily, she says Emily didn't deserve me anyway. Well, that's what she *would* have said, and even though I know that's what she's *supposed* to say, it still makes me feel better.

She tells me I should be happy that I'm *capable* of being in love. She says a lot of people aren't. *If you can fall in love once, you can fall in love again.*

What I want to know is this: If love's so great, why do you fall into it? You fall into a puddle. You fall into the mud. You fall into the abyss.

It is not very promising company.

She tells me not to get hung up on semantics, even though she probably doesn't know what semantics are.

If it weren't for Annika, I never would have spoken to Emily in the first place. I could hold it against her, but I really have her to thank. After all, I was seventeen and I'd never been kissed. I needed all the help I could get. We were at a basketball game at Chelsea High, getting a Coke at halftime, and Annika told me *that girl* was staring at me. "Go up and talk to her," she said. I wanted to, but I'm a chicken. I'd seen her before and I always thought she was pretty. Too pretty to approach—even though she's not that kind of pretty. Cheerleader pretty. Stuck-up pretty. Emily had them all beat and she didn't even have to try.

Annika made it look so easy. While we were walking back to the bleachers, passing Emily, Annika told her what a beautiful shirt she was wearing, and the next thing I knew, we were all sitting together, watching the game, talking with an ease I'd only thought possible in retrospect, like when I'm by myself, alone, restructuring the wreckage of another lost conversation. I know it's lame only being able to get a date through your little sister. But it's not as lame as not having any date at all.

I tell Annika about Katie. It would have been practically lying not to. She just says, "If it wasn't for me you'd never meet *anyone*."

As if I didn't already know.

Besides baseball, that's the kind of stuff I talk about with Annika. She says everything I'm too afraid to admit to myself. I ask her how I could still hold out hope for a relationship that's completely dead, but can't bring myself to believe in God.

She says she doesn't know either.

Chapter 17

TUESDAY THROUGH THURSDAY we're the main attraction in Chelsea. There's no advertising. No yelling from the rooftops. But they keep coming. Father Ferger's complimentary shuttle bus brings in a new crop of twenty pilgrims every fifteen minutes. That's 160 people three times a week. This endeavor is not endorsed by the Catholic Church. I repeat *not endorsed*. Not the bus. Not the public showing. And most definitely, not Annika. *Especially*, not Annika. As far as the Church with a capital *C* believes, she doesn't exist. That's their specialty—denial. They may look like penguins, but really they're ostriches. They just hope Annika will go away. It's a no-win situation for them. If they say it's not really happening, they alienate all the believers who swear to God it is; and if they say it really is happening and it turns out it's not, they end up looking even more primitive than they already are.

When the pilgrims get off the bus, Mom welcomes them each with a hug and leads them through the front door. They file in, careful to stay on the plastic mats that cover the Oriental rugs in the hall. The only thing Mom worries about is germs, so she had a sliding glass door put in, sealing Annika off from her admirers.

Once safely inside, the believers gather around the doorway to Annika's room, but they can't look in. Not yet. A red velvet curtain hides the view. Besides, first Father Ferger has a few words for the congregation. He says, "God is using Annika to get our attention. We live in a throwaway society where death is pervasive. It's all around us: executions, abortions, homicides, suicides. Annika is telling the world her life is useful. Her life has meaning. *All* life has meaning. God does not make mistakes."

As the pilgrims nod their collective head in agreement, Ferger hits the button of a boom box, offering up choral accompaniment that prompts the believers to fall to their knees—at least, the ones who can. Then the curtains open, revealing Annika in her bed, as peaceful as a girl can be.

No one would blame you if you called her the Bubble Girl . . . well, maybe Mom and Maggie and Father Ferger. They wouldn't like that at all. Dad, on the other hand, he probably wouldn't care; mainly because, well, he's not here.

The pilgrims smudge their faces against the glass, pointing and praying. Annika lies there, her hair cascading around her face, styled with curls and red bows. Everyone says how pretty she looks. *What a doll.* Then Father Ferger tells them the story about all the miracles that Annika has left in her wake. As if they haven't heard it all before. As if that's not why they're here in the first place. They pray and gawk for a few more minutes before Father Ferger finally shuffles them along. All they leave behind is their greasy prints on the window and the faint scent of sickness—nothing a little Lysol can't take care of. Then, they're led to the garage . . . I mean the *chapel*. There, they pray and leave their offerings until the bus arrives to take them away and bring in the next batch.

And that's the way it goes. For those six hours a week, Annika is an animal at the zoo. The difference is, an animal will at least move if you tap on the glass and sometimes, if you're lucky, the beast might even put on a show. Sure, Annika can bleed, which is the show everyone wants to see, but she can't do it on call. You can't just tell her some horrible story or show up suffering and expect the blood to flow. It doesn't work like that.

When I look at her through that window, I think of those exhibits at the natural history museum—fake saber-toothed tigers and giant ground sloths. They were around so long ago, it's hard not to wonder if they ever really existed at all, if they were just figments of some archaeologist's imagination. It's not like they ever found a giant ground sloth stuck in ice. That huge sloth is really just someone's best guess of what might have been; that saber-toothed tiger is just an echo of scattered bones from long ago.

Anyway, it doesn't matter what I think, so I don't say anything. At least it's all quick and efficient and everyone gets a glimpse of the girl who they believe somehow feels their pain. Her suffering is for them. Maybe this reinforces their faith. Maybe it makes them better people. Maybe they're just fooling themselves. But that doesn't stop me from envying them.

When people come to visit Annika, they bring gifts: religious knickknacks, I guess you could call them. Flowers, candles, and incense are popular; but mostly they bring pictures, statues, and tapestries of the Virgin Mary. They fill Annika's room, the rest of the gifts overflow into the garage/makeshift chapel. Dad says he's okay with the arrangement for now; but when it starts to snow, he's going to want to have some place to park his Mercedes.

The visitors are generous, but they steal stuff too. Nothing valuable, just proof they were here. A *souvenir*. Mom gives out postcards with a picture of Annika before the accident. On the other side there's a prayer you can say for her. Apparently that's not enough for some people. Mom saw a woman cutting off a piece of the drape that covers Annika's sliding door, but she didn't stop her. I asked her about it later and she said if she wanted it that bad, she could have it.

That's not the only thing they take. People cut our flowers. They steal our *dirt*. They go through our *garbage*. You let them get away with it once; they just keep coming back for more. I guess if I really cared, I'd stake out the situation, bust the dirt stealers in the act, but that would be demeaning to everyone involved. Like Mom says, if they want it that bad, they can have it. It's bad enough to steal dirt, but being the guy who tells someone to stop stealing dirt may be even worse.

~~~

IT'S ONLY EIGHT in the morning and it's already the hottest day of the summer. It doesn't help that the air conditioner is broken. When I come down the stairs, Maggie is on her knees. That's typical, but usually you don't see her doing it here—in the hallway. She's in front of Annika's sliding glass doors where the pilgrims gather. The doors are open and a fan is going back and forth, barely cutting through the heat. Annika lies there. Like she always does.

If you ever go to the Ohio State Fair, you have to check out the butter cow. In fact, it may just be the best reason to go at all. It's not like it's a secret; the butter cow has its own building, a bona fide shrine to butter. They say the cow is life-size, but it looks bigger than any cow I ever saw. Two thousand pounds of butter; no matter how you slice it, that's a lot of cow.

If you do Ohio proud, you too can graze in the refrigerated pasture with the butter cow. Buster Douglas. Bobby Rahal. Jack Nicklaus. They've all been honored with butter sculptures. It's something to aspire to.

Annika, behind the sliding glass doors, looks like she's about halfway there. She's the butter princess for the new millennium. It's about time for Ohio to catch up with the times. In Minnesota, the Queen of Dairy and her courts' likenesses are carved in butter. They don't do that here, but it's never too late.

The power went out last year and the butter cow almost died. Maybe you heard about it? Beyond the ongoing saga of Ohio State football and before Annika, it was the biggest story to come out of the Buckeye capital in years. With the electricity down and the temperature soaring into the nineties, the cow was in jeopardy of melting. Clearly drastic measures were required. The power was down for long enough that CNN not only picked up the story in progress, but they featured an ongoing ticker in the corner of the screen indicating just how long the cow had gone without proper refrigeration. A suicide bomber killed seven people in Tel Aviv that afternoon, a tornado took out a shopping center in Oklahoma, and a dozen whales beached themselves in California, but that ticker just kept on ticking. That's the kind of respect the butter cow gets.

But it wasn't just about the cow, it was more than that. Liberty and freedom were also at stake. A butter replica of the Liberty Bell, as well as a soaring bald-headed eagle, shares the refrigerator with the butter cow and her calves. Clearly, the metaphorical ramifications were potentially disastrous. Everyone takes their freedom and liberty for granted, but they're really just ideas that can melt away.

Breathe easy, now. Just breathe. Everything is going to be okay. The butter cow was saved and you will be too.

Above the parted velvet curtain, in the middle of the doorway is a bust of Mary. I hadn't noticed it before. There are so many statues and pictures of Mary around here, it's like being in one of those fun houses full of mirrors and all you see is yourself from a thousand different angles and every one is different. But in this case *yourself* is the mother of Jesus. It makes it easy to get confused, you know, if you're inclined to be that way.

This Mary, though, is definitely different. She's crying blood.

Each drop splats red on the plastic mat in front of Maggie, who greets each drip with another round of prayer. Maggie's on her knees so often, it's easy to imagine her in an entirely different profession.

Still, statues don't cry blood every day. I should be amazed. I should be blown away.

I should tell Mom. She's got to see this. Of course, I'm just fanning the flames, but she's going to see it anyway. Maggie is her second pair of eyes. "One of the Mary busts is crying blood," I tell her, matter-of-fact. Mom tells me to get the video camera and then she calls Father Ferger. Nothing surprises her anymore.

I videotape it all—Mary's tears, Maggie's prayers, Annika's stare. Then the camera floats to the snow globe on Annika's nightstand; it just takes me there. There's a blizzard going on in the glass dome and I didn't touch it. I swear. The flakes are swirling a halo around Mary's head. I probably shouldn't keep it to myself, but I do.

I'm still shooting when Father Ferger comes through the door. It takes him only about ten minutes to get here. He knows a good thing when he sees it or hears about it or *whatever*. He's here.

The first thing Father Ferger says when he walks in the house is how hot it is. Then he wipes his brow. "You don't know how lucky you are not to be wearing one of these," he says, pulling his collar from his neck.

Mary's still crying. *Splat . . . splat . . . splat*.

Father Ferger stares at her. He's not getting down on his knees. He's not praying. He's just staring. Not in wonder. Not in awe.

"Where'd she come from?" That's what he wants to know.

Mom says it could be from anyone. So many people send things, bring things, make things. "They're all so sweet," she says.

Father Ferger removes the bust from its perch, an action whose shear nonchalant audacity shocks Maggie, the horror on her face a flicker of my own slack-jawed disbelief when Ben removed my autographed 1990 Cincinnati Reds team ball from its protective case and began tossing it against the wall—an act of heresy if there ever was one.

Father Ferger studies the bust from all sides. He taps it. He shakes it. He tastes the tears.

He says it's beef blood and vegetable oil. He says it's the oldest trick in the book. Crying statues. "All in the name of Jesus," he says, shaking his head.

"I was just reading about a case down in Argentina," he says. "We don't see it much up here, although in divinity school we used to play tricks on the freshmen. It's pretty simple: You just take a statue, it could be Mary, it could be Napoleon—it doesn't really matter. Then you coat it with a mixture of vegetable oil and cow blood; chicken blood works too. After that, all you have to do is sit back and wait. When the room gets hot, it'll start dripping and everyone thinks they're seeing real tears. But really it's just a trick.

"And the best part about it is that it usually happens when a lot of people are in the room. Their body heat makes the oil melt and the group dynamic, I guess you could call it mass hysteria, has a way of making everyone believe they're in the middle of a mystical experience."

Maggie's off her knees now, sitting on the steps, her chin in her hand. Listening. She can't believe it. You start getting used to miracles and you get spoiled.

"It's pretty funny. At least, in school it was," he says, happy for the opportunity to reminisce. "Thank goodness this didn't happen in front of a crowd. All of God's *real* work here would have been put into question."

I don't mention the snow-globe blizzard next to Annika's bed. It's over now anyway. Mary is looking to clear skies; the snow has settled over the town of Bethlehem.

Chapter 18

WHEN THE PILGRIMS come to visit, they don't see Annika eating her meals through the tube that goes into her stomach. They don't see Maggie cleaning out her diapers. They don't smell Annika's bad breath. They don't hear the Bible stories or the Neil Diamond being piped into her head. They don't see how hard it is to give a girl a bath when she's just limp. They don't see the hours my mom combs her hair every day. They don't see all the work it takes to put on this show.

They just see a doll in the window. They just see how beautiful she is. They say, *She's so pretty, look how gorgeous her hair is.* They used to say these things before all this happened and now they say it even more.

Sometimes it seems like Mom is either brushing Annika's hair or working her rosary beads. The beads must wear down over time, but Annika's hair just gets more and more beautiful. She could be a model. She really could.

But, I guess, in a way, she already is.

THE DOORBELL CHIMES "Gloria in Excelsis Deo" and I answer the call. Aunt Sally hasn't been around much, but her extended absence hasn't really occurred to me until right now, seeing her face-to-face. She's wearing her trademark pearls and holding a stuffed teddy bear in her hands.

"Monroe, you're getting so tall," she says, kissing me on the cheek.

I can see where this is going. "Mom," I yell, "Aunt Sally's here."

Mom's coming down the stairs and she looks surprised. "Sally? Is that you?"

They're looking at each other, reticent, like there's something holding each of them back. Mom's face says, *So what brings you here?*

"Thought I'd stop by to see how our patient's doing," Aunt Sally says as she kisses Mom.

"We don't like to call her that," Mom says, pulling back. "It makes it sound so *clinical*."

"Oh, right," Aunt Sally says. Apparently, she's heard it before.

The two go into the living room to see Annika and I follow. It's odd, the frequency between them. Sally can barely look at Annika. The only way I'll figure out what's going on here is to leave. "Well, I guess I better get to work," I say.

I can hear everything from around the corner.

"Everyone misses you at the club," Aunt Sally says. "*I* miss you."

"It's funny how fast time goes by when you're really immersed in what you're doing. Isn't that right, Annika? . . . Look who's here to see you, it's your Aunt Sally. She brought you a bear. *Roar*."

"Jeannie, and please don't take this the wrong way, but maybe you need to get out of the house once in a while. How about if we go out to lunch?"

"There's some tuna in the kitchen. I could make you a sandwich. . . ."

"That's not really what I had in mind. Come on, Jeannie, you could use a break."

"I've rested enough," Mom says. "I feel like I'm wide awake and I never want to go to sleep again." Then she laughs, "I know how ridiculous that must sound."

Aunt Sally says, "We all feel awful about what happened to Annika, but you don't have to let it completely change your life. Even God took a day off for rest."

"Oh, honey, I know you don't understand and that's okay. I know what people say about me; I realize I'm one of those people we used to make fun of. But don't worry, I'm not going to preach to you."

"Honey, no one's asking you to give up God. I'm just asking you to come out to lunch."

Mom tries to figure out a way to be polite. "Maybe next Thursday?"

But Aunt Sally doesn't let up. "Okay, how about this: Margot, Courtney, and I were talking about going to Hilton Head for a week, you know, how we used to. We'll play tennis, lay out on the beach. . . . We'd all love it if you'd join us."

"I don't think I could leave Annika for that long," Mom says. "No, you wouldn't like that? Would you, sweetheart?"

I HAVE THIS theory: Annika's hands bleed only on days when Barry Larkin goes hitless. She's bled four times since she's been home and every one of those days Barry has been shut down, sent home with a collar around his neck. A big zero. If she's feeling any pain, it's not Jesus's suffering she's emulating, but the pain that Barry Larkin endures when he goes 0–4.

I wrote Barry Larkin a letter and told him all about Annika. I told him what happened and how she's in a coma. I told him how he's her favorite player and how we listen to every game together. I didn't mention that she bleeds Cincinnati red on the days he doesn't get a hit. I didn't want to freak him out. He's got enough on his mind as it is, but I figured he should know what he means to his fans. I didn't ask for anything from him, not even an autograph. I just wanted him to *know*.

I wasn't expecting anything from Barry Larkin. I'm sure he gets about a dozen make-a-wish requests a day, half of which are probably made up by some pathetic thirty-year-old autograph-dealing creep. I don't need an autograph from Barry and I'm sure Annika feels the same way. We just want him to go out there every day and lead the Reds to the World Series. I think maybe if he knows about Annika, it'll give him an extra push. Maybe it will inspire him to know that there's a little girl somewhere out there stuck in this odd place between life and death and that when she was *living, breathing, jumping,* the Reds brought her much pleasure and that she always said Barry Larkin was her boyfriend. I told Barry how we listen to the games together and that maybe, *just maybe*, it's making its way into her head.

I think if I were Barry Larkin, a letter like that might put a smile on my face.

I guess it did, because he wrote back. He said he'd read about Annika in the paper. He sent along his best wishes, a ball autographed by the entire team, and a genuine replica jersey—just like the one he wears with number 11 and LARKIN on the back, but sized to fit a ten-year-old girl. How cool is that?

Annika wears that jersey now whenever we listen to a game. Maggie dresses her in it an hour before the first pitch and she takes it off when the game is over and hangs it up in her closet, covering it in plastic.

I sent him a picture of her wearing the jersey, you know, as a thank-you. I hope it wasn't too creepy.

We never heard back.

THEY SAY LOSING a child is the hardest thing that could ever happen to a parent. You lose your spouse and you're a widow. You lose your parents and you're an orphan; but when a parent loses a child, you're a *survivor*. That's what the obituaries say. That's how close you are to death when you lose your kid—you just made it. It could just as easily be *your* funeral. Who knows? You might just be *next*.

Father Ferger tells Mom there's a reason for this: it's all part of God's *plan*—the oldest excuse in the book. He says that Annika's suffering will bring people closer to God. He says that when Annika bleeds, she bleeds for *everyone*.

Mom loves to hear that so much, she tells the same thing to anyone who'll listen.

It's a pretty high price to pay, isn't it? To steal a girl's consciousness so people she doesn't even know can learn a lesson? Why does everything have to be part of God's plan? Couldn't it be that He just gave us this world and wished for the best? Couldn't it be that there is *no* plan?

Surely someone must believe this world is a gift with no strings attached. Like Buddhists or someone like that. All I know is that the Catholic God must have some pretty bad manners, giving away presents, then attaching strings to them like He's some gazillionaire who sets his kids up in paradise and says it's all theirs as long as they follow the rules. As long as they do what Daddy wants them to do. God should be smart enough to know, that doesn't make His children love their good old Dad; it just makes them fear Him.

We don't see much of Dad since the accident. Not that we ever did. He gets up earlier and comes home later than he used to. Other than that, it's pretty much the same. When he gets home, he scrubs down the kitchen counter, even though it's already clean. He cracks open a beer, drinks it fast, and opens another, thinking no one will notice. He used to hang around downstairs and eat dinner with us, but now he's usually home so late he eats over the kitchen sink, if he eats at all.

On his way upstairs he'll look in on Annika. It'd be hard not to. The living room is right there by the stairs. But he doesn't go in and talk to her. He doesn't hold her hand and tell her everything will be all right. He doesn't tell her about his day. He just pauses for a second and looks at her—like he's doing math in his head, figuring out the calculus of just what he can do to solve this riddle. But there's nothing he can do, so he turns his back and drags himself up the stairs, a briefcase in each hand.

Someone should pay for all of this, shouldn't they? Someone should be sued. If there's a thought in his head, that must be it.

In the safety of his bedroom, he'll bury himself in work. He'll carefully arrange his briefs over the bed, fire up the television, and let its chattering voices filter out the rest of the world.

Annika and I are listening to the Indians and the Reds going at it when Dad comes in and sits down. "Listening to the game?" he wonders. He's just passing by on his way to the kitchen. It's not like he really wants to be here, he just thinks it's what he's supposed to do. Stop by. Put in his time. "The Indians aren't looking so good this year," he says. He barely even looks at Annika. In fact, he'd much rather look out the window. It's just starting to get dark, but that doesn't stop him from noting, "The hedges are looking a little ragged, don't you think, Monroe?" I tell him I'll take care of it tomorrow. "Good, very good," he says, as he wanders into the kitchen. When he comes back, he has a glass of orange juice spiked with vodka in his hand.

The liquor loosens him up, but not in a good way. He can be a charismatic drunk, but tonight he's just mean. Fortunately, he directs his anger at the Indians. He's a Cleveland Indians fan, always has been. They had a nice run of success once they opened their new ballpark, but not so much lately. Annika and I never got into the Indians, which I'm sure Dad takes as some sort of betrayal. Not that he's ever said anything.

"What the hell is he thinking?" Dad wonders when C.C. Sabathia gives up another walk. "The kid *obviously* doesn't have it tonight. Why doesn't Manuel get him the hell out of there?"

"Because he's a moron?" I ask, sarcastically.

"Damn right, he's a moron," he replies. "I don't even know why I bother."

It's nothing new; Dad's always blaming everything on the manager. If you listen to him long enough, you'd think the manager pitches and hits himself.

It's not exactly a life-or-death situation here, but from the vein bulging in his forehead, you'd never know it. There's not a whole lot you can say to make Dad feel better about anything these days. Even with Annika being the way she is, his life isn't so bad. If he just looked around, he might see that. But right now he's seeing everything through the bottom of a cocktail glass. No wonder it all looks so fucked-up.

With the Indians down 4–1 after the fifth inning, Dad drains his glass and says he's heard enough.

The Indians end up winning the game. I go into his room to congratulate him, hoping it'll put him in a better mood. He's asleep on his king bed, surrounded by carefully laid-out papers and documents, each in their own special place. That's where Mom used to sleep, right where the piles of briefs from the epic legal struggle *Ferguson v. Consolidated Products Inc.* now rest.

Dad's talking now—in his sleep. *Goddamnlowdowndirtycocksuckingmotherfucker* . . . It's like that, a never-ending stream of profanity. It's nothing new—Dad's been trash talking in his sleep for years, saying all the awful things that rattle around in his head all day but never actually come out of his mouth. It's nice to think that at least when he's asleep, he can relax enough to be himself.

There's a sign above the workbench Dad never uses in the basement that says HE WHO MAKES THE LAW HIS MISTRESS, MISSES HALF THE FUN. It's ironic, but I don't think it's meant to be. Mom moved into the guest room a few years ago. It just happened. They drifted into their own separate places—and where they once had each other, now they're alone . . . well maybe not *exactly*. Now Mom has God and Dad has one more mistress to keep him occupied—booze.

GRANDPA MEANS WELL, he really does. I don't know why Dad has to be so mean to him. He talks to him like he talks to me. Like he's a kid.

It's Sunday night and we're all having dinner. Annika's here. She always is. Mom props her up in her wheelchair and sets a place for her. After you see her sitting there a few times it seems perfectly normal. You don't even notice.

Grandpa's doing what he can to liven it up, to fill in the empty spaces that make up our traditional family dynamic. Innocently, he asks Dad what's going on at work. As I may have mentioned, Dad hates that question. Seriously, he *hates* it. It's not like it's a secret. I learned not to ask a long time ago. Dad says, "Oh, nothing too interesting." He says that to anyone who asks. That's his answer.

Grandpa is undeterred. "Oh Larry, I think you're holding back.

You couldn't spend fourteen hours a day working if it wasn't at least *interesting*." It's not like it's a challenge. He's just trying to be nice, to show that he cares.

"Okay, Jim, tell me: Which would you prefer? The case about the five-year-old boy who died in a fire because his mother's cigarette burned the house down, but who's suing the smoke alarm company because she was too drunk to hear the alarm? Or the one about the woman who's suing Nestlé because her husband was crushed when the candy machine he was trying to break into fell down on him?"

"The candy machine story sounds like a good yarn."

"Believe me, *it's not*."

Grandpa, however, is determined to get a conversation going, so he asks Dad what he thinks about the upcoming senatorial election.

"They're both morons" is his reply.

"What this country needs is a new John F. Kennedy," says Grandpa, citing his solution to every conceivable political crisis. Grandpa *loves* Kennedy. Back home, he's got a picture of him by the desk where he pays his bills.

"The best thing that ever happened to Kennedy was getting a bullet in his head. It made everyone forget what a failure he was," Dad says with the nonchalance he generally reserves for telling me to rake the lawn.

"Excuse me?" says Grandpa.

"Let's see, Kennedy got us into Vietnam—that was constructive. He almost got us all killed with the Cuban Missile Crisis. Oh yeah, and let's not forget the Bay of Pigs. Brilliant." Apparently, Dad doesn't have a problem with sarcasm when *he* uses it.

"Kennedy was a great civil rights leader."

Dad has an answer for everything: "He was a civil rights *follower*. The writing was on the wall and he just read it. At least his Ivy League education was good for something. . . . How about this? Tell me three good things the man ever did—and Marilyn Monroe and the Peace Corps don't count."

I'm shocked to find out Dad thinks the Peace Corps was a good idea.

"As a Catholic, I really don't know how you can say that."

"It's not that hard," Dad says. "You forget, Jim, I went to Vietnam because of that bastard."

It's true. Dad went in 1969. He never talks about it and I mean *never*. When I was in tenth grade, I had to do a report for school on Vietnam; Dad wouldn't even sit down and dish out one measly story. He told me to watch *Platoon* instead. "That will tell you all you need to know." So I just made it all up, everything but the Purple Heart. That part is true. He keeps it in the back of his sock drawer. I found it one rainy afternoon, but I never said a word, even though I'm dying to know where he got hit. Anyway, Dad came out looking like a real hero in my school report. He probably figured that's what I'd do.

"Kennedy was a good man." That's all Grandpa can come up with in his defense.

Dad just shakes his head, chewing his last bite. "That was delicious, honey," he says to my mom. Just like he says after every meal. "I better go upstairs and get caught up on some work."

When Dad leaves Grandpa says, "Annika, you like Kennedy, don't you?"

She's been staring at the salad bowl for the last twenty minutes.

"Of course, you do."

Chapter 19

THE SUMMER AFTER Heidi Morgan was murdered, I rode my bike by her house every chance I got. I'd go by slow and pretend I wasn't looking, but I was. Not that there was anything *special* to see. Not that there was anything *different*. Unless you knew who had lived there, you'd think nothing of it. But once you knew, you couldn't *not* look. At least, not me.

It was the inside, though, that I really wanted to see. Ben said the Morgans had a *huge* shrine for Heidi above the fireplace. He said there were pictures of her *everywhere*. And more importantly, he said I'd be a pussy if I didn't check it out.

It was a sticky August night and fireflies were lighting up the shadows. Nights like that, we used to play ghost in the graveyard, but after what happened to Heidi, those days were over. Even though Heidi was killed well before the sun went down, once the streetlights came on, we had to be inside. At least I did. Ben could still do whatever he wanted.

Mom and Dad were at a party when we snuck out of the house. This was a mission that would require the cover of darkness. That's the only way to look into windows without the people inside being able to look back at you.

The living room was lit up blue. That's where I found Mrs. Morgan staring at the television, eating potato chips. One after the other. A buzzer was buzzing in the distance, but she didn't move. She just kept eating the potato chips, like she'd been doing it *for days*.

From upstairs, "Mom! Are you going to get that or what?"

No response.

Allison came stomping down the stairs and said, "What are you doing? The cookies are *burning*." But Mrs. Morgan didn't say a word. She put another potato chip in her mouth. Then another. Then Allison shook her head and disappeared into the kitchen.

I didn't see a shrine, let alone a picture of Heidi. Just Mrs. Morgan eating potato chips. One after the other.

It's not what I wanted to see. It wasn't titillating. It wasn't exciting. It was just sad.

Then Ben chucked a tennis ball at the window, blowing my cover. Mrs. Morgan sprang up off the couch, her bag of potato chips falling to the floor. I don't know if she saw me or not. I kept running and never looked back.

Did I mention that Ben is the biggest jerk in the world?

Only two years later, on a sunny spring day, would I return to Holly Lane. I figured by then the coast was clear. The house was pretty much the same, but the hedges were overgrown and ivy was beginning to creep onto the windows.

Mrs. Morgan was on her knees, surrounded by groceries. Cans of food were rolling all over the driveway and she wasn't doing anything to stop them. She just watched, like that was it—the last straw. There's nothing more she could do. She'd given up.

Not even canned food could save her now.

I know I should have stopped and helped, but I just kept pedaling, pretending I didn't see a thing.

Now look at us. We're the freaks in the neighborhood. We're the ones they stare at. It can happen to anyone.

Most people just wish we'd leave, people who used to be our friends. At least, that's what I thought they were, but really they're just *neighbors*. It's not so hard to be a neighbor. It's a role people play. Neighbors wave and smile and bring over casseroles when you're sick. They'll give you pancakes on Saturday morning and they'll lend out their power tools, but when your problems become bigger than a scraped knee, they're not there anymore. They disappear.

I've taken Annika on her walks, pushing her wheelchair down the street. I've seen the neighbors scurry back into their homes. I've seen them pull out of their driveways and wave without even rolling down their windows. I've seen them vanish behind their garage doors. I've seen them peek through their blinds.

Even the Shepherds pretend we don't exist. Mrs. Shepherd always used to stop Annika and tell her how beautiful she was. How *perfect* her hair looked. The Shepherds are big on perfection. Mr. Shepherd spends so much time telling me how to cut his yard, he might as well do it himself.

A few years ago, the Shepherds had a little boy with Down syndrome. And there's nothing perfect about that. So guess what they did?

They sent him straight to Oakside.

As far as they're concerned, he might as well be dead. They adopted another baby right away. Like Down Syndrome Boy never even existed. A lot of people don't know William is adopted, they just assume he's the Shepherds' real flesh and blood. I wouldn't know myself had I not overheard Dad telling Mom. That's the only way to get any good information around here. You have to be sneaky.

The traffic has only gotten worse since Mr. Oester's campaign banned on-street parking. People still cruise by and point. Then they circle the block and do it again. Now, they just don't *stop*. You get used to living in a fishbowl a lot faster than you might think.

When I cut lawns, sometimes they ask about Annika. *How is she? Has anything changed? We've been praying for her. She's such a sweet girl.* It's really nice of them, I suppose, to be so concerned. Then again, maybe they're just being polite. Or maybe they're just fishing for gossip. Something to spice up the conversation while they pick through Caesar salads at the country club. Either way, I say, "She's the same. We're hoping for the best." They say they are too. Then we move on to more pleasant topics of conversation, like the importance of mulch or how watering in the middle of the day can burn the lawn.

~~~

MOM DOESN'T FEEL like cooking, so I'm picking up Chinese for dinner. Allison Morgan, Heidi's sister, is in front of me. She's slowly
shaking her head as she flips through the seemingly oxymoronically
titled alternative weekly rag *Columbus Alive!*

Chong's isn't the only Chinese food around here, but it might as
well be. It's the only place we ever go. It used to be pretty good, at
least I *think* it was, but the more you eat there, the more you begin to
wonder what was so good about it in the first place. I guess we just go
there out of habit. It's easier to do the same thing over and over than
it is to try something new. Maybe that's what it means to get old. You
keep *doing, eating, buying, watching* the same old things over and over
out of some duty to ritual, but in the end you're not even satisfied. All
you get back is familiarity in a world seemingly out of control. Maybe
it's a fair trade. I don't know.

I heard somewhere on TV that psychologists say that love only
lasts for eighteen months. After that it becomes *something* else. I
wonder if that *something* is the same thing that makes me order Filet-
O-Fishes at McDonald's, even though they always make me sick.

Allison is standing there picking up her order, checking to make
sure everything is in there. She's wearing an old Rolling Stones shirt
and sweatpants. It looks like she might have just gotten out of bed. I
bet she doesn't even know my name. Everyone knows hers, though.
Ever since her sister got killed, it's hard not to look at her and think
of Heidi and the way she died.

That class picture. Her crooked teeth. The way she was left in a
ditch, her head smashed with a rock.

"No fortune cookies?" Allison asks.

Mrs. Chong apologizes profusely and fills up her bag with a
handful.

Allison explains, "The future just seems so murky without them."

"Your future bright like the sun." Mrs. Chong smiles.

Allison brushes by me on her way out. She smells like cocoa butter. Our eyes meet for just a flicker of a moment, but she keeps going.

I want to follow her, but they're asking me what I want; so I just let her go. I don't know what I'd say to her anyway.

I never know what to say to anybody.

IT'S MY BIRTHDAY and my boss, Paul, wants to take me out to celebrate. I'm surprised when he suggests we go see August West. They don't play any Grateful Dead covers, but they might as well, and Paul frequently points out how the Grateful Dead have no soul. Paul never asks me to do anything, so it's not like I'm going to say no.

Paul's off getting us beers when I spot Emily hanging all over some greasy guy wearing cowboy boots.

She has beads braided in her hair.

She's tan.

She looks so happy I want to die.

The cold metallic taste of a thousand pennies gurgles in the back of my throat, the taste of all the things I imagine they've done together.

I head to the bathroom, but I don't make it. Instead, I lose it in a garbage can full of empty beer bottles. I don't think anyone sees me, not that I hang around to make sure. I just keep moving.

In the bathroom, thankfully the mirror's too scratched for me to see my face, but it feels like I'm on fire. I douse myself with water, but the flame's not going out.

That's when *he* comes in the bathroom. Emily's poncho-wearing boyfriend. He says to me, "Hey man, you look like you could use a joint. You wanna help me out with this?"

I guess he doesn't get high in front of her either.

"Sure," I say. *Like an idiot.* That's all I've got. *Sure.*

I take a long hit, hoping maybe it'll give birth to a half-decent thought. But all I manage is "Thanks."

"Just don't tell my girlfriend," he says.

"Okay," I say. Even though this is the last guy I want to talk to in the world, he's already made me his confidante. I'm just that much of a tool.

"What do you guys do for fun around here?"

"Not much. I guess there's always cow tipping," I say. "Or smashing mailboxes." Not that I've ever done either.

"I'll tell you one thing, there sure are some hot chiquitas in this neck of the woods. Kerouac was right when he said the most beautiful girls in the world are in Columbus, Ohio."

"Des Moines."

"Huh?"

"Des Moines—in Iowa—that's where Kerouac said the most beautiful girls are. Not here."

He looks bummed. "Fuck, man, I've been telling everyone it's Columbus."

Despite that he likes Kerouac enough to misquote him, I'm surprised to find that I don't completely hate him. I wish I could just go up and talk to people like that. I don't know why it's so hard.

After saying good-bye, I head out to look for Paul and tell him maybe we should go somewhere else, but Emily is headed straight toward me. I would have hoped she'd have had the decency to pretend I don't exist. But instead she squeals "Monroe!" as if she's really happy to see me. And I'm so weak-kneed at the sight of her, I almost let myself believe she is.

"You're back."

"Something like that," she says. "I just talked to your mom about an hour ago, but she didn't say you were going to be *here*."

"You talked to my mom?"

"Yeah, I wanted to see how you were doing. Maybe have lunch."

Lunch. Even I know nothing good can come from *lunch.*

"I feel pretty terrible about the way things worked out, breaking up in a letter. You didn't deserve that."

"Thanks."

She says she hopes we can be friends. You know, the kind of friends who have *lunch* together.

"Sure," I say.

"I came back with Billy. He's the guy I met down there. He's really sweet. You'd probably really like him. He's a lot like you."

Right now, I pretty much hate myself, so you can imagine how I feel about him. But I don't say that. I don't say anything.

"He's a musician."

"That's great." Musicians traditionally make wonderful boyfriends.

"You know Dolphin?"

Yeah, I know Dolphin. They're like the number one Grateful Dead wannabe jam band in the world. It's a dubious distinction. Ever since Jerry Garcia died, all the Deadheads who still had the munchies for senseless guitar solos and disharmonious vocals jumped in the ocean and landed on Dolphin. But I don't say that.

"Dolphin?" I ask.

"Monroe, I think you may have mentioned that they suck before."

"Oh. *That* Dolphin. That's right, they do suck."

"Well, Billy's their singer." And as that bit of info sinks in, she adds, "I missed you, Monroe. I missed you a lot." Then she hugs me.

This is way too easy for her. Isn't being friends something you should have to *earn*? Not an afterthought like, "Oh sure, I'd like fries with that"? Then again, it's not like I have any friends. I'm not exactly in a position to be picky about it.

Billy's on his way over with a couple beers, all smiles. Emily's face lights up at the sight of him. She used to look that way when she saw me.

"I know that dude," he says. "We were just hanging out in the bathroom." As if to thwart any reefer smoking allegations he adds, *"Discussing literature."*

Emily says, "Billy, this is Monroe. His sister is Annika, you know, the girl in a coma I told you about."

"Cool."

Cool? My face must have *What the fuck?* written all over it.

"Dude, don't get me wrong. The coma's totally *not* cool, but that whole healing people thing she does is pretty rad."

"Yeah, I guess. If you believe in that kind of thing."

"She cured that girl with cancer. I saw it on Guatemalan TV. Can you believe that shit? Guatemalan *fucking* TV." I'm not sure if he means whether I believe they have televisions in Guatemala or if I can believe the story traveled so far.

He's talking about the eight-year-old girl from the farm outside Dayton who was in town to get chemotherapy. Naturally, her parents brought her by to see Annika first. They sat with Annika for about fifteen minutes and prayed. They weren't the first, but they'd be the last who'd get that close. At least for a while. The next day, Annika was covered in sweat, her lymph nodes were popping off her neck, and her feet were covered with bruises. Meanwhile, the little girl from Dayton had gone into remission and she hadn't even gotten the chemo yet. Annika's symptoms went away the next day. The doctors couldn't explain it; she was completely fine. People think this episode makes Annika a true "victim soul"—she's able to *literally* take on the suffering of others.

"I don't know," I say. "Cancer goes into remission all the time. You're in a band, right? Let's say a hundred cancer patients are at one of your shows. Odds are a few of them would get cured whether they went to your show or not. So if one of them does get better, would that make you a healer?"

"I don't know, man, but it would be pretty cool. We could put a live album out and call it *The Healer.* It would be *awesome*," he says. "Hey man, you think I could meet her? I have that carpal tunnel syndrome. Every time I rip into a solo it feels like it's ripping into me. You know what I mean?"

"That's why Billy was in Guatemala. Resting his wrists," explains Emily.

"Just getting away from it all, you know?"

"Maybe you should try surgery," I suggest.

"And have them cut me? No way. Besides, the band's already pissed at me for making us hang low this summer."

"Acupuncture?"

"No way, man. Didn't you ever listen to 'The Needle and the Damage Done'?"

"Yeah, it's about *heroin.*"

"*Exactly*. And once you start playing around with needles it's a slippery slope. Don't think I don't know; I watch *Behind the Music* like everyone else."

"Yeah, that must be something, being in a band. Girls must be throwing themselves at you all the time."

For some reason, I find the glare in Emily's eyes encouraging.

Billy turns to me like we're the only ones there. "Yeah, it's kind of ridiculous—what girls will do. But it's not like they want to sleep with *you*, they want to sleep with this *idea* of you. After you do it a few times, it's just *depressing*. Kinda like acid. It's fun at the time, but then you pay the next day, you know? Dwayne—our lead guitarist—he keeps saying we oughta get some eunuchs to work security—you know, those dudes from Egypt with their balls cut off? Dwayne says the yellow jacket security bastards are always skimming the best chicks for themselves." He looks all doe-eyed at Emily with an approximation of soul that's almost convincing. "But I don't really care anymore. It's like I'm completely happy with my life."

Then he gives Emily a kiss on the cheek. Like that's proof, that he, *you know*, has *changed*.

"I always used to think I'd never change for anyone. It's like I'm a fuckin' rock star, right? It's like what can be better than this? What guy in America wouldn't give his left nut to have what I have? You know?"

"Maybe they could work security for you."

"Hey, you're funny. . . . The thing is, I'm living the dream. It's like why would I want to change?"

"I can't imagine."

"Me neither—until Emily came along. She's really helped me see what really matters. It's like we were on the plane yesterday and Emily was reading the paper—which is something that most people don't even do, it's like a lost art or something. And she's reading this story about how the Russians rounded up every male Chechen in—I don't know, Chechnya, I guess—and hooked them up to electrodes and started questioning them and this one woman was like, *Please don't take my son, he's retarded,* and they're like, *Well, we'll see just how retarded he is* and they cart him away. And I'm thinking like, *What the fuck are we supposed to do about it? Man, I hate the news. It's such a letdown.* And Emily is like, *Well maybe you can do something about it.* And I'm like, *How?* And she's like, *Maybe you could make up some T-shirts for the Chechen resistance, like in tie-dye, and you could sell them on your Web site or whatever and send them the cash.* And I'm thinking, *That would be cool.* It's like we're in a unique position, you know, because of all our fans, to change the world."

Emily interrupts. "So would it be cool if we stopped by tomorrow and hung out with Annika?"

"Sure."

"I really miss her."

"Me too," I say, thinking this is getting a little too personal. "I guess I better get going. It was great seeing you." Which is a lie. If only I'd seen a glimmer of a regret in her eyes, then maybe it would have been true.

Billy says they're having a party at the Hilton after the show. Maybe we'd want to stop by?

"Sounds cool." Once I start lying I can't stop.

"We're registered under Jack Cousteau."

Emily knows there's no way I'll show up. "If we don't see you later, we'll give you a call in the morning, okay?" And they disappear into the crowd, leaving me with nowhere to go but away.

I'M SITTING BY the pool, reading the box scores, when I hear, "Hey Monroe." It's Emily sticking her head over the fence. She says it all sweet like she used to talk to me back when the world was our own private joke. My heart is racing and my face is flushing. It's amazing I can even corral a single thought in my head. There's nothing quite so humbling as thinking you're completely over someone, then realizing you're not even close.

I try to be all nonchalant, like it's no big deal. "Emily, is that you?"

But then Billy sticks his head over too. "Hey dude," he says. "You should have come to the party last night. There was this little raven-haired honey there that was *perfect* for you."

As Emily leads him poolside, she says, "Billy, that *skank* wasn't Monroe's type." It would be nice to think Emily is sticking up for me, but the truth is, I might as well not even be here.

Billy's all sunglasses-hungover-greasy and Emily's all Guatemala dress-wearing, patchouli-smelling, flowers in her hair. Basically, they're all over each other. "Emily, that girl was *everyone's* type.... She was like Grace Slick with dreadlocks."

"Billy, she doesn't wash her hair."

"You say that like it's a *bad* thing."

Emily pouts and Billy says what he's supposed to say. "Oh Baby, you know you're the only one who's perfect for me." Then he kisses her. As if I want to see *that*. I wonder if she ever even told him that we used to go out. I bet she said I was just an old friend. He doesn't seem particularly threatened by me, not that anyone ever is.

"So this is where it happened?" Billy asks.

"A lot of people think if you say Annika's name backward three times in a row, rap the final verse of 'Stairway to Heaven,' then jump in the water—you'll be cured of all your ills." But I don't say that. I just say, "Yeah."

"That must be wild, saving someone's life."

"You probably would have done the same thing."

Billy says he can't swim, which makes me think maybe, on second thought, I *should* tell him about the curative powers of our swimming pool. But I don't. Instead, I just feel stupid standing there with my skinny legs and sunken chest, while Billy's all decked out in rodeo gear, looking like he's just walked in off the range. "So, I guess you guys want to see Annika?"

Billy starts talking about his wrists and how much they hurt and how every doctor in the world has looked at them and they all want to cut him open, and he can barely even *look* at his wrists, let alone contemplate slicing into them. *Yeah, yeah, yeah,* he went to an acupuncturist, but the needles completely freaked him out. Then there was the Hindu mystic and the Pentecostal faith healer and the rattlesnake blood he got on the side of a road from an Indian in Arizona. None of it worked. So far, he says, only the endorphin rush he gets from the crowd kills the pain.

"I just want to see Annika," says Emily.

"In that case, on to the main attraction," I say as I walk them back around to the front door. "But, I'm not promising any miracles."

In the front yard, two guys with a video camera are shooting the house. "Wave to the parasites," I say.

Emily sheepishly confesses, "Well, actually, they're with us."

"You guys brought a camera crew?"

Billy says, "It's cool. They're doing a documentary. I'm playing a benefit tonight at the Newport, you know, for the Guatemalan textile workers. *Solo.* It oughta be pretty rad. You gotta check it out."

That's when Mom comes outside. I'd like to think if she wasn't in the equation, this is where I would have kicked them out and said, "What the hell is your problem? Bringing a camera crew to see my sick sister like you're at a fucking zoo?" But I probably wouldn't have said that. I probably would have let them in, but I'm pretty sure I would have made them leave the camera behind. I just would have blamed it on my mom.

Like I said, I'm a pussy.

When Mom sees Emily, she gives her a huge hug—bigger than she's ever given me. I don't read too much into that—she hugs everyone now. It's not like she's forgiving Emily for the way she blew me off, not that she could—she doesn't even know. Mom and I never talked about what happened. There were a few weeks there when I would have spilled my guts, but after a while it didn't seem like it mattered much anymore. Mom tells Emily it's so good to see her and it seems like she really means it.

Mom hugs Billy too, and the camera crew moves in closer.

Then Mom asks, "What's with the cameras?"

I explain, "Emily's new boyfriend, Billy, is a rock star and he starts to literally disappear unless his every move is documented."

Billy eyes Emily and says, "That's not such a bad idea, putting *everything* on tape." That's what I get for being a smart-ass. The image of the two of them making their own pornos projected into my head.

Emily says, "Actually, Mrs. Anderson, they're filming a documentary on Billy and a concert he's doing tonight. It's *a day in the life* kind of thing. We can send them away if you want. We don't want to intrude."

So far, Mom's only let Cheryl Hanover inside with a camera. There's *no way* she'll let these jokers in.

"If they're friends of yours, I'm sure it will be all right," she says. For some reason, it doesn't seem like it's worth arguing about, so I roll my eyes and follow them inside.

I'm not going to pretend it wasn't funny when Billy walked right into the sliding glass door, because it was. Maybe I laughed a little too much and a little too long, but it's not like the door broke and the glass cut his jugular, leaving him a convulsing mess on the floor. It wasn't like that at all, although that would have been nice. Instead, Billy is only momentarily stunned, a condition he is seemingly quite comfortable with. He laughs it off and Mom slides open the door. "We really should put some decals on there, like roses or crucifixes. Wouldn't that be nice?" wonders Mom, who's completely lost all sense of interior design.

Emily starts crying at the first sight of Annika. It would be easy to assume this display of emotion means she has a heart, that she is capable of empathy. But people cry all the time when they see Annika; it's a pretty common reaction. Of course, those people are *believers*. Emily isn't. At least, she didn't use to be.

"I guess I kept thinking that by the time I got back from Guatemala, she'd be awake."

"She looks so beautiful," Billy says, in a testament to his powers of original observation. He wants to know if it's okay to touch her and Mom says that we all touch her all the time, which comes out a lot creepier than Mom would ever understand.

As I'm looking at Emily, I'm thinking, *Get your grimy mitts off my sister.* But, still, I want to kiss her more than anything in the world.

Billy's guitar *somehow* materializes and he wants to sing Annika a song. "What kind of music does she like?" he asks. I tell him she likes Parliament and he says as far as British music goes, he's partial to the Beatles. Mom volunteers that Annika really likes Neil Diamond.

So, to Maggie and Mom's delight, Billy sings "Sweet Caroline." But instead of *Caroline* he sings *Annika*. The women are really into it, and the truth is, he doesn't suck nearly as much as I want him to—which only makes me hate him more. Emily is all smiles while Mom and Maggie tap their toes along to the whole humiliating melody. I would bolt, but I can't. It's like my feet are stuck in buckets of concrete, paralyzed by the mediocrity of it all.

After the song is over, Emily whispers in my ear, "Is everything all right?" The way she says it and the way she touches my shoulders is so sweet, it's cruel.

There are so many things I want to say to Emily, but all I can manage is, "I'm fine." She whispers, "I think you're being really great," then goes back to Annika's bedside. She's holding Annika's hand and I'm looking at her, wondering how it all went wrong.

Billy asks Mom if she thinks Annika can do anything about his wrists. She tells him, "Honey, Annika can't do anything about something like that, only God can do that. . . . Then again, who knows?" Mom adds, "Maybe Annika can pass along the message," nonchalantly elevating Annika to saint status.

Billy takes her hand and thankfully prays silently. I'll have to talk to Annika later and give her the lowdown on Billy, which is not to say I'll try to get his prayers reversed. I just think she should know all the facts.

"How about a Beatles tune?" Billy offers, stupidly smiling at Emily. He picks up his guitar again and breaks into "Twist and Shout." Everyone knows the Isley Brothers broke that song; the Beatles just made it okay for white people to listen to it. But I don't say that. Some people simply can't be helped.

As Billy's really getting into it, Annika's head starts rocking back and forth. A vein on her neck bulges. Her arms start to shake.

"Come on now baby, work it on out."

Emily says, "Look. She's *dancing.*" Then she sees the little pools of blood forming in her hands and all she can say is, "Oh my God."

Billy's eyes are closed. He keeps playing. Annika keeps bleeding. The camera keeps rolling.

When Billy finally finishes, he opens his eyes and sees what he's been missing. What's left of his mind is completely blown. He doesn't know what to say.

It's a wonderful development.

Mom tells the cameraman to make sure he gets a good look at her hands. "I just hate it when people act like it's something we make up. Who would ever want to do that?" she asks to no one in particular.

Once the event is sufficiently documented, Mom wipes down Annika's forehead with water. "She's burning up."

"It smells like roses," Emily notices.

"After a while," Mom says, "you get used to it. . . . Isn't that sad?"

Of course, Mom asks them to stay over for lunch. Mercifully, Emily says Billy is supposed to do a radio interview over at QFM-96, the favorite radio station around here for people who can't quite get their mind around the idea that there are other bands besides the Stones, the Who, and Led Zeppelin. Billy offers to put us on the list for the benefit concert.

Mom says he's already given her such a beautiful memory, she wouldn't want to ruin it. Then she gets her checkbook. She's a sucker for a benefit.

I say I have other plans, but otherwise it'd be great. Obviously, if Emily wanted me to go, she would have asked me herself.

She leaves me with a kiss on my cheek. It doesn't feel like much of a consolation prize.

But that's what it is.

~~~

RATTLESNAKE BLOOD MAY not have cured Billy's wrists, but Annika's seems to have done the job. At least, that's what he's telling everyone, from Uncle Daddy Skaggs at the radio station to the scribes at *Rolling Stone* magazine. Billy's acoustic show that night was considered "epic and combustible." At least, that's what the music critic at *The Dispatch* wrote under the headline "Dolphin Escapes Net."

Then, of course, there's the videotape of Annika bleeding. Some people think it's proof. Some people think it's fake. Some people think if they see it one more time, they may never watch television again. (That someone would be me.)

I don't know if anyone has actually been healed by Annika. They say they have been, but people get better all the time. Cancer goes into remission all on its own, hearts mend, and the endorphins of heightened expectations wash the pain away in the moment. That's what Paul says and he probably would be in medical school by now, you know, if he'd bothered to go to college in the first place. Maybe he's right. Maybe just coming to visit Annika means they have the will to get better, so they're already halfway there before they even come through our door.

Chapter 20

NOT EVERYONE IS a fan of what's going on here. I don't think Mr. Oester, our neighbor, was speaking just for himself when he sent the following letter to *The Columbus Dispatch*:

To the Editor:

In the future, please try to resist the urge to further lionize Annika Anderson in your pages. Perhaps her story helps you sell papers, but your coverage merely makes you a participant in her exploitation. Annika's near drowning and current state of coma is obviously a tragedy, but this tragedy has been compounded by the delusional brand of religious fanaticism promoted by her mother as well as Father Ferger of St. Victor's. I can understand Mrs. Anderson's need to make her daughter's life have some meaning, but Father Ferger should be defrocked for perpetuating this gross violation of a young girl's dignity. To claim that an eleven-year-old girl in a coma is a "victim soul" who is here to take on the sufferings of the world is nothing short of child abuse. What kind of God is it that heaps suffering upon an already broken child in order to strengthen people's faith? Are we so desensitized by politically correct notions of tolerance that we're not offended by the site of a persistently comatose girl being displayed for the edification of hundreds of desperate, damaged believers, grasping at the last straws of hope? Annika, indeed, is a victim—the victim of misguided

religious fanaticism. The public abuse of a healthy child would
never be accepted, but the abuse of the defenseless is celebrated in
your pages. Everyone who participates in this charade is an accessory
to child abuse, including you. The local bishop's refusal to loudly
condemn this mockery is a disgrace. Then again, perhaps he's too
wrapped up in his own problems with sexual abuse allegations to
pay attention.

Thomas Oester
Chelsea

It's pretty harsh, sure. And, yes, other people have said that Mom *likes* Annika this way, this little living miracle. Mr. Oester is not alone. We get hate mail *all the time*. But those people don't see how every moment of the day is dedicated to waking Annika up. They don't see the massages and the baths and the feathers on her feet and the ice on her skin and the songs we play in her ears and the stories we read. They don't see how a moan can be interpreted in so many different ways or how you can have a conversation with a series of blinks. They don't see the prayers and the tears, because if they did, they'd know there's nothing my mom or any of us wants more than for Annika to just come back.

SURE, I THOUGHT it was a stupid idea to take Annika to France; but considering everything else that's been going on, after you think about it, it doesn't make any less sense than anything else.

I guess we have Mr. Winchell to thank. Mr. Winchell is the CEO of a waste management company up near Cleveland and he's lucky he isn't in jail. If it weren't for Dad, that's where he'd be. I'm not saying that's a *good thing*. I'm not *bragging*. After all, you probably shouldn't be able to poison an aquifer that serves a population of three million people and walk around your thirty-thousand-square-foot lakefront mansion like nothing happened.

Anyway, Mr. Winchell heard all about Annika and wanted to

come and see her. In fact, he's the first person Dad has brought home since the accident. It's not like Dad wanted to bring him home; it's more like he *had* to.

The first thing Mr. Winchell says, when he sees Annika, is that she looks just like Bernadette. Everyone's like, "Who's Bernadette?"

He looks pretty shocked that no one knows. Maggie would have known, but she has a way of disappearing when Dad's around.

We're all sitting at the dinner table when Winchell tells the tale. He says it all started in Lourdes, France, in 1858, when a fourteen-year-old peasant girl named Bernadette Soubirous was fetching some wood down by the river with the help of a sister and a friend. Bernadette saw a white apparition, but the other girls didn't see anything. Just Bernadette. Ordinarily, that would be that, but Bernadette must have been quite persuasive. Three days later she went back with a posse of several more girls. They knelt down and said the rosary and once again the apparition of a young woman appeared, but again only Bernadette saw her. Bernadette stood there like she was in a trance, her lips moving as if she was in deep conversation. The other girls didn't see a thing, but they were nonetheless impressed.

I'd really like to interject here that this tale sounds suspiciously like when Angie Hume down the street got an Ouija board and started telling everyone she could talk to their dead pets. But I don't say that.

On the third day Bernadette said the spirit told her to come back for fifteen days in a row. By the end of her engagement at the cave there were *thousands* of people enraptured by her every word. The crowd showered her with kisses and, if they couldn't get their lips close enough to her, they settled for the dirt she walked on. The newspapers at the time concluded Bernadette was "the interpreter, if not the image of a superior being."

Winchell laughs and says, "It was like she was a *rock star.*"

Two weeks after her first sighting of the ghost, who was now believed to be the Virgin Mary, Bernadette knelt down and pawed at the ground. She said Mary told her to. People laughed at her as if she were a pig digging for truffles, dirt smeared across her face. But they didn't laugh for long. A spring bubbled up from the dry earth and a peasant girl, who had lost the use of her right hand, slipped it in the water. When she pulled it out, her fingers moved for the first time.

It just takes one.

Ever since, the water from that spring has been thought to have the power to heal the sick and lame. Now, four million people come to Lourdes each and every year to cure their ills. Mr. Winchell notes, "That's more people than go to see the Yankees."

Mr. Winchell says he didn't really believe the whole thing, but for some reason while he was in Paris on business, he decided to make the trip. "It was just a lark," he says. "I guess I didn't realize it at the time, but I was kind of depressed. I'd look out my office window and I'd imagine jumping out. When my plane landed in Paris, I was hoping it would crash. I wondered, *What's the point?*"

I'm thinking Mr. Winchell was probably just feeling guilty about all the environmental devastation he's left in his wake. But I don't say it.

Mr. Winchell says that ever since he soaked his head in the waters at Lourdes he hasn't been depressed at all. "Lourdes changed my life." I want to point out the irony of a man who contaminated the drinking water of the greater Cleveland area resorting to the healing waters in France, but I don't say that either. I just nod along.

Mom thinks it's a great story, but I think if he'd really changed he'd have a different job. He probably still dumps the same shit in all the same places.

Then Mr. Winchell has an epiphany. "Why not take Annika? Maybe, it'll work on her."

Dad says, "I don't think she really travels so well."

"You can take the company jet," offers Mr. Winchell.

Dad says, "That's a really kind offer, but—"

Mom cuts him off, "We'd love to think about it, if that's okay."

"Of course," he says. "The offer's always open."

I feel compelled to do a little research on Lourdes. And while it's true that four million people go there every year, the Catholic

Church has certified only sixty-five miracles since people started flocking there almost 150 years ago. Those aren't very good odds—certainly, not as good as the chances that your local priest is a pedophile. Strangely, many Catholics won't admit a priest would ever molest an altar boy, but they're willing to believe you can stick your crippled arm into a babbling brook and be cured.

Like Annika, Bernadette was a rather sickly young woman herself. You might think that if the waters of Lourdes were going to do their trick on anyone, it would be her. But Bernadette died at the age of thirty-five from complications due to tuberculosis and a whole bunch of other stuff they probably hadn't even figured out names for yet. The "healing" waters of Lourdes couldn't even save their illustrious founder. Some might call it ironic, but it didn't stop the Catholic Church from calling Bernadette a saint. She was canonized in 1933. Now, her dead body is laid out for everyone to see at a church in Nevers, France. A wax mask covers her face. How sick is that? That's about one step ahead of those freak shows where you can see a pickled two-headed baby in a jar of formaldehyde. I swear, if they ever try to pull a stunt like that with Annika, I'll burn the place down.

Oh, wait. They already *have* done that to Annika. The only difference is that she's *still alive*. But, rest assured, as long as that's the case, there will be no burning down of the house.

After Mr. Winchell leaves, Mom and Dad fight. Ordinarily their fights are battled in silence, but this one is vocal enough to easily eavesdrop on. Basically, it's like this: Dad thinks it's a waste of time. Mom thinks they have nothing to lose.

She yells at him. "Don't you see what's going on here?"

"The less I see, the better."

"You're standing in the middle of a miracle and you won't even open your eyes."

"Maybe the more you close your eyes, the more of a miracle you see."

"Just for once in your life, try not to be such a *lawyer*. We're talking about your daughter here. If there's a chance something will happen there—no matter how small—isn't it worth it?"

IN LESS THAN a week they're on their way to Lourdes.

That's right, they're taking the circus on the road. I figure I'll be able to miss the festivities. After all, it'll all be available in bite-sized morsels on TV.

Click. I'm eating pizza, watching on the little kitchen television. To the cheers of a crowd of well-wishers, they load Annika onto the Waste Incorporated jet. Before takeoff the congregation surrounds the plane with the circle of prayer. One woman tells Cheryl Hanover, "And I'll be here when she gets back to see her *walk* off the plane."

She may be a nut, but I hope she's right.

Click. I'm smoking a joint in my bedroom, watching the baseball scores scroll across the screen, when a CNN *newsbreak* interrupts a story about wild parrots attacking tourists in San Francisco's Golden Gate Park.

A near riot has broken out in Lourdes and Brittany Whatever-her-name-is, the late-night newsreader, can't contain her glee. Cut to: footage of Dad carrying Annika in his arms, pushing his way through the cobblestone streets of the seemingly quaint French village. There's blood streaming from Annika's forehead and her eyes are bouncing all over the place. Mom's by his side and they're encircled by people. *Hundreds* of people. And they're all trying to get their paws on Annika. They're hungry for her blood.

How did it come to this? After a brief commercial break, CNN will happily explain in a sixty-second digestible chunk and they'll keep doing it all night long. Rewind to Annika at the healing waters surrounded by a crowd of curiosity seekers. Father Ferger and Mom dabble the water on her forehead. Right then, right there, Annika sprouts wounds just like the ones Jesus got from the crown of thorns. The camera is a bit shaky and the focus slightly suspect, but what you see is what you get.

Women faint. Children squeal. Grown men cry. Everyone wants to get *closer*.

Click. I'm having a cup of coffee in the family room with Katie Couric. She can't believe it. "It really does look like a little girl up there," she says. Cut to: a full moon hanging big and low over a crowd of people in the streets. The camera focuses in on the moon. I guess you might be able to see a curly-haired girl's face etched in there—if that's what you're looking for.

Turns out, that crowd of people is outside a hospital. Katie's talking to Mom via satellite. "And I know this sounds crazy," Mom says, "but we have reason to believe Annika communicated with an apparition of the Virgin Mary."

The footage of the crowd gathered in front of the French hospital is eerily reminiscent of Annika's first days at Riverbend after she fell in the pool. The camera pans up to the window and you can see Mom with her hands on the glass, as if she were a human antenna for the crowd's prayers.

Click. After a day of cutting yards, I'm drinking one of Dad's Heinekens in the pool house. Ordinarily, *The Larry King Show* would require another *click* to escape, but this time I'm stuck. Mom and Father Ferger are in a studio in France talking to Larry. Larry says, "Now there have been many cases of stigmata throughout the years; but what makes Annika Anderson especially interesting is that she's in a coma. Essentially, she's dead to the world."

Mom is a big fan of Larry King; so big, in fact, she frequently refers to him as a *journalist*. But Mom *hates* when people say Annika is dead to the world. "Actually, Larry, Annika is kneeling by Jesus's side. She's with him every day, taking on His pain and spreading His word. There's nothing *dead* about her."

In the guise of sympathy, Larry acknowledges how hard all this must be. Then he asks, "Do you really believe that your daughter is suffering like Jesus suffered?"

Mom says, "For those who believe, there is no explanation needed. For those who don't believe, no explanation will suffice." An embroidered pillow couldn't have said it better.

Then Father Ferger chimes in. "I couldn't agree with Mrs. Anderson more. After his death, Jesus appeared to Thomas and chided him for demanding proof of his resurrection. Jesus said to him, 'In your belief, will be your salvation.' "

Click. I'm watching ESPN waiting for the lowlights of a Reds loss and the next thing I know, Kevin Costner is at the anchor's desk with a special news report. Cheryl Hanover is at his side. He says Annika's plane went down over the Atlantic. There were no survivors. He says, "Not even God could save them. It makes you wonder, doesn't it: What's the point to it all?" Then Costner breaks down, crying. Cheryl Hanover tries to comfort him, first by rubbing his back, then by kissing him hard on the lips. The color bars of technical difficulties appear on the screen and I wake up.

I'm not sweating, I'm not panicked. It's just a dream. I'm happy, although I suppose it would have been nice if my brother had been on the plane with them.

You can't have everything.

I guess this makes me a pretty shitty person, dreaming about the death of my family. Maybe I am. But it doesn't mean I don't love them. Maybe it just means I love them more when they're not around.

Everything else, though, is true. It must be. I saw it on the news.

Click. I'm fresh out of the shower, watching Cheryl Hanover in my room.

She's such a tease. "Annika Anderson returns tonight from her pilgrimage to the healing waters of Lourdes, France. Stay tuned for live footage as she gets off the plane." Even if you weren't infatuated with Cheryl Hanover, you might half expect Annika to walk down the runway all on her own. It's a prospect that keeps me watching through a stream of local car ads, weight loss miracles, and once-in-a-lifetime discount warehouse sale extravaganzas.

When Cheryl returns, she doesn't deliver the goods. Annika gets off the plane just like she got on—on a stretcher. I admit it; I thought she might walk off the plane all by herself. I know, *I know.* It's like hoping the Reds will come back when they're down by five with nobody on and one out to go. Sure, a rally is *possible*, just not very likely, but that doesn't mean I'd change the channel because if they did come back and I was watching a rerun of *Seinfeld*, I'd never stop kicking myself.

A reporter sticks a microphone in Mom's face. He asks if she's disappointed. Mom says she has more hope now than she did before. She says, "Just because Annika's not walking on the ground, it doesn't mean she's not walking with God." You can tell she has a lot more to say about God and faith and the power to heal, but they cut away to a story about who's watching you undress in the changing room at area department stores.

Click.

Chapter 21

IF THE SUMMER HAS a bright spot, it's that Ben was gone for most of it. On tour. I told you how he's a big-shot golfer, right? The best around here since Jack Nicklaus? If I mentioned that already, forgive me. If so, you've only heard it twice. Me? I hear it all the time. I hear it practically every *fucking* day.

Ben was runner-up at the U.S. Amateur Open. Despite not even being on television, it was pretty monumental. I don't know why, but for some reason he wants to graduate from Ohio State before he turns pro.

Turns out to be the stupidest thing he's ever done. School hadn't even started yet and Ben was hanging out, drinking vodka on the roof of the fraternity house where he lives.

He fell. He shattered both his arms. His hands too. His blood alcohol level clocked in at 0.27.

That's a lot of drinks.

It probably didn't hurt as much as he deserved, it being that he was so drunk. What hurts the most, I imagine, is that he'll probably never be the golfer he once was. And without golf, Ben is nothing.

There's a word, apparently, for the way I feel. It's *schadenfreude*. According to the dictionary it means "the malicious satisfaction in the misfortunes of others." But it should be pointed out, *the other*, in this case my brother, has been nothing but malicious to me for my entire life. So really, *schadenfreude* should be thought of as a celebration of karma, a satisfaction in seeing some sense of order arise out of chaos. Quietly approving of karma—that's the way I feel, which is not nearly as sinister as "malicious satisfaction" might otherwise suggest. Really the definition should be *satisfaction in the misfortunes of others who had it coming.* My satisfaction is not malicious at all; it's full of *hope.* It's hinged on an appreciation of this display of cosmic reckoning, on the idea that every once in a while someone gets what he deserves.

I'M AT THE HOSPITAL. *Again.* Not because I really care, but because it's expected. No one notices me here, but if I weren't here, I'd never hear the end of it. After all, *everyone* is here: Mom, Dad, Grandpa, Ben's entire frat house too. The frat boys are all pretty bummed out. Father Ferger, mercifully, is in Cleveland, which means somehow we'll have to get through it all without the benefit of a prayer circle.

Everyone around me is talking about what a great guy Ben is, how they'd do anything for him. It makes me wonder if I can think of one good thing to say about him. It's not easy. I have to spend a while on rewind, flipping through years of tears and humiliation. That's when it hits me. Remember lawn darts? They don't make them anymore, but Ben and I used to play with them at our grandparents' farm. I look fondly back on those days, being carefree and young, tossing lethal projectiles into the air. There were a bunch of times Ben could have tossed one *at me,* but he didn't. Sure, sometimes he'd *pretend,* but he never went through with it. It was almost as if in those few fleeting occasions, Ben actually had a heart. He realized just how much damage a lawn dart could do. And because of Ben's compassion, I've never had a lawn dart stuck in my head. For that small kindness, I'm forever grateful to my brother.

Dad's talking to a bunch of Ben's pals, telling them the story about how he used to golf with Ben and how Ben beat him when he was only nine years old. Dad says he quit playing golf after that. He figured if he couldn't beat a nine-year-old, he had no business being out on the links. "Of course," he says, "Ben shot a seventy-three that day." That gets a big laugh, but not from me.

Dad tried to make a golfer out of me too, but I can understand why he'd rather forget. I sucked. The last time, when I was eight, I lost a dozen balls before we finished the first nine holes. We got cheeseburgers and called it a day. I haven't picked up a club since.

It's okay; he was probably doing me a favor. People make such a big deal about golf, like they're out there splitting atoms, but as I look around at all of Ben's brain-dead golf buddies, finally it all makes sense to me. Thinking on the golf course can only cause problems. The key is just to hit the ball toward the hole. It's no more difficult than that. Thinking only screws everything up. No wonder Ben is so good at it. Or *was.*

As if I'm not already on the verge of puking, Dad goes on to talk about Ben's "infectious love of life." For so long, I thought Ben's main love was making my life miserable. But maybe I'm the only one he treats that way. Maybe to everyone else he's just a burst of sunshine. At least, that's what you'd think from what his friends have to say. *Oh Ben. Always there with a funny joke. Ben, always there to help you out. Ben, always there to drink a beer. Ben, always thinking about everyone but himself.*

I wish I knew that Ben.

You'd think we really were at his funeral, all the nice things people are saying.

By the way, you might as well know, Ben almost died doing what he loves—playing golf. He was hitting balls off the roof of his frat house. His brothers bet him he couldn't hit a sorority about three hundred yards down the street. Indeed, he could. With one swing, he shattered their bathroom window. He's just that good.

But nothing could break his fall.

I KNOW BEN is Dad's favorite. The writing is on the wall. Literally. At Dad's office, the pictures of Ben outnumber me and Annika about five to one. I never wanted to read the obvious out loud, but it's true. I might as well. Dad can always brag about Ben if he wants, but he doesn't have to. People know about Ben. They do the bragging for

Dad. They know he's a great golfer, *the best around here since Jack Nicklaus*. All Dad ever has to do is bask in the praise.

There's nothing about me he can brag about, even if he wanted to. They wouldn't even let me be the equipment manager for the *junior* varsity baseball team, let alone play. And no one really cares if you make the honor roll. That's pretty much expected. A given. Even Ben gets great grades. I don't mean to sell myself short. Sometimes people compliment us on how nice our front yard looks and I guess I am responsible for that. It's true; I do have a way with the weed whacker. And no one can take that away from me.

Dad's not taking Ben's accident well. Like something was stolen from *him*, like it's *his* arms that are in casts. Sure, he pretends he's all right, but he isn't. For a lawyer, he's not a very good liar. He walks around like he's holding his breath, waiting for the next bad thing to happen. It seems like every minute, he lets out a lungful of air, a loud exasperated breath, like it's all just too much to bear. Maybe if he would just breathe in and breathe out, *breathe in and breathe out*. Maybe if he could just do that, he wouldn't feel like the world was collapsing on him. Someone should tell him that. He can go to Father Ferger. He offers his services all the time; he always wants to *talk*. But somehow, I doubt Dad'll take the bait. If there's someone in his life he can talk to, I have no idea who it might be. All I know is that he doesn't want to talk to me and even if he did, I wouldn't know what to say.

Mom has convinced herself Ben's accident is part of God's plan. "This is an opportunity for Ben," she says. It's a nice thought and I envy her capacity for believing there's some order in a world where everything seems so arbitrary. There's a kid down the block and he's probably seven or eight years old. His parents are so afraid something might happen to him, they make him wear a helmet wherever he goes. He looks like quite the special spirit, but at least you know someone loves him enough to make sure he doesn't crack his head open on the pavement. I'm not saying I wish Mom and Dad would have slapped a helmet on my head and I probably wouldn't have worn one if they had. But it would have been nice if they'd cared enough to try.

THE DAY BEN MOVES back into the house is supposed to be the day I move into the dorms at Ohio State, but I don't. I stay. Why not flee? *Get out. Get a life. Move on.* It's not like my mom really needs me. She's got plenty of help. Despite everything, she's happier than I've ever seen her. And Dad, well, he doesn't *need* anybody.

This will probably come out all wrong. If it does, I'm sorry. I know this is Mom's show; she's the lifeline here. Even skeptics say so—*the biggest miracle going on at the Anderson house is Jeannie Anderson's love for her daughter.* Maybe that's true, but without me here, I think Mom's love would probably kill Annika. She'd be toast. I know that sounds drastic and possibly quite self-serving, but think about it: Annika would be on a diet of Bible stories and sad miserable letters from sick people plus Neil Diamond and show tunes. And that's all she'd get. After a while, that would warp anyone. If someone doesn't feed Annika Otis Redding records and ball games and box scores, she'll become completely brainwashed. At least with me around, she has a chance.

That's why I don't move out of the house. While living at home isn't exactly how I expected to spend my freshman year at college, I'm probably not missing much. The dorms at OSU are notoriously nasty. They corral the freshmen into an architectural monstrosity affectionately known as the Suicide Towers. Residents used to routinely jump out of the windows, especially in the wake of a defeat by the football team, but after calculating the loss of tuition versus the cost of fixing the problem, the university eventually decided to seal the windows up. Now if you want to kill yourself, you have to be a bit more creative.

Before all of this happened, there was a story in the paper about this guy who was driving on a rural road in Nebraska. The sun was setting and a deer jumped out of a patch of corn. The guy missed the deer, but he ended up landing his car in a ditch. It wasn't a well-traveled road and it was getting dark. Pinned in the car and unable to move his arms, it looked like it was going to be a long night. At first he was happy his favorite Lee Greenwood CD was there to keep him company, but somehow during the accident, the repeat button was pushed and he was left listening to "I'm Proud to Be an American" over and over. And over. And over again. Catch a sliver of it flipping through the radio and it can ruin your whole day; just imagine what listening to it all night can do.

Four and a half hours after the sun came up, someone spotted the car. At that point, the victim in question had been listening to "I'm Proud to Be an American" for fourteen hours. That's like 250 times. He used to love that song. He used to love Lee Greenwood. The man admitted it himself. In Nebraska, apparently it's nothing to be ashamed of. But now whenever he hears that song he can't move all over again. He's literally paralyzed. Play the magic chord and he's stuck on pause. For many people, it might not be so hard to avoid that song, but as a fan of both NASCAR and Fox News, sadly, the man from Nebraska has found it virtually impossible, leaving him to spend his days just one patriotic outburst away from freezing in place.

If music has the power to paralyze you, is it so crazy to think the whole process could work in reverse?

I COULD TELL you about how the seasons change, but everything stays the same. I could tell you how the doctors say the longer someone is locked in a persistent vegetative state, the less likely it is to be reversed. I could tell you all about how even the most remarkable circumstances don't feel that way when you're in the middle of it all. I could tell you all about these things, but it seems I already have.

Besides, I'd be wrong. Because while some things stay the same, some things *don't*.

Like Ben.

The way he's acting, you'd think he fell on his head, not on his hands. In fact, he's been so *nice*, you might think he's retarded. A nice retard like Forrest Gump, not the mean retard of Ben's former glory. It's a Ben that's easy to like. He hasn't called me a stupid fucker since he's been back. Not once.

There's not a whole lot Ben can do besides watch television. Both of his arms are in casts from his armpits to the tips of his fingers. He's completely helpless. He can't feed himself and he most certainly can't change the channels. It would be easy to say that that's why he's being nice to me. Because he's helpless. But the truth is, he doesn't *really* need me at all. The infrastructure for around-the-clock care is in place. I'm just an appendage.

Television brings families together or, at least, sometimes brings them together in the same room. Sure, Ben and I have watched television together over the years, but it hasn't exactly been a binding force. Ben always ruled the remote with an iron wrist, but it was a reign never worth rebelling over. In this house, if you don't like what's on, you can always find a TV in another room more amenable to your tastes. There are so many TVs around here, anyone can preside over their own little corner of the TV world. As you move from room to room, it's like flicking through the channels without ever having to lift a thumb. But right now, Ben's thumbs aren't able to do the job. So here I am.

Ben, it should be no surprise, likes to watch golf. There's a channel where that's all they show twenty-fours hours a day. It seems to be relaxing for him to call everyone a *stupid fucker*. Even Tiger Woods. "What a dumbass," Ben says.

As long as he's not calling *me* a dumbass, I don't mind. Not so surprisingly, Ben has an excellent eye for golf. He's always saying how someone should *go for it* here or *lie up* there. Someday, he might just make a really good caddy. But I don't say that. Right now, everyone's supposed to talk about how Ben will be better in no time. How this is just a bump in the road. It's hard to say that, though, after seeing the X rays of his powdered bones. It looks like he has about as much chance of playing golf competitively again as a shattered piece of Waterford crystal reassembled with glue has of holding water.

Controlling the remote is a big responsibility; you have to be on the same wavelength with the other viewers. Knowing when to change what's on is as important as what's on in the first place. Ben's wavelength, fortunately, is not such a difficult code to crack. Think cleavage, explosions, golf, beer commercials, ass shots, and more cleavage and you're riding the rail of the lowest common denominator that is the engine for the bulk of American commerce. It's not so tough to get with the program, but smoking pot seems to help.

It's Ben's idea to get high. He's so desperate for a buzz he doesn't seem to mind the humiliation of my holding the joint to his lips. Sadly, the pot smoking only lowers the bar further, landing us in the heady terrain of trying to juggle a *Beverly Hills, 90210* marathon with reruns of *Growing Pains*.

Maybe Ben's newfound civility isn't because he saw the light as he fell off the fraternity roof or because he can't fend for himself or even because he's stoned. Maybe it's because he's in love.

Remember that hot nurse from the hospital when Annika first had her accident? Nurse Finnerty? Ben's been dating her ever since; even when he was on the road they'd still see each other. Her real name's Lisa and she's not nearly as stuck-up as I assumed she was, you know, from being so pretty. Every time she comes over, she remembers my name and gives me a hug. Mom says she's a sweetheart and it's hard to disagree.

Her sweetness must be infectious; Ben doesn't kick me out of the basement when she comes over. Obviously, if he needs the channel changed, she can do it for him. The last time I was down there with him and a girl was when he was in high school. It was there, as I hid inside a trunk, that Ben unwittingly gave me an aural lesson on the finer points of seduction. The highlights of the seminar included: Saying "I love you" is fair game even if you don't know the girl's last name, it only takes two to play strip poker, and if all else fails, *no* means *yes*. I also learned it's best not to get caught hiding inside a trunk. You might end up staying there a lot longer than you bargained for.

But with Lisa, it's different. I don't have to hide in the trunk, not that I'd really want to. Lisa doesn't seem to mind having me around at all. Maybe it's because she likes to smoke too. That's probably it, but I don't mind. I don't feel used, getting them high, but maybe that's just because I'm so used to being ignored.

Lisa's not all into God like she made out when we first met at the hospital. When I ask her if she really thinks the air conditioner splooge Jesus on the side of the building was the work of God, she says, "No more or no less than anything else," which seems like a nice way to say you believe, without jamming it down anyone's throat.

It used to be I didn't understand what any girl could see in Ben beyond the small degree of celebrity his exploits on the golf course accorded him. Now that Ben's claim to fame is stuck knee-deep in a sand trap, it might seem especially shocking that someone like Lisa would *still* be interested in Ben. They've been together for about five months and now that his future is in jeopardy, it'd be a perfect time for her to bail, but she's sticking around. In fact, she's been very supportive. It's not like they sit around praying about his recovery, but I've heard her tell Ben how a little faith goes a long way. The thing about Lisa is that she doesn't need Ben to be who he was. She doesn't need him to be a star. She's got her own life. She's raking in the cash as a nurse and once she has enough, she's going to enroll in med school. She's so smart and beautiful; if she wants respect, she doesn't have to rub it off someone else to get it. Maybe that's why Ben likes her so much, but it still doesn't explain why she puts up with him.

Lisa likes to tease me. While we're watching *The Graduate,* she says, "Hey Monroe, has Maggie ever made a play on you?"

"She'll barely even look at me," I say. *"Thank God."*

"Well, God must have it out for me," Ben says in his closest statement to self-pity since his accident. "Maggie keeps asking to give me a sponge bath."

"Hey, that's *my* job," says Lisa.

"That's what I told her," he says. "But she keeps asking. What can I say? I know it's sexy, being an invalid. Like how chicks are all into *The English Patient.* They love it when you're helpless, like in handcuffs or something. Isn't that right, baby?" he asks, angling for a kiss.

"When was the last time you brushed your teeth?" she replies.

My completely involuntary laughter is repaid with, "You know, Monroe, maybe if you had a broken arm, Maggie might be into you too," eliciting the familiar fear in my eyes he's looking for. Before he can be berated, he says to Lisa, "I'm just kidding. I used to be kind of a dick to my brother."

I can't believe he actually said that. It's almost like an apology.

"But not anymore, right Monroe?" he asks.

"Being handicapped has really brought out the best in you," I say.

"It was all for his own good—what doesn't kill you makes you stronger, isn't that right, bro?" he says, cocking his plastered arm, like he's going to hit me again.

While the question of whether or not Ben is a dick is still up in the air, it doesn't stop people from sending him get-well cards and presents all the time. The phone is always ringing. His friends are always coming over. He made Mom promise not to tell the pilgrims he's here. She doesn't tell, but they find out anyway. Despite Ben's protests, they still have a prayer vigil for him. If you've seen one vigil, you've seen them all, unless, of course, roses start falling from the sky. But that doesn't happen when people pray for Ben. Whatever grace Ben picked up when he fell quickly goes out the window in a stream of profanity. He yells at the pilgrims from his room and tells them all to get a life. "I don't want your fucking prayers," he screams. But that doesn't stop them. It just makes them pray more.

After that, Ben gets out of here as soon as he can and moves in with Lisa to convalesce in peace.

In eight weeks they'll take off his casts and he'll be as good as new. That's what the doctors will say. They'll be shocked. They'll be awed. But they won't say it's a miracle.

They'll leave that to everyone else.

Chapter 22

IT'S BEEN A YEAR since Ben fell and I still haven't moved out of the house. Annika still bleeds about once a week. People still come, hoping to get healed. And some of them do. We still bombard Annika's senses and sometimes it feels like she's about to break through, but she never does.

Sometimes I catch a whiff of Dad's cologne, but that's about the extent of our interaction. He spends a lot more time out of town than he used to. When he is here, he drinks. He still thinks he's being sly, sticking with vodka, but his habit is as obvious as the spiderweb of capillaries forming on his nose. I used to find the bottles hidden in the bottom of the trash can, but I don't bother looking anymore. I *know* he's a drunk; it's not like I need to gather evidence. There will be no trial. Dad convicts himself every day all on his own.

Grandpa still lives with us. He says, "The best thing about getting old is you can just be yourself and no one can say a damn thing about it." Everyone, that is, except Dad.

Dad wants Grandpa to move into an old folks home or, as he calls it, *a retirement community*. He says it'd be for his own good. I heard him making his case to Mom. It's not that he *wants* him to leave; it's just that the evidence demands it. Exhibit A: Grandpa leaves *Playboy* magazines around the house. Exhibit B: He walks around naked, especially when Maggie's around to see him. Exhibit C: Despite repeated objections, he skinny-dips in the pool. Do you see a pattern here? That's hardly evidence of a man who's losing it. It seems to me, he's *living* it up.

Good thing for Grandpa's libido, slightly spry widows on the prowl are among Annika's biggest fans. They show up at our door three days a week and Grandpa's always there to check out the latest batch. You know how snapping turtles just sit at the bottom of a pond? How they have a little wiggly piece of flesh in the back of their mouth that looks like a worm? All they have to do is sit there and wait. Eventually a little fish will swim right in their mouth and snap goes the trap. Annika's kind of like that little worm, inviting the fishes to come on in, and then Grandpa goes in for the kill.

That's right, I'm not the only one around here who's slept with a pilgrim. Which brings us to Exhibit D: I don't know how many notches Grandpa's carved in his bedpost since he's been here, but there's been at least one. Dad busted him in the garage/chapel going at it with a blue-haired vixen on the offering table.

I don't think Dad *wanted* to see Grandpa's naked white ass in action. He just got lucky. Certainly, it's an indignity an eighty-two-year-old man hardly deserves to endure; but that must have been part of the fun, the possibility of getting caught. I'm not exactly sure how it went down. I imagine Dad mumbling his apologies and getting out of there as fast as he could. I really don't know. I heard Dad tattling to Mom about the whole thing, like it was the end of the world. Like he'd just witnessed the mushroom clouds of the apocalypse coming this way. And the beauty of it all was that Mom didn't even really care. "Oh, Larry. I'm sure you're *exaggerating.* Let him have his fun," she said.

That's about as exciting as it's gotten around here lately.

PAUL'S DAD GOT REMARRIED and Paul decided to leave town. He said it's time to go, even though he's not sure where to. He figures he'll know when he gets there. He asked me if I wanted to take over the lawn-cutting business. I said, *Sure why not?* I've been taking classes at Ohio State, but I have a lot of free time. So I bought his Scout, two lawn mowers, and a snowplow. As a bonus, he anointed me the keeper of his vinyl collection. It's not mine to keep; I'm just in charge of making sure nothing bad happens to it while he's gone. From Cannonball Adderley to Stevie Wonder, everything that matters is just a needle drop away.

While cutting lawns is seasonal, people need work done for them all year long. Like shoveling snow in the winter. Especially *last* winter. I'd have a driveway cleared in the morning and I'd be back that night to do it again. Like Paul says, "When it snows, it snows cash."

Which is not to say Paul cares about money. It was just something he did because it's what he *always* did. And if you want to know the truth, I think Paul liked being sixteen a lot more than being twenty-two. I expanded the operation, not because I'm some huge capitalist, but because it makes the day go by quicker. The key to this job is to become indispensable, and it's really not so hard. Rich people can't do anything for themselves, so I do whatever needs to be done, and if I can't do it, I find someone who can.

Within the first few months, I expanded into odd jobs and hauling away junk—that's where the real money is. This isn't the kind of neighborhood where people have garage sales. They give away their old junk, usually to Goodwill, but sometimes to their maids. Basically, they want someone to make it disappear, and the sooner the better. That's the kind of instant gratification my clients crave. People give me the greatest stuff—from broken Tiffany lamps and paintings, to boxes of baseball cards and comic books, to designer clothes and old watches. I sell it all.

People are always asking me what I'm going to do with my life. I feel like I'm already doing it, that this *is* my life. But I don't tell them that. It'll just disappoint them. I tell them how much I enjoy my classes at OSU. I tell them I'm thinking about medical school, which is the last place in the world I'd ever go. But it's what they like to hear, the implication being that if the current state of modern medicine can't save my sister, I guess I'll just have to do it all by myself. That makes them feel good. And since they pay me cash, it makes them feel like they're contributing to the cause.

But really, I think to myself—why do I bother with school? I'm happy doing what I do. Besides, it's not like I'll ever be someone who changes the world. I don't even know if it's possible. Sure, it's easy to screw the world up—people do that all the time—but cleaning up the mess they leave behind is an entirely different matter. If it meant cutting one yard at a time, if that's what it took to make a difference, maybe I could lead the charge; but somehow I doubt that's the answer.

After all, people don't even notice the changes in their own back-yards. Take the Irvings. They live in an ivy-covered brick house, so I cut their lawn with the exact meat and potatoes geometrically precise lines found at Wrigley Field. Or there's the Baxters. They live on Camden Street, so I gave them the diagonal crisscross cut pioneered by the groundskeeper at Camden Yards in Baltimore. And let's not forget the Banks. Since they're from New York and never shut up about the Yankees, I gave them the star cut like they do at Fenway in Boston. You know, just to stick it to them. And do any of them ever notice?

No.

Changing the world one lawn at a time is clearly not working.

In fact, the people with the nicest yards are probably the biggest part of the problem. Tell me what to do and I'll do it, but sometimes it seems the best thing anyone can do for the world is to just do nothing at all. At least then you're not screwing everything up.

When I was a kid, I thought the famines and the murders and the genocide and the wars and greed—I thought that they were just stories that landed at our front door and got in the way of the sports page. Stories that made me change the channel on the TV. I used to think that maybe those stories weren't even real, that maybe all those tales of pain and suffering so far away were just there to make us thankful for what we have.

But that seems like a long time ago.

And the stories still come to our doorstep, but now they're people—living, *breathing* people. They're all sick. They're all broken. They're all grasping at straws. And they're here, practically every day.

It's been going on so long that it feels practically normal. If they bring with them a lesson, it's to be thankful for what you have before it goes away. Sure, everyone knows that already, but nobody *really* knows until it's too late.

People still always ask me how Annika is and I say, "The same." And they say they're sorry and then we move on to something else. The thing is, she just turned twelve years old. Soon she'll be hitting puberty and I won't be able to say she's the same anymore. Soon I'll be saying, "Oh, she's just a typical teenager—kind of shy, withdrawn, sleeps a lot."

I DRIVE BY the Morgans' house about once a month and leave a flyer on their door advertising my services. It's not the kind of street I usually troll for new clients. The people on Holly Lane tend to take care of their own lawns. It's something they look forward to. Except, apparently, the Morgans, who seem to be going for a more natural, overgrown look. If not for the same station wagon that's been sitting there for the last ten years, it'd be easy to think no one lives there at all.

With all the bad memories just a block away, it's amazing they haven't packed that car up and driven away. This is a dead-end street; you can't leave here without going by the scene of the crime. With every trip to the grocery store, with every run to the bank, they *must* think about the day she died. I know when I drive by, I do.

Then again, maybe *everything* makes them think of Heidi and that ditch is just one more reminder. Maybe after a while, it doesn't matter anymore.

After leaving ten flyers, Mrs. Morgan finally calls me. She says she has a few odd jobs around the house.

I tell her I'll be right over.

Mrs. Morgan has hair that runs down to her waist. It's not often that you see an older woman grow her hair so long and I guess by looking at her you know why. It's brown and stringy with slivers of gray and probably chock full of split ends. Maybe she thinks if she grows her hair long enough, she'll be able to pull herself out of the hole she's in, but that's probably being a bit too optimistic. She looks like she could walk into traffic any minute.

We sit down in their living room and she goes over a list of chores she needs to have done: *Fix the banister, put in a towel rack, snake the kitchen sink, clean out the attic* . . . The usual. Nothing out of my league. I'm barely listening though. I know she'll hand over the list—they always do. Right now, my focus is on Heidi's shrine. After all these years, I can't believe I'm looking at it. That it actually exists.

It revolves around a picture of Heidi above the mantel. She's in a forest looking shyly at the camera, trying to hide behind a dried-up leaf. There's a stretch of woods by the ditch they found her in. It's hard not to imagine that the picture could have been taken minutes before she was killed.

Dozens of pictures fan out from the mantle like a trail of crumbs leading you through Heidi's life. No matter where you sit, she's always looking at you and you're always looking at her—a budding beauty trapped in time.

It must comfort the Morgans to have her around like this. I always thought it would be creepy, but it's not. After all, we have a shrine in our home too. It's a living shrine, I suppose. Not only does its subject still breathe, but at the root of our shrine lies some hope that Annika will come back to us.

The Morgans, though, have no hope. Heidi will *never* come back, so they've memorialized her to the point that you can feel her presence, you can almost *hear* her. Her life was cut short, but the Morgans are still grasping at the strings. Mrs. Morgan's eyes say the longer she holds on to the threads of her lost daughter, the more her own life unravels.

Mrs. Morgan sees me looking at the pictures of Heidi and asks me about Annika. She tells me she'll never forget seeing her face in the moon, even though it was only the moon on television. "She had that look like everything was going to be all right. It's so hard to believe that sometimes, you know?"

I tell her I do.

"There's a man in Kansas who says he can see Heidi's face in the clouds. He says she waves to him every day. Can you believe that? I know he's insane, just another nut. I *know* that. I do. But he sends me pictures—every week twenty-four new ones. A brand-new roll. They're just photos of clouds, that's all. Storm clouds, fluffy clouds, clouds that don't look like clouds at all. Allison tells me I shouldn't open them at all. She thinks I should just throw them away. But I can't do that. I look forward to those photos. Every week I try to find my sweet little girl's face, I do. But I never can. I know it's crazy," she says.

I just listen. That's all most people seem to really want. She tells me how blessed we are that Annika's still alive. She says she prays for her every day. I tell her I do too, even though I don't. I don't think this makes me a liar. It just makes me easier to talk to.

"Allison says you were in her class."

"I didn't get to know her as well as I would have liked. How's she doing?"

She says I can find out for myself. She's upstairs. She'll probably be down in a few hours. She likes to sleep late.

Mrs. Morgan looks around, surveying the room. "This place has gone to hell since Jack left," she says, like it's the first time she noticed.

They're divorced. This happens all the time when parents lose a child. That's what Father Ferger says. I used to listen in when he'd counsel Mom and Dad back when all this started. When you need someone the most, they're too wrapped up in their own grief to be there for you . . . or maybe they've gotten over it and you haven't . . . or maybe they blame you . . . or you blame them. Father Ferger said losing a child is the hardest thing a parent could ever face. I guess that's where I first heard it. Looking at Mrs. Morgan, it must be even harder to face alone.

She's wearing a housecoat. It's old and frayed. Her pasty legs are peeking out. She smells like cat food, but I don't see a cat anywhere.

I tell her she has beautiful hair and she laughs. She says she hasn't cut it since Heidi "left." It stopped growing years ago. She says she thinks maybe she should cut it again, but she hasn't gotten around to it.

It looks like the days go so slowly around here, it must all be a blur.

I get to work cleaning out the garage. *Everything must go.* I love it when people say that, but in this case she's right—there's nothing in here worth saving.

As I'm hauling the last of the junk out to the curb, Allison walks up to me with a glass of lemonade in her hand.

"My mom said to give you this," she says, handing over the glass.

"Thanks, Allison."

She seems momentarily surprised that I know her name, like it's been so long since someone called her that, she'd forgotten it herself.

"You're welcome, *Monroe.*"

"This is really good lemonade," I say.

"It's concentrated. You might as well be drinking Kool-Aid."

"Oh."

"I never pegged you as the blue-collar type. Hauling garbage."

I'm surprised she pegged me as any type at all.

"I never really pegged myself that way, either."

She says she's so glad high school is over. It was a nightmare. "College would probably be a lot better if I didn't live *here.* Man, it sucks to be a Buckeye."

Truer words were never spoken.

She says, "OSU turns everyone into a cow. There must be like five hundred kids in my psych class."

"Me too." Turns out we're in the same class and don't even know it.

"So, is our house anything like you thought?"

"What do you mean?"

"I *know* what people say. How it's a shrine to my sister. How my mom is like completely insane. I know how people are around here. Of all people, I'd think *you'd* know what I'm talking about."

"It's not as bad as I thought, I guess."

"Yeah, well at least we don't charge admission."

A lot of people think that, but it's not true. Mom practically gets a rash when people think we're putting on this show for profit. She likes to say the only currency she deals in is *faith*. I tell Allison we don't charge admission, but I wish we would. Then maybe not so many people would show up.

"So what's up with the stigmata?"

Most people don't bring that up. It's the elephant in the corner, the boil on your nose, and the hair on Dad's back all rolled up in one.

"I wish I knew."

"If you're the one who slices her palms, it's okay—you can tell me. It's not like I'm going to blow your cover."

"Believe me, I *wish* it was a hoax. Then everyone would leave us alone." She looks at me skeptically, her eyebrow arched. "And that's the truth," I say, not altogether convincingly.

"The truth only fucks everything up," she says. "It's lies that make the world go around. It's lies that make people happy."

Between saying that and the way she arches her eyebrow, it would have been impossible not to ask her out.

Chapter 23

WHEN ALLISON GETS IN my car, the first thing out of her mouth is, "I could really use a drink." Clearly, she has a knack for saying all the right things.

Within a minute, I'm pulling into the parking lot of the closest bar. There aren't any bars in what you'd call Chelsea *proper*, but the Leopard Spot is on the *other* side of Route 33, less than a minute away from Allison's house. It attracts an older crowd, mainly singles who live in the condos that line the river. It's nothing special, really: dark booths, lame jukebox, fried appetizers. Unless they're slumming, people from Chelsea don't come here.

We beeline through a maze of chairs to a booth in the back. Allison says she's never been here before, but she's always wondered what it was like inside. Behind the gauze of smoke, she's a different girl than the one I met earlier today—she's not so sure of herself, out of place.

It's easy not to notice how pretty Allison is. Her dusty brown hair is limp, her face is plain, and her skin is pasty, but the more I talk to her, the better-looking she gets. I've barely even put a dent in the drink, so I can't even blame it on that. And the better-looking she gets, the more, it seems, she can see right through me. The bar, though, has an amber glow. Everyone, it seems, is basted in honey.

"People never know what to say to me," she says.

"Maybe you don't make it very easy."

"That's only because I never know what to say to them either."

Sometimes I think the only good conversations I ever have are with myself. That's when it comes to me. "You ever feel like you're completely invisible, but if you weren't around everything would fall apart?"

At first, she looks kind of surprised. Then she searches my eyes to see if I'm just making fun of her. I'm not.

"Welcome to my life," she says.

Once Allison starts talking, there's no way I'm going to stop her. It all just spills out, a secret she's been dying to tell.

"Ever since my dad bailed, all I ever hear from my mom is *You're all I have left*. She says it like it's a good thing. Sometimes I don't even blame my dad for running away. I wish I could do it all the time, but he beat me to it. He moved to Arizona a year and a half after the murder and all we got was a fucking note. Can you believe that? A *note*. After fifteen years of marriage and two kids. His clothes are still in the closet, like my mom thinks he's going to come back or something. Like that would be a *good thing*. The night he left, I found Mom in the garage sitting there in the car, the engine still running. It's pathetic. She'd only been in there for like five minutes, but I just *knew*. She must think I'm as stupid as she is. She said she was listening to a song on the radio, like she wasn't doing anything wrong. Can you imagine wanting to die to Simon and Garfunkel? Anyway, I haven't seen my dad since. Don't really want to. Now my mom walks around like a ghost and if I leave, I'm afraid she'll just disappear. I know she's fucked-up and everything, but I love her. I could be at Northwestern right now. When I told Mom I got in, she swallowed a whole bottle of aspirin. What a bitch, huh?"

Then she catches herself. "So, like I said, welcome to my life. I can't believe I just told you that. I'm sure I just broke every dating rule ever written. I'd totally understand if you wanted to bolt. My shrink says I'm a self-saboteur, but I think you should know the truth. It's only fair." Panic flushes her face. "This is a date, right?"

"Unless you want to pay for your own drinks."

"A date it is, then," she says, smiling.

That's when I see Dad at the bar. He's not alone.

"I spooked you, didn't I?" she asks.

"Fuck," I say. "My dad's here."

"So?"

"He's with a woman. Not my mom."

"Men are such pigs."

I want to defend him, say it's not the way it looks, that he's *not* a pig. It's probably just a client, *it's business.* But I don't say that.

That wouldn't be so convincing. Not when he's nibbling on her neck.

"Let's get out of here."

Allison says, "Sure, we can leave. But first, let's think this through. I bet right now you're thinking you don't want him to see you. That's what I'd be thinking if I were you. But if you don't let him know that you know, you'll hate yourself. Guaranteed."

"How do you know?"

"My dad left town with his secretary—fucking pathetic, right? Well, I knew—months before anything ever went down. I used to go downtown in the summer and have lunch with him once a week and I could just tell, it was so obvious—so obvious that there wasn't even some detail you could point to and say, *See? I know what you're up to,* so I never said a word. I guess I didn't want to believe it, as if somehow by not saying anything, it would make it less true . . . but now I think that maybe if I had said something, maybe he would have caught himself, you know? Maybe he would have never left."

I tell her it's not right for her to blame herself.

She smiles *thanks,* but says, "It's like life's this slippery slope and we're never really in control and sometimes it seems like running into a tree is the worst thing that could ever happen, when really it's what stops us from going over the cliff."

The waitress comes up and asks if we need anything. I tell her to bring two strawberry daiquiris to the couple at the bar. I give her a twenty and tell her to keep the change.

"Daiquiris?"

"Yeah, Dad used to make them for my mom all the time during the summer."

"Nice touch."

Dad's looking around, squinting his eyes, as the waitress points out the origin of his frothy tropical bounty. He sees me and I wave. Allison holds up her glass.

Cheers.

Chapter 24

DAD FILLS UP a suitcase and drives away. I guess he'll come back and get the rest of his stuff later. If not, a few decent consignment shops around here will be happy to take away the contents of his closet. He's got some pretty nice suits. Nothing flashy. Just *nice*.

But before we get to the fallout, maybe we should go back to the explosion that preceded it.

Back at the bar, Dad thinks he can smooth it all over by talking to us. That's what he does. He negotiates. He settles. He makes everything all right. *A good lawyer never lets it get to trial.* That's what he always says. But I'm not going to let him talk his way out of this one.

He brings his friend over. Actually, he doesn't call her that. He says she's his "colleague." Her name is Elanna Baxter. She's probably thirty-five. I guess you could say she's hot, but it looks like she puts some work into it. And when you start thinking about someone going to all the trouble—primping and preening—all of a sudden they're not so pretty anymore. He says they've been "taking depositions."

"So how long have you been sleeping with my dad?" I ask.

I can't believe I said that, but I did. I swear, those exact words. I figure I'm safe here. It's not like he can hit me. After all, we're in public and he's with his mistress.

"I apologize for my son. It seems he's had too much to drink," Dad says in a feeble attempt to turn the tables. Like this is all about *me*.

"I hope we get a chance to meet again under more favorable circumstances," she says. Truth is, she seems *nice*. She probably doesn't deserve this; but then again she is an adulterer, so I spit out, "I don't. I hope I never see you again." Looking back, I realize I probably sounded like a six-year-old all broken up over a dropped ice-cream cone.

Before Dad can scurry her away he says, "I'll look forward to seeing you later, *Monroe*. And don't expect the circumstances to be *favorable*." He says it all sinister, like I'm going to be grounded for the rest of my life, even if I am nineteen years old.

I'm certainly in no rush to get home now, so Allison and I get as drunk as Dad thinks I am. It takes us only about two hours to collect enough umbrellas to weather this storm. But I'm not the one who should be afraid. He is. After all, I saw him kissing *her*. I have all the proof I need. He's the one who should be worried, not me.

"My dad's going to kill me," I say.

"I doubt that," she says. "At the rate you guys are going, you may just be the best bet to keep up the family name."

"It's not like there won't be any more Andersons."

"Well, when you put it that way, maybe we should have one more drink."

When we pull up to Allison's house, there's a police car in the driveway.

"Did we break your curfew?" I ask.

"Oh, that's Officer O'Neill. It's no big deal. He came over to have dinner with my mom tonight." As if on cue, the front door opens and the cop's now saying good-bye to Mrs. Morgan.

"Your mom's dating a cop?"

"It's the closest she comes to having a date, but actually he's the lead detective on Heidi's case. He comes over about once a month and tells her how the investigation is coming along. He's pretty much Mom's last hope they're ever going to find out who killed Heidi. Truth is, at this point, he's the only one in the Chelsea Police Department who really cares."

I'd really like to kiss Allison, but O'Neill is making his way to my car. I roll my window down and he says, "So you're Monroe Anderson?"

"Yes, sir," I say.

He's leaning over, making sure I can see his holstered gun. "You better treat this young lady right."

"Of course," I say.

"I know where you live," he adds, menacingly, eliciting what must be a look of complete horror. "Ahh, I'm just screwing with you," he laughs, slapping the top of the Scout. "Hey there, Ally, how's it going. This young man behaving himself?"

"Shouldn't you be getting back to your wife?" asks Allison. "Oh right, she left you. I almost forgot."

"You got a real firecracker on your hands," he says, nudging my arm. And with that, he hitches up his trousers and ambles off to his cruiser.

Then Allison kisses me. It's a nice kiss. It really is; but it's hard to enjoy, considering that O'Neill is looking at us from his car's rearview mirror. But before it can get weird, Allison's out the door, saying, *See you later, good luck, let me know how it goes.* As she's heading up the driveway, I'm thinking it wasn't so weird that I couldn't have handled kissing her a little bit longer.

I'M SURPRISED DAD'S car isn't in the driveway when I get home. I guess the meeting with his *colleague* ran late. So I wait. Everyone's asleep and the house is quiet. I go into Annika's room and check on her. She's the same as she ever was. Mom's got her listening to the Bible on tape for like the millionth time. Tonight she's on Revelation, and despite all the fireworks that book entails, I'm not taking any chances it will drown out whatever's about to go down between Dad and me. She doesn't need to be exposed to that.

I slip her a dose of Parliament, which I just can't get enough of and neither can she. *Make My Funk the P. Funk / I wants to get funked up.*

Who can resist that? I still like to think these beats, these funkadelic grooves are a drug, an antidote to the monotonous ramblings of the Bible. It gives her a fighting chance against the Armies of God, which is not to say that this is a battle of good versus evil. It's a battle against boredom. A battle against brainwashing. All Annika needs to do is let the soldiers of funk roll in. All she needs to do is succumb to the commandments of the grandmaster of Funk, the sage George Clinton—and maybe then all that ails her will be cured.

> Now this is what I want you all to do:
> If you got faults, defects or shortcomings,
> You know, like arthritis, rheumatism or migraines,
> Whatever part of your body it is,
> I want you to lay it on your radio, let the vibes flow through.
> Funk not only moves, it can re-move, dig?
> The desired effect is what you get
> When you improve your Interplanetary Funksmanship.

I wish I could board the mothership with Annika and fly far away from here, but instead I go in the family room and wait in silence. Annika will have to take this journey on her own.

I sit in what technically would be Dad's chair, but he spends so little time in here, it's really not his anymore. The only reason I know he'll come in here is because this is where he keeps the vodka.

I might as well admit it; I'm pretty drunk. This is the first night I've had any hard liquor since the night I threw up a bottle of tequila all over Dad's shoes four years ago.

I don't have to wait long. He heads straight for the bottle, so predictable for a man I hardly know. He pours himself a glass and gulps it down. Hard. Then he looks out the window, but all he sees is his reflection looking back at him. That must be a *disappointment*. He cushions the blow with a deep breath and another drink. He has no idea I'm there.

So I say, "And just when I thought you were going to break your curfew. Have I ever told you how proud Mother and I are of you?" I had that part planned, but that's about as far as I got. From here on out I have no script.

He looks at me blankly and takes another drink, as if maybe the booze will fuel a worthy comeback.

"Tough night of work with your *colleague*? Did you go over your *oral* arguments together?"

Okay, I admit it. I'd already thought of that one too.

"Jesus, Monroe, are you ever going to grow out of the miserable sarcasm? It's really getting *old*."

Technically speaking, what I said wasn't even sarcastic. It was more of a double entendre. But I don't say that. Instead, I go with. "Oh gee, sorry, *Dad,* what I meant to say was—*how's the new fuck*?"

He looks at me hard, his jaw quivering like it could grind glass back into sand. "Is that shooting straight enough for you, Dad?" I say, standing up to him for the first time in my life.

"Watch yourself, Monroe, you're treading on thin ice."

"Maybe you should watch where you put your dick." I'm happy to report that retort was merely the product of quick-witted improvisation.

He rewards my wit by hitting me. In the face. *Hard.* It hurts. I know, it's not like I gave him much of a choice. I just wanted to see how far over the line he's willing to go. He's broken his vows and now he's hit me for the first time—in the last two hours he's become someone else entirely. Before, he was just another boozing lawyer who works too much. Now he cheats on his wife and beats his kids.

"Gee, Dad, you're becoming more and more of a *man* every day. I'm so proud of you."

It's amazing I'm still standing. He recocks his marine-tattooed gun and I'm ready to take the hit, even though the tears running down my face betray me. I don't care, I'm not going to duck. And I *could* if I wanted to. His right hook is about as subtle as the *beep beep* of a garbage truck backing down the street.

What would Jesus do?

His fist connects with a crack. It's my jaw. It's not bone, just the pop of cartilage. I may not be willing to defend myself with my fists, but my mouth has a reflex of its own. My back to the wall, I spit out, "That's great, Dad. Kick my ass just because you're cheating on Mom. That'll make it go away."

The truth, succinct and clear, catches him as he's about to unleash another blow. He doesn't look so tough, just another loser punching at the world. It's a fitting time for my mom to come in and ask, "What's going on in here?"

But she doesn't.

It's just him and me. I have nothing more to say. So I walk away, leaving him there to think about what he's done. To think about what he's become.

The dining room door hits Grandpa on my way out. He's been listening to the whole thing. He pats me on the back and nods his head. Not saying a word. The tears are really flowing now and it's about to get worse, so I run up the stairs. It feels like I'm handing off the baton, like maybe Grandpa's going to go in there and kick Dad's ass, finishing what I wasn't man enough to do.

After a few minutes, Grandpa comes up to my room with a towel full of ice. He says what I did took guts. And that only makes me cry more. No one ever told me I had any guts in my entire life.

I'm still awake at four in the morning when I hear the car door slam in the driveway. It's Dad closing the trunk of his car and driving away.

I fall asleep before he turns onto the main road.

Chapter 25

I'T'S BEEN A WEEK since Dad left and Mom has been acting like nothing's wrong. Like nothing has changed.

And in a lot of ways, it hasn't.

"So, when's Dad coming back? It's been a week," I ask. It's not so much that I care. I'm just making conversation.

Mom's snapping her jaw on a bowl of Grape-Nuts. She's staring out the kitchen window at a squirrel ransacking her squirrel-proof birdfeeder. "We gotta do something about those squirrels," she says.

It's seven a.m. and I'm just here for the coffee. "What about Dad?" I persist.

"I really don't think laying down poison is the answer."

"You know what I mean."

"Your father left us a lot longer than a week ago. You know that."

"You mean, like since the accident?"

"Your father and I were drifting apart for *a long time* before Annika's accident. The accident just made everything a lot clearer. That's all."

It'd be easy to look at Mom and figure she measures out her life in teaspoons of delusion. That's what I used to think. But I don't anymore.

She continues, "I've changed a lot. I know that. And I understand how not everyone else is necessarily going to be on board with what's going on here. Your father isn't a religious man and the truth is, I don't need him to be. But I do need him to respect the choice I've made. He thinks what's going on here is a joke and because of that I'm not sad to see him go."

"I'm not exactly very religious either," I say.

"Neither was I when I was your age."

"So you think I'll come around?"

"I don't know, Monroe. You'll do whatever's right for you. That's all anyone can do. Personally, I think you're a lot more suspicious of the institution than you are of the message. And there's nothing wrong with that. But being Catholic is about a lot more than the Catholic Church. Institutions are like a cover of a book, or a person's body."

"It's what is inside that really counts." I say it a lot snottier than I mean to only because I'm so annoyed that she's right.

"You don't miss Dad?" I ask.

"I've missed your father for a long time. Sometimes I think I fell in love with the idea of who your father could be and not who he really is."

"Is that why I never saw the two of you kiss each other?"

She laughs. "There's a lot more to a relationship than the physical. You'll come to realize that someday."

I guess that's what I'd tell myself too if my husband was just busted cavorting with a younger woman. But I don't say that.

"Do you think he's going to come back?"

"Your father is *not* coming back. He's already offered me a settlement. I get the house, a healthy alimony, and Annika will have a trust that ensures she'll always get the best care, which was really the only thing I was worried about."

My face must say, *What about me?*

"Louise said he'd call you later this week and schedule a lunch."

WE MEET AT a steak house downtown. Dad eats here at least twice a week. He's a regular. I guess he's not worried about me making a scene, about being embarrassed by what I might have to say.

It's noon and I find him working on a beer.

"Well, looks like you're the man of the house now," he says. It sounds cheesy and forced, just like the smiled pasted on his face.

"Sure that doesn't make you want to hit me?"

I know he won't try anything in public, so I figure I can run my mouth with impunity. Then again, I never thought he'd hit me in our own living room either.

"This isn't easy for me, you know."

I'm not just being a smart-ass, but I don't think it should be easy. When you get married, it's supposed to be *forever.* I don't have to tell him; he knows all about the law, promises, and pledges. In fact, he's an expert on how to break them. That's why he gets the big bucks.

"Gee, Dad, if it were *easy,* then I'd have *another* reason to lose respect for you."

"I deserve that," he says. If he was one of those punching-bag clowns that weeble and wobble but don't fall down—that's what it would say. *I deserve that.* Over and over again. "I'm really sorry about the other night, Monroe. I don't think I'll ever be able to forgive myself."

"For which part?"

"For hitting you."

"You mean for hitting me *twice.*"

"Okay, Monroe, I see where this is going. I don't think I'll be able to forgive myself for hitting you *twice.*" He's pissed. But he's trying not to show it. "Anything else?"

"Well, when you were my Little League coach and you only put me in right field for one inning for the championship game—you could apologize for that."

"I shouldn't have done that. I'm sorry, but you really should have said—"

"I'm not done," I say. "There was the time in sixth grade when you told my teacher I had a bed-wetting problem. That really wasn't necessary. Not to mention, factually incorrect."

"I really don't recall . . . I mean I'm sorry."

I'm really starting to enjoy this. "Then there was the time you fell asleep at my school play."

"You were in fifth grade."

"Second grade. I was in *second* grade."

"Monroe, I'm sorry I fell asleep at your play."

Who can blame him? It was pretty boring. I was a rabbit.

"Don't worry about it. It's not like you'll get a chance to do it again."

"The other night," he says. "I wish I could explain."

"We're not done yet. Remember how the Reds went to the World Series in 1990?"

"Yes."

"And how you had tickets and you took Ben and not me?"

"I apologized about that at the time, if I recall."

"And now's your chance to do it again."

"I'm really sorry I didn't take you to see the World Series."

"Why's that, Dad?"

"Because you love the Reds."

"And?"

"Ben doesn't."

"You're getting good at this, Dad."

It's fun to see him so cowed, knowing that he screwed up and not being able to talk his way out of it. He can't make any excuses. All he can do is sit there and take it. Unfortunately, once I realize that, it only makes me feel sorry for him. I know I shouldn't, but I do. But sitting there, defenseless, looking at the foam fizzle in his beer, he's fish in a bucket. And when you realize that's what you're taking shots at, it's not that much fun anymore—unless, of course, you're Ben.

I ask him a question I always wanted to ask but never did: "I wonder, have you ever felt like Mom was cheating on you with God?"

He laughs and says, "I guess she's been looking for something more too."

"When do I get to meet your girlfriend again? I sure hope I didn't make a bad impression."

He says he wouldn't call her that, his *girlfriend*. She's just someone he blows off a little steam with—an image I really don't need to have rubbed in my face. "Your mother and I grew apart." He says it like it's the first time it's ever happened to anyone, like it's some sort of masterful deconstruction of the relationship that took months of therapy to figure out. "When you're in a relationship, it's easy to forget who you are," he says.

"I guess you could say the same thing about working sixteen hours a day."

"Yeah, I guess you could," he says.

"So does this mean you're not going to work so hard?"

"Considering the settlement I offered your mother, I don't think that will be an option." He takes another drink. "The Clippers are back in town next week. Maybe we could go?"

"That would be nice," I say. It's the first time he's ever *asked* if I wanted to go to a game; usually he just *tells* me.

We spend the rest of the meal discussing the Reds and the Indians and their play-off hopes. Despite the fact that Dad would rather be talking about the Cleveland Browns or OSU football, he makes it easy to believe that baseball is all he ever has on his mind.

Chapter 26

WHILE ANNIKA MAY NOT be a vegetable, sometimes it feels like she's a piece of meat. Every time people come to see her, it's a big all-you-can-eat buffet. It's hard not to wonder if there'll be anything left of her when she wakes up, but Mom says it's not like that. She says that while Annika indeed does nourish the pilgrims, it's a two-way street. It's better to give than receive and all that. They nourish her too. "What's happening to Annika is a gift to the world. It would be wrong not to share."

Even when we get bad reviews, like on *Dateline NBC,* the people keep coming. Father Ferger said it was like being mugged, but muggers generally don't pretend they're your friends, like they're on your side. That's the way the *Dateline* people were, at least according to Mom. And I'll have to take her word for it, because once I heard they were coming, I disappeared. After seeing myself on TV the first time, I wasn't about to make the same mistake twice. At the end of their report they concluded: "It seems as though Annika is just a placebo, but everyone treats her like she's a miracle drug," which was enough to make Mom turn off the television. I'm not sure why she was so upset: Whether people are really getting better or just *think* they're getting better, it doesn't really matter, does it? They're *better.* The placebo effect, you know, doesn't just happen when you take a sugar pill and think it's a real drug. It also happens when you take a real drug and think it's going to cure you. People are suggestible; that's just the way they are.

I don't know why Annika's hands bleed or why it always smells like roses or why people keep getting cured. But I do know that *Dateline NBC* isn't going to get to the bottom of it by spending the whole day at our house. In the end, maybe Annika's real purpose is to be a cog in the pop-culture amusement machine—file under: a wonder to be marveled at, an aberration from the norm. *See? We live in a wonderful world full of limitless possibilities. Isn't it crazy? See? We're not all the same. See? Everything can't be so easily explained. Now be happy and go buy some more stuff.*

When Annika wakes up, I'm sure Oprah will get first crack at her, or maybe Barbara Walters. They'll treat her like the third coming and if there's any justice in the world, maybe she'll have something to say that will make people look at themselves and wonder what they're doing with their lives before they change the fucking channel.

I MIGHT AS WELL just admit it; I once cut Annika's palms. It was with a pocketknife Grandpa gave me when I turned sixteen. It featured a moose made of mother-of-pearl embedded on its side. Grandpa said he got it in Montana, which seemed so far away then—just like it does now.

The cutting, I should point out, was Annika's idea. Not mine. Emily and I had just started dating. And as stupid as it sounds, in retrospect I only now realize, maybe Annika was a little jealous I was spending so much time with someone else.

She said she wanted to be my blood sister. I told her she already was, that we didn't need to cut each other to prove it. She didn't care about that, she wanted to make it *official,* and the only way we could do that was by joining blood. She'd seen something on TV and once Annika got an idea like that in her head, she wouldn't let it go until it happened. Despite sharing parents, she was convinced that for her to be my *blood* sister and for me to be her *blood* brother, our blood *had* to mix. It was as simple as that and I figured it was easier to spill a little blood than to resist.

Even though it was freezing out, we performed the ceremony in the tree house in our backyard. Annika put Billie Holiday singing "Strange Fruit" on the boom box and we let the cutting begin. I slit my palm first. It didn't hurt. It didn't feel *at all*. Well, not at first, but once the blood started to flow, it stung like salt in the eye. Still, I didn't let on.

"Now me," she said.

I asked if she was sure and she said to hurry before I stopped bleeding.

Her hand was so small and delicate, like it still is now, that it seemed wrong to alter it in any way.

"I'm not getting any younger," she said.

I sliced the knife across her right palm, blood chasing the blade. She smiled her snaggletoothed smile and we joined hands, the blood squirting between our fingers into the two cups of grape juice sitting in front of us. You're supposed to use wine, but there wasn't an open bottle in the house and that's just the kind of thing Mom would have noticed, so grape juice it was.

We held up our cups of juice and blood and Annika said, "Now joined in blood, two becomes one and one takes on the power of two." Then we drank the juice blood and slammed the cups down.

"Does it hurt?" she asked.

"No. You?"

"Of course not," she said. And in case I didn't believe her, she asked if I wanted to play some catch.

"It's snowing," I said.

"Oh, right," she said. Then she looked down at her hand. "Do we have any bandages?"

Those scars healed in about a week, but not so fast that Mom didn't want to know what happened. Annika told her she cut her hand on a fence and Mom believed her. In fact, Mom believed her so much she took her to the doctor for a tetanus shot. I remember watching out the window as they got into the car and Annika smiled at me. Our secret was secure. She was taking a hit for the team and she couldn't have been happier about it.

Now Annika's hands bleed about every ten to fifteen days. There's no real rhyme or reason to it. Once you think you see a pattern, like Barry Larkin not getting a hit, it turns into something else, like days when a priest gets indicted or days when someone TP's our yard. Some stigmatists will bleed only on religiously significant days. Some just bleed whenever. Some have their wounds open all the time. Some heal soon after the bleeding begins. Sometimes there are no scars at all; the blood just seeps through their hands, like water beading up outside of a glass on a hot day.

Annika's wounds open and they close. Just a couple days after a bleeding, her hands look none the worse for wear. It's like she has Neosporin in her veins.

ALLISON IS HANDING out parking tickets. Well, they're not *really* parking tickets; they just look like they are. She's putting them on the windshields of SUVs. The citation says the driver is guilty of crimes against the environment, aiding and abetting terrorism, as well as generally poor aesthetic taste. If you ask Allison, which I don't necessarily recommend, pretty much everything wrong with the world goes back to SUV drivers.

We're supposed to be going to a movie, but it turns out watching people pop an artery over a fake ticket is a lot more entertaining than you might think. Technically, my Scout is an SUV, but she says it's exempt since it has a legitimate commercial purpose. Besides, she likes to stick with big game—Navigators, Durangoes, Humvees. "Although everyone around here deserves a ticket for *something,* that's for sure."

We're watching the squint-eyed owner of a mammoth Navigator peel her freshly minted ticket off the windshield. She's reading her citation, but she doesn't think it's nearly as funny as we do. "That's Libby Green," notes Allison. "She came to our house after Heidi's funeral and acted like she was my mom's best friend and then we never saw her again."

"What a bitch," I commiserate.

"She's no different than anyone else." She says after Heidi died, people rallied around their family. They were always bringing over food. The day of the funeral, the house was so full that people filled the front and backyard. "But after about a week, no one came over anymore. I don't blame them, it was pretty depressing."

Our house *always* seems to be full. It's a wake that never ends.

She asks me if I remember going to field trips at the Ohio Historical Society when we were kids. Of course I remember. I tell her about Sam and the milk shakes and how if they ever close Lazarus, maybe that's where he'll end up.

She says, "I used to feel so sorry for everyone who worked there in the village, stuck in the same day every day. But when you think about it, they're no different than anyone else. Maybe the trick is to find a day you like and stick to it."

"I can't imagine that Annika likes this day she's stuck in."

"But then again, maybe she likes it so much she doesn't want to wake up. Like when you have a dream that you wish would go on forever."

There's this one window at the Historical Society you can look through and see a little girl in her bedroom from like 1850. I guess they must have been kind of rich; she had the room all to herself. It's not like they were on the edge of the frontier out there fighting with the Indians; she could have been in England with the patterned wallpaper and the lace on her bed. She was playing with a doll, caught in a state of perpetual awe. In fact, she was *surrounded* by dolls, but her unblinking eyes said the one in front of her was the only one that mattered. That girl at the Historical Society, she was just a doll looking at a doll and every day people look at Annika through that window and pray, the two girls become more and more alike: twins stuck in time, even though they're a century and a half apart.

"You can do something about it if you want," Allison says. "If people thought it was all a scam, they wouldn't come anymore."

Chapter 27

WE'RE AT A Clippers game, Dad and me. We made the plan about a week ago, but he's called me twice today, just to make sure I'm coming, which is not like him at all. We arrive while they're singing the national anthem, about an hour later than usual. You might think Dad likes watching the players warm up more than actually watching them play the game, but really it's all about avoiding the traffic—very possibly the same reason he used to head to the office at six-thirty in the morning and come home after eight at night. That's when the coast is clear.

Everyone looks so stupid, singing the anthem, their eyes fixed not on the flag, but on the bouncing ball on the video screen that leads them through the lyrics. It's really difficult, apparently, to memorize *the national fucking anthem*. From their bumbling, you'd think they were trying to decipher the Dead Sea Scrolls.

There's really no reason for me to be here. Usually, Dad goes to games by himself; I've seen the ticket stubs on his dresser. I'm not sure what's going on in his head, although sometimes you can see his lips just barely moving. He's talking to himself, which is only slightly more unusual than the four beers he's already downed by the third inning.

It's not like we argue a lot. After all, he's a pro. So there's really no use in trying. Maybe that's why we mainly just talk about baseball. I've tried to school myself on Ohio State football—that's what he really cares about—but I still can't manage enough enthusiasm to have a convincing conversation.

Dad sounds all innocent when he asks, "Wouldn't it be great for the Reds if the National League had the DH? Griffey Junior could just hit and maybe then he wouldn't get hurt so much." But he's not being innocent at all. If there is one core belief that binds us more than our DNA, it is the notion that the designated hitter is bad. A cancer. Downright evil. An affront to a great game. This is a principle that Dad maintains, despite the humbling fact that his favorite team, the Cleveland Indians, is subject to the designated hitter rule. The Reds, being in the National League, where *real* baseball is played, are not.

I wish he'd keep murmuring to himself. *That,* I could respect. Instead, he has to open up a can of worms. Just when you think there's one thing you can count on, it turns out you can't rely on anything.

I say, "You're kidding, right?"

And with a completely straight face he says, "I've been thinking about this a lot, Monroe. It's not like anyone wants to see the pitcher hit anyway. It's actually kind of cruel to even put them in that position."

"So, I guess tradition means nothing to you," I offer, thinking I'm throwing the high heat when really I might as well be sitting the ball on a tee.

"For the game to grow it has to evolve. They've changed everything about it—the gloves, the balls, the bats, the mound. Hell, it used to be four strikes and you're out."

It did?

"Monroe, I thought you believed in evolution."

"I do, but . . ."

"You know, Monroe, it used to be a tradition to not let black people play either, but you think bringing Jackie Robinson into the league was a good thing, right?"

"Yes, Dad, I think letting Jackie Robinson play was a positive development."

"But, an aging star with aching knees who can still hit, but puts his health in danger by playing the field shouldn't?"

"He can always pinch hit."

"So you're saying that the handicapped should just be allowed to work part-time? I don't think that would go over so well with the Equal Rights Commission. I didn't realize that was the way you feel about the disabled."

"It's not."

"Good. I'm glad to hear that. So after all he's done for baseball, you think someone like Ken Griffey Jr. should be able to DH?"

"Sure, in the American League."

"I thought you wanted the DH abolished in the American League?"

"I do."

He laughs and says, "Me too. I'm just kidding with you, I hate the DH too." As a reward to himself, he waves the beer man over.

Then Dad says, "You hear the one about when the Devil visits a young lawyer's office?"

"No, Dad, I don't think I have."

"The Devil says, 'I have a proposition: You'll make millions. Your partners will love you. Your clients will respect you. You'll have four months of vacation each year and live to be a hundred. All I require in return is that your wife's soul, your children's souls, and their children's souls must rot in hell for eternity.' The lawyer thinks for a moment and he says, 'What's the catch?' "

Whenever someone brings up a lawyer joke, Dad always says: *You want to know what's wrong with lawyer jokes? Lawyers don't think they're funny and everyone else thinks they're true.* The thing is, lawyers like to tell lawyer jokes, they just don't like to be told them, unless it's another lawyer talking. It's kind of like how black people are allowed to call each other *nigger,* but no one else can.

But I don't mention that. Instead, I change the subject. "Dad, how come you haven't come over to see Annika?" I expect him to say that he's been really busy, something about work and how time flies and how he's been meaning to, but it just hasn't worked out that way.

"It hurts too much to see her like that." That's what he says. "And besides, it's not like she even knows anyone is there."

"That's not true," I say, somewhat surprised at how adamant I am.

"Monroe, I've talked to the doctors. As you know, Annika is in a persistent vegetative state. I know those are just words, but basically it means that several parallel, segregated cortico-straitopallidal-thalamocortical loops in Annika's frontal lobes have been disabled. There may be bilateral loss of basal-mesial cortical tissue. If so, the prognosis is not good. Keep in mind that bilateral lesions of the globus pallidus interna are unusual in that this structure contains each of the identified cortico-straitopallidal-thalamocortical circuits involving the frontal lobe, striatum, globus pallidus, substantia nigra, and thalamus. That's what the doctors say, but your mother won't even listen to them anymore."

"I can't imagine why."

Oblivious, he continues, "She doesn't want to hear *the truth*. I know how much everyone wants to believe that Annika is trapped in there. That she can hear us . . . and maybe she can. But do you know how rare it is for someone to come out of a vegetative state when they've been in it as long as your sister has?"

I know, *everyone knows*, it's rare. Practically impossible. But it does happen. You can read the stories on the Internet; you can hear them in our halls when people come to visit Annika. A girl in Austria wakes up at a George Michael concert after being in a coma for seven years. A man wakes up from a motorcycle accident when his friend plays him his favorite Neil Young song. A little boy wakes up when his nurse leafs through a Green Bay Packers yearbook and starts reading his favorite player's stats. I start telling Dad about the girl who woke up at a George Michael concert, how no one thought she had a chance. How it seemed so impossible . . .

"Sounds like a great story. I'm sure it'll make a heartwarming movie," he says, finishing off another beer. "But even though a bilateral pallidal injury can disable all of the parallel networks, at least partial cognitive function can recover following *some* bilateral injuries to the paramedian thalamus and mesencephalon—so it's not completely a lost cause. But, then again, doctors are paid to say stuff like that."

Attempting to steer him away from using any more medical jargon, I say, "It's not like I've fallen for the whole religious thing, but that doesn't mean it can't happen. It doesn't mean that she's still not there. She does seem to enjoy Aretha Franklin and when we're listening to baseball . . ."

"I admire that hope, I really do," he says. "I wish I could share in it."

"Just the other day, a woman who was in a coma for twenty years came out of it and on the news a doctor said that forty percent of the time when patients are called persistently vegetative, the diagnosis is wrong."

"Whatever you want to call it, the results are the same. She's just lying there."

"So you think talking to Annika is like talking to a wall?"

"I wouldn't say that," he says as he pays for his fifth beer in four innings. "I think it's more like talking to yourself."

AFTER THE GAME, we go to his new apartment. Actually, the game's still going on. Like I said, Dad never wants to stay until the end. He's obsessed with beating the traffic, even when no one's there.

Dad lives downtown in a big glass tower just a block away from where he works. If he could, he'd probably just sleep in his office. Unfortunately for him, despite the opportunity for billing more hours, the firm looks down on that kind of thing; so it's apartment living for him.

I don't expect much, but when we walk in the door, I can't help but be impressed. He has art on the walls and plants in the corners, books on the shelves and pillows on the couch. It's almost as if an actual living, breathing person lives here.

"Nice place," I tell him. "Your girlfriend fix it up for you?"

"A—I don't have a girlfriend. And B—the place came this way. I didn't have to do a thing."

Turns out, he bought the model condo, the one they use to show off the units and all of their endless possibilities. Now that I see that, it all makes sense. From what I can tell, the only personal addition he made is the liquor in the wet bar.

"The only thing I had to replace was the cardboard television," he says proudly, pouring a drink. "Basically, it's a place to sleep. I don't really spend a lot of time here."

Dad wants to talk, but it's not like at the baseball game, looking out on the field with ninety-mile-per-hour fastballs and sacrifice flies and doubles off the car ads in the outfield. There's no crowd cheering, no peanut man punctuating the conversation with, "I got your peanuts. Who wants some peanuts?" At a ball game, there's just enough going on to distract you from real life, but enough space to give you time to reflect on what really matters. Even if it is just a game. Even if it doesn't really mean anything in the end. That's the beauty of baseball, the freedom lies in the spaces in between. Baseball gives you a chance to *breathe*.

It's not like that in Dad's apartment. There are no roots. We could be *anywhere*. We could be in a room with a blue screen, stuck inside a virtual world, where everything is right in front of you but just out of reach.

Dad leads me to his balcony, a drink for him in one hand, a Coke for me in the other. On the slab of concrete, sitting in two teak chairs, we look at the lights of Chelsea laid out in the distance. When one light turns off, another one might turn on for a late-night snack. But either way it doesn't really matter from here. They come and they go, each one erasing the memory of the one that came before.

Dad's talking about how he envies me, how I've got my whole life before me. He says I can do whatever I want with it.

"The only thing that really matters is being happy," he says. "I don't mean that in a hedonistic way, like you should get wasted all the time. I'm just saying, it's easy to get in a rut where all you think about is the future; but the future never turns out the way you expect. It's not a news flash, I know. But maybe it should be. Then maybe it wouldn't be so easy to forget."

I guess this is what they call a midlife crisis, but I don't say that. This balcony worries me, but I don't say that either. I hope he doesn't spend a lot of time out here. He's had his head in the sand for so long and now he can see for miles. But in a lot of ways, the view's the same. Either way, it's pretty hard to see what's right in front of you.

It's not like we're really having a conversation. Dad might as well be talking to himself. I just happen to be here. He says I have everything in the world to live for, like it's the first time he's said it. Like he's not repeating himself.

I tell him, "You do too," but what I really mean is, "Have another drink and go to bed."

Maybe if I'd said what I was thinking, things would have turned out differently.

Chapter 28

IT'S SIX IN THE MORNING, the darkness fading, when Chelsea's finest knocks on the door. With stunning efficiency Chelsea's police force manages to break up keg parties within thirty minutes of the keg being tapped. Noise complaints are resolved before the offending CD moves on to its next track. Outsiders are tracked with the efficiency once only thought possible in gated communities. And they manage to do it all without mustaches, like real cops. They're much too clean-cut for that. Still, this force has an albatross around its neck. They never solved the mystery of who killed Heidi Morgan and they probably never will.

His name is Officer Romine. He wants to talk to my mom, but I tell him she's not here. There's no point in waking her up, that's what I figure. In retrospect, maybe I should have.

Basically, Dad tried to kill himself. *Suicide.* There's no reason to sugarcoat it. Everyone else will do that later. The cop does it now. He says he found him in his car out by the river, drunk. Like *that* was the problem. Like he's got Dad in the back of his squad car and he's just dropping him back off at home. Like he's doing us all a big favor.

But that's not the whole story. Officer Romine saves the best for last. Sure, Dad was drunk by the river, but not so drunk that he didn't manage to rig a hose from the exhaust pipe into the back window.

"It would have worked too, had I not come by."

"Thanks, you're a real hero," is what I'm thinking, but I don't say that. I just say, "Thanks."

"I'm really sorry," he says, almost convincingly. "Just part of the job, doing this kind of thing."

That's everyone's excuse for everything.

When you hear news like that—your father tried to kill himself—you might think you know how you'd react, but you don't. I don't feel bad for him. I don't wonder how he's feeling. I don't want to hug him or even shake his hand. Even though I saw him only hours ago, I don't start thinking of all the things I could have done differently.

Basically, I want to take a baseball bat and jack him in the knees for being such a dumbass.

Dad's at the hospital now. The cop says he's going to be okay, which I take to mean there's no need to wake up Mom and tell her what happened. Instead, I brew up a pot of coffee. It's going to be a long day.

It's not really a surprise. *Suicide.* I always thought that's the way Dad would end it. Just not so soon. Just not *now.* I figured he'd be an old man who couldn't bear the thought of someone taking care of him. It'd be too much, giving up that kind of control, so he'd take matters into his own hands.

He once mentioned a lawyer from his firm who killed himself in his office. Mr. Briggs was his name. It's the first name on the long list above the law firm's front door, *Briggs,* but he wasn't the one who put it there. His dad was. Anyway, he was seventy-three years old and full of cancer, so the end was coming soon. That's what he figured. Dad spoke about it like it was a good thing, like it was noble to go down that way. Maybe it was, I don't know. Maybe it is *more* noble to have a Honduran cleaning lady making minimum wage find Mr. Briggs's head splattered across the wall, instead of his wife. Maybe it is better to desecrate an anonymous office than to ensure that no one will ever want to go into the living room again.

To Dad, Mr. Briggs was a martyr. His demise was somehow stoic, something to aspire to. Dad would have you believe it was the unselfish thing to do. There's a cartoon in Dad's office. Two guys are sitting at a bar and one says, "I shot a man in Reno just to watch him die. After that, law school was pretty much a given." So true, it's funny.

Lawyer jokes are like that.

Anyway, Dad said that when it was time to go, he'd "take care of the situation." He said, "There's nothing worse than a slow dive." It made sense to me then, but it doesn't make so much sense to me now. If that's the standard—that slow dives are bad—how does he really feel about Annika?

I go into Annika's room. Her eyes are open. I tell her what Dad tried to do, but she just lies there like a fish on the beach, but there's no flipping or flopping, just open eyes so deep that if you jumped in they'd make a splash.

It shouldn't be a surprise when I find that her hands are bleeding, but it is. *It always is.* It's one of those things I can't get used to. And I hope I never do.

MOM TAKES THE NEWS hard. A lot harder than I thought she would, so much so I wonder if she's really upset that he *didn't* succeed. But that's not the case at all. She's mad that I didn't wake her up. Like forty-five minutes is a big deal.

"It's not like you could have done anything."

"I could have prayed."

"Prayed for what? He was already stable. He didn't need your prayers."

"What we need and what we deserve are two different things."

"I don't think Dad *wants* to be prayed for."

"All the more reason to do it."

There's no reasoning with Mom. This conversation, in fact, takes place in the car on the way to the hospital. That's how unhinged Mom is. Dad abandoned us, but she can hardly wait to get by his side. She can hardly wait for a chance to save him, a chance for him to see *the light.* That's why those forty-five minutes matter to her so much; she wants to get there while he's still vulnerable.

~~~

WHAT I'LL ALWAYS remember is the shame in his eyes. Dad had never failed at anything in his life, but he couldn't even pull off the weakest thing a person can do. I can hardly wait to say, "People always talk about how it takes guts to kill yourself, but what really takes guts is *not* killing yourself. That's the hard part, finding a reason *not* to do it every day."

When he sees us walk in his room, he starts to cry. Not blubbers. Just tears.

"You didn't have to come," he says. He's looking at Mom, her eyes already wet.

"I tried to tell her that," I say.

"But I'm glad you did," he says. And she's looking back at him. They're floating in each other's tears.

"You know how she is; she doesn't listen to anything."

"I'm glad you came anyway," he says again to his wife. It's like I'm not even there.

Mom trips over herself to hug him. I've never seen them do *that* before, holding each other like they really mean it, like nothing matters more than the bond between them, no matter how bruised and battered it may be.

I guess it's *nice*. Like 250-thread-count sheets. Like a new Toyota Camry. Like puppies and flowers and Easter bonnets. *Nice* like that.

I'm not going to let him get off that easy.

Mom does what she does best and prays to God to give them the strength to see this through. Dad doesn't resist. He doesn't say a thing. He just lies there. He looks tired, like he aged ten years overnight. He closes his eyes, like maybe he's praying along; but I think I know him well enough to say this (and I really don't know him at all): he's just biding his time.

"I love you, Dad," I tell him. I say it because it's what I'm supposed to say, not because I actually believe it. At least not in this moment. Love is not what's coming to mind. I really should *hate* him right now. After all, if he had succeeded, I would have been the last one to see him alive. Dad must have considered that if he'd pulled off his suicide, I would have blamed myself, at least at first. That could have really fucked me up, but apparently that possibility didn't even cross his mind. Maybe he thought I'm such a lost cause, it didn't matter. Or maybe he just didn't care.

After an hour, he's lying there smiling, his eyes closed. Asleep. Not a bad pose if you're shopping for a casket. I should be happy he's not dead, thankful he's alive. I really should. That's the way a good son would feel, but I'm not feeling like a good son. Seeing him there all peaceful, I feel like smothering him with a pillow. Not that I'd kill him — I'd just like to see him have to fight to stay alive.

But I don't do that. I just tell Mom I'm going to look for some coffee.

Chapter 29

Before I can get an infusion of caffeine, Allison calls me on my new cell. She says her mother has lost her mind; she needs me to come over. To come over *now*.

When I get there, the place is trashed. "She started pulling up the carpet and once she started she couldn't stop. She says it's infected with memories of my dad. She gets an idea in her head and she might as well have a tumor."

It's a mess in here, sure; but Allison never looked so beautiful. It's nothing I could really point to and say, *Look how rosy her cheeks are* or *Look at the way the light catches her hair.* Maybe it has nothing to do with any of that. Maybe just being wanted by her is enough for me to see just how beautiful she is.

I tell her, "You look good."

"You're a pathetic liar, you know that?"

I tell her she really shouldn't let the dominant beauty paradigm define her self-worth.

"Fuck you, Monroe," she says.

She always knows just the right thing to say.

The living-room ceiling is full of clouds. Not painted clouds, but all those color photos Mrs. Morgan showed me last time I was here are pasted up there. I'm looking up at them when Allison says, "You see my sister?"

"Not really."

"Me neither. Someone keeps sending them to my mom."

"Yeah, she showed me."

"Well, the guy's an *asshole*. He says he can see Heidi in the clouds. Every photo comes with a description: *See Heidi doing the laundry . . . see Heidi waving to the crowd in her tiara . . . see Heidi play catch with a beagle*. The guy's a sick fuck, but Mom wanted to see her so much she put them on the ceiling. She thought that might make it easier. More *natural*."

"Can she see her now?"

"So she says. It was such a pain in the ass putting them up there, I'd say I saw her too."

I keep looking, but I come up empty.

"When you think of Heidi, what does she look like?"

"I wish I was like everyone else and just saw her class photo, but the truth is when I think about her, she looks *dead*."

That's not the sort of memory I was hoping to conjure up.

Allison says, "This is my advice to you: Never have an open-casket funeral. They say that it's supposed to make it easier to say good-bye. But it only makes it *worse*. That's how I remember her now, lying there dead, surrounded by flowers. She looked pretty, she really did, maybe prettier than she ever was when she was alive. If that makes any sense. Anyway, that's what I think about when I think about her—lying there in her casket."

"They must have done a pretty good job putting her back together."

"Yeah, *too* good of a job. That bastard who killed her smashed her head in with a rock. Everyone knows that, I guess. But the thing people don't know is that the killer also slit her throat, ear to ear. The cops never told anyone about that part. I guess they like to hold back details for the investigation. Like it mattered."

"Then he left her there in the ditch. When my dad found her, he said it looked like she was sleeping. Sounds stupid now, but that's what he thought—that she'd fallen asleep on her stomach by the creek. He was so happy when he saw her. He said he started to cry—tears of joy, you know?—then he turned her over and saw that her lips were blue and her head had been smashed and her throat had been

cut and the tears kept coming until he started to choke on them. I
don't think he ever stopped. That's probably why he left . . . we
should have just had a closed casket. That's what my dad said we
should do, but Mom wanted them to put her back together. She
wanted to see her whole again. But, it's like by putting her back together, it made what happened not so bad, like it could be fixed, you
know?"

I just nod. I don't really know what to say, other than I'm sorry.
I'm really, really sorry.

"But it can't be fixed. Either way she's dead and there's nothing
you can do about it." She looks up at the ceiling for a moment,
searching the clouds. "How's Annika doing?"

"My dad went on forever last night about how he doesn't think
there's much of a chance she'll come out of it."

"What do you think?"

"I just wish she'd hurry it up. I really miss her."

We're lying on the floor, looking at the clouds, when Mrs. Morgan
comes in. "Jesus Christ on a stick, Allison, you sure don't waste any
time."

"Mom." She says it like she's said it a thousand times. What it
means is— *You don't understand anything.*

I say, "We were just looking at the ceiling."

The house is a wreck. Rolled-up shag carpet is everywhere, the
furniture seemingly rearranged by a tornado.

"You think you can move all this carpet out of here by yourself?"

"I thought I'd give it a shot," I say.

Allison says she can help. She's wearing overalls and a sleeveless
T-shirt. Her skin is so white, I'm afraid my hand will disappear if I
touch her.

Mrs. Morgan says she's going back to bed, but first she needs to
get her medicine. Allison whispers, *"Whiskey."*

As she heads upstairs with her coffee cup full of booze, Allison
says, "Good night, Mom."

Once she's out of earshot: "She sleeps so much, it's like living with
a bear."

"I heard that," she says down the stairs.

"She's such a freak," says Allison, illustrating the obvious. *"Parents."*

For some reason, I feel the need to trump her. "My dad tried to kill himself last night. I just got back from the hospital."

"So what the fuck are you doing *here?*"

I tell her not to worry, that he's okay. He screwed the whole thing up.

"How'd he try to do it?"

"With the exhaust fumes from his car, but a cop found him. All he got was a bad headache."

She contemplates that for a moment. "Your dad and my mom oughta get together . . . well, I guess it's not such a bad way to die, but it's a pretty shitty way to be found. The fumes kill you pretty fast, but then you start to bake in your car. You can't just leave a car in idle like that, it gets really hot—like an oven. After a few hours you melt into the seat. It's no way for someone to find you. I guess if you make sure there's not a lot of gas in the car, it's probably not so bad. But either way, it's hell on the resale value."

Apparently she's done some research. "They make you disclose suicides when you sell a car?" I ask.

"They don't have to. The smell never leaves. It doesn't matter how many pine trees you dangle in there either. People just *know.*"

I probably should be sad about what Dad tried to do, but I'm not. I'm not even mad anymore. More like somewhere between numb and disappointed. Dad said he felt the same way about me when I crashed the driver's ed car. *Disappointed.* But there's no joy in having the tables turned. It seems so long ago that I used to think he was so strong and powerful. Now I see that he's just as broken as everyone else.

Allison says that's the most freeing feeling in the world, the moment you realize that your parents are just people. They're not heroes, they're not Gods—they're just *people.* Maybe she's right, maybe it is freeing, but it's not giving me that kind of comfort, at least not yet. I'm not saying Dad was my hero or a God or that I even wanted to be like him, but he was always someone I could count on—he was always consistent, even in his inconsistencies. Heroes are there to be loved, but not to love you back. How can anyone respect you when you put them up on a pedestal? They'll always be looking down at you. I'm not saying that heroes are a bad idea, even if they do disappoint you in the end. Maybe that's what they're there for in the first place. Maybe that's the whole point. As your heroes fall away and you're left standing, you realize you can do whatever you want. You realize the only person you have to live up to is yourself.

I ask, "You know how the speed of light is so slow that some of the stars in the sky burned out thousands of years ago, but we'd never know it because the light is just getting here?"

"Yeah."

"So if you wish on one of those dead stars, does that wish count?"

After scrunching her nose over it for a moment, she says, "Maybe that wish counts *more* since you're wishing on a memory and after all is said and done, memories are all we ever have left. When something is still around, no one appreciates it anyway."

I want to kiss her. I know I'm supposed to be working and it's completely unprofessional, but it feels like the right thing to do. She must be thinking the same thing because the next thing I know, we're making out on the couch. My eyes are closed and I'm floating in her embrace, but I can feel we're being watched. I'm sure of it. It's like wearing the softest cashmere sweater in the world but it itches your shoulder blade. I look around, expecting to see Mrs. Morgan standing there watching us. But she's not there. Heidi is. Staring right at us. *Finally,* I can see her. She's right *there.* I can't believe I didn't see her before.

Allison wants to know, "Is something the matter?"

Dead sister talk is not an aphrodisiac. I know that much.

"I thought someone was watching us."

"Don't worry about my mom, she had like half a bottle of whiskey for breakfast. She's down for the count."

But I'm not worried about Allison's mom, not with Heidi right there in the sky. She's not just in one picture—that's where I was going wrong before. In the corner there are about twelve photos together; that's where she's hiding. It's so obvious once you realize what to look for. She's peeking behind a tree. Blink. And she's running. Blink again. She's jumping rope.

Maybe I should say something, but I don't. Instead I kiss Allison's neck.

Allison unbuttons the straps of her overalls and pulls off her shirt. This is what you get when you don't say what's on your mind.

And with one good look at Allison's chest, Heidi disappears back into the clouds.

MRS. MORGAN COMES down in time to see her daughter tugging at my belt buckle.

"Mom, you're supposed to be *passed out*."

But she's not even looking at her daughter; no, her eyes are on me. "*Monroe,* I hope you're not going to charge me by the hour."

"Ummmm . . . of course not," I say, buckling myself up.

"What are you trying to say, Mom? That I'm some sort of whore?" And then Allison turns to me. "*I'm not a whore.*"

"I never thought you were," I say.

Then Mrs. Morgan chimes in. "If you are a whore, then the least you can do is give me my cut. It is my house, after all."

I can't find my shirt.

"Oh, I see, Mom, now you want to pimp me out?"

I say, "Maybe I should start hauling that carpet."

"Maybe you should," says her mom. "By the way, *Monroe,* you should know, I caught her doing the same thing with the chimney sweep." She says *Monroe* like it's some sort of alias. Like everything I say is a lie.

"Now, you're just making stuff up," Allison says in her own defense. She assures me, "We've never had our chimney swept. We've never even had a *fire.*"

"Oh young lady, I *know* who started the fire," screams Mrs. Morgan as I drag a roll of carpet out the front door, the tacky-textured cardboard back sticking to my skin. *"I know!"* she screams.

Once I get the carpet loaded on the truck, I'm ready for another load. I look back at their house. They're screaming at each other now. "How did I raise such a slut?" Mrs. Morgan yells. "It's not like you ever leave the house."

"Jesus, Mom, if you hadn't broken all the mirrors in the house, maybe you could take a good hard look at *yourself.*"

"Don't mind me," I say as I come in for another roll of carpet.

"When you get that to the landfill, you tell them to burn it," Mrs. Morgan says.

"Sure thing," I say.

"You know, Mom, if they burn it, all the evil spirits will float into the air and then you'll be *breathing* Dad in and you won't even know it."

"Fine," she reconsiders. "Tell them to bury it."

"And the next thing you know his essence will be seeping into the groundwater and you'll be *drinking* him."

"Is this what I get for sending you to college?"

"Last time I checked, Dad was paying for my college."

"I'll be back in a little while," I say as I drag another roll out of the house. But they don't see me go; they're blinded by each other's glare.

I get in my truck and my back sticks to the vinyl seat, like microwaved meat to cling wrap. But it's a small price to pay for my freedom. I turn the key and fire up the Scout. Even though the car is moving, their house disappearing in the rearview, there's no escape. In seconds, I'm driving past the ditch where they found Heidi and I think about her shy, class-photo smile. I think about her eyes and how it still feels like they're looking at me. I look up through the sunroof to see if I can see her up there, but I don't. There's not a cloud in the sky, which is strange. It's always cloudy in Columbus.

The light is red. Heidi was last seen alive right here at this corner. There's not a marker or anything. Most people I'm sure have forgotten all about it. Each one of these homes must be worth a half million dollars. It's a nice neighborhood. *Really* nice, nicer than what I'll ever have on my own.

I'm looking across the street and there's a girl in a big yard, playing catch with a dog. It's a golden retriever, a purebred just like everything else around here. The dog is looking at the ball like it's the only thing that matters in the entire world. The little girl moves the dog's head around like a remote control, up and down, back and forth. She knows that the dog will do anything for that ball and she's going to make him work for it. She's going to make him want that ball more than he already does. She probably barely knows her multiplication tables, but she's determined to add to infinity. I wish there was something in my life that mattered as much as that red ball matters to that dog. Maybe that's what it means to be a man. You have a ball to keep your eye on and a woman who makes sure you do.

Chapter 30

Mom says, "Your dad is going to be moving back in." She delivers the news like the dried toast that just popped out of the toaster. She's in the kitchen fixing a bacon, lettuce, and tomato sandwich. "You want some?"

She makes the best BLTs. "I guess, if you're having one," I say. I can't help but to add, "It's very Christian of you to take care of Dad until he gets better."

"Monroe, just because I've found God does not mean that I'm oblivious to your sarcasm."

"Really? I thought for sure that you were."

"Your father and I are going to give it another try."

"So you're in love again?"

"Your father and I have always loved each other. That was never in question."

"So it's going to go back to the way it used to be?"

I don't know why I'm being such a jerk. It's not like I feel threatened, my role as "man of the house" in jeopardy. Biologically speaking, I'm just a man *in* the house.

"It's going to be different that it used to be. Your *father* is different than he used to be."

"So are you."

"And I thank God for it every day."

"I'm just a little confused. I didn't realize that suicide was so sexy."

"Monroe, this is not about sex."

"So why'd he do it?"

"He says he was tired, that he just wanted to rest."

"So he tried to kill himself? What's wrong with a trip to Saint Croix?"

"I don't know, *Monroe*, you might want to ask him that."

"I'm sure he doesn't want to talk about it," I say. "But then again, he never wants to talk about anything."

"He's pretty embarrassed."

"So what are you saying? That Dad found God?"

"That's what he told me."

"Was he all loopy on medicine?"

"Actually, Monroe, he was quite lucid. He said he wants to change his life. He said he wants another chance. He deserves that. Most people do."

"I guess that's better than waking up and wanting to kill himself again."

Maybe I'm being a little harsh. If he wants sympathy, he's already found it from my mom. He doesn't need mine.

"Maggie says you dressed Annika's hands last night."

"Sorry, I forgot to mention that."

"It's amazing, isn't it?" she asks.

"You say that like it's a *good* thing."

"Your sister is suffering, but she's with God, so her suffering is not in vain."

What a Great Guy, God. It really makes me want to get to know Him better. Forcing a little girl to suffer for the sins of all mankind. That's just one step above a priest sacrificing an altar boy's ass for his own gratification and saying it's God's will. But I don't say that. Why bother?

Mom continues, "What's amazing is that she bled when Ben had his accident, she bled while your father was sitting in that car . . ."

"You think Annika knows Dad tried to off himself?"

"Not only do I think that, but I think she summoned help."

"Like a spiritual call to 911?"

"Monroe, I know you're mocking me, but yes, kind of like that."

She doesn't even look at me when she says that; she just turns over the bacon.

I try to break through the sizzle of fat and ask, "So, when's Dad coming back?"

"I'm not sure; they want to keep an eye on him for a few days."

"I thought he was fine."

"He is fine."

"So why are they keeping him there?"

"They just want to make sure he's fine."

"He was barely even passed out when they found him. . . ." That's when it hits me. "Oh, I get it, Dad's a *mental patient*."

"Your father's in the *psychiatric* ward. It's standard procedure after someone tries to uhmmmm . . . engage in self-destructive behavior. He needs our support right now." And as if she's convincing herself more than me, she adds, "And your father is *not* a mental patient. He just had an unfortunate lapse of judgment." An *unfortunate lapse of judgment* that could have been the last judgment he ever made.

"You're taking this all very well, Mom."

"God never gives us more to deal with than we can handle."

It is this thought that made me never want to go to church again, this notion of a compassionate God where war, rape, murder, starvation, and genocide—it's all part of His plan. Surely, no one has ever endured more genocide than they could deal with. We're just too insignificant and small-brained ever to understand the wisdom of His ways. But there's no use bringing that up. I have so much more restraint than people give me credit for. Instead I answer, "I guess not, Mom."

Then she laughs, "That's the kind of thing that makes me sound like a nut, isn't it?"

"Yeah, Mom, it kind of is."

"That's the tricky part about seeing the light. Sometimes it blinds you to everything else . . . now, you did say you wanted a BLT, right?"

Chapter 31

THEY MAKE IT HARD to get in the psych wing, but what they're really worried about is the patients getting out. I make my way through a gauntlet of phone calls and suspicious security officers. Lists are checked, my ID is scrutinized, and soon I'm in. Once they're convinced I'm not here to start a revolution, they tell me to go down the hall to the TV room. There I can meet Mr. Anderson. *Mr. Anderson* — I guess that's their way of giving dignity back to those who have thrown it away.

Patients aren't allowed to have visitors in their rooms. They like to keep an eye on you or at least promote that illusion. A disinterested nurse looks up long enough from her Egg McMuffin to ask me who I'm here to see. I tell her and she says to take a seat, he'll be right there. But she has more pressing matters to tend to, most notably the hash brown in front of her. Once she's finished feeding, she makes the call. Meanwhile, I sit in the corner as far away from the TV as I can. It's on loud, *too* loud, but no one seems to be watching — *seems* being the operative word. I want to get up and turn it down, but I'm sure if I do some patient will have a fit. *The Price Is Right* is on and, considering the lack of intellectual rigor required to participate, I suspect their main demographic may very well be waiting rooms for the mentally challenged.

On the other side of the room, there's a guy sitting in hospital pajamas. His hair is greasy and his glasses are crooked. He's talking to himself, but I can't hear what he's saying. He looks really sad, like people are supposed to be visiting him, but they didn't show up—*they never do*—so now he's just visiting himself.

There's another guy, walking in circles. He keeps clearing his throat, and each time whatever thoughts I had in my head scatter like marbles bouncing on a linoleum floor. He looks Middle Eastern and I can't help but wonder if he's involved in a low-grade terrorist campaign to drive everyone around him completely, irrevocably insane.

I'm sitting here, scratching my face, when I see blood on my hands. No, it's not a *sign*. I haven't been chosen to carry the burden of humanity's suffering. I cut my face shaving yesterday and I've opened up the wound. It's as simple as that. I'm trying to stop the bleeding when a woman spots me and comes over, asking what happened. I think she'd like me to think she's a nurse, but her blue slippers give her away. She's a patient.

She wants to know if there's anything she can do. She looks kind of slutty, maybe in her late thirties. Nice rack. I tell her what happened and she says she cut her face once too. She was getting ready to go on a first date and she was shaving her armpits and somehow she pulled the razor all the way up and sliced open her lip. Sounds suspicious, I know, but she acts out how it happened and I can see how it might be possible. She doesn't sound unhinged at all. She says she was bleeding all over the place, but she got it under control enough to go on the date. It was okay as long as she didn't smile or it would break open again. I ask her if she ended up going on a second date and she says, yeah, they did. Once they started drinking, she says everything was fine, they were both laughing and the blood didn't seem to matter anymore. It was just *funny*.

Finally, Dad arrives. He's wearing a warm-up suit, like he could be on his way to a game of tennis. He smiles when he sees me. The slutty woman asks him if I'm his son and he says, "Yes, he is," to which she replies, "He's very handsome." Then with a wink she goes away.

Dad rolls his eyes and whispers, "She has AIDS."

"Really?"

"Probably other stuff too. Did I ever tell you about how when I was in the marines they used to show us these movies about what would happen if you had sex with the natives? Pretty nasty stuff. Sores, lesions—that kind of thing."

"No, Dad, you never mentioned that."

I look over at the lady with AIDS; she's wrapped up in *The Price Is Right*. "No no no NOOOO," she says. "You only bid a dollar when you're the *last* one up. You fucking idiot."

It's not fair, disarming me like that. I'm ready to dish back all the *disappointment* he's ever spat my way. But he looks so sad there in his tired old warm-up suit. It's probably ten years old—in that gray zone of being out of fashion, but maybe it will come back in another ten years. I see now that it's useless being upset with him.

"You know, you could have at least *tried* to make it look like an accident."

"I guess I just wasn't thinking."

What can you say to that? Me? I say, "I've got doughnuts, the kind you like."

"Powdered jelly?"

"I thought you liked bear claws."

He smiles wide and says, "Those are good too." He opens the bag like his long-lost childhood football card collection might be inside. It makes me happy to see him this way.

"So what happened to you? Get in a fight with a razor?"

"Something like that," I say, still holding a napkin to my cheek. It's hard to feel superior when you don't even know how to shave.

"I guess I should have taught you a little better," he says, his face sprouting stubble. Actually, he never taught me at all; I'm still picking it up on my own in a trial-and-error kind of way. He must be thinking of Ben, but I don't remind him. It'll only make him wish Ben were visiting instead of me. He feels his chin. "They won't let me have a razor around here. You have to get one of the orderlies to do it for you."

The Middle Eastern–looking guy comes up smiling and says, "Larry, is this your law partner?"

"No, Babou, it's my son."

"I am Babou," he says, smiling. He shakes my hand, his eyes rolling around in his head like pinballs. And like that he's gone, back to circling around the room, hacking out a lung.

Dad shakes his head. "I can't believe I'm here."

"Me neither. What do people do around here all day, anyway?"

He says earlier in the morning there was a group therapy session and everyone had to say what his goal was for the day. "I told them mine was to be discharged, but they said that wasn't going to happen. Not today."

"What are you supposed to say?"

"I don't know—take a shower, have a nap, watch some TV. The standards are pretty low. Babou says his goal is to get rid of his phlegm and believe me, everyone is very supportive of his vision of the future."

As if on cue, Babou reaches deep within, searching for the goblin stuck in his throat. But he comes up short.

"They still use electroshock therapy. Did you know that?"

I say, "I thought that was something they only did in the movies."

"Me too," he says.

He's scared. I've never seen him like this before. Not when Annika first went into the coma—then he was *concerned*. Not when Ben fell off his frat house—then he was *sad*. But now, the uncharted waters are in his own head and he's flailing, looking for something to hold on to. It makes me like him a lot more. No wonder he told Mom he wants to play on Jesus's team. He looks so pathetically *alone*.

Meanwhile, on the TV, it's time to spin the big wheel. *Click click click click click* . . . but it doesn't make it all the way around. The crowd groans and the woman with AIDs yells, "You fucking *loser*! Spin the *motherfucking* wheel. How tough can it be? What are you? A *gimp*?" If you were able to come up with a thought in here, I swear it would slip away before you even knew it.

"So Dad, Mom says you found God? Was it a light-at-the-end-of-the-tunnel kind of thing?"

"No, actually, it's more of a nothing-else-is-working kind of thing."

Chapter 32

ANNIKA BLED AGAIN, but this time it probably won't make it into the weekly newsletter Maggie posts online. Annika's a real woman now, that's what Mom says. She just had her first period. Thirteen years old, right on time.

Sometimes I pray for Annika. Even though I'm not quite sure *who* I'm praying *to,* it feels better than doing nothing. I ask for her back, nothing fancy. I don't make promises. I don't try to strike a deal. Dad once told me praying is like paying insurance, but with insurance at least you know who to make the check out to. But I think my prayers are more like a message in a bottle. Who knows who'll pick them up? Most likely, they'll end up in the garbage. But you can say that about just about everything.

It should be no surprise; a growing segment of believers pray *to* Annika. As disturbing a trend as that is, there is some consolation in knowing there are people running around loose who are a lot more confused than I am. The Church doesn't like the idea of people praying *to* Annika very much and when I say *the Church,* I mean the archdiocese in Chicago.

That's right. Today they're bringing in the big guns. So big, Mom's been cleaning the house all week, even though I seriously doubt they'll be checking to make sure the Christmas decorations are properly sorted and stored. Cardinal Mahoney is the esteemed company. He's from Chicago and lives in a sprawling mansion on the lake. We get a lot of priests, nuns, and occasionally a bishop, but he is the first cardinal to come through our doors.

The cardinal has assured Mom this isn't an *official* inquiry. He's heard so many great things about Annika, he wanted to come and see for himself. *60 Minutes* did a big story on the cardinal a few months ago and they didn't even try to nail him for being a child molester or for nefarious real estate deals. They actually made him out to be a pretty good guy. That's considered a news flash these days—a Catholic Church leader who isn't a complete scumbag.

We've already eaten a lunch of poached salmon and asparagus, and we're sitting out on the patio where no one ever sits. It's just Mom, Maggie, Annika, and me. Dad really would have liked to be here, but he's in Baltimore. Grandpa's in Branson with Betty and Uncle George. Father Ferger's absence, however, is not an oversight. His pronouncements against the Church for their handling of the sex scandals have made him a bit of a pariah among his fellow clergy. I'm sure he took the dismissal with a stiff upper lip, but he must feel like a teacher whose prodigy is giving a recital at Juilliard and he's not allowed in the building.

"Some tea would be lovely, Mrs. Anderson," says the cardinal.

Mom brings in tea like it's something she does every day—God knows, nothing dusts off the drudgery of around-the-clock caretaking like breaking out the good china.

Cardinal Mahoney is old, gray, and personable enough. The way Mom's rolled out the red carpet, you'd think he was *the pope*. Mahoney smiles the smile of someone about to sell you something you don't really need, but has you thinking you can't live without.

Mahoney has a couple of other priests in tow. There's a fat one and a skinny one. The fat one has a bullfrog look to him, although surely the idea of jumping must be a faraway memory. The skinny one is younger and thoughtfully jots down much of the proceedings in a little black book. His scribblings make it quickly apparent that while this visit may not be official in nature, it is investigatory. They must have talked to Maggie alone for almost an hour and it's hard to imagine anyone talking to her that long about anything—even the one topic that matters to her the most—Annika.

Now it's my turn. Mahoney has done his homework, but little does he know—so have I. He starts out by tossing me a softball. "The Reds are looking good this year," he says. "Of course, it'll all come down to the pitching."

No duh, I think, *it always comes down to pitching.* But I say, "So I guess you must be a Cubs fan?" But there's no guessing about it. It's amazing what you can find out about someone on the Internet.

"Those seem to be the cards I've been dealt," he replies. "God willing, this may just be our year."

I'm thinking, "The Cubs are a persuasive argument for the futility of the power of prayer." But instead I nod along like an idiot and say, "Tough loss against Saint Louis last night."

"Indeed it was," he says.

"Hard to believe it was 1945 when the Cubbies last went to the World Series," I say. But I'm thinking, I sure hope it doesn't take another nuclear bomb to drop for it to happen again.

"Good things come to he who waits," he says.

I hold up my teacup. "Here's to your health, Father. It could be a while."

He laughs a self-deprecating laugh. "That Sean Casey sure can hit," he says, picking out the most likely Catholic in the Reds' lineup.

The Cubs and the Saint Louis Cardinals are pretty huge rivals. I wonder if Mahoney sees the irony in rooting against a team called the Cardinals from a town named after a saint, but I don't mention it. If I just said what's on my mind, I'd probably be a much better conversationalist. But I'm waiting for the other shoe to drop, for the interrogation to begin. Mahoney has his small talk down, but he didn't come all this way just so we could discuss baseball.

"I understand you've become estranged from the Church, Monroe? Do you like Father Ferger?"

"He's been very helpful to my mother," I say, not even lying.

"Well, Monroe, you were baptized, so you'll always be a child of God," he says.

When I told Allison about it later, she said, "To say that getting baptized makes one a child of God is like saying when a women gets raped it makes her the rapist's wife." It's that kind of on-the-spot analysis that explains why she's getting an A in women's studies.

I wish I'd been that quick. Instead I spit out, "So you guys bury any pedophile allegations lately?"

The fat one is the first to parrot the Church's official line: "Those are *isolated* incidents."

"Yeah, isolated to the cloakroom."

"Monroe, you seem like a very angry young man."

This is where I'm supposed to say, "Well, Father, there is a lot to be angry about," but instead I just glare.

"You know, son, I used to be like you, enraged, swinging wildly at the world, thinking it was me versus everyone else. But it doesn't have to be that way."

This is where he's going to start talking about faith, the freedom of faith, how faith will fill in all of these holes in my life. But I don't want to hear it. I really don't. "Maybe we should just talk about Annika. Obviously you guys didn't come all the way down here to talk about *me*."

The way they look at each other suggests talking about me was, in fact, rather high on their agenda. The fat one says, "So tell us, Monroe, do you have any theories about what's going on here?"

The skinny one says, "Specifically, the *stigmata*."

"Not really," I say.

"You must have some sort of *idea* of what it could be," says Cardinal Mahoney.

"Like some sort of medical explanation?" I ask.

He nods his head *perhaps*.

"Just because they haven't been able to figure out a medical reason for it doesn't mean there's not one. The doctors may know a lot, but it's not like they've cured cancer and doctors have spent a lot more time trying to figure *that* out than they have figuring out what's going on with Annika."

"You do realize many of these cases are hoaxes," says the thin one.

And apparently 321 are not—that's how many stigmatists have received the Church's official seal of approval since Saint Francis kicked off the festivities in 1224. But I don't say that.

"Which is not to say we're suggesting that," adds the cardinal.

Which *is* to say, I'm a prime suspect. I guess I have motive. I'm not a believer and, as an infidel, one might think I'd like nothing better than to make the Church look bad—despite its well-documented ability to do a fine job of that all on its own. They sure don't need my help. Still, they think that's my diabolical plan—to somehow destroy the Church's credibility. They're just big enough ego pigs to think I'd sacrifice my sister in order to make them look ridiculous. When you have a private party line to God, narcissism knows no bounds.

Mahoney probably tries to do the best he can within the scope of his limited worldview. Little does he know that if I could, I'd prove this is all a scam. Then the circus would shut down and Annika could be left in peace.

Mahoney looks so silly sitting there, with the tea and biscotti in front of him. And the fat one looks so serious with his interrogation asides straight out of *Law & Order*. And the skinny one looks so earnest with the little black pad in his lap, thinking that whatever he jots down will somehow add up to *the truth*. It's all so funny, I don't feel bad that I'm about to give them exactly what they want, the lifeblood of their vocation—*lies*.

"So, Father, can you explain how a computer works?"

"I believe it has to do with zeroes and ones, but beyond that—no."

"How about television?"

The three shift nervously, looking at one another, wondering where this could be going.

"Radio?"

The three largest instruments of mass media and these geniuses have no idea how they work.

"It's almost like magic, wouldn't you say?" I ask.

"Monroe, what are you trying to get at?"

"Have you ever dabbled in the black arts?" asks the fat one, with the deftness of a bloodhound picking up a false trail.

I confess, "Yes, magic has been a hobby of mine for quite some time."

The skinny one leafs through his notes and says, "That's never come up before." I tell them that's because I've plied my trade in secret. I didn't want people to think I'm a geek. Especially girls, who for some reason, I lament, don't embrace magic as an aphrodisiac. "I tried to learn guitar," I say, "but the magic kept pulling me back in." The priests nod as if they understand my dilemma.

Mahoney's brow itches that he's on to something, he's cracked the code. He wants to know if I can show him a trick. While I've never performed an act of magic in my life, I'm happy to give it a try. With the nonchalance of a saxophone player improvising a jam he's practiced all afternoon, I ask him for a single. I say, "I would ordinarily ask for a twenty for an illusion of this caliber, but I understand you've made a vow of poverty." Without the help of a laugh track, my joke falls flat.

Mahoney rifles through his wallet and comes up with a single. I twirl a magic marker in my fingers and I ask, "Cardinal Mahoney, do you have a dog?" He says he does, he *loves* his dog Izzy. I can just see him down on his knees saying, "Izzy a good boy? Yes he is." So I write down Izzy's name across George Washington's face in bold red ink. I show it to the priests, who pass it around. Then I put the single in my wallet. They're looking at me, skeptical. Is that all there is? "Oh yes," I say as if I almost forgot. "Now for the hocus-pocus." Then I clasp my hands together in the fashion of a Buddhist monk and mutter the holy babble of a believer speaking in tongues. "Now, if you go into Annika's room and look under her pillow, you'll find your money."

The thin one says he'll go, leaving the others sitting there smiling, nibbling at their biscotti. In just a few swallows a loud "Oh my Lord!" rattles through the house.

"Come here, you have to see this," he yells. So, dutifully we all head to the hallowed ground where my sister sleeps. The skinny one is standing over Annika, his jaw hanging in awe.

Annika's hands are bleeding again. But they're all looking at *me*.

"Look, I have nothing to do with *that*," I say. "My magical abilities stop at sleight of hand . . . uhhh no pun intended."

Annika's head is twisting back and forth, the tendons in her neck popping. "Just look under her pillow."

Mahoney reaches under the pillow and finds a crisp dollar bill with his dog's name on it.

"See, I told you you'd get your money back."

By now Mom and Maggie have arrived. Maggie's immediately on her knees and Mom has the glow of someone who expected vindication all along.

Mahoney, meanwhile, is looking extremely bewildered—*what's magic and what's real?* Mom sees the confusion on his face. "It's hard to believe, isn't it?"

"I really don't know what to say, Mrs. Anderson," he replies.

"Some people like to say the Lord's Prayer," Mom says.

Annika's head is moving back and forth. It's obvious she's in pain. I realize now, looking at her, why Mom finds these episodes so comforting. When Annika's in pain, you know there's *something* there, that she's not just a vegetable. There's no guesswork about it, like a blink or a possibly involuntary twitch of her hand. You're not just looking into her big blue eyes and seeing whatever you need to see.

As her head tosses back and forth, I'm thinking of the one time I tortured her. I had her pinned down on the ground and I was hawking huge loogies in the back of my throat and I was letting them dangle from my lips, hanging over her face, and then I'd slurp them back up, a trick I learned from Ben. She'd writhe and wiggle and I'd do it all over again, until finally the loogie fell in her face. And she looked at me, like *How could you be so cruel?* It's not like I wanted to spit in her face; I just wanted to scare her. I just wanted her to think I would.

And after that she always *knew* that I would spit in her face, which is a big difference from thinking I just might. Between spitting in her face and putting her goldfish in a blender, it's amazing she ever talked to me at all.

Annika's contortions ease and she returns back to her old self. The wounds in her hands are fresh. Earlier in the day her hands were pink; Mahoney examined them himself. Now it looks like nails are sticking through them. The cardinal rakes his hand through her hair and tells Annika everything is going to be all right, that God is with her.

Then the cardinal looks up and says to me, "If you're behind this, you're a very sick young man."

"All I said was that your money would be under her pillow. How was I supposed to know she was going to bleed?"

Mahoney looks closely at his precious dollar bill. It has blood on it now. "My bill came from the Philadelphia mint. This one is from San Francisco." He has the satisfied look of a grown man who has all of his candlesticks and knives lined up in a game of Clue. *Silly.*

"Oh well," I shrug. "It was worth a try." I suspected he'd be carrying money from the city of brotherly love. I just didn't get the right one.

"I hope you're satisfied with yourself, young man."

I ask him, "You didn't really believe I could somehow transport a dollar bill across the house and put it under my sister's pillow, did you? Because if you did think that, it says a lot more about you than it says about me."

"Look, young man, we're just trying to get to the bottom of this."

The fat one chimes in, "The cardinal is a very busy man."

"I don't know what you're complaining about. You got your miracle." Here these guys are whining about a magic trick, when everything they could possibly want to see is just lying there in front of them.

Mom's now the confused one. One can hardly blame her when she asks, "Monroe, what have you done?"

~~~

ONCE THE CARDINAL leaves it only gets worse. It's not like Mom *yells;* she merely wants to know what has gotten into me. I tell her it was just a prank. *It's not like anyone got hurt.* Still, she's *disappointed,* but she won't say it. She doesn't need to. Instead, she looks at me like she doesn't know who I am.

"I'm sorry you're not proud of me. I'm sorry I've never done anything you can brag about to your friends, like winning a worthless golf tournament or taking on the suffering of Jesus Christ. I'm sorry all I do is cut people's lawns."

Then she says, "But I *am* proud of you"—of course, that's what she *has* to say. She has no choice.

The kitchen is thick with silence. It seems there's nothing left to do but take the knife from the counter and slash it across my hand. So, I do—obviously without much thought at all. The knife is so sharp, it doesn't even hurt. Not yet.

"Are you proud of me now, Mom? Are you?" I say, holding up my bloody hand for her to see.

But she doesn't freak out. That must be what I want, because her calm reaction only gets me more upset. When she says, "Is this another joke?" I respond by slashing the other palm as well.

I hope she's happy now. But she's not.

"I look at you sometimes, Monroe, and I don't even recognize you."

That might have been when I called her just *another lemming for Jesus,* just *another brainwashed pilgrim.* That might have been when I told her everything she thinks is a figment of her imagination. I might have mentioned that she's living in a fantasy world. I might have told her that *anyone* can bleed for Jesus; it's not that fucking difficult. *See?*

I definitely say, *It's all right, Ma. I'm only bleeding,* and just when I think the Dylan reference eludes her, I see a look on her face, like she's just picked me out in a crowd at the airport after a long trip and I'm hiding behind a beard. For a second there I think maybe she's about to come to the realization that for two years she's been obsessed with a daughter in a coma while the rest of her family has fallen apart, but she just says, "But, honey, you're bleeding *all over the place.*"

And that's all it takes to get me to see how ridiculous I've become.

She says, "I don't understand you, Monroe. I really don't. There's a miracle going on here in this house, right under your nose, and you just pretend nothing is happening. You've seen the blood flow from her precious little hands for yourself. You've seen people come here sick and leave here healed, but it means *nothing* to you."

That's when Dad comes in, a suitcase in his hand, back from Baltimore. If he didn't look like he always has, you'd never recognize him. Ever since he quit drinking and turned himself over to God, he's actually not so bad. He doesn't scrub counters that are already clean—although all that blood must be tempting. He doesn't sweep up imaginary piles of dust; he just lets it all go. He's whittled his workday down to a mere twelve hours.

He wants to know, "Monroe, what happened to your hands?"

"I cut them."

He looks relieved. "Hmmm . . . Two cases of stigmata in the same family would have been quite an odd coincidence."

My hands are bleeding all over the place and no one seems to really care. Not that there was a lot of planning involved, but this is not going down at all like I expected.

Dad looks at me, like he's searching for a part of himself in my face, but he doesn't see it. I'm a stranger to him too. "Son, what exactly were you trying to accomplish by cutting yourself?" He has never called me "son" before. It sounds so strange, as if he's trying to convince himself that's really who I am.

What did I think I was trying to accomplish? I've heard that so many times in my life, I really should start keeping a list. *Monroe, what were you trying to accomplish when you painted the Albertsons' cat red?* I don't know (I was trying to warn the birds, although I realize now a bell would have been more effective). *Monroe, what were you trying to accomplish when you infested the McEnaneys' lawn with dandelion seed?* I don't know (but maybe Mr. McEnaney should have thought twice about banning his backyard as a shortcut). *Monroe, what were you try-*

ing to accomplish when you got the principal a subscription to Barely Legal? I don't know (but I sure didn't think I'd get caught). *What were you trying to accomplish?* . . . It's one of those things where if you have to ask, you'll never understand.

"I don't know."

"You should put some Neosporin on that." Old Dad would have lost it on me; new Dad takes everything in stride. Nothing ruffles new Dad: no more choppy waves—just smooth sailing. It's all going to be okay, it's not in his hands anymore. God is now on his side. He opens the refrigerator and pours himself a glass of orange juice. Straight up.

While Dad doesn't drink anymore, I should mention, he is on drugs. It's not a big deal, just Prozac. I saw the bottle in his medicine cabinet, hidden behind a jar of suppositories. I don't know why he thinks he has to keep it a secret—everyone's on it. You know that moment after the second drink? That calm that proceeds the buzz? Dad's like that now—*all the time*. Mellow, but not a zombie. High, but not wasted. He's what passes these days for *happy*.

I haven't seen Dad clean the kitchen counter since he got back. There's blood all over the place, but he just asks, "You guys want to watch *Survivor* tonight?"

We eat dinner with the TV on. We never used to do that before the accident. Annika still sits at the table; she's just not so talkative now. Like Annika used to, the TV smoothes over every edge, every silence, giving us all the impression that it's not so empty in here as it might otherwise seem.

Chapter 33

IT'S THE NEXT MORNING and I'm sitting at the counter of the Chef-O-Nette, the only diner in Chelsea. It's been here so long, you could call it old-fashioned, even if they do serve their milk shakes in Styrofoam cups. I'm drinking coffee, waiting for the morning dew to burn off so I can get to work. I'm reading *The Columbus Dispatch*. Usually I head straight for the sports page, but today the headlines are hard to miss. A Chelsea cop was arrested yesterday for exposing himself to an eight-year-old girl. His mug shot is plastered above the fold. I recognize him immediately; he's the lead investigator in the Heidi Morgan case. He's the guy who told me I'd better be good to Allison or he'd hunt me down and kill me. It's Officer O'Neill, also known as CPD 59843-04.

There's also a picture of Heidi, the same third-grade class photo she will forever be trapped in. The paper says that "Detective Warren O'Neill, who as recently as six months ago claimed to be on the verge of a 'big break' in the seven-year-old Morgan murder case ... but now it is O'Neill himself who has been arrested on an unrelated charge." The charge? Indecent exposure at the playground of my old elementary school.

Everyone at the counter is talking about it.

"For the love of mercy," says one.

"I think he coached my kid's football team," says another.

"They should castrate the bastard," offers the waitress as she fills my cup.

"Looks like there'll be no need for that," says a man eyeing the morning newsbreak on the television that hangs above all our heads.

Perky Cathy Halloway reports that Detective O'Neill was just found hanging in his cell.

"They should still castrate him," says the waitress as she fills my cup. "As an example to all the other scumbags out there."

I LEAVE MY COFFEE full and pay my bill.

I'm at Allison's house in less than a minute. A crowd of three dog walkers assesses the situation safely from across the street. If you were just casually driving by, you might think that the place has been TP'd, but instead of toilet paper, the contents of a filing cabinet have been unleashed on the yard. Newspaper clippings, handwritten notes, snapshots, pages and pages from yellow legal pads—*everywhere,* all pasted in place with the help of the circling automatic sprinkler. A closer look reveals that the picture window is broken, very possibly caused by the chair that is now precariously perched on a bush. Lest one get too close, the sprinkler makes its rounds, warding off any interlopers. Allison is waiting for me at the door.

"I heard the news and I thought maybe I should come over."

She offers her thanks with a hug and then she asks about my hands. I tell her I cut them on a fence, which she seems to swallow, and then I change the subject. "Guess your mom isn't taking it so well."

"You don't know the half of it. Not only is O'Neill a fucking pedophile—he's the one who killed Heidi—at least that's what he said in his suicide note. The pathetic fucking cockroach."

"That wasn't on the news."

"Well, it *will* be."

"When they called to tell her about O'Neill, she lost it. She ripped down all of Heidi's pictures, threw all her files everywhere . . . I wanted to take her to the hospital, I thought she might hurt herself, but that just made her flip out even more. Finally, I got her to take some Valium. She's asleep now. Look, if you don't want to deal with this, I totally understand."

"What can I do?"

"Before you say that, you might want to see what it's like inside."

She's right; the inside is worse. "It's like a hurricane came through here."

"Shhhh . . . she's still asleep. Not that I blame her. She completely trusted O'Neill and I guess I kind of did too. I mean, who would have ever thought?"

"That guy's beyond sick."

"What's *sick* is that O'Neill slept in Heidi's room for a week after it happened. He said it would help him to, and I quote, 'get to know her better.' *Sick* is feeding my mom hope that someday he was going to catch who did this. What's *sick* is that O'Neill was pretty much closer to my mom than anyone other than me since my dad left. She thought he was the only person on the police force who was still interested in finding out who killed Heidi. Everyone else had just written the whole thing off. They just wanted to forget it. He didn't want to forget it and now we know why—he got off on the whole thing."

"I'm really sorry." I don't know what else to say.

Allison says that O'Neill gave her mother copies of everything in the police files. *Everything.* "It was pretty much all she ever did, read over the files, the interviews, staring at the pictures all day. It was like she thought that if she only looked hard enough, the answer to everything would just appear, like everything would suddenly make sense."

"Sounds like the way my mom reads the Bible."

"All my mother ever wanted was justice."

"At least O'Neill is dead," I say, trying to look on the bright side.

"The bastard got off easy." Mrs. Morgan's up, coming down the stairs. "This place is a fucking mess."

Mrs. Morgan is modeling a new look as well. She's cut her hair into a sort of frenzied bob. Despite still looking like she wants to die, she's snipped at least ten years off her age.

"Don't worry about it, Mrs. Morgan, we'll take care of everything."

"Monroe, do you realize how lucky you are, having your sister still in a coma?"

"I never really thought of it as luck," I say.

"Maybe not, but it's better than being dead."

"Mom, I see you've regained your optimism." Allison may have a smart mouth, but at least there's some sincerity behind her sarcasm. She really does love her mom, maybe too much.

Allison hugs her and when she says *everything is going to be okay,* you know she's going to stick around and try to make sure it's not another empty promise.

Then Mrs. Morgan turns to me. "Is it true your sister can cure the sick?"

"It seems some sick people have gotten better after seeing her," I say, diplomatically.

"Do you have to be Catholic?"

"I don't think so. I think you just have to believe in *something.*"

"I wish I could be like that. A believer. I used to be, but it got lost somewhere along the way," she says.

"Mom, don't say that."

"You're right, honey, I shouldn't say that. I believe in *you.*"

EVERYTHING IN HERE has been destroyed. The only things left are the pictures of clouds on the ceiling. It's almost as if the roof was ripped off and all that survived were the four walls and the splattered junk inside.

"Just throw it all away," says Mrs. Morgan. "There's nothing worth keeping in here."

Allison picks up a picture, the one that used to be the center of the shrine, the one of Heidi looking at a leaf, like the mystery of the world can be found in its veins. "Mom, don't you want this?" she asks.

"I don't think I need one that big anymore. . . . I'm going to go up-stairs now."

And with that she's gone. "Hopefully she'll just go back to sleep."

I stand there looking at the junk, overwhelmed with the task at hand. "You heard the lady, everything goes," she says. But looking around in here—at the broken glass, torn pictures, and scattered candles—it's just too depressing.

Allison must think so too. She says, "Let's start outside."

If it weren't for the sprinkler wetting down the papers, we'd be cleaning up the whole street. Allison surveys the scattered remains of a pointless investigation. "Mom used to look over these files all the time, trying to make some sense of them. She'd come up with all these theories and O'Neill would keep bringing more, every time he came over for dinner. Sometimes he'd have another folder, some-times a whole box. It made her so happy, not just the information but seeing O'Neill. It was like proof that something was being done. Like she wasn't the only one who still remembered. That fucker's lucky he killed himself, otherwise I would have done it for him," she says, tying up another garbage bag with the lack of sentimentality one generally reserves for cleaning out a car.

We're almost done out front when the news van shows up. Local "newshound" Cindy Baker jumps out and makes her way straight to the front door, her camera crew in tow. It's like we're not even there. She's Cheryl Hanover's replacement. Cheryl moved on—as Grandpa says—"to smaller and worse things" as a host of a morning show in Los Angeles.

"Hi, I'm Cindy Baker, Channel 10—"

"Look, I know why you're here and I really don't think my mother wants to talk to you."

Apparently, Mrs. Morgan doesn't need her daughter to run inter-ference for her. She's at the front door, still in her dingy bathrobe, her hair all over the place. She asks, "Is the camera ready?" and the cameraman nods. She holds her head up high, looking as noble as a woman can in her bathrobe and no makeup, and says, "My heart was broken when Heidi was taken from us; now that her killer has been revealed, my heart feels like it was put through a blender. . . . There, you got your goddamn quote. Now please leave me alone."

Cindy looks at her cameraman and shrugs her shoulders. "It should always be this easy." They get back in the van and go.

There will be others.

Chapter 34

IT'S THE NEXT DAY and we're in Heidi's room. It looks a lot like it probably did the day she was killed. "She was a really clean kid," says Allison. "She would have been really pissed the way the cops trashed it, but O'Neill made them put it all back right where they found it. . . . I guess now we know why."

Stuffed animals huddle in the corner while an aquarium gurgles on the desk, but there aren't any fish in it. The bureau mirror is lined with badges from the Girl Scouts, friendship bracelets, and pictures of Jewel cut out from a magazine. There's a poster of a panda eating some bamboo. The only thing astonishing about this room is how ordinary it is.

The really disturbing part is that Mrs. Morgan has been sleeping here since her husband left, probably even before. The full ashtray on the bed stand and the smoke-stained ceiling are the only clues she's left behind.

Mrs. Morgan wants it all thrown away. She says she'd do it herself, but she's *just so tired*. All she really wants is to go to sleep, back in her own bed.

Heidi's bed is made and we're sitting on the yellowing lace spread. Allison wants to know, "You ever wonder what it's like to be in a coma or a vegetative state or whatever?"

"All the time," I say.

She says she does too. She wants to know what I think it's like. I tell her I think it's like having one of those dreams where you're being chased and right when they're about to catch you, you realize you're dreaming, and all you have to do is wake up and everything will be all right. But you *can't* wake up. Sometimes I think a coma is like that. You're stuck in that dream and you can't escape. Then it's not a dream anymore. *It's your life.* I tell her that I hope I'm wrong; I hope that it's like floating on a cloud.

Allison says she thinks it's like being wrapped in gauze. "You can hear what's going on, but it's muffled. You can see forms, but you don't really know who they are. You want to reach out and touch them, but you *can't*. You want to run, but your legs are stuck in place. It would be like being at your own funeral, but it never ends."

Allison wants to know if I'd trade places with Annika if I could, just for a day. I guess a day wouldn't be so bad, but I tell her I'd rather be dead than have all those people praying for me.

"You never know," she says. "Maybe that's what's keeping her alive. There are scientific studies, you know, that say prayer actually works, even when someone doesn't realize they're being prayed for. Of course, they were probably conducted at Oral Roberts University."

Allison wants to know if she can hypnotize me. In high school, when she was living in the cracks, she experimented with Wicca. You know, witchcraft, which she is quick to point out does not make her a Satanist or a Devil-worshipper or anything like that. Not that I thought it did. Wiccans, apparently, are a little touchy on this point. "It just means being hooked into nature," she says. "And there's nothing evil about that." On that note, she says she wants to do an experiment.

I say, sure, why not? But I say that only because I don't think it will work—I'm not the hypnotizing kind. She asks, "Why not? Are you a schizophrenic? A mental patient? Only people who can't concentrate on something for more than fifteen seconds can't be hypnotized. Considering how long you're willing to work on unhooking my bra strap, I think you qualify."

Fine. "I'm at your mercy. Just don't make me do anything stupid."

"Don't worry. You won't do anything stupider than you're already inclined to do. The key is that you have to want to be hypnotized. Do you want it?"

"Oh, *I want it*," I say.

It's just like you'd think it would be. She tells me to look in the eye of the panda on the wall. *Keep looking at the eye. You will notice a pleasant feeling coming over you. Your body is getting heavy. This soothing sensation of warmth starts in your legs and rises . . .*

It's futile to resist. It's like when you're watching TV late at night and you say you're just going to rest your eyes, and the next thing you know you wake up on the couch at three a.m. with Tony Robbins telling you to get a life, and you're so disoriented you'd swear he may actually be onto something.

I'm almost like that when I come out of it; I don't remember a thing. Judging from the look on Allison's face, it's probably better that way. She's scared.

"I thought you were just screwing around. Seriously, I didn't mean to hurt you, swear."

I feel okay. I don't have any idea what she's talking about. "*I* was screwing around with *you?*" I ask, confused.

"I thought you might be faking."

"What made you think that?"

"That's not important. The point is, I thought you were just messing with me."

"What'd I do ? Cluck like a chicken? Oink like a pig?"

"I'm sure you would have . . . but no."

"So what was it?"

"It really doesn't matter."

"Then just tell me."

"Fine, Monroe. If you must know, you told me that you love me."

How do I know she's not screwing with me now?

She says, "No one ever said that to me before. You know, someone I'm not related to."

Okay, I believe her. Truth is, I *do* love her, but I had planned on keeping it to myself, at least for another year or two.

"And I thought you were just messing with me, that you weren't really hypnotized, that it was all just a big joke to you. So I told you my hand was so hot that it was burning. Then I told you when my hand touched your chest, it would burn, but it wouldn't hurt. . . . Anyway, now you have my palm imprint burned onto your chest. Sorry."

I pull up my shirt, revealing a perfect reflection of Allison's hand in a very disturbing shade of red speckled with bubbling white welts. I run my fingers over it and it tingles. "Couldn't you have figured out another test, something, you know, that wouldn't scar?"

"I put your arm to sleep and pinched it, but nothing happened."

"Which would suggest it was working, right?"

"Yeah, but I just wanted to make sure. So then I got a cup of bleach and held it under your nose and told you to inhale the roses. You didn't flinch, you said it smelled like Annika."

"And that didn't convince you?"

"I guess I just wanted to see how far I could go."

"Is there anything else you want to say?"

"I love you too," she says.

You might think it would be creepy making out in your girl-friend's dead sister's bed, but it's not. Once you get going, it's the last thing on your mind.

After a while Allison comes up for air and asks, "Was Annika like really into the story of the crucifixion?"

"Besides obsessively acting it out with her doll collection? You know, tacking Ken up on a cross while Barbie, in her black fuck-me pumps, cries over the blood. But all kids do that."

"Monroe, is it so tough to be serious, just for a minute?" She says that a lot of stigmatists want nothing more than to feel the suffering that Jesus felt because they believe that by suffering like him it will make them *understand* and therefore love Jesus even more than they already do. "They actually *will themselves* to bleed."

"So when they bleed, it's like some sort of self-hypnosis?"

"Unless they're just cutting themselves, which I imagine Annika probably isn't doing."

While Annika may not have been preoccupied with Jesus's suffering, she has been surrounded by people who are. All day she lies there as my mom, Maggie, and Father Ferger read stories from the Bible. Annika has heard the story of the crucifixion and the resurrection about a hundred thousand more times than most little kids see *The Lion King*. Even if she's not conscious, it must get in there somehow, like people who listen to foreign-language tapes while they're sleeping and the next thing you know they're speaking Italian. If a pet rock were sitting there listening to it all, it would probably bleed too.

Allison says the burn on my chest, as incredible as it may seem, isn't so unusual. She says there was a hypnotist who convinced a woman that in a past life she was an urchin on the streets of London who died of a brutal beating. He instructed her to relive the moment of her death and, as she did, bruises appeared on her body in the exact places she said she had been beaten. In another case, a woman believed that in her past life she hanged herself. The hypnotist had her relive the moment when the chair fell out from under her and the rope tightened. Witnesses watched as a red welt circled her neck.

If people can sprout blisters and bruises with nothing more powerful than a few words, what's to stop Annika from replicating Jesus's wounds in the same way?

"When you think about it," Allison says, "it's not so completely strange; the whole country is under hypnosis. People say they believe in God, but they pray to celebrities, name brands, and cold hard cash. Instead of going to church and taking Communion, people go to the mall and consume some more. There's no greater sacrament than a mortgage you can't afford and a new car in your garage. They're always preaching freedom and independence. And maybe money can buy you those things, to an extent, but really they're selling self-imprisonment. The more tethered you are to things, the less free you are."

"Are you trying to put me to sleep again?"

"Fuck you, Monroe."

Chapter 35

Dad's finally got himself a hobby—suing anyone and everyone even marginally involved in Annika's accident. It's not like his other cases; he actually *likes* talking about his crusade to avenge those responsible for Annika's condition. You know, the way hunters like to talk about the trophy heads they have mounted on the wall? It's like that. He's already gotten a $250,000 settlement from SkyHigh Dive, the manufacturer of the diving board that Annika cracked open her head on, with an additional $100,000 from the makers of the board's sandpaper-esque covering, which apparently failed to prevent any slippage that may or may not have occurred. The company that put in the pool coughed up another $75,000. What they did wrong, beyond *existing*, I'm not sure. Dad says it was enough cash to make them hurt, but not so much that it was worth it for them to go to court over the whole mess.

Dad also bled the ambulance company for $75,000. After all, they really should have arrived at our house about two minutes faster than they did—two minutes that, one could argue, made all the difference. Sure, it's an argument that would have to overlook the fact that Annika was breathing on her own by the time the ambulance arrived, but *still*. They probably would have gotten away with it had they not started making excuses. When they got the call from the 911 dispatcher, they were stuck in a drive-thru line at McDonald's and couldn't get out. They were *trapped*. The real culprit here, of course, was McDonald's, who not only failed to live up to their commitment to fulfill the ambulance driver's order in the allotted two minutes, but, more perversely, they had installed a concrete curb that made fleeing the drive-thru line essentially an impossibility. As a result, the golden arches kicked in an extra $50,000—twenty-five for the curb and twenty-five for not living up to their promise of truly fast food.

Dad says he could have gotten more, but as part of the settlement McDonald's agreed to universally revamp the way they make their Filet-O-Fishes. That was really where it all went so terribly wrong. They were tossing the frozen fish patties directly into the fryer, requiring an additional thirty-eight seconds of cooking time, not to mention the extra time it took to fetch the patties from the freezer. It seems Filet-O-Fishes aren't exactly very popular. Or, as McDonald's likes to call them—*a specialty item*. Now, in a bold move, the Filet-O-Fishes are thawed out *before* they're cooked—a sea change that apparently not only cuts down on fat content due to less time in the fryer, but also makes for an overall tastier fish sandwich experience. Dad considers this a big victory, allowing him to faithfully argue that at least something good has come from all of this.

It should be noted that while none of the defendants actually had to admit any liability, *that's not the point*. Dad says money talks and those companies can tell their stockholders whatever they want, but their checks tell a different story. And it's the only story that matters. Dad says money is *always* the bottom line. He even squeezed $500 from the diving teacher Annika took a couple lessons from about two years before the accident. While Dad concedes it barely made it worthwhile to pick up the phone, he just wanted to make sure the guy didn't think he was going to get off scot-free.

So far, Dad has not served me with any papers for my involvement in the day in question. However, until the statute of limitations runs out, there's really no reason to gloat. He could come down on me at any time.

Dad says all of those other settlements are just milk money. The big fish is Dr. Singh and Riverbend Hospital. They've offered to settle for a cool million but Dad says that's *nothing*. He says it's an *insult*. There are equations for figuring out how much a life is worth and that's not even close. Not only does Dad want to go to trial; *he's looking forward to it.* He says when he's through with them, Father Ferger and Saint Victor's will be running that hospital and no one will ever get harassed over having a prayer circle again. Basically, Dr. Singh's big mistake was sitting there and doing nothing while Annika's swelling brain deprived itself of much-needed blood. Dad says Dr. Singh might as well have watched a puppy choke on a tangled leash and just sat there, patting the puppy's head and taking pictures, doing everything but untangle the leash. All Dr. Singh needed to do was perform a simple procedure that would have drained down the cushion of spinal fluid in which Annika's brain floats, and her brain would have gotten all the blood it needed. Dr. Singh, of course, did not do that. Dad likes to say it's an idea simple enough, even a jury can understand.

The trial is scheduled for this fall.

Chapter 36

THE SECOND ANNIVERSARY of Annika's first bleeding is coming up and everyone's making a big deal about it. Bigger than they did last year. Maybe this time around *USA Today* will document it all with a pie graph. Thirty-two percent of attendees have a terminal disease, 8 percent have untreatable STDs, 15 percent are off their meds, 30 percent are hypochondriacs, 15 percent are there for the free wafers and juice.

That first year the church was so packed, Father Ferger had to do three services. Mom says it really wore Annika out. "It's not like she's just lying there," she explains, anticipating an argument. After all, Annika is a *victim soul,* so theoretically she's feeling the pain of those who come to her for comfort. If I actually believed this notion, like my mother, there's just no way I would put someone I love in that position, especially when they have no say.

I've tried to be mad at Mom, but you know where Annika would be right now without her? She'd be warehoused in Oakside. That or dead. If she bled at all, they'd just write them off as bedsores. No one would care. Maybe we'd visit her on her birthday and afterward we'd go out to lunch at a little country inn and eat potato leek soup. We'd make a whole day of it. Maybe hunt for some antiques. Maybe buy some corn from a farmer on the side of the road. Whatever Mom is doing, she's doing it out of love. At least, her heart's in the right place. Sure, love just screws everything up. Most stalkers think they're in *love.* Mothers who kill their kids talk about how much they *love*

282 ~ Brian Strause

them. Men who beat up their wives, it's only because they're so in *love*. People slowly suffocate each other with love all the time. Love is a weapon we use to hurt the ones we love. I think Eminem said that and maybe he's right; but still, love probably should still count for *something*.

I asked Mom if it shouldn't be Annika's choice whether or not she wants to share her so-called gift. After all, she's the one feeling the pain. Mom said the strangest thing. She said, "It's not Annika's choice and it's not my choice. It's bigger than all of us." That's a pretty serious bomb to drop on your kid. *Sorry about your pain; I could protect you from it, but there's something bigger at work here, so you're just going to have to suck it up.* After all, it's God's will. It's hard to argue with that, not because God's will is so supreme, but because it's so irrational. "God's will" sounds like a legal document left behind by a crazy millionaire after he dies. He promises his son a gold-embossed mansion, but only if he agrees to kill the family dog in front of the kids.

I'm as guilty as anyone, I know that. All I do is stand around and watch. I used to think I'm like Switzerland—neutral. But there is no such thing. For so long, Switzerland got away with flying the flag of neutrality, like it was something to be proud of. The Nazis were rampaging across Europe, killing all the Jews they could, and we're supposed to think the Swiss were special because they didn't do anything about it?

Sometimes you have to choose sides. You can't just sit there. If you don't say no, you might as well be saying yes.

That first anniversary celebration was awful and I really don't want to go back. It's not just because Father Ferger singled me out last time and said I was a *hero*. He said if it wasn't for me, none of us would have been there celebrating such a joyous occasion. It sucked, but seeing Annika up there like that sucked even more. It's already creepy enough, in a peep-show kind of way, seeing her in the comfort of her own room with people passing by her window, but to see her in the *church*, propped up on the altar in a hospital bed? She might as well have been the roast beef at the Sunday brunch buffet at the country club. *Would you like a slice of my sister with your Communion wafer?*

They laid Annika out on the altar and right next to her there was a big picture of her from before the accident. The smile popping off her face in the photo stood in stark contrast to the drool coming down her chin. The photo was there to remind everyone she wasn't always that way; she used to be so full of life. They do the same thing at funerals, although the unheralded pioneers of juxtaposing lively photos with the dead are the marketing wizards at Denny's. Their meals look so tantalizing in their Technicolor renditions, but when the food arrives, they might as well be slapping down a plate full of roadkill.

But this was no all-you-can-eat buffet. The pilgrims couldn't get their mitts on Annika, thanks to the security offered by a red velvet rope. To Catholics, always reverent to authority, that rope might as well have been the hand of God. While the pilgrims couldn't touch her with their hands, there must have been a ton of germs flying around. After all, most of the people who came were there because they were sick or lame. Naturally, some must have been contagious. Meanwhile, they prayed Annika's ability to heal was contagious as well. It was a match made in heaven.

Despite the precaution provided by the red security rope, Annika got sick, and the scary part was that no one knew what it could possibly be. She had a rash all over her body. If it was Halloween she could have gone as a topographical map of Mars. The doctors were stumped. Tests were conducted. Biopsies were taken. They brought in a skin specialist from California and even he didn't know. No one could figure out the puzzle, until a cancer doctor from Minnesota got a look at her. He concluded it's a very rare rash that occasionally occurs in cancer patients who are going through chemotherapy. They don't know why, but sometimes it happens. Chemo is strange that way, but Annika has never been through chemo. The rash disappeared in two or three weeks. On the day it went away, Mom got a letter from a man who was at the anniversary service. He said he had tried everything to get rid of his cancer, but nothing worked. He almost lost all hope, but he thought one last try was worth it, so he came to see Annika. Two days later, he'd gone completely into remission. He wasn't the only one; there were others who said the same thing—they came to the anniversary service with cancer and now it's gone. Around our house, that's what we call documented proof of a miracle.

If that means nothing to you, Annika's supporters never fail to mention that Annika's hands started to bleed on July 16—the anniversary of the day the United States tested the first atomic bomb in New Mexico. Some might say that's a coincidence, but there are no coincidences when it comes to Annika. Everything that happens, happens for a reason. Everything is a piece of a puzzle, a puzzle of clouds that we'll be able to fully decipher only when we're dead, but until then, *have some faith.*

Enter Annika—the latest innocent chosen to suffer for the sins of us all. News about that rash and the chemo patient circled the globe. The waiting list to see Annika at our house is now three years long. I wonder if the people at the end of the list pray that Annika is still vegetating when their number comes up? Not that they're bad people, but they probably do.

Thanks to the the atomic bomb connection, there are people who think Annika's bleeding is a call for peace, that she's a living sign telling the world it should rid itself of nuclear weapons. It's not such a bad development. If you're going to be a living symbol for something, you could do a lot worse.

Chapter 37

Pᴇᴏᴘʟᴇ ᴅᴏɴ'ᴛ ᴛᴀᴋᴇ getting cured of cancer lightly. Saint Victor's isn't going to cut it, no matter how many services they conduct. That's why this year the festivities are moving to Clipper Stadium. Father Ferger figures they'll be able to fit twenty thousand pilgrims in there.

Celebrating the day Annika's hands first bled, I guess it's supposed to be like Good Friday, the day they tacked Jesus up on the cross, but the day I'm waiting to celebrate is Annika's Easter, the day she comes back—her resurrection. That's when I'll believe we really have a miracle on our hands.

I wasn't planning on going to the service, but Allison wants to see what it's like. When her sister, Heidi, was killed, fifteen hundred people showed up for her funeral; they overflowed out of the church. Most of the people had never met her. It's okay they didn't; it's not like they were there getting their kicks. When Heidi died, part of the community died along with her. That's what people said. That's what they were there to mourn.

Allison says she wants to be there for Annika's anniversary because at least it's about *hope*. When she lost her sister, hope was an immediate casualty. It's hard to find any hope when a little girl is found raped and killed in a ditch just a long fly ball away from her back door. All you can really hope for is the strength to overcome the loss. And, I suppose, you can hope it never happens again. So when

Allison asks if we can go and see what all the fuss is about, I don't argue with her. I just say, "Okay."

People come from all over the world, which is why the festivities are supposed to last for about four hours. Mom figures we might as well put on a show if people are going to come from so far away. If it's possible for there to be an adequate explanation as to how the embarrassing local band Annika's Sleeping got on the bill, that will have to suffice.

Mom has been doing Annika's hair since six this morning. She looks beautiful. She usually does, especially when her mouth's not hanging open. It's been more than two years since her hair has been cut. It's long, blonde, curly, and full of life—just like it always was. Today, it matches her face. Perfect skin, rosy cheeks. She really is a Sleepy Beauty. That's what the pilgrims always call her.

When we get to the stadium, there are already fifty buses in the parking lot. Pennsylvania. Indiana. Michigan. West Virginia. Tennessee. Massachusetts. School buses. Chartered buses. Church buses. But the bus that sticks out is the one that says PRO-LIFE FOREVER on the side. I was hoping they wouldn't be here. I guess I haven't mentioned it before, probably because they're so annoying, but you might as well know—the so-called right-to-life movement has adopted Annika as their poster girl. Fortunately, they've taken a backseat to the antinuclear crowd, but they're always around. To the antiabortion crowd, Annika represents the sanctity of life, how even a girl in a coma has something to offer. Hopefully today they won't be foisting photos of aborted fetuses in everyone's face; they'd only be preaching to the converted. That, however, won't stop them from setting up an information booth in hopes of attracting more fanatics to their cause.

The scene in the parking lot isn't much different from an Ohio State football game, except that no one's running around drunk, with his shirt off, screaming "Fuck Michigan!" A church from Bucyrus is serving pancakes. One from Kentucky has doughnuts and coffee. The matrons of Saint Victor's are dishing out a notoriously dry pecan roll. They're also selling shirts with Annika's picture that say EXPECT

A MIRACLE. The pro-lifers are also selling T-shirts with Annika's picture on it with the message EVERY LIFE COUNTS. The antinuclear people have T-shirts that say ANNIKA IS THE *REAL* BOMB, with a mushroom cloud providing the halo behind Annika's head. There are tables with buttons and candles and pendants and rosaries—all with Annika's picture on them. The proceeds supposedly go to Catholic charities, which at this point might as well be code for paying off sexual abuse settlements.

That's when we stumble into Katie. She looks even more beautiful than she did when I first met her almost two years ago. Her smile is brighter; her hair is shinier. She's got a baby in a pouch and a man by her side.

"Monroe! I was hoping we'd see you here," she yelps. "Bet you thought I was dead," she adds, laughing.

"The thought crossed my mind," I say, but the truth is I never thought of her as dead. I never really thought of what happened to her or even if she made it back to Canada. When I think of Katie, I think of her kiss and the way she held my hips. I think of her smile and the way she wrapped herself around me with her legs. I think about the way I held her breast in my hand and the way she shivered in response. It's a revolving loop, moments that project themselves over and over again in my head so often that if they were on film, they would have disintegrated long ago. They'd be scratched and the sound would pop, but in my memory it might as well have happened yesterday. After all, when it comes to sex—*real* sex, it's the only reference point I have.

She hugs me, her baby sandwiched between us. "Don't worry, she's not yours," she whispers, dispelling a thought that had never entered my mind.

"I meant to write you and tell you how everything is going," she adds, prompting a smile from the man I presume to be the baby's father. "But I didn't want to jinx it," she says.

"Don't worry, I totally understand."

Then she introduces her child and her husband. Her child, it should be no surprise, is named Annika. Her husband's name is

Randy. He's big, strong, and bearded—basically, the opposite of me. He seems nice enough, though, even if he is a cop. He practically crushes my hand when he shakes it, but I don't think he means to.

Allison has wandered over to a stand of votive candles; she's not exactly the most social person in the world.

"You guys look great," I say.

"What can I say?" says Katie. "It *worked*. I'm better and I've never been happier." As if to add an exclamation point, she rubs the back of Randy's grizzly bear neck.

"That's really fantastic," I say, and I'm not being sarcastic. It really is.

Randy says, "I never really believed in miracles before, but you can only close your eyes for so long."

Katie adds, "Every day is such a gift."

"We just wanted our little Annika to have a chance to meet her namesake."

I tell them they could have just come to the house.

"We thought this would be more festive, you know, being with other people whose lives she touched. There's going to be a testimonial section, right? That's what it said on the Web site."

I tell her, "I don't know," but I'm thinking, "I sure hope not."

Katie says they should probably go find a seat and I tell them I'm sure I'll catch up with them later, inside.

As they walk away, Allison pops up next to me. "I didn't realize you fraternized with the pilgrims."

"When I first met her, I didn't know any better."

"Well, she's pretty."

"She used to have leukemia," I say. Allison doesn't have anything to say to that, but I know what she's thinking. *That I had sex with her.* Women can just tell; they can smell it. That's what it says in *Maxim* and, according to them, there's not enough cologne in the world to cover it up.

Either way, Allison lets it go at that. In appreciation of her bitten lip, I take her hand in mine. The ceremony is about to begin, so we head inside. The place is packed and it's the hottest day of the year.

The crowd is quiet, reverent, like they're at church, even though many are wearing shorts and tank tops. It feels like a festival for the sick, a lollapalooza for losers: the place is cluttered with crutches and wheelchairs and people rubbing their rosaries. Handicapped parking must have filled up three hours ago.

Father Ferger starts it all off with a prayer and then he actually says, "Without further ado, I'd like to welcome Annika's Sleeping."

The band takes the stage with their acoustic guitars and a little drum kit that looks like it's from Kmart. They're strictly a coffee-house act, but there's no reason to be nervous. The crowd is full of the people who keep Wonder Bread in business, lovers of Jell-O salad, and avid devotees of *Wheel of Fortune*—so they'll be happy with just about anything as long as they stay away from feedback. You look at the kids in this band and it's hard not to wonder how they make it through their days without getting beaten up. The Birkenstocks, the peach fuzz, the friendship bracelets: it's like they were all hanging around at some church retreat breaking it down to "Puff the Magic Dragon," when someone must have thought, "Wow, we sound really good; we could do this in front of an audience." Remarkably, there is a girl in the band. She's even kind of cute. She plays the Casio, effectively coloring the proceedings with a gloss of electronica.

They start it off with their hit "Annika, Save Me," which, until now, I don't think I've ever actually listened to all the way through.

> *Annika, you may be sleeping*
> *But we know your heart is weeping*
> *It's a tragic world*
> *And you're just a girl*
> *But I know you can save me*
> *Annika, won't you save me?*
>
> *Annika, I can see in your eyes*
> *That someday you will rise*
> *And when that day comes*
> *You will walk with God's Son . . .*

As the song's saccharine chorus strips the enamel off our teeth, Allison holds my hand and squeezes it. And with that small gesture, the pain of the moment effectively subsides.

"I love you," I say. It's the first time I've said those words since she put me under hypnosis. It's the first time it felt like the right thing to say. I take off my sunglasses and look in Allison's eyes, so she knows I'm not joking and she says she loves me too. No hesitation at all. Then a terrible thought crosses my mind: Does that mean "Annika, Save Me" is now "our song"?

THE BAND KEEPS AT IT. Ordinarily, if I'd heard a song like "Annika, Feel My Pain," I'd feel inclined to jam a fork in my hand; but when you're with someone you care about, you can be anywhere and the rest of the world just doesn't matter. Maybe that's what it means to be in love.

"We've got a very special guest—Billy Hoboken from everyone's favorite jam band Dolphin."

A section of the bleachers rises in tie-dyed solidarity. Hippies, it seems, are always able to find one another.

"Annika Anderson changed my life," Billy says. "She showed me the light and when I heard about this anniversary, I just knew I had to be here." He's up there with his guitar, poised to serenade us with his newfound inner glow. "I used to think drugs were the only way to get high. Now I know that was just the Devil talking. I used to think I could only function in a band, but thanks to the strength I've gotten from Annika, I'm pleased to announce I'm going solo."

The hippies look around confused, unsure whether this is a positive development or the end of their world.

"Isn't that your ex-girlfriend?" asks Allison.

Sure enough, Emily is off to the side of the stage, a tambourine in her hand. She's wearing a Yoko Ono–esque kimono with what I presume is a lack of irony.

"Oh, so it is," I say. "What a pleasant surprise."

"Sarcasm is so sexy," she says. "Did I ever tell you that?"

There's an empty concession stand underneath the bleachers. It wouldn't have exactly been my first choice of places to make out with Allison, but it works out surprisingly well. The only detail that really matters is that I'm not thinking about Emily and I'm not thinking about Katie. I'm just thinking about kissing *Allison* and how all I want in the world is for her to feel as good as I do.

By the time we're back with the crowd, Billy and Emily have vacated the stage. They've been replaced by a line of pilgrims there to offer their testimonials. They want to tell everyone how Annika has changed their lives. The first woman says her five-year-old son got attacked by the neighbor's pit bull. "He lost so much blood, it's hard to believe there was any left. Even the men in the ambulance said so. . . . I'm crying and screaming and just out of my mind. He's my baby, *my only baby*. And it just came out of my mouth, I don't know where from—it must have been God—but I said, 'Annika Anderson is a living saint.' It was me talking, but it *wasn't*. And once I said those words, everything was okay."

Then there's the man who says he lost his little girl to muscular dystrophy and wanted to kill himself. He didn't see what the point was anymore, but that was before he saw Annika on TV. "There was a halo of light around her head." . . . And there's the high school boy who got dragged behind an eighteen-wheeler on his motorcycle for *two miles*. He had to have skin from his ass grafted onto his face. Sure, people made jokes, but after visiting Annika, he realized everything he has to be thankful for. . . . And there's the teenage girl with anorexia who says she'd look in the mirror and see the fattest girl in the world even though she weighed only eighty-three pounds. Her mom brought her to see Annika and the next time she looked in the mirror, she saw her true self for the first time.

Those are the kinds of things people have to say. Every story is different, but like snowflakes, they might as well be the same. The line snakes around the outfield wall. Over by the sign for McGeiger Ford, I see Katie and her new family patiently waiting.

When my brother, Ben, takes the stand, I can't help but be surprised to see him here at all. He quickly recovered from his fall and his golf game only got better. He won the NCAA Championship by seven strokes and turned pro the next day. There are people who say that what happened to Ben is a miracle. And many of them have taken to following Ben around on tour.

When he takes the microphone, he's instantly recognized with a loud semi-standing ovation.

"I'm Ben Anderson, Annika's brother. It seems many of you know my story, so I'm not going to recount it here. I know a lot of you think what happened to me was a miracle. I think it was luck. A miracle is when the laws of science are suspended. But believe me, gravity works."

The crowd laughs, falling into a typical Ben trap—the lull before the storm.

"The thing is, no angel helped stop my fall. A hedge did. My bones broke. I drank my milk and I healed. It took work, not prayers. I'm a golfer and what I do requires concentration. And that's why I'm standing here today. I've asked you people in person and I've asked on Annika's Web site. Now I'm asking again—*please quit coming to watch me play*. I appreciate the support, I really do, but I don't want to see your posters with scripture from the Bible. I don't want to hear how God is on my side after I jack a three-hundred-yard drive off the tee. I don't want to hear your prayers when I'm stuck in a sand trap. Seriously, it creeps me out. It creeps *everybody* out. So, please, just quit it, all right? . . . Oh yeah, and by the way, I'm not the one who saved Annika from the pool. That was my brother, Monroe—so thank him."

They're not standing for Ben anymore. They're just sitting there, looking perplexed, like a dog that was told it was bad for the first time in its life.

Father Ferger, though, has a biscuit to pick their spirits back up.

"I've always said that golf courses are no place for the faithful. I can't think of another place where the Lord's name is taken in vain so often." That gets them laughing, the sting of Ben's admonition behind them. Meanwhile, the line for testimonials hasn't gotten any shorter.

There must be forty or fifty priests here. They're smiling, completely oblivious to what many say is the abuse of my sister. To them she's a vessel, another symbol in the roulette wheel of Catholic icons. She's not a person to them. After all, if that's all she is—*just a person*—no one would be here.

Busloads of nuns stack the box seats over the third-base dugout. They're suckers for this kind of thing. Most of them probably wish they were Annika. Since they'll never have a man, the penetration of stigmata might just be as close as they ever get.

The nuns are indistinguishable from afar, just a mass of black and white. If you stare at them hard enough, it's like looking at a newspaper for too long, and it all just blurs together into streaks of gray, which is kind of funny since there are no grays in the life of a nun; everything is black or white, wrong or right, good or evil. If you stare at anything long enough, it breaks down—beauty turns ugly, ugliness becomes beautiful. I bet if you put a cancer cell under a microscope, then blew it up and put it on a wall in the Museum of Modern Art, people would look at it and say how beautiful it is.

Instead of looking at blocks of people, I think maybe I'll just focus on them one by one. Maybe that won't be so bad. As I scan the crowd, it becomes clear that so many of these people are used to being invisible. Especially the ones in wheelchairs. People think that by *not* staring, they're being compassionate. And just to make sure that no one *thinks* they're staring, they don't look at all. Maybe they think that makes them *good people*. But I wonder which is better—being ignored or being stared at? To be invisible or to be an eyesore?

I see eyes rolling around, mouths wide open, goiters that are about to burst. I see rashes, bald-headed girls, and little blind boys. I see tremors, lesions, and full body casts. I see pasty faces that haven't seen the sun, smiles that probably haven't broken in years. I see hope in eyes that have been accustomed only to flickers of resignation.

It's an island of misfits.

These are my sister's people.

I'm looking at a woman in a wheelchair. She must be in her sixties. She's wearing a simple dress with blue flowers and her hands are shaking and her head is bobbing back and forth, all in perfect rhythm, to what I'm not quite sure. She's a mass of tics and shakes, her body gradually flopping to the side. There's a woman next to her, probably her sister, who's there to help. She props her back up, but the shaking never misses a beat. Allison says the woman probably has Parkinson's, she's probably too far gone to remember it didn't always used to be this way. Allison bets it's her sister who prays that she will get up and walk away—then maybe she can have her life back. "Even though there's only one person in that chair, two people are attached to it," she says.

Whether you look at this crowd as a whole or just in pieces, it's depressing. I thought that having Allison with me, I might be immune, but I'm nauseous. It's kind of like last week when two guys who work for me took me to a strip club. I'd never been to one before, which they thought was some sort of crime, so they insisted I come. And it was fun at first. We were drinking and there was a moment there when I would have sworn that the girls were really *talented*, that they really knew how to dance. But by the time I was getting a lap dance, it wasn't so much fun anymore; it was just sad. I tried to drink through it, but each drink boomeranged, making me *more* sober, and pretty soon it was obvious that there was no way I could ever get drunk enough to enjoy the delights of some broken girl shaking her rack in my face.

Maybe Annika isn't so different than those strippers. It's not like either one set out to be that way; it's just what happened. As far as I know, Annika never thought of pursuing a career as a religious icon, just like most strippers probably never thought they'd be getting naked in front of a bunch of scumbags for a fistful of dollar bills. They're both victims of circumstance. People come to see Annika to heal their pain. People go to strip clubs to forget about their pain. Some people say Annika brings them closer to God; a good lap dance supposedly has a similar effect. Strip clubs provide a fantasy that makes promises it can't keep and the Church does pretty much the same thing. It's no wonder the believers are always trying to shut down the titty bars; it's their competition.

THE EXPERIMENTAL DANCE troupe from Ohio State takes the stage and performs their original dance, choreographed especially for Annika. It's called *The Butterfly*. While it prompts the gag reflex in me, everyone else seems to be swallowing it fine. When the butterfly emerges from its cocoon, the crowd stands on its feet and cheers, that is, the ones who are capable of standing.

Allison says maybe we should take a walk.

We work our way through the back into the restricted area behind the stage, and there's Annika. She's sequestered in a little hut made especially for today. Actually, it's a storage shed; but they cut out a hole and filled it in with a picture window so everyone can look in. I knew this was in the works, but it's one thing to hear about something and it's another to see it for yourself. The idea is to keep Annika protected, not only from the sun, but also from the sickness of the crowd. I see Mom through the window, brushing her hair. From here it looks like a mother ape picking bugs out of her little baby ape's head.

When Mom sees us, she emerges from the hut and asks, "Doesn't Annika look beautiful today?" She knows the answer all too well.

"She *always* looks beautiful, Mom," I tell her.

Mom's beaming, looking at her daughter in the storage shed, and it takes me back, back to a place I've only been to in flashes of 3" x 5" black-and-white photos. Back to when Mom was a kid. She's wearing the same smile she wore when she was a 4-H'er and her cow won the blue ribbon, *pure joy*. Now she's got another prize on her hands. Lying there in her holding pen, Annika's a heifer, a veal cow stuck in a stall. And this afternoon, she's the main course.

Mom says, "Doesn't that dress look nice on her?" She's talking to Allison, not me. Allison says it's really *beautiful*. She says it brings out the blue in Annika's eyes. Mom and Maggie made it themselves, just for today. Allison smiles along. She's either a real good sport or a real good liar.

Annika's hut is hooked up to a tractor. That's how they're planning to bring her out. Father Ferger's up on the stage, talking about healing and salvation and the power of prayer. He's talking about the beauty in small things and the miracles that happen every day without anyone even noticing. You'd think he'd get sick of saying the same things over and over again, and maybe he does, but he says them like he's saying them for the first time.

I'm not quite sure what Allison is up to when she says, "Mrs. Anderson, there's the most amazing quilt of Annika by a church group from Indiana. Did you see it?"

"Not yet," says Mom.

"Would you like to go take a look at it? I'm dying to see your reaction," Allison replies.

Mom thinks for a moment and asks if it would be okay if I stayed with Annika until she came back. "Sure, no problem," I say.

As Allison and my mom head out of the hut, Allison winks at me, sealing our unspoken conspiracy, a conspiracy that doesn't yet actually exist.

I'm left alone with Annika. She's glowing, her face lit like a lantern. Her shine makes me forget the ridiculous ivory dress, her hair's manufactured luster, and the hut's plywood panels. It makes me forget, for a moment, what we're here for.

I can't keep my eyes off her. I feel warm, like a winter morning, and I'm covered in blankets and the cold floor, just inches away, makes it impossible to get out of bed.

If *I* can't stop from staring, how can I blame anyone else? I realize what I need to do. I can't sit by and stare anymore. I have to do *something*. I have to get out of bed.

I already hate myself for letting it get this far. These last two years have been like when you see a glass falling off the counter and you're actually close enough to make the save, but you can't. Or maybe you just *don't*. It's not like it's happening too fast to react. If anything, it's the opposite. You're so close and the end result is so obvious; everything slows down. You could grab that glass and tragedy could be averted, but instead you just watch, its contents sloshing in slow motion—and then, when it hits the ground, real time explodes shards of glass everywhere. It's not like there was nothing you could do—you were paralyzed by the moment. It's not like you *wanted* it to happen. It's not like you didn't want to be helpful. Only when you're cleaning up the mess can you see how easy it would have been to stop it.

What I *should* have done is always so obvious when there's nothing left to do. What I *should* have said comes to me only when the conversation is over.

It's not going to happen this time. This glass has been falling for far too long and the only way I'm going to catch it is if I finally hold out my hand.

Chapter 38

I'M AT THE WHEEL of the tractor and the engine is running. It's not like I see a sign. But if there were one, it would say *go*. It's not like I'm being moved by the spirit. But if it were moving me, it would be putting the pedal to the metal. It's not like I hear a voice, but if it were talking it would say I better do something, and I better do it before it's too late.

I've never driven one this big. Besides the enclosed cab, it's not much different than my Cub Cadet. In no time we're in the parking lot, heading for the exit.

I go by Ben and Lisa walking back to his car, holding hands. I honk the horn, which mysteriously comes out as "The Battle Hymn of the Republic." I won't make that mistake again. They see us and Ben yells, "What the fuck are you doing?"

"I don't know, just taking a drive."

"Nice day for it," says Lisa.

"Is that Annika in there?" Ben asks.

"Yeah," I say. "I was just taking a drive," I mention again.

Ben smiles. "Well then, what the fuck are you waiting for?"

It's a pretty good question. And I think Ben might just be happy with my answer, which is to keep driving. After all, Ben is all about results. That's one thing, I guess, that golf is good for. At the end of the day, you always know your score.

As I turn the corner, I'm greeted with the vision of Emily and Billy making out by the Porta-Johns, a sight that propels me to the exit—not out of longing or regret, other than the longing to get away and the regret that the past can't be undone. I don't look back; I keep going forward.

Mom must have sent Maggie out on an errand; she's pulling in as I'm leaving. I wave and smile and she waves back, continuing along her way. That was easy. *Too easy.* With Maggie out of the way, the dozen or so cops lining the perimeter are a breeze. Then again, cops aren't too tough to fool. Years of television viewing have taught me that cops are like dogs; they can smell fear. Look like you know what you're doing and cops will let you get away with just about anything.

Once we're out of the parking lot, we're driving down Broad Street, heading toward downtown. I want to get Annika out of there, but I'm not sure where to go. For now, *away* will have to do.

I'm driving about twenty miles per hour in a tractor through the worst neighborhood in town. At least, the worst one *I've* ever been to. It's so bad there's a boarded-up McDonald's. When your neighborhood McDonald's can't stay in business, you know you live in a dump. There's a ton of graffiti everywhere I look, but I don't know what any of it means. The gangs around here really ought to spend a little less time staking out territory and a little more time making their territory worth staking out.

It's still Sunday morning and there aren't a lot of people out, just a few gray hairs parked on their porches. They've probably seen *everything* already. They wave when we go by. Even though Columbus is a cow town, farm machinery doesn't often cruise down Broad Street. Not anymore. You'd think we'd be cause for alarm, but they just look like they're wondering what happened to the rest of the parade.

The sound of dogs barking is drowned out by the whirl of a helicopter's blades. It could be the cops or it could be the news. It doesn't matter. It's only a matter of time before I'm busted. At the first overpass I see, I pull over.

I'm going to have to ditch the tractor . . . but not until I get Annika out of there. She's still in her hut, seemingly oblivious. I barely even looked before, but Mom really did do a great job with her hair. And I'm just going to mess it all up.

"Annika, you really do look beautiful today. I'm sorry no one's going to get a chance to see it."

She's looking at me all doe-eyed. Actually, she's not really looking at me, more off to the left a little bit. But, at least, she's gazing in my general direction. I tell her, "You're going to break some hearts someday." Then I lift her up. You might think she would be dead weight, but when she's in my arms it's like holding a load of balsa wood. She's so light, she might as well be floating.

Thankfully her wheelchair is in the hut; otherwise we'd be at a dead end. We've got to keep moving. The helicopter is hovering like a vulture that knows there's something dead down there; it's just not quite sure where. There are sirens in the distance, but in this neighborhood, maybe there are *always* sirens in the distance.

It's not too late to go back. It's not too late to pretend this never happened. All I need to say is that we took a wrong turn.

It would be just like me to do that, but I've been *like me* for too long. Sure, I could leave the decision up to Annika, but I don't have the time to wait around for her to blink. Besides, I *know* she wouldn't want this anniversary party. This is no time for doubt, but it is time for a decoy. That's what we need. That's all I'm thinking about when I lock the tractor in drive and send it on its way. The cab is enclosed and the glare from the sun is blinding. Maybe no one will realize there's a ghost at the wheel.

What I'm *not* thinking about is how much damage an unmanned tractor can do. The death. The mayhem. The destruction. That's *not* on my mind. And it's probably best that it's not. Otherwise I'd undoubtedly chicken out. Like I always do.

The cops are coming our way. These sirens are for us. So I turn into an abandoned gas station and roll Annika between a Dumpster and a chain-link fence. We'll be safe here. *I'll figure out a plan,* that's what I'm thinking. But we're face-to-face with a rottweiler. He's inches away, his mug pressing against the chain-link fence. His hot breath in my face. One of his ears has been torn off, but he's wagging the stub of his tail. He just wants to *play,* at least that's what I think it means when he tries to lick Annika's face through the fence.

Once the cops go by, we keep walking. I tell Annika, "It may not seem like I know what I'm doing, but it's all going to be for the best." I swear not on the Bible, not on our mother's grave. "I swear, it's okay. Everything will be all right." I keep saying that, more to myself than to Annika. I say it over and over so much, it might as well be a prayer.

We're going down a side street, the sirens bouncing off the corrugated tin of abandoned warehouses. They're not so far off. The first two cops have been joined by others; it's a symphony of sirens, although around here the tune is probably getting pretty old.

A white guy in a rusted-out Olds Delta 98 pulls up right next to us; his window is down. "You ain't from around here," he says.

"Not really," I say.

"You know what they do to white people down here?" he asks, but he says it like he knows the answer. He looks like Tom Waits circa 1983 after a bar fight. He's almost handsome in a down-and-out kind of way; but when he smiles, it's all gum.

"No, what?"

"They eat 'em. Just like fried chicken."

"But *you're* white."

"I'm sourdough, you're *Wonder Bread*," he says.

"I didn't know black people like sourdough. I thought that was more of a San Francisco thing."

"Fine, I'm *corn bread*," he says. "Not that it fucking matters. They're looking for *you*."

Corn bread is more yellow than white, but I don't say that. "So why don't you turn us in?" I ask.

"And help out the pigs?" he laughs. "Fuck that, they ain't never done nothing for me."

I refrain from pointing out his use of the triple negative. This is not a situation where one can be picky. What we need is a car.

"Car trouble?" he asks.

"Yeah."

"But I don't see no car."

"That's the trouble," I tell him.

He says to get in. I push about a case worth of empty beer cans off the backseat and lay Annika down, her wheelchair folded up by her side. I hop in front and before I can close the door, we're burning rubber and he's offering me the biggest joint I've ever seen. I tell him no, maybe some other time, and he says, "Your loss. I'm not going to ask you again. By the way, I'm Stan."

"Stan the Man."

"Yeah, I guess so." I knew it was a stupid thing to say before it came out of my mouth, but that didn't stop me.

"I'm Monroe and this is—"

"The less I know, the better. In fact, as far you're concerned, Stan's not even my real name. Where to?"

I don't know where else to go, so I ask him if he wouldn't mind driving us back to Chelsea.

"A Chelsea boy, huh? Man, I would have cleaned out the car had I known I'd be having such esteemed company."

When you say you live in Chelsea, people pretty much automatically hate your guts. I should have told him we live in Fairview. It's not so far away and not quite so rich; we could have walked. "I know this all probably seems kind of weird to you," I tell him. "But it's not what it looks like. She's my sister. She's in a coma."

He looks up at the rearview like he doesn't realize there's someone else with me. "I don't know what it looks like and I don't really care. I just like to drive," he says, popping in an Al Green eight-track. He takes a long drag off his reefer and continues, "People don't like advice, but I got some for you anyway: don't ever get married. That's my gift to you. They say a man is the king of his castle, but that ain't the way it is anymore . . . fuck, maybe it never was. All I know is this: if I want to be the king, I gotta drive."

"King of the road," I say. It comes out patronizing, but I'm just trying to stay on his good side.

"Maybe you shouldn't talk so much," he says, cranking up the music, leaning back into his chair. Fifth Avenue is a ghost town on a Sunday morning: closed-up Chinese restaurants and pizza parlors with their dead neon signs. As Al is singing about how it feels like winter and the snow is falling in his improbably titled single, "Feels Like Summer." Stan turns onto Stoneridge Road and I direct him to our driveway. Before I get out I offer him a twenty for his time and he scowls. "It's *you* who did me a favor," he says. "Taking me down a street I never been before. . . . I'll take your money," he says, snatching the cash away. "But what I really need is some cans. You got any cans?"

"Have I got cans?" I say, lighting up his neon bloodshot eyes. First, I get Annika out of the car and put her back in her chair. Remarkably, her dress is still clean. "We've got *a ton* of cans in the garage. I'll get them for you." Ever since Dad quit drinking booze he downs half a case of Coca-Cola a day and that's just when he's home. Who knows what kind of habit he has at the office? The recycling bin is pretty much always full. I roll the bin out to his car and Stan couldn't be happier. He pours them through the window, filling up his backseat. "You just made my day," he says, his face lit up.

"Maybe we'll blow down a joint sometime," I say.

"My daddy once told me," he says, trailing off as he lights up another big fat one. He inhales the smoke into his lungs, his chest rises, and his nose glides high, searching for the scent of what he is about to say. And as he lets the smoke out through his nose, it comes back to him. "My daddy, he told me so many things—but this one is true: there are no second chances." And with that, he guns his engine and pulls away.

I push Annika around to the back of the house and park her by the pool. She's wearing all white and her hair is golden in the sun.

Here we are where it all started, but it won't be for long. If we were still kids we'd hide in the bushes out back. That's where I'd go when the going got rough—when they made me practice piano or wear a suit or when Ben had tortured me and I didn't want him to see me cry anymore. There were secret tunnels back there—they went through the whole neighborhood—but they're probably overgrown now. You could see everything through the bushes, but no one could see you. That's where I'd go when I'd run away, but I never lasted past dinner. I guess that's all it would take today. By dinner, everyone will be on their buses headed back to wherever they came from, that is, if they haven't formed a posse looking for us.

That's probably what they'll do. If they figure out what happened, they're going to want to crucify me.

Chapter 39

GRANDPA'S IN THE living room watching a John Wayne movie. I thought for sure he'd be at the stadium with everyone else.

"Hey, Grandpa, what's going on? Why aren't you down at the anniversary party?"

"They're playing John Wayne movies all day."

Grandpa, by the way, is not senile, even if it sometimes seems that way. His priorities are simply shifting.

"There's a lot of hot older women down there," I say.

"What can I say?" he says. "I like it when they come to me."

That's not senile, just practical.

"Was that Annika I saw with you by the pool, Monroe?" he asks.

"Yeah, Grandpa, it was."

"What? You kidnap her from that celebration?"

"Something like that."

"Good for you," he says.

"Really?" I ask.

"You want to know something else?"

"Sure."

"John Wayne's pretty much an asshole."

"Yeah?"

"They're going to come looking for you, you know."

"Yeah, I guess they will."

"But the less I know about it, the better." And then he pauses and says, "Your mother put my car keys in the peanut jar above the refrigerator." Grandpa's not supposed to drive anymore, but instead of laying down the law about it, Mom hides his keys.

"You're the greatest," I tell him.

"Stay out late," he says. "Get in lots of trouble."

IT'S NOON AND the streets are empty. We're in Grandpa's Cadillac and I've got Annika strapped in the passenger seat, her head nodding off to the side. If you don't look too closely, we almost look normal. I'm flipping through the AM dial to see if we're on the radar. It's a wasteland of religious babble, get-rich schemes, and oldies molding all day, all night. Then I hit it, the news. *News you can use.* And for the first time they're right. WCAP, *the heartbeat of the capital,* is at the scene. Pamela Vargas—who, according to the morning anchor, has "a face for radio and a bod for sin"—has the scoop. She says the tractor went over the bridge into the river. Search crews are looking for us right now. Better yet, "It doesn't look good." She's got a witness, but it sounds like he's drunk. "One second I'm enjoying my morning constitution and the next second I'm watching a tractor fall into the river. I heard a scream, but it might have just been me."

Thanks Pamela, that's the news from the scene.

I don't know where to go. I just know we have to keep going. We're on Route 33, driving along the river, the most dangerous road in central Ohio. It winds and curves and it always freezes before everything else. People die here all the time, leaving only skidmarks and white cross echoes behind.

You know how smart the radio thinks you are when they try to sell you Hooked on Phonics. They're telling a story about how little Adam Fisher's life turned around at age fifteen once his parents finally did for him what his teachers couldn't. They taught him to read. Well, not exactly. They got a deluxe CD set to do the job for them. The point is not that Adam Fisher can read and that life is full of possibilities, or even that a semi-retarded boy can pull himself up from the muck with just the help of a box of CDs retailing for $299 (or twelve easy payments of $29.99). The point is that the radio stays on long enough for them to remind me that the Reds are playing at two-fifteen this afternoon.

In a matter of minutes we're on the 71 heading south to Cincinnati. We should be there in less than two hours. No one will ever think to look for us at the game. Especially since they're looking for us at the bottom of the Scioto River. It's really the perfect place to go.

I tell Annika we're going to see the Reds. She's wearing a pair of Grandpa's sunglasses, the kind cops wear. Since she doesn't have the capacity to blink in a way that would protect her eyes without some shade, Annika's retinas would bake in the sun. So when I tell her the news, we can't play the blinking game. But what I see now is more definitive than any series of blinks will ever be. The sign for BARRY'S BAIL BONDS—which is coming up as it looms over the Third Street overpass—is reflected in her lenses, specifically *Barry* beating in red neon.

If that's not a sign, I don't know what is.

There's nothing to listen to in here, just a bunch of inspirational cassettes wrapped in plastic. Mom gave me most of them too, but I sold mine online. I can't imagine that Grandpa has ever played a tape in his life. I'd be doing him a favor if I tossed them all out the window, but I'll just wait for the first rest stop. In a little while it'll be time to change Annika's diapers. In the meantime, news from the Reds radio headquarters peels the miles away.

Jose Rijo will soon be taking the mound. He was the MVP of the 1990 World Series, the last time the Reds won it all. A few years later, Jose blew out his elbow and now he's making his forth or fifth comeback. He's had so many surgeries he says they might as well put a zipper on his arm instead of using stitches. Once they took a ligament out of his wrist and wrapped it around his elbow. The next time they took a tendon out of his leg. Every time Jose Rijo throws a pitch, it could be his last, but he always has a smile on his face.

There's not much going on between Columbus and Cincinnati. Once you pass the rendering plant and the tire dump, you could be sailing on an ocean of corn. Instead of ships, sometimes you see a tractor. Instead of sharks, sometimes you see a cow. The corn's about four feet high now. Every farmhouse and barn along the highway looks abandoned, but the corn keeps growing.

And on the radio, they keep talking. About trades the Reds *could,* *should,* but probably *won't* make before the deadline. About how Danny Graves gives everyone a heart attack. About how if only Ken Griffey Jr. could stay healthy, then maybe everything would be different.

We stop at Jasper's Farm, an old-time general store, produce market, and fireworks showroom. That means we're halfway to Cincinnati. We stopped here once when Dad took Annika, Ben, and me down to see the Bengals play the Browns three or four years ago. Ordinarily, Dad would rather go to Cleveland to see his beloved Browns, but a client gave him some tickets, so we went into enemy territory. On the way back, Dad bought a pecan pie for Mom. He said she wouldn't let us back in the house without one, as if she really would have liked to come to the game, but she wasn't allowed, and a pecan pie was the only way to make her forgive us for leaving her at home while we went off and had all the fun. But the truth is, Mom hates football almost as much as she hates baseball. She says it's boring, it takes too long, and you always end up disappointed. It's pretty much the same way I feel about going to church.

At Jasper's, they also sell apple fritters. That's what they're famous for and that's why we're here . . . well, that, and it smells like it's time to change Annika's diaper.

Contrary to popular belief, Annika does not shit roses. I haven't had to change her diapers before, but I've seen Mom do it. As far as instruction, that's going to have to do. When Maggie does it, she always makes me leave the room, like she's somehow protecting Annika's dignity. Ordinarily if you were knocked out, you'd be outfitted with a colostomy bag, but Mom prefers diapers. It's all part of the immersion therapy. Basically, anything that makes you *feel* is a good thing, even if it is shit.

If I'm going to be a hero here, I better get some credit for it.

Grandpa's cell phone is charged in its resting spot; it's sort of a safety net in the event that he finds his keys, but if it ever came to that, I seriously doubt he'd know how to use the phone. "The latest newtangled contraption," that what he calls cell phones.

Anyway, I dial up Allison and she answers. "Monroe, is that you?" The reception is pretty lousy. "Where are you? At the bottom of the river?" she laughs.

I tell her we're at Jasper's Farm, that everything is okay.

"Bring home an apple fritter for me, won't you?" she asks, fading in and out.

"You weren't worried about us?" I ask.

"I knew you would be okay," she says.

That's when the line goes dead. And I didn't even get to tell her what I'm about to do. I was really hoping for a little moral support here.

While there's a big turd in her drawers, Annika doesn't seem to notice. Nonetheless, I go into the store and buy some diapers. I'll spare you the details; it's not like it really matters anyway. Anyone would do the same thing—changing his sister's diaper—even if she is thirteen years old. The trick is to just hold your breath and it's over before you know it.

After we're both cleaned up, Annika's mouth is open, like a bird waiting to be fed. She must smell the fritters. As I slide the glazed doughnut over her lips, across her tongue, the sugar melts, leaving just the dough with bumps of apple coming through. A little drool drips down her chin. That's nothing new, but when she licks her chops, it feels like we're getting somewhere. I've never seen her do *that* before.

Maybe when we get to the game, we'll try some ice cream.

I KNOW WE'RE GETTING close to Cincinnati when I see the Confederate flag. It's painted on a barn's roof by the highway. You might think it would be faded and peeling, that you're looking at a relic from a long time ago, but it's fresh, like it was painted yesterday. It used to be accompanied by a burnt-out cross, but it's not there any-more. Slowly, with a stutter, they're almost catching up to the twenty-first century.

We're only thirty miles from the stadium.

The week after I graduated from high school Annika and I were going to see the Reds. That was the plan. It's not like I'm trying to turn back time. I know that doesn't work. The last time we drove by that burnt-out cross she wanted to know what it was all about, so Dad told her all about the Ku Klux Klan and how they used to burn crosses in black people's yards to intimidate them. Annika was like, "They didn't like that the black people believed in God?" and Dad told her how the KKK did what they did *in the name of God* and An-nika just sat there for a second before she finally said, "God must not have liked that very much."

Then Dad said, "Yeah, you'd think if God were around, he'd strike them down in their tracks."

Annika thought for a moment. "Maybe living by the freeway is punishment enough. Cars go by all day, but you're not going any-where."

THANKS TO GRANDPA'S HANDICAP PLATES, which apparently come standard with Cadillacs, we get to park right next to the Reds' brand-new stadium, Great American Ballpark. And it being that we are on the run, Annika's going to need a disguise. It's not like she's a major celebrity, but people definitely know who she is. The sunglasses help, but if anything, it's the blonde hair people recognize. It goes practi-cally down to her waist. I tuck her hair behind her shirt, but that's not going to do the trick, so I sacrifice my Reds hat to the cause and perch it on her head. Between that and her sunglasses, we're practi-cally incognito. While you wouldn't necessarily think Annika was vegetating, you'd probably think she was very sleepy. Some things you can't fake.

We roll up to the walk-up ticket window and in a matter of minutes we're inside. When you're with a little girl in a wheelchair, people fall all over themselves to help you out. It's not such a bad way to travel.

A nice old man brings us to our seats—me to my seat, a folding chair, and Annika to her wheelchair's designated space. He says, "What a beautiful young lady." He's ancient and very possibly half-blind, but he's right. He's wearing a red vest and a straw hat. All the ushers do. At any moment they could break out into an a cappella version of "Take Me Out to the Ball Game." While that might sound sarcastic, it would be pretty cool if they did.

We're behind the Reds dugout, last row of the field box, about twenty-five rows up. *Nice.* Lots of leg room. For the most part, like I mentioned, no one really looks at someone in a wheelchair. They're anonymous. If we weren't in a section full of other cripples, it'd be like we didn't exist at all. It's them I'm worried about, the other gimps. They're not afraid to stare at one another.

It takes the boy sitting next to us about twenty seconds to spit out his name—DadadadadaDennis. He's with his mother, a mildly attractive feather-haired devotee of Guns n' Roses. That's what her T-shirt says, GUNS N' ROSES WAS HERE scrawled like graffiti over a girl slumped in an alley, her panties ripped around her ankles. She says, "He's not stupid. It just sounds that way."

Dennis, who is probably eleven or twelve, can't stop looking at Annika. "You are very pretty," he says. Or something like it. "What's your name?"

I tell him her name is Anne.

"Anne, you look like a dream I once had," he says. Or something like that.

His mother says, "He's a real Johnny Depp. Just like his dad."

I tell her, "Anne's just really shy. She was in a tragic fishing accident in Lake Erie. She hasn't said much since. Actually, she's quite lucky to be alive."

"Aren't we all?" Dennis's mom says. "By the way, my name's Stacy."

"I'm Luke," I say. I've always wanted to be a Luke.

"Dennis just has a stutter."

"I'm paralyzed too," he spits out.

"That too," she says. "Ever since he fell off the motorcycle. His idiot father didn't even realize he fell off until he got home. The stupid bastard."

"I—I—I—I'm sorry," says Dennis.

"You're not the stupid bastard. Your father is," she reassures him.

"What a terrible accident," I say.

"Don't feel sorry for me." At least that's what I think he says.

Stacy beams, "A mute and a stutterer. They make a pretty cute couple—don't you think?"

That's really something I don't want to think about, so I just say, "I guess."

Dennis is trying to ask Annika, "Who's your favorite player?"

I tell him she likes Barry Larkin best.

"Me too," he says. Or something like it.

This is Barry's nineteenth year as a Red. He's the captain, but he's hardly the best player on the team anymore. Before I can pop a peanut in my mouth, Larkin rips the first pitch over the left-field wall. It's the fourth time this year he's started a game out like that. Annika doesn't stir as the fireworks go off and Larkin trots around the bases. On the big screen you can see him smiling as he rounds third and heads for home. I wish Annika could see his face. I hold her hand and whisper in her ear, "That one was for you."

She squeezes my hand, but her openmouthed grouper glaze doesn't change. It feels like maybe, just *maybe,* she might be happy.

Or maybe it's just *me.*

I'm becoming more and more like my mother and it terrifies me. I know it shouldn't. A lot of people talk about what a saint Mom is, but I don't want to be a saint. I just want to do the right thing.

Not a lot happens for the next six innings, other than that Jose Rijo has yet to give up a hit. I can say that now, but at the time no one was saying a thing because everyone knows if you do, you might as well just kiss the no-hitter good-bye.

Everyone except for Dennis. He declares, "The Cardinals don't have any hits." Or something like it.

People in front of us—the people who can get up and walk whenever they feel like it—look back, annoyed.

His mom says, "What he means is the Cardinals don't know how to spit. Isn't that right, Dennis?"

"Nananananana—NOOOO," says Dennis. "Zero hits zero hits." Or something like it.

"Zero *zits*. That's what he means. The Cardinals have nice complexions for such bastards, isn't that right, honey?"

That's when the foul ball tips off Barry Larkin's bat. No one sees it coming; we're all distracted by Dennis and his mom. There is no flash of lightning, just the dull implosion of cowhide on flesh. Now all eyes are on *us*. No one cares about Dennis anymore; but it's not like anyone can really *see* anything. The force of the ball has knocked Annika out of her chair.

"Oh my God," says the usher in a panama hat. He's the first on the scene.

Annika's on the ground; her hair is everywhere, covering her face like a yellow sheet. A lady screams and drops her chili cheese dog, the splat of ground meat hitting the cement an exclamation point, echoing the grotesque thud that has left the entire crowd silent, straining to get a glimpse. I try to hold Annika in my arms but the medics pull me away.

Everything is happening in slow motion. Everything is happening so fast.

She's sprawled on the ground; her wheelchair's wheels spinning on its side. As the medics put her in a stretcher, she lets out a long anguished moan that silences the crowd. Even when her hands bleed, nothing comes out of her mouth. She must be in a lot of pain. She must be *in there*.

As they take us away, I look back at Stacy wrapping her arms around her stuttering son. He he he he he he he he's absolutely freaking out. You'd think he just saw his puppy get run over.

THEY TAKE US through a door marked with a red cross. As far as they know, Annika is knocked out. I would have said something, but the Reds official is peppering me with questions. *Do I know where her parents can be reached? Am I her legal guardian? Does she have insurance?*

Naturally, I don't want them to call my parents, so I lie. It's not like I have a choice . . . besides, when you're on the run, the truth is the first casualty—unless, of course, the reason you're on the run is because you killed someone, in which case, truth would be the second casualty. The first lie is always the hardest and after that, they just keep coming. *Oh yes, our parents are dead. That's how she got in the wheelchair in the first place. . . . Yes, it was a terrible crash. So, now I'm her legal guardian. . . . Yeah, it's hard, but what are you going to do?. . . No, the insurance company cut us off last year. I know, it's just not right. . . . Our lawyers are looking into it.*

They've called an ambulance; they want to take us to the hospital. It's not like I can really decline and say, "Oh, don't worry, she'll be fine. She gets knocked out all the time." I just hold Annika's hand as she lies there on the stretcher next to me. I have no choice but to wait and see how this plays itself out. There's nothing to do but watch the game on the television in the corner. The score is still 1–0 and Jose Rijo still hasn't allowed a hit.

In the movies and in books, coma patients are always just waking up, but that's not the way it really happens. Doctors have told us that about a hundred times. *Don't expect a miracle.* Waking up from a coma takes awhile, sometimes weeks. That's what the experts say. But that's not how it happens here.

Annika's eyes are open. A deep dark blue ocean with no bottom. Usually you can see whatever you want in there, but right now I see a rogue wave coming to the surface and there will be no getting out of the way.

What I see is that Annika is awake.

The wave crashes over me, leaving my face wet with tears and my head swimming for high ground.

You might think her first words would be "Oh my God, where am I?" but they're not. What she wants to know is: "Can I have some water?" Her throat is scratchy like she's been hanging out with Jesus, playing poker and smoking five packs a day.

The doctor puts a cup to her lips and she drinks.

"This is a really good sign," he says. Little does he know just how *good*.

I'm on my knees, hugging her, touching her, making sure it's not a mirage. You think you know how you'll respond when you get what you've always wanted, but you don't know until it actually happens, and when it does, you might not even believe it's happening at all.

The doctor wants to know why she's in a wheelchair and I don't know what to say. I don't know if I should tell him what's happening or if I should lie. Annika says, "It was the only way to get half-decent seats."

"She's just kidding," I somehow manage to say.

"Monroe, did you get the ball that hit me?" she says, winking my way.

"Um, no, I didn't," I say.

There's an official from the team with us. He's eager to please. "We'd like to give you a ball autographed by the *whole* team."

"Cool," she says. "But you know what would be *really* cool? A bat."

He says, "We can do that."

Annika announces, "I'm feeling better already."

That's when they bring in another casualty. He's on a stretcher, his shirt covered in puke, passed out. His buddy's with him, a typical frat boy: Ohio State hat, Abercrombie T-shirt, neon orange Converse high-tops. He says his friend just had a little too much to drink. He explains, "I guess not everyone is up for the Great American Challenge."

The doctor says, "I hate to ask, but what's the Great American Challenge?"

The kid's like, "One beer and one chili cheese dog every inning. It's not too tough. I guess the sun got to him. *The pussy.*" It sounds like something Ben would do.

There's a television in the corner and we can see the game. Jose Rijo continues his dominance, striking out feared Cardinals slugger Albert Pujols. Annika asks, "Did Barry get a hit?"

The doctor says Larkin got a double off the wall, but got stranded out there. Annika says, "Well at least he hit that home run." Her voice is clear, one cough and the cobwebs disappear.

I'm looking at Annika, stunned. She's acting like she's up from a nap, perhaps a little bleary-eyed, but still shockingly lucid. After two years and almost three months, you might think she'd be at least a little disoriented, but she's sitting in her wheelchair, smiling like she's about to tell the funniest joke in the world.

The drunkard wakes up, wondering where he is. His buddy tells him to chill out. And then he looks at Annika and he says, "Don't I know you?"

Annika laughs and says, "Aren't you a little old for me?"

"Really man, that's *sick,*" says his buddy.

"No, not like *that,*" he says. "I've just seen you before, that's all. . . . Man, my head hurts."

Thankfully, the guy comes back with Annika's bat. They must have quite an arsenal ready for such occasions. He says, "It's Barry Larkin's. I'm sure he would want you to have it." Annika runs her fingers over Barry's engraved signature; her eyes are open but it looks like she's reading Braille. *"Barry,"* she says. "He hit me and it felt like a kiss." Clearly, her night with the Crystals was not spent in vain.

Annika says, "Thanks a lot" to the Reds official, then she whispers in my ear, "Want me to get you a jersey?" I tell her that's okay. "You'll be kicking yourself," she says.

The doctor asks, "Are you feeling nauseous? Dizzy?" He has a flashlight and tells Annika to follow the beam as he looks into her eyes.

"I'd really just like to get back to the game."

"Well, your eyes look good," the doctor says. "But if you like, we'd be happy to take you to the hospital for more tests, you know, just to be sure."

Annika says, "I don't think that will be necessary. At least, not until *after* the game."

As I'm pushing Annika out the door, the drunk is like, "I know, I know. She's Ben Anderson's sister. *You know*. The chick whose hands bleed." He then breaks into the Rolling Stones' "Let It Bleed": "*We all need someone we can bleed on . . .*"

Thankfully, his buddy's not buying it. "Ben's sister is a *vegetable*, you dumb ass. Why don't you just shut up so we can get back to the game?"

I practically pop a wheelie as we head out the door. Once we're in the hallway I say, "We better get out of here. The car's out front."

But Annika has other plans. "You're kidding, right? Leave? A game like this? It's only the eighth inning. And Rijo's pitching—" she catches herself, careful not to be a jinx, *"out of his mind."*

I'm speechless. "You do realize I hear *everything*, don't you, Monroe?"

"Everything? All this time?"

"By the way, I should thank you for turning me on to Parliament. They rock. Otis Redding, though, he kind of bums me out."

"What if someone recognizes you?"

"People think we're dead; we might as well live it up. And if anyone recognizes me, so what?"

"They said you wouldn't just wake up, that it would take weeks. That it would be baby steps."

"People say so many things," she says, quoting Stan. "By the way, thanks for getting me out of that anniversary party, although I must say, I was kind of looking forward to it. You know, just for the change of pace, getting out of the house and all. But this is *better*."

"So you could hear *everything*?"

"Sometimes it felt like you were right there and I was having a conversation with you and sometimes it just felt like everyone was so far away, like I was buried underneath a bale of cotton. And, other times, well, I had to sleep."

"We really should get home."

"Since when did you turn into Dad?"

THE REDS ARE getting ready to bat when we get back to our seats. Stacy says, "I never thought we'd see you again." Stacy has one of those voices that carries. It's as if all her life she's been trying to be heard above the din of a crowd or a band or a motorcycle engine and now she can't turn the volume down. And it's hard to ignore. First, the heads in our section turn and when they see that Annika is back, they're like dominoes in reverse, wave after wave of people standing on their feet, clapping, happy that she's all right. And they don't even know who she is. She's not a budding saint. She's not an icon suffering for the sins of all mankind. She's just a girl in a wheelchair who took a foul ball off the side of her head.

Annika smiles and waves; she's the queen of the crippled section. Even behind her now-crooked sunglasses, her face lights up the big diamond vision screen. The whole crowd is standing, thirty thousand people—a bigger crowd than they could have ever fit into Clipper Stadium.

All I'm thinking is that we've got to get out of here before anyone figures out who she is. I'm not sure exactly what would happen if they did, but I don't want to find out.

The ovation lasts only about fifteen seconds, but it feels like minutes. Once Ken Griffey Jr. comes to the plate, everyone sits down.

Dennis is more excited than anyone to see Annika back. "Barry Larkin was looking for you," he says with barely a stutter. Stacy adds, "We were *all* real worried about you."

Dennis assures Annika that she's still very pretty. Intent to focus on the game, she sticks with the mute story, takes off her sunglasses, and beams back her reply. The glow on Dennis's face says no one has ever looked at him that way before.

The Reds go down fast, but the score is still 1–0 Cincinnati. Rijo must be completely exhausted, but he may not know it. At least not yet. The longest he pitched all year was into the seventh against San Francisco back in May. Rijo gets the first two outs fast, leaving only the pinch-hitting Jim Edmonds between him and the record books. Edmonds works the count to 3–2 and fouls off ball after ball, rattling at least seven souvenirs throughout the stands. And with each pitch Rijo is getting weaker. His shoulder is slumping, the weight of baseball history in the air. The catcher Jason LaRue starts to come out to talk, or maybe just to give his pitcher a rest, but Rijo waves him off. He's earned the right to dictate the terms. He wants to pitch.

And it should be ball four, but Edmonds swings anyway. He launches it square, a line drive to deep left-center field. . . . Griffey is going back, back, back, until he's out of real estate. That's what Marty Brennamen says, his voice rising up from hundreds of transistors. There's nowhere left for Griffey to go. At the wall he leaps, coming down hard, like a marionette whose strings were just cut. Edmonds is rounding second in his home-run trot, not looking back.

Silence.

The crowd can't believe what they've just seen, their hearts suspended in their throats. Their dreams dashed. Then Griffey looks in his glove, pulls out the ball, and the cheering begins.

It's a perfect game.

Chapter 40

Y OU EVER HAVE A FRIEND who you haven't seen in a while and when you see him it's like it was just yesterday and you pick up where you left off? Well, until now, I never had a friend like that, but I've heard about people who do. That's what it feels like right now. There's no rush; everything we missed will eventually be filled in.

We're only about ten miles outside of Cincinnati, headed back to Columbus, when Annika says, "I think I just peed myself."

"You want me to change your diaper?"

"Not really. At least not if you're planning on doing it in the middle of a parking lot again."

"No one saw."

"Well, they could have."

"Are you telling me you could see too?"

"Not in the way you're thinking."

"Could you feel anything?"

"Usually I couldn't, but sometimes I could."

"Like when you were bleeding?"

"Yeah, I guess," she says, watching the fast food–auto dealer–Wal-Mart world go by. It's an endless loop like this until we get past Kings Island, then the never-ending mall will be swallowed by the sea of corn.

I let her rest and listen to the radio. Marty and Joe are delirious as they go through the highlights over and over, but when they cut to the news, it turns out we're the big story of the day. They're still looking for us on the banks of the Scioto River. The crowd from the stadium has relocated and they're all praying for us. They say there must be five thousand people, maybe more. There's an amphitheater next to the crash site and the pilgrims have filled it up and are overflowing along the river's banks. Mom is being interviewed at the scene and says she won't believe we're dead until they pull our bodies out of the water. Until then there's *hope*. She says, "I have faith in God that everything is going to be okay."

Dad's standing next to Mom, not that I can see him; but he must be and I'll bet he's a mess. His religion came to him with a gun to his head. I'm sure he would really like to fall back onto God like a safety net, but he can't quite do it. The reporter asks him if he has anything he'd like to say and all he can come up with is, "I just want my children back."

Annika's either not listening or she doesn't care. "You remember Ping?" she asks.

"Your goldfish?"

"Yeah."

"The one I put in a blender?"

"That's the one."

"I'm really sorry about that," I say.

"I know. You just never said it before."

"I'm sorry about that too."

After a few minutes of silence, Annika wants to know, "Do we have to go home?"

"I don't know. Where do you want to go?"

"Somewhere else. *Anywhere* else."

I tell her, "Mom's going to lose it when she sees you."

"You say that like it's a *good* thing . . . when the thing is, I should lose it on her."

I'm really not so sure what to say to that. She's kind of right.

"Monroe, are you having one of those conversations with yourself? I'm right here, you know."

"I know, I know. I was just thinking."

"It's not healthy to keep everything inside," she says.

I always thought it would be like Rip Van Winkle, that when Annika woke up it would be like she had been stuck on pause. That she'd be like she was right before it happened. I thought that while everything else had changed, at least Annika would be the same.

"This whole thing is so screwed up," I say.

"How do you think I feel? As far as I know, this all could just be another dream. You know how when your foot falls asleep and when you try to move it around, it feels like it's on fire? *My whole body* feels like that and there's nothing I can do about it."

"Blink once if this is a dream, twice if it's real."

"Screw you, Monroe."

"I would have thought you'd be in a little better mood."

"I don't mean to be such an ogre," she says. "I've got kind of a headache."

"Maybe we should get you to a doctor."

"What's a doctor ever done for me? If it was up to doctors, I'd be just another rotting vegetable in Oakside. Don't even talk to me about doctors."

"Okay," I say. "I can't believe you're back." We pass a sign saying Columbus is only ninety-eight miles away.

"Do we really have to go home?"

"You have any better ideas?"

We're driving through Cincinnati's sprawl, mini-mansions hiding behind cement walls. No matter how high those walls go, they're still living on the highway. Sure, maybe they can mask the constant roar of the road with waterfalls and white-noise machines, but the carbon monoxide is still going to get them.

"When you were in the coma, what did you think you wanted to do, you know, when you came out of it?" I ask.

"Mainly I wanted people to quit talking to me like I was retarded. I guess I should thank you for not being like that."

"Did I ever tell you how pretty your hair looks in the sun," I say. "It must be so soft."

She ignores my attempt to talk to her like a retard and says, "You know in Funkadelic's 'Maggot Brain'? How in the beginning when he says, 'I have tasted the maggots in the mind of the universe. I was not offended for I knew I had to rise above it all or drown in my own shit'? The last two years were like that. *Exactly* like that."

"That's not quite like Mom's official version. You know, being by God's side and everything."

"Well, Mom had to believe what she had to believe. And in a way I guess she was kinda right. I was just *being*. I wasn't really thinking about the past and I wasn't thinking about the future, I was just *there*."

"Maybe that's what it means to have the funk. You're there, you know, in the moment."

"*Maybe*," she says. "But, Monroe, that whole power-to-the-pussy stuff at the end of the album? You're lucky Mom never heard that. She would have lost it on you."

"The funk experiment was done in secret for a reason."

Annika says, "I'm *starving*. I could really go for a cheeseburger."

"I thought you were a vegetarian."

"You try eating nothing but cardboard wafers for over two years and talk to me about not eating meat."

"Seriously, Annika, we probably should get you to a doctor."

"Monroe, I'm *fine*."

"You can't even walk."

"You really shouldn't tell people what they can't do. Some of them might believe you. I can walk *fine*."

WE PULL INTO the Country Kitchen just past Kings Island. It's an old diner with an exit all to itself, an orphan on the interstate.

The parking lot is full of pickups accented with gun racks. As I'm getting Annika's wheelchair out of the back, I find her *standing* right behind me.

"What are you doing?" I ask.

"You also shouldn't believe everything the doctors say," she says, showing off her pedestrian abilities with a catwalk flourish. She's a little wobbly. A colt taking its first steps comes to mind, but she's *fine*.

"They said you'd have to learn how to do everything all over again . . . you know, if you ever woke up in the first place."

"Massages twice a day do wonders for a body," she says. "I suppose that'll stop now that I'm awake."

She does a pirouette and stumbles.

"Maybe you should hold my hand," she says. "Before someone comes and recruits me for the Special Olympics."

So, I take her warm hand in mine and we head inside where Annika promptly spreads herself out in a booth and orders a cheeseburger. "And a chocolate milk shake. The thicker the better."

There's one of those personal jukeboxes at our table. I feed it all the quarters I have and put on Al Green's "I'm Still in Love with You."

"I *love* this song." Annika perks up. "I really should thank you for introducing me to Al at the dawn of my sexual awakening. Did you know that twenty-two percent of the girls my age have already had oral sex?" she says.

"Where did you hear that?" I manage to ask, practically choking on an ice cube.

"Mom was telling Maggie, I think. Or maybe it was on *Ellen*. I'm so *behind*. I've never even kissed a boy."

"Boys are really bad." I cough, the image of Annika going down on little Josh Gorman imprinted in my head.

"But *you're* a boy."

"And the same way you don't want to kiss me should be applied to boys everywhere."

The food comes out fast and Annika's slapping the bottom of the ketchup bottle, knocking out its contents in gulps of red.

"I bet you want to know if it was real when I bled, don't you?"

"I know it was *real*. I was there."

"Two thousand people might be in the audience when David Copperfield makes an elephant disappear, but that doesn't mean the elephant really disappeared, does it?"

"I guess not," I say.

"But I'm not David Copperfield," she concedes. "All I know is that it hurt. It hurt a lot. And if Jesus was sitting there with me—like Mom always says—the least He could have done is slipped me some aspirin."

"You didn't have visions of being up on the cross?" I ask.

"Whatever was going on in my head might as well have been a dream. Besides, no one really cares about other people's dreams. They only care about their own."

"I practically never remember my dreams," I say.

"See?" she says. "You don't even care about your *own* dreams enough to remember them. Why care about mine?" And with that she takes a stab at a French fry . . . with a spoon.

She looks up at me and laughs. "It's probably best I stay away from sharp objects for a while."

WE'RE DRIVING BACK toward Columbus, *back home*. But I'm not quite sure what that means anymore. Just being with Annika feels more like home than the idea of walking into that house on Stoneridge Road.

We pass a landfill. It's *huge,* rising high above the fields that surround it. On the top sits a sign declaring GOD BLESS USA in big cutout block letters. Above it flies an American flag, the stars and stripes hanging limp above a mountain of trash, an image so painfully perverse I couldn't make it up if I wanted to. "God bless this mound of trash," says Annika. And there's really nothing to add to that. My English professor said irony is dead, but everywhere you look, there it is. My biology professor said the same about God—dead; but He's everywhere too. In fact, up on the next exit, there's an outlet mall. They've got everything you could ever not want at bargain prices. Including Bibles at the Bible Liquidators Warehouse.

"I thought Bibles were free," I say.

"Whatever," Annika says. "I could really use some new underwear. These Depend undergarments aren't really working for me anymore. Mind if we stop at the Jockey Store?"

"Sure," I say.

*   *   *

Once we're back on the road, Annika says, "I think I'll pretend I've fallen asleep for a while."

Annika closes her eyes and I listen to the radio. They're still talking about the Reds triumph and the amazing Jose Rijo. People are calling in from a fifty-thousand-watt radius and every one of them agrees: *It's a miracle.*

And it's hard to argue. The six surgeries? The tendons taken out of his leg and wrapped around his elbow? It's incredible that he can lift up his arm to drink a cup of coffee, let alone throw a baseball. Even his doctor says so.

The corn rolls by as the day fades away. I've heard the commercial shilling Hooked on Phonics so many times, I'm beginning to think maybe it might really help my vocabulary. As I fumble for a pen to write down the toll-free number, it's like waking up from a shame-filled dream. I almost turn off the radio, but another newsflash from the scene stops me: "As the sun begins to set here by the banks of the Scioto River in the heart of downtown Columbus, hundreds, if not thousands, of people are gathered for a candlelight vigil. As we've reported throughout the day, Annika Anderson and her brother were in a tractor that crashed into these waters late this morning. . . ."

"Annika, you want to check out your vigil?"

But Annika doesn't respond; she's sitting still, her mouth slightly open as we pass by a cluster of fast-food emporiums and cheap motels.

"Annika?"

Nothing. Not even the gentle rise of her chest as she breathes. Not even that.

I jostle her bony knee and my voice jumps an octave. "Annika, you want to check out how the search is going?"

"Sure," she says, her eyes not opening.

~~~

WE PULL OFF on Broad Street and head to the scene of the tractor's fatal downfall. It's getting dark, but the banks are lit up with hundreds of candles.

"Wow," Annika says. "Don't those people have anything better to do?"

In order to remain incognito, we drive across the bridge to the other side of the river and park the car. Here we sit safely perched above the muddy waters, the candles' light reflecting off the surface.

"Looks like your fans haven't given up."

"It's really the least they could do for me," she says, presumably infused with a heavy dose of sarcasm. But as she looks at the candles flickering down below, a tear invades her eye. "You know, I never wanted any of this."

"I know," I say. "That's why I kidnapped you."

"Yeah? So what took you so long?"

"I'm sorry," I say. "I guess I was pretty lame."

"Better lame than never, *I guess*. God knows what they were going to do with me next."

"Next week they were planning to get a video camera in your room and blast it out to the World Wide Web all day and all night. Nothing sexual, I'm sure. Purely for *spiritual* purposes."

"I heard Maggie say something about that."

"Yeah, well did you hear that if Ohio State goes to the Rose Bowl this year, Waste Disposal Incorporated was going to put you on a float and parade you through downtown Pasadena? I'm sure it would have been very tastefully done."

"I always wanted to be a Rose Princess."

"Well, now it looks like you're going to have to get it done on pure talent."

"Like there's no skill in being everything to everyone. If it's so easy, you try it," she says.

"I think there was talk of auctioning off vials of your blood to raise funds for earthquake survivors in El Salvador."

"Seriously?"

"No, *not* seriously. But I wouldn't mention anything about it. It might give them ideas. Everything else, though, unfortunately is true."

"The river looks so beautiful," she says, her eyes mirroring the candles dancing on the river's lazy ripples.

"I'm supposed to start seventh grade this fall," she says. "I bet they're going to try to hold me back."

"If you're lucky. Junior high sucked," I say.

"For *you,* maybe. *I* was looking forward to it. You know, someone could have piped some info I could *use* into my head. Don't get me wrong, I appreciate the music and the baseball games, I really do. They may have saved my life. But all those letters from the sick people and the Bible? What was I supposed to do with that?"

"I don't know, teach Sunday school?"

"Yeah, *right,* my life's ambition. . . .Oh Jesus, do you think Mom's going to make me go to Saint Victor's?"

"I think she's going to be so happy to see you, she's going to let you go wherever you want."

"Maybe I should switch to Islam and start wearing a burka. That'll show her for trying to turn me into some sort of religious freak."

"Yeah, but then you'd be the one wearing a burka," I say.

"It'd probably be too much like being in a coma anyway . . . but *still,* someone could have at least put a foreign-language tape in the mix. Something *useful.* Being able to quote the book of Revelation in its entirety isn't exactly going to make me Miss Popularity."

"You're *already* Miss Popularity. All those people down there sure aren't looking for *me.*"

"They're not looking for me either. Just some idea they have of me."

"That's very philosophical of you."

"Let's lock you in a room for two years and see what kind of ideas *you* come up with."

"You want to go over there and see what's going on?" I ask.

"Not really," she says. "Sittin' by the Dock of the Bay" is playing on the radio.

"Remember how we used to dance?" she asks.

"Yeah," I say.

"Well?"

"I thought you didn't like Otis?"

"He made me feel lonely, but I'm not alone anymore, so it's okay."

Annika cranks up the stereo and along with the crashing wave accompaniment to Otis's finest, yet most overplayed song, we find ourselves on the sidewalk. In addition to its view of the vigil, the sidewalk's main claim to fame is that it's lined with every state's flag, all fifty of them. It used to be my favorite part about going down-town, looking at all of these flags of places I'd never been. Places I've *still* never been. We're under Hawaii, but when I take Annika's hand in mine, we could be back in our living room or in the Lazarus tuxedo department. We could be anywhere. Time is slipping back onto itself, like some animated explanation of quantum mechanics that seems so simple, yet makes absolutely no sense. It's all I ever wanted, for her to come back and have a moment like this, where it's like it used to be, and now that it's here, my head's swimming with all the little use-less details that screw everything up.

I'm thinking about the wind flapping in the breeze, wondering how often they have to replace those flags. I'm thinking about the cracks in the sidewalk and wondering if anyone ever broke their mother's back by stepping on one. I'm wondering what people would think if they saw me, practically a man, dancing here with a little girl.

"It's okay," Annika says. "No one's watching." It brings me back in the moment and we glide on Otis's sad voice, a voice that's weary at only twenty-six, singing a song about having nothing left to live for. Annika hasn't lost a step; her wobble is long gone. "Dip me," she says. And when I do, her spine pops like bubble wrap.

Before I can feel the dread of personal responsibility for turning my sister into a paraplegic she says, "That felt so *good*."

Otis is done with his song, but that's where he'll always be, sitting by that dock, *watching the tide roll in, wasting time.* He'll be stuck there forever. Only three days after Otis recorded that song, he died in a plane crash outside Madison, Wisconsin. But I don't say that. It'll just bum Annika out.

Now they're selling mail-order pet medication on the radio. Annika says, "I guess we should probably go home and get it over with."

"Yeah, I guess. Unless you want to go play putt-putt golf or something."

"That's okay," she's says. "But a Blizzard might really hit the spot—that Country Kitchen shake was kind of lame."

WE'RE AT THE DAIRY QUEEN, sitting at the picnic tables out back, spooning our Blizzards. We're not really talking, just enjoying the summer evening. The family over at the next table isn't saying much either; each one of them is lost in his own individually packaged sundae paradise.

"You have no idea how good this tastes," Annika says.

"Considering that all you've eaten in the last two years is the flesh of Jesus Christ, I'm not surprised."

"Yeah, funny how He tastes like cardboard. Might as well eat a poster of Barry Larkin," she says, twirling a glob of ice cream around a sliver of Butterfinger. "He did a lot more for me than Jesus ever did. Those stories in the Bible never change, but baseball is different every time."

This is all I wanted, to be sitting here at the Dairy Queen with Annika on the way back from the hospital almost two and a half years ago. It just took a lot longer to get here than I thought. Even though the Blizzard is a victim of diminishing returns, each bite not quite as delectable as the last. Even though there's a burning in my stomach over the notion of returning home that all the ice cream in the world couldn't soothe. Even though dreams never quite live up to reality. Despite all of that, it's been worth the wait, to sit here wrapped in the intimacy of silence and watch Annika do something so simple, so stupendously mundane as picking through the candy in her ice cream. Something so many doctors said she'd never do again.

"Quit staring at me," she says.

Out of all the so-called miracles that have happened since that day she fell in the pool, watching Annika eat a Blizzard is the one that matters the most; it's the one that has my jaw hanging off my face. It's the one that has me believing maybe there's some higher power at work here.

Chapter 41

WHEN WE GET HOME, the street is littered with television crews. They're on a death watch, waiting for my parents to give up hope.

Annika says, "Mind if I go back to sleep?"

"Don't be such a prima donna."

"Fine," she says, picking up Grandpa's cell. She tries to dial, but can't quite get the numbers right.

"Here, you try. Let's be newshounds," she says, handing me the phone. On the side of Channel 10's van a big dog begs for news tips. *Give the dog a bone, call* . . .

Once I finish dialing, Annika snatches the phone. She rolls her eyes as it rings, then abruptly she says, "Oh my God, someone's got to come here and see this—Annika Anderson just washed up on the shores of the Scioto, you know, right near the bend by the trash-burning power plant? *Mi Casa Su Casa* Mobile Home Park? . . . Yeah, she could probably use an ambulance, but I thought I should call you first. She's standing there all on her own with her arms out-stretched. . . . I think I see a halo. . . . Oh no, I'm breaking—"

She hangs up, but she's got other things on her mind. "So, Monroe, how come you never brought Allison over to see me?"

"I don't know."

"Don't you love her?"

"Well . . ."

"I *knew* it," Annika squeals. "Monroe's in *looooove* with Allison. *Monroe and Allison sitting in a tree . . . k-i-s-s-i-n-g . . .*"

"What are you? Eleven?"

The Channel 10 van races off.

"First comes love and then comes marriage, then comes . . ."

"Do I know you?"

"Monroe in the baby carriage. Sucking his thumb, wetting his pants . . ."

Channel 10 is quickly followed by the rest of the press, leaving Stoneridge Road as calm and ordinary as it used to be so long ago.

"Maybe you should play dead," I say. "Mom could have a heart attack if she sees you up and about."

"Yeah, I guess you're right. We'll ease her into to it. I haven't figured out a way to cure a heart attack yet."

THEY'RE ALL IN the living room when we walk in. Actually, I'm the only one walking, Annika's playing possum as I cradle her in my arms. She's not much heavier than she was when I first pulled her out of the pool, but still, she's a handful. They don't hear us; they're wrapped up in prayer—Mom, Dad, Maggie, and Father Ferger. Even Ben is here, keeping an eye on the television. The others are not exactly asking for favors from God; they're merely suggesting to Him a vision of the future they'd be happy with. Everything will be okay, they say. God is with Annika. He's with *me*. Despite His suspicious track record, He won't let anything bad happen to *us*. God is *good*. On that, they all agree. Except for Grandpa, who appears to have fallen asleep with the Sunday funnies in his lap.

I stand in the doorway for what seems like minutes, but it's probably only a few seconds until Mom looks up and sees that her prayers have come true.

She lets out a scream that could drop a bird from the sky and runs over, hugging us both, saying she never wants to let us go. Dad is speechless, yet dutifully joins the group hug. Maggie babbles scripture. Ben hangs back, cautious like he's surveying a tricky green; and Grandpa, who woke up after Mom's initial shriek, is laughing the laugh of someone who already knows the punch line but likes the joke anyway.

It's warm, this feeling, being hugged, being welcomed back. I thought for sure Mom was going to kill me.

Mom sweeps Annika from my arms and lays her down on the couch, spreading her out like a rag doll, her limp arms and legs falling like tumbling laundry. You really would think she was still knocked out cold. Mom's caressing Annika's face, saying how everything is going to be okay. As she loses herself in Annika's eyes, she whispers, "Sweetheart, please don't ever scare me like that again," but really she should be talking to me.

I don't know what it feels like to be Mom. I have no idea what's really going on in her head. The closest experience I have to go on is when Ben told me our dog Blue was hit by a car and died. Mom and Annika were doing some errands and Ben was supposed to be looking after me. I must have been ten or eleven. Ben came into my room, interrupting a perfectly good game of solitaire, and said Animal Control scraped Blue off the pavement and were on their way to the glue factory. He even took me out to the street and showed me the spot of smeared blood and fur. Before Annika became cognizant enough to have a conversation, that dog was my best friend; I would have traded my life for Blue's in a second. After bawling for two hours, I was reduced to a husk of heaving dry sobs. When Mom returned, Blue came running into my room like he had so many times before. Turns out Mom took him to the vet to get a few shots. Not only was Blue reborn, but I was too. That momentary bliss, though, was quickly replaced by the question—*How could anyone be so cruel?*

It's only a matter of time before the interrogation begins.

Mom wants to know what happened to Annika's head. Apparently there's a bump where the baseball hit her. Maggie assumes her customary position and massages her feet. I can see Annika clenching her jaw, trying not to laugh. She is, after all, quite ticklish.

"Yeah, Monroe, what exactly happened?" asks Dad. He's kneeling by the couch, examining Annika, touching her, trying to make sure this homecoming is *real*.

I had been doing a fine job of fading into the wallpaper. Now I'm a stain on the couch that no one can take their eyes off of.

I realize what I say here is wrong, but I can't help myself. There's a wave of anger about to come my way and I want to dodge its crashing blow, so I say, "Truth is, I was moved by the Spirit. . . . While I was sitting in the bleachers watching all those people waiting to get healed, a voice in my head said if I somehow reversed the situation and Annika was in the stands of a baseball stadium, maybe then *she* would be the one who would be healed."

"You heard a *voice?*" Mom asks with the eager anticipation she once reserved for a sale at Neiman Marcus.

"I wouldn't call it a voice per se—you know in the build-it-and-they-will-come kind of way. It was more of a guiding *feeling.* A *warm* feeling. So I took her. I figured if I said anything, you wouldn't believe me."

"A warm feeling, huh? Like heat stroke?" asks Dad.

I should have just told her the truth. Telling Mom I had a vision is like giving Dad a bottle of vodka; she really doesn't need to be any drunker on God than she already is.

I'm about to start stammering, "Well, *actually* . . ." but Annika beats me to it. "Monroe's just saying that. God didn't say anything to him. He only did it because he loves me."

And with those words, the tables turn; everyone *else* is on pause while Annika shines with life. She's sitting up, the smile on her face glimmering. Her rising has landed a collective sucker punch in the stomach, leaving them all trapped in that moment when you can't breathe, but you haven't yet started gasping for air. Hard to believe a thirteen-year-old could be a knockout, but the evidence suggests otherwise. She might as well hold her arms up in victory; she's a champion. Mom's face, for once, is colored in shades of disbelief. Dad couldn't be more shocked than if a jury had come out against him. If only Ben could get out the words *What the fuck?,* surely he would. Grandpa, however, is sporting a smile so wide he'd need two lanes if he wanted to take it out on the open road.

You can tell by the way Mom's lips are trembling, she desperately wants to say something.

"Hi Mom," Annika says with tears in her eyes.

"Thank you, God. Thank you, God," says Mom, looking to the ceiling. It's white, but you can almost see the Sistine Chapel echoed in her eyes. It's practically like Mom's autistic, she keeps repeating, "Thank you, God. Thank you, God," over and over again. She must be saying it once for every time she's asked God to bring her back. *"Thank you, God. Thank you, God."*

"You might actually want to thank Barry Larkin," Annika says. "He's the one whose foul ball hit me in the head. That's what finally knocked me out of the fog."

Annika's voice brings Mom back. "Your *voice,* it's so beautiful. It's the most beautiful song in the world." Mom's staring into Annika's face, like she's seeing her for the first time. Did she register what Annika actually said? I don't know.

"You were at a ball game?" Dad asks.

"I knew you were in there, honey. I *knew* it."

"I know, Mom. I *know.*"

"I've dreamt about this moment. I've *prayed* for this moment. And now it's here. I knew God was listening. I *knew* it."

"Sure took Him long enough to do something about it," chimes Ben.

Annika says, "He's got a very big to-do list."

Dad says, "I think we better get a doctor over here," as he picks up the phone, presumably to do just that.

"Honey, are you okay?" Mom asks. "We exercised your arms and legs and massaged you every day."

"It felt really good."

"In my dreams it was always just like this. You woke right up. But the doctors told me not to be so unrealistic."

"Gee, Mom, since when did you start listening to the doctors? Didn't they also say you should put me out in Oakside?"

"Honey, I'd never put you in Oakside. *Never.*"

"I know, Mom."

"Oh, sweetheart, I knew you were going to be okay."

"I know, Mom."

Dad says, "Let me just get this straight. While we were all thinking you were down at the bottom of the Scioto River, you were actually down in Cincinnati watching the Reds? Is that right, Monroe?"

Apparently, some people can be right in the middle of a miracle and not even realize it. And I'm just about to say so, but Annika interrupts, "Then after the baseball game we went to a diner and then we checked out the vigil and then we went to the Dairy Queen. It was the best day I've had in years."

"Man," Ben says, "why didn't you guys tell me you were going to Cincinnati? How amazing was Rijo today? I would have given my left nut to see that."

Dad turns to Ben and asks, "Wait a second. You saw him take her and you didn't say anything to us?"

"Jesus Christ, why the hell would I? Looks like they saved themselves fine," Ben says, sticking up for me for the first time in my life.

Mom's voice cracks when she says, "Ben, you know how I feel about that language."

Annika takes Mom's hand in hers. "I love you, Mom. I love you for having faith that I was there. That I knew what was going on when no one else believed it. And you were right." Mom's staring at her all misty, very possibly in shock. "But there's one thing I don't understand."

"What is it, honey?"

"I just want to know how could you believe I was there, that I was feeling the pain of *all humanity*, then parade all those sick people through our house? I don't get it." She says it gently, like she's talking to an idiot, but there's a cruel undertow that says the idiot has no excuse for being so dumb.

"We thought you had a gift."

"We wanted to share it with the world," says Father Ferger.

"The Church's sense of charity is truly inspiring," Annika says, glaring at Father Ferger.

"Father Ferger has been very good to all of us, Annika," says Mom, sweetly, like she's reminding her to wear her coat outside. Annoying, like it's the kind of day when you don't really need a coat anyway.

"Mom, please don't talk to me like I'm a little kid. I hate that. I *know* what happened. I was *there*. What did you think I was? Your own personal Stigmata Barbie?"

"No, honey, I didn't think that." I'd have thought Mom would crumble under such criticism, but her focus remains constant. "God was with us. God was with *you*. In case people couldn't see that, He posted signs everywhere: the roses falling from the sky, Jesus on the hospital wall, the blood on your hands. It's not like I was just making these things up. They happened. I'm not deluded. *They happened*. What was I supposed to do, hide you away from the world when you had so much life left to share? God *was* with you. He still *is*. He brought you back."

"Actually, Monroe brought me back."

Father Ferger adds, "Annika, you changed so many people's lives. Not just the people who came and got better by seeing you, but the people who were brought closer to God through your story. Isn't that better than wasting away in obscurity? After all, look at you, you're okay now."

"That's easy for you to say."

"Honey, if God was trying to speak through you, who am I to try to stop Him? How could I?" Mom asks.

"I hope God can speak for Himself. Jamming wafers down my throat every morning and reading the Bible to me all day? What made you think that would be a good idea?"

I'm thinking, *Gee Mom, maybe you better think twice about what you pray for next time.* But I don't say that.

"Really, Mom? Is that true? You made her take Communion while she was in a coma? That really is sick," says Ben.

Annika pulls herself off the couch and heads over to the window.

"Ben, you really shouldn't talk to your mother that way," says Dad.

"Just for the record, I'd like to interject, no one made Annika take Communion. She stuck her tongue out on her own," says Father Ferger.

"She was probably sticking her tongue out *at* you, not *for* you," notes Ben.

"Really Ben, this day has been long enough . . ." pleads Dad.

"Man," Ben says, "I wish I'd driven Annika away from that fucked-up spectacle myself. I never saw so many freaks in my life."

Mom's jaw quivers. "Don't call them that. They're *not* freaks. They've suffered in ways you'll never understand and I say that knowing full well what you've been through. Those people have been defiled, disgraced, and ignored all their lives. If freaks are what they are, then I'm proud to stand with them."

"Fine, Mom, you're a freak too. No argument here."

Meanwhile, Annika is staring off into the distance through the window, its reflection casting the room back into itself.

"You know what the last two years were like?" she asks no one in particular. Her voice, soft and slightly faltering, cuts through the noise.

"It was like everyone was outside playing and they'd call up to my window, *Come play with us*. I wanted so badly to join them, but I couldn't get up and I couldn't call out. All I could do was listen to them play. I guess that's what I miss the most, just being with every-one else—*being with you*."

"That's all we wanted too," Mom sniffles.

"I love you all very much," Annika softens, "and I'm very tired. I never thought I'd say this again, but I'd really like to go back to sleep, just not for so long this time."

I GO TO the bathroom and when I come out Dad is waiting for me.

"Monroe, you realize this family's been through a lot in the last two years."

"Yeah, Dad, I know. I'm sorry." I swear, it looks like he's going to hit me again.

"And today was probably the hardest day of all of them, thinking we lost the both of you."

"I know, Dad. I guess I wasn't really thinking. You're not going to hit me, are you?"

"You're not following me, son. What you did took some balls. Seeing your sister turned into a sideshow attraction made me sick. I let it happen and I didn't do a goddamn thing about it."

"Really?"

"Don't get me wrong. It was stupid, running off like that, but it took balls."

"Thanks."

"You know, all my life I've been able to make a pretty good argument. That's what I do. But I couldn't do it this time. And all the evidence I needed was staring right at me."

"It's okay, Dad," I say.

"It's *not* okay," he says. "But thanks for saying so."

And then he hugs me. *Really* hugs me.

All this time I've been thinking I couldn't live up to my dad. That I'd never be able to come close to doing what he's done. Building a successful career. Building a family. *Making a life.* Sure he has his faults, but in the end, I wish I could have seen more of them, because if I had, I would have seen more of the good stuff too. That's the unfortunate trade-off. Someone has to pay for all of this. And he has. Over and over again.

Chapter 42

YOU THINK LIFE IS FULL OF CHOICES, but that's not the way it is. Sometimes if you want to be able to live with yourself you have to do things you don't really want to do, things you never thought you'd *have* to do. Sometimes, it's not like you have a choice at all. So even though I took a stand, it wasn't a big deal. It's something anyone would do. Well, not Dad. Certainly not Mom. But if Ben was even *thinking* about it, then *you* probably would have done something too.

I'm not so special.

It's hard to see the truth when everything is designed to make sure you don't see it, because once you do, once you see everything for what it is, there's nothing to believe in anymore. Nothing but yourself, that is. And even that isn't always particularly convincing.

I'm not sure where that leaves God. If it's true that you can't love somebody else until you love yourself, what's the point of giving your love to God? The middleman always screws everything up—even if it is God or whatever you want to call Him. It's not exactly a secret: God separates people more than He brings them together. Maybe you should give your love to yourself and to the people around you. Maybe it's that simple. Maybe we're all alone until we realize that all we have is one another. Maybe that's what God really wants.

Maybe you already know all of this and don't need to hear it from me.

WE'RE WATCHING THE FRONT of our house on television; I can see Grandpa peeking through the blinds. Once the media got hold of the story that Annika didn't really rise from the bottom of the Scioto River and is, in fact, now lucid, they came down on us like the locusts they are, destroying half the plants in our front yard. Last night they got a glimpse of Annika through a window and they've been replaying it ever since.

Annika says, "I can't believe you guys got rid of the diving board." All she's talked about all morning is taking a swim in the pool, but CNN is staked out in the Gormans' backyard. So much for privacy.

Mom says maybe Annika should have a quick little press conference, give them what they want, and let the world know how everyone's prayers were answered. Then, she says, maybe they'll go away.

Annika, though, pleads, "Mom, if you put me out in front of those jackals, I'm going to lose it."

Mom says, "Honey, believe me, I hate the idea of this as much as you do, but I don't know how else we're ever going to get rid of them."

"Fine, Mom, let me take care of it."

Mom addresses the reporters while Annika slouches by her side. Despite her initial reluctance to address the press, Mom seems to be enjoying her recitation about how everyone's prayers were answered, how thankful she is to God for having mercy.

It's not long before the reporters have had enough of the opening act and want to get to the main attraction. "Annika, Annika . . . people all over the world have been praying for your recovery. Do you have anything you'd like to say to them?"

"Yeah, thanks, I guess."

"You don't seem so sure about that."

"Don't get me wrong, I appreciate that people care. Father Ferger says my story brought people closer to God, which I guess is great, but I'll just never understand how anyone could pray to a God they think would make someone bleed on purpose. I know people are hurting, I know people want help. But if someone says they love God, and it's His will that they have cancer, they might as well just say they were asking for it. Mom left the TV on in the afternoon more than once, so I know all about battered wives going back to their abusive husbands. Seems to me that praying to such a cruel God is kind of like that."

"Annika, are you saying God is a wife beater?"

"No, *you're* saying that. The God I know doesn't go around trying to hurt people to prove how powerful and almighty He is. I don't know that God, but if *your* God treats people that way, I'd really think twice about praying to Him 'cause basically you're just getting down on your knees to a sadist."

Mom is struck dumb as a statue. Not a noble or heroic statue, more like a slab of butter formed into a cartoonish approximation of herself, melting on a hot day.

Annika continues, "I wasn't the only one lost in the fog for the last two years. Everyone who came here, everyone who prayed for me or to me, you were just as lost as I was. Seriously, *wake up*. You were all in a coma. The only difference is that at least I had an excuse."

Mom regains the blood in her face and puts her arms around her daughter and angles her away from the microphone. "Clearly Annika has been through quite a bit. Perhaps it was premature of us to put her in this position. . . ."

Annika turns around and heads back to the house, leaving cameras flashing in her wake.

Mom, mortified, continues. "I hope you all will show Annika the kind of compassion she deserves and refrain from publicizing this most unfortunate episode."

File that under *wishful thinking*. There are no second takes on live television.

Once the press packs up and leaves, once the coast is clear, Annika dives back in the pool. She's swimming laps and it looks like she's going nowhere, just back and forth, but really, she's going places that once were possible only in a dream.

~~~

Turns out people, apparently, not only don't like it when you call them mindless drones for believing in you, they also don't appreciate having God compared to a wife beater. In fact, the suggestion got the believers so riled up, it's hard not to think Annika was on to something.

Which, of course, is exactly what Annika was shooting for; she wanted everyone to go away. Insulting them, she figured, was the easiest solution. And it worked. Sure, at first there was outrage and indignation, but it passed. At least they don't come to our house anymore. Sometimes they drive by and point, but that's about it. They don't try to come in. Now that Annika can talk, it's not so easy to put words in her mouth. She's not a blank slate anymore; she's just a teenage girl. She doesn't bleed. She doesn't heal anyone. And she doesn't smell like roses.

But that hasn't stopped Mom from believing she's a saint. Like a doomsday cult leader who wakes up to find that doomsday has come and gone, she sets a new date for the apocalypse. Mom still believes Annika was chosen to take on the suffering of all humanity. She still believes it was all part of God's plan. The fact that Annika doesn't advocate this version of events, she says, is just an obstacle to overcome. Annika will hear none of it; she won't talk about what happened, other than to say it's all just a really bad dream she'd rather forget. Mom says that's just proof that God was using Annika as a vessel for a greater good. How she gets to that, I'm not quite sure.

This fall I moved out of the house and moved in with Allison. I thought Mom might say something about our living in sin, but she hasn't said a word. In fact, she seemed glad to see me go. Perhaps that's because my old room is now the central headquarters for Mom's latest project, Everyday Miracles, a nonprofit public relations firm that catalogs miracles and encourages the media to refrain from taking on a mocking tone when covering the work of God.

You know how they say that after eighteen months, love turns into something else? I never knew what that something else was, but

I do now. And it's not the *something else* that had me ordering Filet-O-Fishes at McDonald's, even though they made me sick. It's not that at all. When love first comes to you, it's like a dream you don't want to end. But you're afraid it will. And like a dream, it should be noted, no one else cares. So I'll just leave it at saying, I'm happy being with Allison. She makes me feel like I can do anything. In fact, she's the one who told me to write this all down. She says that way, I'll never forget, and maybe—if I'm lucky—it'll all make sense.

The real reason I'm writing this down, though, is because I don't want to remember. I don't want to be telling the same story for the rest of my life. Whenever people find out who I am, they ask me about Annika. So now, when people want to know what it was like to be Annika's brother, *what really happened,* they can read this book. And if they don't truly want to know, if they're just making small talk, maybe they won't mind talking about baseball instead.

Epilogue

A FEW YEARS HAVE PASSED and I'm about to graduate from law school. That's right, *law school*. It's not exactly the road I thought my academic career would go down, but here I am: two weeks away from being a multiple degree–holder from Ohio State. After getting my undergraduate degree a year early, Dad said majoring in environmental studies with a minor in landscape design was a major waste of time. "Nobody cares if you have a diploma when you cut their yard," he said. Maybe I played right into his hands, enrolling in law school. Maybe it's exactly what he wanted me to do. Then again, maybe now I'll actually be able to do something about all the corporations polluting the world. And if that happens, I'm not sure who'll have the last laugh, him or me.

Annika and I see each other at least once a week; sometimes we talk on the phone. She's into Goth rock now, a testament to how little influence I've had on her. Her skin is pale and her blonde hair is dyed black. She's running away from her beauty, but no matter what she does, it's never far behind.

Usually Annika calls before she comes over. I guess that's why I'm so surprised when she shows up at my door. The first words out of her mouth are, "I'm sorry to bother you."

Her blue eyes look dried up, like a lake in need of a good long rain. I offer her some coffee and she says, "Sure."

I'm fumbling around with a Brazilian coffee press that's supposed to be so simple, but in reality it's a lot more work than it's worth when Annika sits down at the dining room table, which also doubles as my desk. As she flips through a book on the global population explosion she says, "I've been thinking about sleeping with my boyfriend, but I don't want to screw everything up. *I really like him.*"

"You have a boyfriend?"

"Yeah, I guess I didn't want to say anything until I knew it was serious. We've been seeing each other for like three months. His name is Nick. He's a painter. He's in school at CCAD." That's the Columbus College of Art & Design.

"Isn't he a little old for you?"

"You don't expect me to date someone from Chelsea, do you? They all treat me like a complete freak . . . and besides, he's only nineteen. He's really *nice,* you'd probably like him."

"Yeah, it's real nice of him to try to get you into bed. Isn't that statutory rape?"

"Actually, A: It's *me* who wants to sleep with him. And B: I already looked into that. The age of consent in Ohio is sixteen, so I'm already a year and a half behind. But if I wanted to get the fifth degree or whatever, I'd be talking to Dad right now."

The mere mention of Dad should knock me out of parental interrogation mode, but I persist, "Sleeping with someone is a pretty big step."

"You mean a big step like when you slept with that pilgrim with leukemia after you knew her for like an hour? *Big* like that?"

"You knew about that?"

"Well, yeah, but only because you told me. Remember? . . . Anyway, it's my junior prom this weekend and Nick is taking me. I think it's completely retarded, the prom, but he says I'll regret it if we don't go. He was homeschooled, so I guess this is like his big chance. He says at the very least, it's something we can laugh about."

"You say he's not pressuring you, but you know, guys can be kind of passive-aggressive about stuff like this. Like trying to make you think it's *your* idea when really they're just playing you."

"Yeah, he says we should wait."

"See? That's exactly the sort of mind game I'm talking about."

"I just don't want to scare him away. . . . Guys are kind of afraid of me, you know."

Could it be because you look like a walking corpse? Could it be because you look like you're *trying* to scare them away?

But I don't say that. She hears it from Mom enough as it is.

"Sex is a pretty tricky thing," I say. "So many things can go wrong."

"Yeah, they keep telling us that at school. If you listen to Mrs. Burdett, you'd think rubbers get broken as often as the Ten Commandments. All they ever tell you is to just *say no*. How retarded is that? It's like, seat belts don't always save you from a crash, but nobody goes around saying you shouldn't *drive* because of it."

"That's a pretty good point," I concede.

"Mrs. Burdett didn't think so. She sent me to the assistant principal's office to talk about my *attitude problem* for like the thousandth time. Maybe if they quit treating us like we're *all* idiots. There must be something great about sex or everyone wouldn't always be making such a big deal about it," she astutely points out. "I just want to know what it's like. Why shouldn't I? The only virgins at school are either ugly or lying."

I really don't know what to say, you know, without lying about it. After all, sex *is* pretty great.

"You think that makes me a slut?"

"Uhhmmmm, no I don't think that," I say, balking for no other reason than that the idea sounds so absurd. Still, my hesitation is all she hears. Her pale face, practiced in displays of indifference, can't help but reveal its disappointment.

So I tell her the truth. "The thing about sex is that it *is* great. It's like the most amazing thing *ever*. You know, as long as you're doing it with someone you really care about. And who cares about you. That's the most important part."

I'm surprised to see her blush. "Are you trying to gross me out?" she asks.

"No, seriously, Annika, when two people in love connect in a physical way—"

"*Connect in a physical way?* That's disgusting, Monroe."

"It's the most beautiful thing in the world."

"Look, I know all about reverse psychology. And it's not going to work. I really hope you don't talk to Allison that way."

"I'm not trying to reverse anything."

"I think I liked it better, you just being there for me," she manages to say. "Like a rock."

"A rock?"

"Yeah, the kind you don't look under."

I'm not quite sure what to say. I just know that's not the kind of rock I want to be.

"Well, thanks for the coffee," she says, heading for the door.

"Annika, wait," I say.

She turns around. "Yeah?"

"Annika, forget that whole conversation, okay? I don't know what I'm talking about, hardly a first, I know. But I do know that I love you and that's never gonna change. No matter what you do, I'll always be on your side. You're stuck with me. *No matter what.*"

Her eyes, her beautiful blue eyes, come back to life like that dry lake after a long rain and she says, "Promise?"

I find myself giving her a hug, saying, "You know, if you need me . . ."

"Not *if*," she says. "*When.* Maybe someday I'll be there for you too, you know, like save your life or something . . ."

"You already have," I say.

The smile on her face is the greatest gift I've ever been given. And with that, she kisses me on the cheek and heads out the door.

I watch her leave from my window. Her car's parked out front, a black BMW—its bumper covered with stickers proclaiming her love for Siouxsie and the Banshees, the Cure, and Bauhaus. Meanwhile, the front bumper is freckled with several dents.

Annika trips and quickly picks herself up. She looks around to see if anyone saw her fall. Then she checks her hair in the reflection of her car's window and makes the necessary adjustments. Apparently, her bed-head hair is that way by careful design. From my perch, she looks small, unsure of herself; but maybe that's the way we all look in unguarded moments when we stumble. Moments when we think we look stupid and hope to God no one is looking.

She starts up the car and, like a backfire, Siouxsie's tribal scream breaks through the windows, leaving Annika's head shaking. Seconds ago she looked so out of place and now she's back, one with the world. *Her* world.

I don't know if I've made things worse. If I said the right thing. Or if there's a *right* thing to say. Apparently, I wasn't supposed to say anything at all. She didn't need my answers to questions she didn't need to ask in the first place. She's going to do what she's going to do.

Everybody always does.

That doesn't mean I have to be happy about the idea of my little sister having sex with someone. In fact, the whole idea has my stomach tied up in knots and my head dying for a smoke. For a flash, I'm enveloped in that familiar desire to press the PAUSE button and make it all stop. But instead, I take a deep breath and think maybe it's like how Dad says: *Time moves by so fast, you try to put your finger on it and it gets chopped off in the fan.*

Annika's pulling out. She's got all the room in the world, but she clips the bumper of the pickup in front of her. Yes, she's going to break some hearts someday. I never thought that one of those hearts might just be her own.

I take a sip from my coffee, but it's cold now and I put it back down on the window ledge. I want to do *something* to stop her. I just don't know what that *something* is.

I'm watching Annika idle at the stoplight, my only plan wrapped up in wishing that light will stay red forever. Even from here, she's beautiful. Free. Enveloped in the moment, singing along to her favorite song. I wish I could hold on to this view, keep her here forever, safe . . . happy.

But the light turns green, and when it does, Annika hits the gas hard and cuts left in front of the oncoming cars, their honks mere screams of protest, not of caution.

And like that, she's gone, disappearing fast from my sight.

acknowledgments

I have been afforded the generosity of many people during the journey that has brought this book into your hands. I am grateful to them all.

My parents' faith in me, as faith does, defies logic. Without their belief in me, I can't imagine having had the fortitude to complete this project.

My friend and screenwriting partner, Karen Krenis, read every draft of this book, and I am incredibly appreciative of having had the benefit of her editorial prowess. Her insight into human behavior is quite humbling. Despite this occasionally annoying trait, I am blessed to have her in my life.

Madison Bell, author extraordinaire and, thankfully, the brother-in-law of my good friend Ann Spires, was my sole link to the publishing world, and I am forever indebted to him for paving the way to Jane Gelfman, who has proven to be everything I could have ever hoped for in an agent.

Fortunately, I have several friends who were more than happy to offer their unvarnished opinions as I subjected them to various drafts of this book. Amy Decker, Sandra Neufeldt, Anthippy Petras, Susan Robinson, and Jonathan Rosen were particularly helpful with their sage advice.

It would be impossible to overstate what an amazing experience it has been to work with editor Jonathan Karp. Not only did he champion this book in the halls of Random House and beyond, but also—and more important—his instructive notes helped make this book better than it was when it first arrived on his desk. Of course, that's the way it's supposed to happen; but having been accustomed only to the peculiar ways of Hollywood, it's an experience I never thought I'd have. His assistant, Jillian Quint, has also proven to be invaluable with her aid.

They say writing is a solitary pursuit, but it should be noted that every page of this book was written with the eyes of an awesome and all-knowing dog on me. Jasper, the aforementioned hound, is a constant source of inspiration and wonder. If I ever grow up, I hope to be more like him.

about the author

BRIAN STRAUSE was born and raised in Columbus, Ohio, and now lives in Silver Lake, California.